PRAISE FOR

NO RELATION

Winner, 2015 Stephen Leacock Medal for Humour

"As with his past novels, which include *The Best Laid Plans* and *The High Road*, Fallis employs an easygoing yet compelling writing style. The subject matter turns serious, at times, but Fallis keeps things light, finding humour in dark situations. . . . So what's in a name? When it's Terry Fallis, you know it means a good book." – *National Post*

"Terry Fallis is fast becoming a master of fiction writing. . . . In *No Relation* [he] employs his understated whimsy and sense for irony in a hilarious chronicle about a hard-luck fellow who loses his wallet, his copywriting job and his girlfriend one fateful day. . . . What delightful lunacy Fallis has concocted here, with a dollop of intrigue and even romance." – Montreal *Gazette*

"Terry Fallis writes with a light touch and fine sense of the inherent humanity of humour, while still addressing one of the biggest questions we all have to face: Who are you? Who are you really?" – Will Ferguson, author of *419*, winner of the 2012 Scotiabank Giller Prize

"Fallis fans, rejoice! Terry is back! . . . A humorous and heart-warming tale." – CBC.ca

"Reading a Fallis novel is like watching *The Big Bang Theory* or some other well-scripted TV sitcom. You laugh, you are entertained, you return to your regular life slightly refreshed." – *Quill & Quire*

"An enjoyable romp." – Kitchener-Waterloo *Record*

"Born of a cheerful mood and a clever mind, Terry Fallis's *No Relation* is an endearing book with a big heart." – Trevor Cole, author of *Practical Jean*, winner of the 2011 Stephen Leacock Medal for Humour

POLES APART

Also by Terry Fallis

The Best Laid Plans

The High Road

Up and Down

No Relation

POLES APART

A NOVEL

TERRY FALLIS

A DOUGLAS GIBSON BOOK

McClelland & Stewart

McClelland & Stewart is a division of Random House of Canada
Limited, a Penguin Random House Company

Library and Archives Canada Cataloguing in Publication
is available upon request

ISBN: 978-0-7710-3619-4
ebook ISBN: 978-0-7710-3621-7

Typeset in Electra by M&S, Toronto

Printed and bound in the USA

McClelland & Stewart,
a division of Random House of Canada Limited,
a Penguin Random House Company
www.penguinrandomhouse.ca

1   2   3   4   5   19   18   17   16   15

Penguin
Random
House

For Nancy

"That the principle which regulates the existing social relations between the two sexes — the legal subordination of one sex to the other — is wrong in itself, and now one of the chief hindrances to human improvement; and that it ought to be replaced by a principle of perfect equality, admitting no power or privilege on the one side, nor disability on the other."

John Stuart Mill
The Subjection of Women, 1869

PART ONE

CHAPTER 1

Grounding your wedge in a bunker is normally a two-stroke penalty. But for my father, only one stroke was assessed—the one that caused him to drop his club in the first place and crumple to the sand with empty eyes. This is how the whole thing started.

"Wait, Mom, you mean he just let go of his sand wedge in the middle of his shot and keeled over?" I asked.

"Sandwich? There was no sandwich involved. The doctor just told me he was swinging a golf club when it happened."

"Mom, a sand wedge is a golf . . . never mind. When did this happen?"

"I just got off the phone with the doctor a few minu—?"

"No, not your talk with the doctor," I cut in. "When did Dad have this stroke?"

"Oh, last Thursday."

"*Last Thursday?* Hold on a second! My father has a stroke, and my mother waits nearly a week to tell me? What's up with that?"

I was not happy. Apparently, neither was I in possession of the full picture.

"Whoa, back off, Ev. Don't dump that on me. This is on your father. I just found out about six minutes ago when he called me from some rehab hospital in Orlando. Your dad and I spoke for a few minutes, but then he had to get back to his Jell-O, so he passed the phone over to his doctor. I called you immediately after," she replied.

"Bizarre! Did no one think to call his next of kin? Isn't that standard operating procedure at hospitals?"

I was upping my volume with each word.

"You know your father," my mother replied, clearly exasperated. "It seems he told the doctor that his golfing cronies had already called me with the news. Then he told his posse to keep their yaps shut. They're all idiots, your father included."

"So he's been in the hospital for nearly a week, alone, without telling us?"

"Well, he's actually been in two hospitals," Mom clarified. "He was golfing in Longwood, so the ambulance took him to, um, just checking my notes, to South Seminole Hospital. He spent a couple of days there but was then transferred to the Orlando Health Rehabilitation Institute and he'll be there for a while."

"But why the silent treatment?" I asked, in a tone that was the equivalent of a pout.

"Come on, Ev. We're talking about your bullheaded, proud-to-a-fault, jerk of a father," she said. "A stroke is a sign of weakness,

4

a chink in his armour, a tear in his cape. He got his ass kicked by a blot clot, and he was sensitive about it. They also told him he was already improving, so he kept it from us until he was feeling better. It's completely consistent with your father's past behaviour. Isn't it?"

"Well, when you put it that way, I mean with your impressive collection of metaphors and all, I guess we shouldn't be surprised."

"Well, I wasn't surprised. I'm not sure why you were. We're talking about Billy Kane, here. Remember?"

I suddenly realized that I'd spent time taking offence at my dad's solo approach to stroke management before covering off a question that was certainly more pressing than my own bruised feelings.

"Um, is he okay? Will he be okay?"

She sighed and paused before continuing.

"It seems it was a minor to moderate stroke on the right side of his brain. That's why his speech was not affected. Unfortunately, he sounds the same to me. But, physically, it's done some damage. He has suffered what the doctor calls 'physical deficits' on the left side of his body. He has reduced function in his left arm and particularly in his left leg."

"So it will get better? He will get better, I mean, over time, right?"

"Well, he's now a resident of this rehab hospital and will be for a month or so at least, as he relearns how to use his left side. The doctor says he has to forge new pathways in his brain for walking and other simple tasks that were lost in the stroke. He'll be in daily physiotherapy sessions and is expected to do a lot of walking on his own around the grounds."

"That doesn't sound too bad. But I wouldn't want to be his physiotherapist. That's going to be ugly," I said. "Hey, who's going to pay for all this medical care? We're talking Florida, here. It's going to cost a fortune."

"His Ford benefits cover the whole thing, so there's no financial hit."

"You mean for Dad. But his next Ford might cost a bit more," I said.

"They can afford it." She paused again. "So anyway, um, I need you to do something for me, for us, for the family."

That did not sound good.

"Okaaaaay," I said in my best wary, sing-songy voice.

"Ev, even though he didn't call until today, your father needs you, and I need you, now. I'm asking you to fly down to Orlando and kind of take care of him as he gets through this. You just have to be with him and walk with him and talk with him. Wait, before you answer, I'm stuck here in Vancouver and simply cannot get down there myself right now. I'm in the middle of strat planning and if that weren't enough, I've got a major, major $200-million deal on the front burner and my time isn't my own. I need you to step up, Ev. Your father needs you to step up."

This was not good.

"Gee, Mom, I'd like to help, I really would, but I'm a freelance writer. I can't just pack up my life on a moment's notice and fly to Florida for an indefinite period. I'm in the midst of a big assignment right now."

There was silence on the end of the phone, except for the not-so-silent sigh. Okay, the sigh was quite audible, loud, even.

"Ev, let's go through what you've just said, step by step," she started.

This really was not good. I could see her end-game already.

"I'd really rather not. . ." I began.

"You're living in a condo that I purchased as an investment property and you're paying no rent."

"Just till I get on my feet. . ."

"Are you in any kind of a long-term relationship with anyone right now?"

"Well, um, I see my local Starbucks barista almost every day."

"I think you know that's not the kind of relationship I mean. Are you involved with anyone romantically?"

"Yes, of course! Well, sort of. Um, no, not really. No."

"Oh, I'm sorry, honey. What happened to what's-her-name?"

"Cassie."

"Right, Cassie," she said. "Wait, let me guess. You did it again. I can't believe you did it again. What's this? Three in a row, now? And after I warned you. Still, you went and did it again. Ev, just stop already! The poor girl never had a chance."

I snorted, but there was no heart in it.

"Mom, that's ridiculous!" Good, start strong, I thought. "It wasn't like that at all. . ." Uh-oh. I could feel myself nearing the ledge. "Well, not exactly . . . um, well, sort of. . ." I stepped off. "Okay, it was quite a bit like that," I said, officially in free fall, as I watched the ground race up to meet me.

She sighed, but her tone softened.

"Honey, you got to stop doing that. Promise me you'll stop. It's unnatural. It's not how men work. And it freaks women out. It's just weird. They can't keep up. Dial it back, or keep it under wraps for as long as you can. Or you'll die alone and deserve to."

"Wow, thanks, Mom." I exhaled like it was my last breath. "I don't know when I've felt such parental warmth, encouragement, and understanding."

I suffer from a mild sarcasm habit.

"Honey, the truth is hard to hear sometimes," she said. "Okay, enough of that. Let's get back on track. We're not quite finished here. So what's this new project you have?"

"Well, I've got a contract to write a big profile piece for a national trade magazine. It might even be the cover story," I said, trying not to sound desperate and hoping she wouldn't ask me which magazine. "It's a big deal and will take a lot of work."

"Congratulations, honey, that's great news. And do you have a laptop computer?"

"What? Of course. Every freelancer I know has a laptop," I replied, walking into the propeller. "It's getting old and weighs about the same as a late-model Honda Civic, but it still works well enough."

Actually, I was lying. Not about laptop's automotive weight

class, but about how well it worked. To get it to turn on, I had to use both hands to flex the laptop diagonally while using my chin to hit the Power button—embarrassing while in Starbucks, but almost always effective.

"And do you sometimes carry it places with you so you can write outside of your—I mean, my—condo?"

"Come on, Mom." That didn't slow her down.

"And do you have this newfangled thing, oh what's it called again, I want to say something like . . . 'email'?"

Okay, now you know where I got my sarcasm habit.

"Mom, I know what you're doing, and I know where you're going. . ."

"Stay with me, Ev, we're almost there," she interrupted. "And if I'm not mistaken, they also have this email wonder service in the United States, including in that beautiful and temperate oasis known as Orlando."

She paused to take a breath, but it was a short one.

"Oh yes, and there's one more thing. I seem to recall, given your birthplace, that you enjoy dual Canadian-American citizenship, so you're able to work in either country without risking deportation. How convenient. What a lovely tight little package we seem to have."

She already knew from my breathing that I was unfurling my white flag, but she went for the big finish anyway.

"So in summary, when you said that you're a freelance writer and can't just pack up your life on a moment's notice and fly to

Florida for an indefinite period, what you really meant was that you're a freelance writer and you actually *can* just pack up your life on a moment's notice and fly to Florida for an indefinite period."

"Wow, Mom. I don't remember you being like this when I was growing up. When did you become so tough and ruthless and— cynical?"

"You know the answer to that question."

"Yes, I do, Mom. But I was asking rhetorically."

"So you'll go?" she asked, already knowing.

I moaned a bit, but not for long.

"I guess I could juggle a few things around and head south for a bit." I sighed. "But I'm not going to live with him. That I will not do."

"No, I agree, that would be pushing it too far," she said.

"Remind me never to negotiate with you," I said. "I just caved so fast."

"Ev, honey, you didn't 'cave,' as you so delicately put it. You did what families do in these situations. You did the right thing. These moments of responsibility seldom come at convenient times. And you won't be on your own for long. I'll be down to do my part as soon as I can. I promise," she replied. "And I'm not even married to him anymore. But you're still his son."

"Yes, and you're still my mother."

She took a deep breath.

"Okay, Ev honey, here's the deal. I'll buy you a new laptop of your choosing. I'll cover your return airfare and rent for as long as you're down there. I'll give you enough cash to keep you in groceries and beer. And you'll always have the undying love and affection of your parents, even though it's hard for them to spend much time in the same room together. Deal?"

Ten minutes later, after she gave me Dad's number at the hospital, I said goodbye to my mother and goodbye to my life in Toronto, at least until my father could walk again and pick up a dime with the fingers of his left hand. I also found a moment to visit the Apple website and pick out a new laptop. Finally, I did a quick Google search on strokes. Yes, I know. I should have done my stroke web browsing before I headed to the Apple website. I know. As it turns out, strokes on the right side of the brain don't just affect motor control on the left side of the body but can also impair what Wikipedia euphemistically calls "perception and judgment." I didn't like the sound of that. Then again, I didn't think my father was particularly well-endowed in that department to begin with, so perhaps this wouldn't be an issue.

So, free flights, free rent, free cash, and a brand spanking new MacBook Pro with Retina screen to use while living temporarily in sunny Orlando, Florida. You might think I walked away a winner from the call with my mother. And I confess at the time, I was not that unhappy with the outcome. Then again, you don't know Billy Kane.

———

I am their son, Everett Kane. Somehow, I think my name would be cooler in reverse, as in Kane Everett, intoned in a deep, raspy, movie-trailer voice. But even in its original configuration, it's not a bad handle, I suppose. An only child, I was born in Oakville, Ontario, Canada, thirty-seven years ago. Despite some parental pyrotechnics just as I headed off to university, my childhood seemed quite conventional. But I'm getting ahead of myself.

My father is Billy Kane, the one now with partial paralysis on his left side, and perhaps even lower scores on the "perception and judgment" meter, though he didn't exactly rock that particular needle before his stroke. Billy Kane. I know. It sounds like a name in a novel, or a TV show, doesn't it? *Billy Kane!* He was sixteen years old when he met my mother, Evelyn, in the corridors of the Detroit high school they both attended. She was thirteen years old, and Canadian. Her parents were both visiting professors at the University of Michigan in Dearborn. They moved from Toronto when Evelyn was ten years old.

Billy's father worked on the line at the Ford plant. In fact, he died on the line, too. He was found sprawled out on the rear bench seat he'd been installing in a Mercury Marquis as the car slowly moved down the line to the next station. Heart attack. Billy revered his father and only ever wanted to follow in his footsteps, minus the early coronary. Without getting into all the details, Billy and Evelyn fell in love, early and hard. They were inseparable through their high school years. He wasn't the captain of the football team, and she wasn't the head cheerleader, but their relationship had that vibe. They were certain of their lasting love, and much too young to doubt it. At the insistence of both sets of parents, Billy and Evelyn waited until she graduated from high school at eighteen before the inevitable storybook wedding.

Billy had graduated from high school with grades that just barely secured him a spot in the upper three-quarters of his class. He was actually quite smart but had really only applied himself to Evelyn. College was not really in the cards. He was much more focused on earning money, buying a home, providing for his wife, and starting a family. This all unfolded back in the seventies. But as I describe it now, it feels much more like the fifties.

Right after high school, Billy landed a job on the line at the Ford plant, alongside his father. They looked like father and son. Both were of average height and wore crewcuts. His father's gut hung over his belt. Billy's belly would get there eventually. Soon after he started at the plant, in one of fate's cruel spasms, it was Billy who discovered his father stretched out on the back seat of that Marquis, his hands still pressed over his heart. Billy took it hard, but he was tough, like his father. So after a week of bereavement leave, he went back to work to honour his father and to secure the dream he shared with Evelyn.

Sure, it was shift work. But it was a good job, a great job. It paid well, with benefits and a pension. He also gladly joined the United Auto Workers and embraced the union movement. Billy Kane was a living paradox. He proved it was possible to be a

flaming right-winger and a devoted union brother, simultane-
ously. He sustained this ideological super straddle split jump for
his entire working life without so much as a pulled groin.

By the time Evelyn graduated and they walked down the aisle,
Billy was snagging all the overtime he could and bringing in big
bucks. To his credit, he'd socked away enough money for a down
payment on a modest semi-detached home. Billy and Evelyn
moved in and started living an all-American *Leave It to Beaver*
existence in suburban Detroit. Two years later, when she was
twenty and he just twenty-three, there were two big developments
in the young couple's life together. First, Billy got a big promotion
and a transfer. When the Ford brain trust shifted manufacturing
of the Mustang from Dearborn to their newer facility in Oakville,
Ontario, Billy was shipped to Canada to help set up the new line.
And second, not long after Billy and Evelyn settled themselves in
Oakville, a leafy bedroom community of Toronto, I arrived on the
scene. As you might expect, my parents were ecstatic. Their vision
of the future was unfolding just as they had planned.

Why "Everett"? It was certainly not a play on my mother's
name as some thought. Rather, Mom just loved the TV show
Medical Center and its star, Chad Everett. Dad had suggested
"Billy Junior." But Mom persuaded him that giving me a name
that could and would be abbreviated in the schoolyard as "BJ"
was cruel and unusual punishment. He agreed to "Everett."

Not long after they brought me home from the hospital, Dad
willingly, eagerly, traded in his beloved Mustang Mach 1 for a

used Country Squire station wagon. He was very attached to that Mustang but loved the idea of a family even more. In his mind, real families drove station wagons. So we graduated to that massive faux-wood–panelled metallic monstrosity that George Carlin once dubbed the Ford Country Shit Box. And man, was it boxy. Never again will so many right angles be assembled in one vehicle. It made the Volvos of that era look positively curvaceous.

Over the years, life in Oakville slipped into a routine. Well, I suppose it might have been a rut, but that only occurred to me in hindsight. Dad worked a rotating schedule of shifts at the Ford plant while Mom stayed home and focused on me, the house, the groceries, and three meals a day. As Dad used to describe it to anyone who would listen, he made the money and Mom spent it. He usually chuckled when he said it. But over time, the chuckling dwindled and eventually stopped. When he worked the night shift, spending time with my dad was difficult for me and for my mother. Left to handle all the house-related duties, and most of the child-rearing responsibilities, Mom began to chafe under the ultra-traditional home life Dad expected and eventually demanded. She read voraciously, novels and non-fiction, but wanted more contact with the outside world. They wanted more children, especially Dad, but none ever arrived. I found out why many years later.

Mom and Dad seemed to start arguing more when I was in grade six. They initially kept it behind closed doors, but the tension, the jibes, the glares, and the silence between them was clear, even to a ten-year-old. The cracks my dad always tossed out to make us laugh eventually became sharper, crueller, and deployed to wound. My mother stopped laughing. And I guess I did, too. But we persevered. Things even took a turn for the better when I started high school. I remember the day my mother told me that Dad was finally "allowing her" to take courses during the day at nearby McMaster University while I was in class at Oakville Collegiate, as long as dinner was on the table by six. Liberated from the daily drudgery of housekeeping, Mom seemed like a new woman, at least for a while. She drove to McMaster in Hamilton most mornings to take courses part-time, as a mature student, toward a business degree. Even Dad seemed happier, at least for a while.

High school flew by. I did well. I had friends. I had fun. My best marks were in English and history. I sensed, rather than knew with certainty, that I had some facility, maybe even a flair, for writing. I just seemed to be able to assemble words into phrases, sentences, paragraphs, and stories with greater ease than my classmates. I couldn't explain why, then. I still can't now. But it felt true. So it seemed natural and comfortable to pursue journalism at university. (Even at that age, I knew it was easier to make a living writing news stories than short stories.)

I was tired of being marooned in the suburbs, so I applied to Ryerson University in the "big smoke," Toronto. Ryerson said yes. In my five years of high school, my very organized, goal-oriented mother somehow finished her part-time four-year Bachelor of Commerce. She worked her butt off, if I can say that about my own mother. She redefined the term "part-time," as it was not unusual for mature students to take more than ten years to complete a part-time degree.

I don't think my father understood what was happening. The day after my high school graduation, there he was, looking dazed and confused at my mother's university convocation. Oh sure, he seemed proud on the surface. He smiled for the family snapshots. But it didn't take a Freud scholar to see that he felt his primacy in the family was threatened. His bottom-of-the-class high school diploma didn't quite cut it next to Mom's top-of-the-class, summa cum laude, university business degree. It was only a few months until his insecurity detonated into a mushroom cloud of selfish paranoia. You see, even back then, "perception and judgment" was never Dad's strong suit.

It simmered over the summer as I joined my dad on the line at the Ford plant. But as I packed up my stuff and got ready to head off to Ryerson University, it happened. A letter arrived for my mother from the Faculty of Management at the University of Toronto. I found it in our mailbox when I arrived home from my final Ford shift and handed the envelope to my mother. My father was doing what he usually did at 6:30 after our traditional 6 p.m. dinner. He was having a beer, unleashing a few burps, and watching the sports segment of the evening news on TV in our basement rec room. My mother's high-pitched squeal brought him running, but only after watching the "Highlight of the Night" segment.

"What the hell is all the racket?" he said as he stepped into the kitchen from the basement stairs.

My mother and I were still holding hands and dancing around the room. I'd never seen her quite so happy. It looked good on her.

"I'm in! I'm really in!" she said, waving the letter around her head. "It took a while, but it's happened. They just had a final space open up and I've been offered admission. Classes start next week."

"Awesome news, Mom." I beamed. Dad's look shut me down. He looked . . . angry.

"What are you talking about?" he began. "And your answer better not include the word 'university.' We've been over and over this and you know where I stand."

"Billy, when we talked about it before, I really didn't think I was going to get in. When I missed the application deadline, I thought it was all over. But they let me in. They want me. It's right here. It's late, but I'm in."

"Sorry. Not happening." He folded his arms across his chest.

"Billy, we have to reopen the discussion now that they've let me in. Do you know what a rare opportunity this is? I've been accepted to grad school at U of T. Do you know what that means? In two years I'll have my MBA and then I, we, can write our own ticket. We'll be set for life."

"Sorry. Not happening. We agreed when Ev started high school that you could do your little McMaster courses but that's where it ends," he said, scowling at the floor.

I stayed where I was, still holding one of Mom's hands.

"Are you actually saying that I'm not permitted to pursue a graduate degree now that Ev is completely out of the house? Are you actually saying I must just stay at home and dust, and cook, and do your laundry?" She took a step toward Dad as she said this, her voice low and level.

"I make the money in this house. I work my ass off on the line so we can live in this house and eat three squares a day. I bought you a car. I paid for your classes, and the dough those university assholes charge is a fucking rip-off! We just can't afford to send two Kanes to university."

"But, Dad, I'm paying for my own university," I piped up.

"Yeah, because of the job I got for you," he snapped. "And this is not your discussion, so shut it."

He turned back to Mom and pointed his index finger right at her face.

"I don't sweat on the line every fucking day so you can keep reliving your youth at university. I sucked it up and let you do your little degree, but that's where it stops. You got your stupid diploma, but now it's over. End of discussion!"

She looked at him for what seemed like a long time. I know it wasn't long, but the silence became excruciating. Finally, she took a step closer to him and pointed her index finger right in his face.

"You're right. It is over."

Then she turned her back on him and walked out.

All this happened nearly twenty years ago, yet I can play back that scene in my memory as if it happened eighteen minutes ago. Moment by moment. Word for word. Gesture for gesture. And in my gut, I still get that tight little knot of what I eventually identified as fear.

At the time, Dad didn't know what had just happened. Mom had pushed back before, but never like this. He assumed she'd gone out to let off some steam and would be back in time to unload the dishwasher, set the table for breakfast, and crawl into the matrimonial bed as she had every other time. But she didn't come back.

She called later that night from her parents' home. They'd retired by then and moved back to Toronto. Through his closed bedroom door, I could hear Dad talking to her. It wasn't a long conversation. Years later, Dad admitted to me that when he hung up the phone that night and laid his head on the pillow, he still thought she'd relent and come home. She didn't.

I felt terrible. I felt helpless. But still, I left for Ryerson the next day.

The family unit splintered into its three constituent elements. My father stayed in Oakville while my mother and I packed up and moved to Toronto. I spent my first year in residence at Ryerson while Mom rented an apartment not far from the University of Toronto. Her parents, who had harboured grave doubts about

Billy Kane since Evelyn first brought him home more than twenty-five years earlier, were more than happy to underwrite her rent and tuition. In their eyes, she was back on track, and still only in her thirties.

It took a while, but my mother and father sold the family home, split the proceeds, and inked a divorce. Dad paid some alimony in the early stages, but it wasn't long before Mom was making more than he was, so his payments eventually ceased. Dad worked at the Oakville plant for a few more years but then moved back to Detroit, bought a little bungalow, and returned to the line at the Dearborn plant, for another thirteen years. Then, in the aftermath of the 2008 economic meltdown that hit the auto sector so hard, Ford was looking to reduce its labour force and streamline its operations even more. So at the age of fifty-seven, and after logging nearly forty years of service to the company, Dad took a package and retired. Ford gave him his full pension and lifetime health benefits. It was a deal he couldn't refuse.

As a city, Detroit was spiralling into urban palliative care, so he sold his little bungalow while it still had some value and headed south. It helped that he hated the winters more and more each year. Besides, Florida real estate was cheap then. Still is now. He bought a nice little condo in Orlando, cash on the barrelhead, and did what he could never do when he was married and working shifts. He golfed, almost every day. His pension was more than adequate to keep food on the table and golf balls in his bag. He no longer drove a Mustang but was quite happy with his top-of-the-line Ford Focus purchased with the employee discount. Hanging out most of his waking hours with a bunch of golfers cut from the same cloth gave him a certain sense of belonging, while his language and jokes regressed to late adolescence. To my knowledge, he has never dated after Mom, though I can report as a first-hand witness that he still leers and flirts, a lot. (Of course I call him on it each time. I can't help it.) But after everything that's happened, he seems okay. He even seems happy.

On the other hand, my mother seems more than okay, and more than happy. She found her place, too, in a big way. Her only regret is that she didn't find it sooner. She finished her MBA on schedule and with top marks. She'd gravitated to the tourism and hospitality sector during her studies and quite quickly landed a marketing job at the Toronto headquarters of the Pearson Group, one of the leading developers and owners of luxury hotels and resorts in North America.

She was born to the business. She was a star. Within two years, she was running Marketing. Then she spent five years climbing the ladder in the Property Management division. Finally, she took over the New Property Development team and learned the ropes, fast. She negotiated land deals, oversaw the design of resort properties, and then managed the construction phase from sod-turning to ribbon-cutting. She was tough, and smart, and worked harder than anyone else in the company. She racked up success after success, added a few coups along the way, and two years ago, at the tender age of fifty-five, was named the Pearson

Group's CEO. Yes, it's true. My stay-at-home mother is now running a global company.

When the appointment notice ran in the *Globe and Mail*, her parents were bursting with pride. I was bursting with pride. Dad? Not so much. I think, deep down, he was proud of her. But I don't think he had any idea how to push through his own insecurity, unearth that tattered shred of goodwill in her success, and express it. So he golfed instead.

It's been eighteen years since my mother walked out on my backward father. Since then, I've made it my mission to be a son, an only son, to them both, equally. It hasn't been easy. My father is, well, difficult, and my mother is, um, difficult, too, for different reasons . . . and for some of the same reasons. I guess I probably knew I'd be going down to help my father even before my mother asked me. I really didn't want to go. But I'm the son. I'm their son. And this is what good sons do, even if they don't want to.

I know what you're thinking. Haven't I left something out? What's happened to me since I headed off to Ryerson eighteen years ago? All in good time. All in good time.

I picked up the phone and dialed the hospital.

"Hello, stroke central."

"Dad? Is that you?"

"Everett! How the hell are you? How's it hanging?" he replied, as if he were calling from a bachelor party.

"Dad, are you okay? Mom just called me."

"Yeah, I figured you'd be on the blower to me tonight. What kind of son would you be if you weren't?" I assumed he was asking rhetorically. "Hey, how was your mother? Did she seem upset? Was she concerned? Was she crying at all?" he asked with what seemed like anticipation.

"Dad, of course she was upset. She wasn't really crying, but you know she's very good, um, at internalizing emotions. She's a CEO now. I don't think she's allowed to cry anymore."

"Oh."

"Dad, I'm kidding. I think she probably was sniffling a bit when she told me," I salvaged. "So how are you feeling?"

"Well, I can't walk worth a shit. My left hand is fuckin' useless, and my left leg feels like a broken drive shaft from an F150. I just drag it around behind me."

"Holy shit, really? Is your leg, you know, totally paralyzed?"

"Kind of half-paralyzed, I guess. I've got some feeling there, but not much. It kind of feels like pins and needles, but not exactly," he said. "And what's worse, my golf game is in the crapper and won't be getting better any time soon."

"Sorry about your golf game, but I'm more interested in your prognosis."

"Yeah, well, my prognosis wasn't affected. It's still working fine," he said with an edge. "I have no fuckin' idea what the word prog-fucking-nosis even means."

"Sorry. It sort of means what's going to happen to you. Are you going to get better?" I explained.

24

"Well, why didn't you just say that," he snapped. "The docs say I'm going to get better, but it's going to take some time and I got to relearn stuff like using my crippled hand and my cement leg."

"Okay, so what do they have you doing?"

"Well, in the mornings I do a couple hours of physio, or what I call Torture Time. Then in the afternoon, I got to walk around the big backyard at this place until my left leg starts to keep up with my right. And I got to squeeze my balls with my left hand."

"I beg your pardon."

"I love saying that," he said. "They gave me these two little black rubber balls. I got to spend all day squeezing them with my left hand."

"Okay, got it. I was confused for a moment there . . . well, you know . . ."

"Yeah, well, I guess if I squeezed my own balls all day, they'd be black, too."

"Thanks, Dad. That's just the image I was hoping to have stuck in my head." I paused, but not for long. "So, do you have your own room?"

"Yep, and it ain't half bad. The bed's kind of hard. You know, somewhere between old carpeting and three-quarter-inch ply-wood. But I got a TV on this funky boom gizmo so I can watch it in bed. Hell, I could yank it down and watch it under the bed if I wanted. And my physioperists are mostly hot. They're always coming in and cooing in my ear, and rubbing my left arm and leg. A shame I can't feel much there yet. But give me time. One day a guy came in to work on me, so that was a little weird and uncomfortable. But the rest are fine. Anyway, the women are all over me, you know? Three and four times a day. Who can blame them?"

"Physiotherapists."

"What?"

"Dad, they're called physiotherapists."

"I know what they're fucking called. I was just messing with you."

"Dad, why did you wait so long to call?"

"I was just waiting to see how long it took you to call me," he said.

"I'm coming down, Dad," I said. "I'm moving down for a while. I'm going to help you walk it off. We're going to do it together."

"Hey, thanks, Ev. That would be nice. To see you, I mean, and talk a bit," he started. "But, listen, rather than saying 'We're going to *do it* together,' how about just saying 'We're going to *get through it* together.' Okay, son?"

"Ah geez," I said to no one in particular. "So have you gotten to know any of your fellow patients?"

"Well, I got my eye on a few of the women limping around the grounds. I think they're a little older but I figure that just means they got more experience."

"Dad, I wasn't asking if you were cruising the patients, or scoring with them. I just wondered if you'd met any of them? You know, and had a normal, civilized conversation, the way people sometimes do."

"Oh, I'm working on it, Ev. I think my gimpy left leg might be a turn-off. But I'm working on it."

———————

My father is nothing if not predictable. By the time I said good-bye, we were on pretty good terms, though it's often hard to tell with my dad. But I think he was looking forward to spending some time with his only begotten son. I might even have been looking forward to spending some time with him.

Just before I headed to bed, I received an email notice of a bank transfer. I opened my online banking and accepted the transfer from my mother, moving it into my chequing account. Beforehand, there had been a grand total of $632.88 in the account. I wasn't exactly flush. When I shut down my soon-to-be-replaced laptop a few minutes later, the bottom line in the account was $10,632.88, and I'd ordered my new MacBook Pro. Why thank you, Mom.

CHAPTER 2

My flight arrived in Orlando in the early evening. Visiting hours at the rehab hospital were flexible enough that I probably could have visited my dad right then. But it was too late in my mind. Or perhaps it was too soon, for I didn't quite feel ready to see him yet. The concierge at Dad's condo was expecting me and handed over a key. Dad's unit was on the fifth floor overlooking a somewhat weedy golf course. The fairway was brown in spots, waterlogged in others, and cut too long. You can often judge an entire golf course by the condition of a single fairway.

I turned on the lights and surveyed my father's rather confining unit. It could not have been more than six hundred square feet. I'm not sure how to describe the decor. Early American Frat House might be a start. Yes, it definitely had a kind of Tappa Kegga Beera vibe to it. I can't say I was surprised. In fact, it was just about what I expected. Dad had been freed from the burden of Mom's housekeeping eighteen years earlier, and his condo was, well, not in great shape. There were dust bunnies auditioning for tumbleweeds, and enough clutter to sustain several garage sales and a shot at an episode of *Hoarders*. Without Mom, Dad had regressed, which is saying something, given his starting point.

On the walls, I found a mix of golfing prints and Ford product publicity posters, with a clear bias toward the Mustang. I discovered an alarming number of empty beer cans and Doritos bags scattered about the place. A stack of porn mags sat on the floor beside a mucous-coloured recliner. My dad was kind of old school. I tapped the touchpad of the laptop on the kitchen counter, and a porn site awoke on the screen. Okay, perhaps my dad wasn't completely old school. I was impressed that he had a laptop, porn site or not. I shut it down.

He had made some effort to put his own personal stamp on his home, I mean beyond the Coors empties and skin mags. On the living room wall was a flat-screen TV the size of a freeway billboard, with an array of speakers and subwoofers powerful enough to rattle windows all the way to Miami. Dad loved his TV sports. The kitchen was quite nice, though I was unable to picture my father turning on the front burner, let alone preparing a meal. The dishwasher was filled with plates and glasses. Some of them were even clean. As I suspected, I could find no trace of dishwasher detergent anywhere on the premises. As for the fridge, I cannot accurately describe what I found resting on a paper plate on the top shelf, but it seemed to be moving all on its own.

(I was unable to determine if the movement was an attempt at locomotion or just respiration.)

The bedroom was in a similar state. The king-size bed was unmade, although "unmade" was a serious understatement. The chaos of the sheets, blankets, and pillows suggested the bed had never been made. Not once. There was another colossal television mounted on the bedroom wall to allow viewers the convenience of retinal damage in two different rooms.

I did find a high-end vacuum cleaner in the front hall closet. It might be that my father actually pushed it around the wall-to-wall broadloom on a regular basis. I made a mental note to remind him to try plugging it in next time. You know, just to change things up a bit. After slipping out to buy some dish soap, I spent a solid hour vacuuming, dusting, washing dishes, wiping counters, and generally tidying. With much of the clutter and garbage gone, it was easier to see just how badly Dad had decorated his home. Nothing, and I mean nothing, matched. The whole look, and you couldn't call it a look, made me wonder if Dad might be colour blind. Exhausted from my efforts, I dug out a clean sheet I was amazed to find in Dad's linen closet, and crashed on the living room couch.

The next morning, as we had arranged, a rather nicely turned-out realtor named Graeme Harris met me on the sidewalk outside a prospective apartment. He had that used-car-sales-guy swagger and a mouth that wouldn't stop.

"Nice to meet you, Everett, my man. I'm telling you, you are going to like this baby. All your boxes are checked," he soothed. "It's close to the hospital. It should be quiet because there's only one apartment. It's quite new. It's clean and mucho spacious. It's just been painted. And you'll get sun streaming in the afternoons. The rent is reasonable for the area. The wood floors are freakin' awesome. The bus runs from the corner. And you can take it month to month if you want. Like I said, checkmarks everywhere."

He paused to take a breath.

"Hi, Graeme. Nice to meet you, too."

He blathered on about the unit for a few more minutes before I held up my hand.

"Graeme, I don't want to interrupt, but how about we look at the apartment since we're right here, rather than you just describing it."

"I like your style, Everett," he replied. "I was just setting the scene for you. Let's have a look."

"Thank you."

There were two ways to get in. You could go through a door adjacent to the double glass doors of the vacant space on the first floor and then walk up the inside stairs to the front door of the apartment. This was probably the route I would usually take. But there was construction going on downstairs and the door to the stairs was blocked off. So we had to climb the outside staircase, really a fire escape in the side alley, to the small second-floor veranda, and enter the apartment's back door into the kitchen.

For all of Graeme's frenetic hyperbole, I liked the apartment. I liked it a lot. It was in an okay part of town. Not too upscale, but not sketchy-ghetto either. It was big and airy, and as Graeme explained, over top of a restaurant that had closed down recently. It was the only apartment in the building, as Graeme had said. Hardwood floors all over, including in the large kitchen. It was open-concept layout with the living room, dining room, and kitchen all spilling into one another. This made it feel open and spacious. Built-in bookshelves ran the length of the living room wall, with a space for a TV in the middle. This would save me buying and trying to assemble an Ikea bookshelf. I had quite a few books that I just couldn't leave in Toronto. In fact, they were en route. The bedroom was large and so was the bathroom. The fixtures and appliances all looked quite new, and the scent of fresh paint hung off the walls.

"So what's going in downstairs, and when?" I asked.

Graeme hesitated before answering.

"Well, to be honest, we don't know yet. I know that sounds strange, but the building owner has been sworn to secrecy by the new tenant. I did see industrial kitchen equipment being unloaded earlier this week, so I'm assuming it's another restaurant. Nothing to worry about. Renovations resume next week. So it might be noisy for a bit, but whatever's going in is supposed to be up and running within the month. Then things should settle down."

"Is it possible it's a fish restaurant?" I asked. "I hate seafood and the stench that goes with it."

"I asked them the same question and you'll be pleased to hear the answer is no."

Graeme showed me three more apartments in the next two hours, but for one reason or another, none of them matched the first one. Not even close. So back we went to do the deal with the landlord who'd agreed to meet us there. It didn't take long. On the spot, I signed a month-to-month rental agreement, laid down first and last month's rent, and held the keys in my hand ten minutes later. Other than the minor question of furniture, plates, cutlery, and a shower curtain, I could move in anytime. I'd been in Orlando for less than twenty-four hours and had already nailed down my accommodations. Though the thought of spending much longer at Château Billy Kane was great motivation to do the deal quickly.

———

Dad wasn't in his room when I got there just after lunch. I knew he'd been tied up in physio all morning, hence my early afternoon arrival.

"Hi, I'm Everett Kane, Billy Kane's son. Do you know where I can find him?" I asked the older black woman filing charts at the nurse's station. Her name tag said Yolanda Robinson.

She wore a mint-green, um, nurse's outfit, a pantsuit I guess you would call it, with Nike running shoes. Her gold-rimmed glasses rested up above her forehead as if assisting a second set of eyes nestled in her closely cropped black hair.

33

"Well, there you have it! The big man was telling the truth, after all," she said, stepping back to give me the once-over and a big smile. "We had a little pool going on on the floor based completely on whether he'd been able to extend his unique line of DNA."

It was clear to me she meant this in a nice way. For the uninitiated, this might have seemed an odd opening line. But remember, she was talking about Billy Kane.

"Did you win?" I asked.

"I surely did," she replied. "I always try to see the best in people."

"Well, you must have very good vision."

She laughed.

"Well, sir, you have got quite a father there," she said with just the slightest suggestion of an eye-roll.

I was still pretty sure her tone was good-natured, but a less discerning observer might have called it exasperated.

"Yes, I know, he's a bit of a character," I replied. "Sorry about that."

"No apology needed," she said. "I can see beneath his macho bluster, overt leering, and constant flirting. And there's good stuff there, I know. I can see it."

"Really. Well, I'm glad you can see it. He doesn't always make it easy to find," I said with a sigh. "So he hasn't escaped, has he?"

"No, no, sorry, I should have mentioned, he's out walking the grounds. He's been very committed to his treatment, and he's making pretty good progress, so far."

"Will he get back to normal? I mean, his walking?" I asked.

"Everett, right?"

I nodded. She leaned her elbows on the counter top of the nurses' station and leaned toward me.

"Everett, it's hard to tell at this early stage. But if he does make a full recovery, it'll be because he's really worked hard at it. So far, he has." She pointed down the hall. "If you take a right at the Exit sign and go out the doors, you'll see the walkways criss-crossing the property. Don't push him too hard. He's teaching his leg to walk again. It's hard, boring, exhausting, and it's going to take time."

I nodded.

"Thank you."

I headed off toward the stairs.

"I hope we'll be seeing you around these parts more often," she said.

"For better or worse, that's the plan, Yolanda," I said.

"Trust me. It'll be for the better."

The grounds were quite lovely—well-manicured lawns, lots of trees and gardens, all interspersed with paved paths about ten feet wide. The paths were coded with little splashes of colour every fifty feet or so. A legend of sorts at the entrance to the grounds gave the length of each winding walkway. Blue was a quarter mile. Green was an eighth of a mile. Red was just a six-teenth of a mile. Yellow was only a hundred feet or so. Half a dozen patients, of varying ambulatory competence, were out on the paths. Many of them were accompanied by family, friends, or orderlies. It was a warm and sunny afternoon. It was Florida, after all.

An older man sat almost motionless in a wheelchair parked just outside the doors at the start of the Blue path, the brim of a battered Corvette Stingray ball cap shielding his eyes. He wore a frayed Chevy Malibu T-shirt that should have been retired long ago. His inert left arm curled in his lap, his hand closed in a fist. His right arm was resting on right wheel of his chair. His legs hadn't moved in the time I'd been standing next to him. With some effort, he leaned forward a bit and looked down the path.

I spied Dad from a distance, shuffling along the Yellow path wearing hospital-issue shorts, a loud, fluorescent green Ford Mustang T-shirt, and sturdy-looking New Balance running shoes. I just watched him for a while, his crew cut bobbing up and down as he kind of undulated along the path, a youngish orderly next to him. It was a far cry from walking. Calling it a limp would be lily-gilding in the extreme. He was pushing one of those walkers you see in seniors' residences. It was odd to see my father using one. He'd push the light metal frame a foot or so along the path on its two front wheels. Then he'd step forward with his good leg, before dragging his left leg up to join it. And I do mean dragging it. His left knee didn't really bend. And he had to lean to his right to reduce the friction of his left foot on the ground enough to move it. When he pushed the walker ahead again, I noticed that only his right hand was gripping it and doing most of the work. His left hand, the one affected by the stroke, seemed to be resting limply on the top rail of the walker, making only a slight contribution. I could see we had our work cut out for us.

I noticed that the older man next to me in the wheelchair was craning his neck so he could look at me.

"Hello," I said. "Are you trying to get someplace? Could I push you somewhere along the path?"

"What I'd like is for you to leave me alone and go and stand next to someone else for a while."

His voice was a little high-pitched and breathy.

"Oh, I see. Gee I'm sorry," I said. "Was I blocking your sun?"

"You're too short to block the sun. You're just standing too god-damn close to me."

"Sorry, I didn't realize I was crowding you here. I'm on my way. Sorry about that. That's my dad just over there. He had a stroke on the golf . . ."

"Hey, how about you stop talking and start walking."

"Right. Sorry."

Five-foot-nine and a half is not that short. In fact, it's exactly the average height of the Canadian male. I know. I've checked – often. That means I'm the same height as most other men in Canada. I'm right in the fat part of the curve. Would I rather be six-one or six-two? Who wouldn't? Yes, I know. I doth protest too much. But I'm fine with five-nine and a half. Just fine. Plus, I have good hair – and nice-looking hands. People tell me that all the time.

I moved down the path a little farther and sat down on a bench I hoped was far enough away from the cranky guy in the wheelchair. You never know, but I might be in a bad mood, too, if I were stuck in rehab hospital with my left side feeling like it belonged to somebody else.

I followed Dad's progress until he reached a bench about fifty feet down the path from mine. It had taken him nearly ten minutes. He sat down on the bench to rest. I heard the orderly tell Dad to sit tight and that he'd be back in a few minutes. Dad nodded, leaned back, and closed his eyes to the sun. I got up and walked over.

"Dad," I said as I approached. He looked up, blinking.

"Ev! You're here!" Dad said as he started to get up.

"Don't get up. Don't get up." I sat down beside him. "I'll join you."

"Come here," Dad said, as he wrapped his good arm around me. "It's great to see you. Thanks for coming."

I hugged back. We hadn't hugged for a very long time. In fact, I couldn't remember the last time.

"I was watching you," I said. "You look like you'll be running marathons in no time."

"You must have been watching someone else. I'm huffing and puffing after ten minutes and we've only covered a few yards. It's goddamn depressing, pardon my French."

"Dad, you've had a stroke. It's going to take some time. Maybe a lot of time to get your strength back and to teach your bum leg how to behave. We're starting from the very beginning here. I'm amazed you're out here on your feet at all so soon after you chunked that bunker shot."

"Shit. And my game was just starting to come around, too. I had the senior tour in my sights, and then this. It just ain't fair."

We sat in silence for minute or so. I reached for something else to say.

"Hey, Dad, who's the ill-tempered guy in the wheelchair over there?" I nodded my head in the direction of the main doors.

"Oh, that's Chevrolet," Dad replied. "I don't know his name but he's a prime, grade-A asshole. He wears a different Chevy hat or shirt every day, just to bug my ass."

"Just to bug you? Come on, Dad. Really?"

"I was wearing a Ford hat on the golf course and I still had it on when I arrived in this joint. When asshole Chevy-boy over there saw it, he flipped me the bird – just like that. I hadn't even said shit to the guy."

I stared at his gaudy green Mustang shirt.

"And now you don't go anywhere without making sure you're branded like a walking Ford dealership in case you bump into him. Right?"

"Yeah, well, when I get my feet under me again, I might do more than 'bump into him.'"

"Should we push on, Dad?" I asked, standing up. "Let's see if we can make it to the next bench."

Dad nodded, gripped the walker with his good hand, and heaved himself to his feet. I walked close beside him, as the orderly had.

"So what do you think of my pad?" my father asked as he shuffled along.

"Dad, I'm afraid no one on the planet still uses the term 'pad' to describe their place of residence. You could try 'crib' if you want to make people uncomfortable, but I think 'condo' is the safe bet," I replied. "And I like what you've done with the place. It's nice. It's fine for one person. And you can sit out on the balcony and heckle golfers. I like it."

"Sorry about the mess. It's usually in better shape. But I wasn't expecting to be cooped up here or I'd have done it up nice for you."

"Dad, it's fine. It looks like my first apartment in Toronto. I tidied up a bit and rented a tractor trailer to return your beer empties."

Dad had the grace to laugh.

"So are you feeling any pain?" I asked.

"Not much. My hips are aching a bit, but I don't have much feeling back in my left side yet. And it might not all come back. We don't really know what's going to come back."

He was starting to breathe heavily again.

"Are you on any medication?" I asked.

"Yeah, they got me on something to keep my blood thin. It helps stop the clots that cause strokes. But it means I got to be careful and not cut myself shaving or I'll bleed out fast."

"Really! That's not true, is it? You cut yourself shaving a lot."

"Well, it's sort of true. They want me to switch to an electric razor to reduce the risk of bleeding to death."

Dad was breathing hard now, making normal conversation more difficult. So we just ambled along in silence. Well, I ambled. Dad shuffled and dragged, shuffled and dragged. We were almost at our next objective. A quite attractive, older woman with a cane was sitting at the far end of the bench, writing on a pad of notepaper. She looked up as we approached and smiled. She somehow looked familiar to me, but I had no idea why.

"Afternoon, ma'am," my father said as he lowered himself onto the bench, a little closer to her than was necessary. "Can we join you? I need to take a load off before we start back."

"Of course. You're welcome to," she replied, turning back to her writing. Dad kept his eyes on her.

"You sure write a lot of letters," Dad said. "Every day I'm out here dragging my sorry butt and gimpy leg up and down this road to nowhere, and you're out here writing."

Again, she looked up and smiled.

"I'm handicapping the patients so I know who to bet on at the hospital track meet next month," she replied with a perfectly straight face. "You're coming along, but I need to see more progress from you before I consider risking any of my money."

She went back to her writing. Dad was flummoxed, but only for a moment.

"Well, the problem is, you're not seeing my best event," Dad countered. "The fifty-foot sprint was never my game. The pole vault is my specialty. We start training for that tomorrow, and I'm looking for a good spotter to help me plant my pole, if you know what I mean."

Yes, that's really what he said, while leaning over toward her. Unbelievable.

"Jesus, Dad, please," I hissed and swatted his arm. He looked back at me, puzzled. "I'm so sorry," I said to the woman. "He's recovering from a stroke and he's not himse —"

"What?" he interrupted. "I'm just having a nice chat with this young, attractive woman. Nothing wrong with that. And you'll have to whack my right arm if you want me to feel it."

She just smiled at me and shook her head a little.

"It's okay, young man. I deserved that. I foolishly set him up. And I should have known the inherent weakness of the male species would lead him to such a ribald, albeit clever and amusing, response. I do understand," she said, before turning to my father. "You, sir, are a live one."

"You got that right, ma'am. And it's only my left leg and part of my left arm that are temporarily giving me trouble. Everything else, and I mean *everything* else, works just fine."

I think I physically cringed.

"Okay, Dad. That's it! I can't believe this." I stood up. "Let's leave this miraculously patient and forgiving woman in peace. We have to get back now so I can have you sedated. Come on, up we go."

I positioned the walker for the return fifty-foot sprint and hoisted Dad to his feet.

"I hope to see you again, ma'am," Dad said solemnly.

"Well, I'm not going anywhere anytime soon," she replied, turning back to her writing.

———

"What the hell was that, Dad?" I hissed, after we were safely out of earshot.

"What? She's a looker. I was just making conversation. Nothing wrong with that! And did you see the pair of. . ."

"Stop, Dad!" I interrupted. "Dad, she is not the sum of her parts. She's a real person."

"Oh geez, here we go again," my father sighed. "Are you still banging that drum? I thought for sure you'd have outgrown that after all these years."

"Dad, it's not something you outgrow," I replied. "Anyway, don't you think she's a little old for you?"

"Yeah, well, who the hell cares? Around here, my options are limited. So I've learned to adjust my standards."

"Give me strength," I said, looking to the sky.

As we approached the door, I tried to steer Dad away from the man in the wheelchair, who was still anchored in the same spot, watching our progress. But Dad kept pulling me toward him.

"Ford dickhead," the old man said when we got close.

"Chevy ass-wipe," Dad replied.

"Hey, you know what Ford stands for, don't you?" Chevrolet asked. "Found On Road Dead."

"Yeah, except for those four Ford victories at Le Mans, against how many wins for Chevy?" Dad taunted over his shoulder. "Let me try to remember. Oh yeah, none, not a single one."

By this time we'd already passed Chevrolet but he managed to give us the finger as we moved through the doors.

Yolanda was waiting for us just inside.

"Mr. Kane, if you two car-nuts ever start a-brawlin', I can't guarantee any one of the staff will leap in to pull you apart."

"Don't you worry, Miss Yolanda. That's just the way I like it," he replied with a wink.

———

I made my escape after getting Dad set up in front of his TV while he rhythmically squeezed the two little black rubber balls in his left hand. His Ford Focus was still sitting in the parking lot, so I drove it back to my apartment.

Over the next week, I spent my mornings hunting down reasonably priced furniture, buying some kitchen and bathroom stuff, and arranging for cable TV and high-speed Internet in the apartment. I spent my afternoons walking and talking with Dad, while he ogled every woman, whether patient, doctor, or staff, who came within his field of view. He also exchanged a few epithets with Chevrolet each time he passed him. Each afternoon, the older woman from our first encounter, who still looked familiar somehow, was on a different park bench, always writing. For three days in a row, she would position herself on the next bench from where she'd perched the day before. I might be wrong, but it was as if she was giving Dad a new target each day, making him walk another fifty feet if he wanted to chat with her. He always made it, though their exchanges were always brief. They never even introduced themselves. They'd just leap into their acerbic jousting. I could only take about a minute of this before I became so mortified that I'd drag Dad back to his feet and make good our escape. She just kept smiling through it all. Dad thought she was playing hard to get, while I thought he was playing hard to like.

Finally, the furniture was delivered, including a bed, basic dresser, a kitchen table and four chairs, a cheap couch and easy chair, and a bland, wheat-coloured area rug for the living room. I picked up a flat-screen TV for an amazing price at a local big box store and set it up myself. Things were shaping up. Just before lunch on about day seven, I arrived at the apartment with the two boxes of books I'd just picked up at the FedEx depot. It certainly wasn't my entire book collection, but I needed at least some of my favourites to make me feel like this was my home, if only for a while. That's what books do for me. I sat on the floor in front of the built-in shelves and started unloading. There were biographies, lots of novels – mainly Canadian – some history, and memoirs. There weren't nearly enough books to fill the shelves, but plenty to make the place look welcoming and a little lived-in. That's what books do for apartments. I was unloading the memoirs from the second box when it happened. I don't know why it had taken me so long to realize it. Even with the passing of so many years, it should have dawned on me long before now. I held the book in my hand and looked at the face staring back at me. I could scarcely believe it, but it was true. I was sure of it. Shocked and excited, I headed for the door, the book in my hand.

It was just after lunch when I arrived.

"Why, young Everett, always great to see your smiling face," Yolanda said as I came through the doors. "That's every day this week. Can't get enough of us, huh?"

"Love it here," I said as I hustled by the nurses' station. "Just love it."

"I'll talk to the pharmacist to see if I can get you something for that," she replied, shaking her head.

Dad was in his room watching TV.

"Hi, Dad," I said as I passed right by his open door without slowing down. "I'll be back in a minute."

I just caught a glimpse of his perplexed look.

I nodded a greeting to Chevrolet as I passed his sentry post just beyond the doors to the walking paths. He grunted something, but I was moving too fast to notice what he'd said.

I found her on a bench at the far end of the Yellow path. She looked up from her writing when I stopped right in front her. She smiled.

"You're Beverley Tanner" was all I could muster.

"Nice to see you again, young man. But you have me at a disadvantage, sir," she replied.

The sun was behind me so she squinted a bit as she looked up.

"Sorry, I'm Everett Kane, son of the lewd and lascivious Billy Kane, your occasional bench mate."

"Everett. A lovely and sadly neglected name. Nice to meet you." She held out her hand and we shook.

"Now, how did you come to discover that I'm Beverley Tanner? No one has recognized me for years."

"I'm a fan" was all I said as I handed her the book I'd been holding behind my back.

"My, my, I haven't seen one of these for a good dozen years. Wherever did you get it?"

"I bought it at a used bookstore about eighteen years ago when I was in university," I started. "And I loved it. It had a big impact on me at a time when I was trying to sort some things out."

"I'm honoured and, well, surprised. I don't think that book was read by many sporting your anatomy."

The book she now held in her hands was her own memoir, *The Funny One*, with the edifying subtitle *Reflections of a Feminist with a Sense of Humour*.

"I can't believe you're here. I can't believe it's you. The odds of meeting you like this are, um, microscopic," I said.

"Yes, they're almost as low as meeting a youngish man who owns, and seems even to have read, my book, let alone liked it."

"Correction, loved it."

She tucked her note pad and pen into her small canvas bag and patted the bench beside her.

"Everett Kane, sit down and tell me your strange story. This, I have got to hear."

I sat down. She held the book on her lap. Suddenly, the world shrank, and I was unaware of anything else going on around us.

"Hmmm, how long do you have?" I asked.

"Well, I'm recovering from my fourth stroke in five years, so I could check out for keeps, any time now."

"No, no, no! That's not what I was asking," I stammered. "I just meant it's nearly four o'clock. When is dinner?"

"Have you had the food here? Trust me, I don't mind missing dinner. And neither will anyone else who's eaten the slop they serve in this place."

I was nervous. I was sitting with a hero of mine. Admittedly, she was not a conventional role model for someone like me. But there you go. I gathered my thoughts for a moment, trying to figure out how to tell her what she'd aptly described as my "strange story."

"Hellooo. This going to take long?" she gibed. "I don't mind missing dinner, but I intend to sleep tonight."

"Sorry, just trying to decide how to start."

"How about you start, say, at the beginning."

"Okay, okay. From the top, then," I began. "I've always thought of it as an awakening – my awakening. It happened while at school. When I started there nearly twenty years ago, Ryerson University was a hotbed of political activism. I suspect it still is. Most universities were. Central America, racism, the Middle East, funding to universities, terrorism, human rights, equality, you name it, the student movement was engaged in it. The Ryerson Student Union, always leaning a little, or sometimes a lot, to the left, played a leadership role in the national student movement. I was doing my degree in journalism. I had a strong interest in politics and got involved after successfully navigating my first year of university.

"When I made it into second year with reasonable marks, I decided I could begin to dabble outside of the classroom. In the fall of my second year, a vacancy on the Student Representative Council opened up when one of the journalism reps transferred to another school. I ran in the by-election against one other student. I printed up brochures and a few posters and asked my professors if I could talk to the class before they started their lectures. They usually agreed. My opponent was far less serious about it all than I. He stopped just short of promising beer in the drinking fountains. Thankfully, my fellow students were a discerning lot, and I won. That was how it all started.

"I spent the next three years immersed in student politics and the national student movement. My outrage at injustice of all kinds grabbed me by the throat and just wouldn't let go. One day I'd be marching for better working conditions for foreign workers. The next, I'd be writing a column in the student newspaper about the lack of diversity on Canadian corporate boards. The day after that I'd join a sit-in protesting the university's investment in companies that despoiled the environment. I was all over the activist's map. And I really felt like I was doing something. In hindsight, I might have been 'doing something,' but I don't think I was accomplishing anything. My colleagues and I were spreading ourselves very thin. Yet I'd never felt more fulfilled and energized in my life. I completely understand the powerful hold social movements can exert over their converts. It was almost like an addiction."

She nodded and smiled.

"Anyway, in my final year, I was burning out, but I didn't want to stop. I realized I needed to change something. I needed to focus in one area and put an end to my scattershot approach to activism. I thought I could contribute more and achieve more if I concentrated on one injustice, rather than all of them."

"A wise call. And I gather you chose gender equality as your personal mission," she said. I nodded. "Why?"

"I attended a powerful presentation about women in advertising given by a woman named Jean Kilbourne."

"*Killing Us Softly,*" she said, nodding. "She's still a good friend."

"Right! That was it. She was incredible. It was a revelation," I explained. "Right after that, I started to see gender discrimination, injustice, inequality everywhere I looked. Not to get too melodramatic about it all, but it was as if the scales suddenly fell from my eyes, and I could see. And I saw it everywhere. Everywhere!"

Beverley just nodded and smiled again.

"Plus, I realized that I'd seen the whole gender-role streaming thing play out in my own family, I guess the same way it does in millions of other families. But it was more pronounced in mine – remind me to tell you about my mother some time – so it struck close to home."

I paused in thought for a moment. Beverley let the silence hang, allowing me to hold the floor.

"But there was something else. I think it was partly a numbers game, for me. I decided if I was going to limit myself to one injustice, I wanted it to be 'the big one.' I figured that systemic gender discrimination prevails in every country and every society. So to put it crudely, I considered it more widespread than discrimination based on race, religion, sexual orientation, economic status, disabilities, and everything else. It won on the numbers. I think of it as the world's most pervasive injustice. For me, equality of opportunity for women became the holy grail of social causes even though I was born into the ranks of those largely responsible for the inequity in the first place. Strange, I know, but not without logic."

"Seems like a sound analysis to me, even for a man," she said. "But quite rare among men. Some might call it downright weird. Not I, but some."

"Yeah, well, plenty do think it's weird, including my own mother, and many of the women I've dated in the last decade or so."

"I'm sorry. I can see how that could pose a problem in affairs of the heart."

"But it bugs me that everyone thinks it's so odd that I should be a committed feminist. No one thought it was weird when so many white students worked on black voter registration drives in the south. Isn't this the same thing?"

"In principle, yes, but in practice, perhaps not," she replied. "Based on your father's daily performances, he clearly has some Neanderthal tendencies. How does he feel about his hardcore feminist son?"

"Well, my dad is a lifelong Republican and spent his entire career, nearly forty years, on the line at Ford, surrounded mainly by like-minded men – not exactly a crucible of progressive social thought."

"Ah, I see. So while you were focused on gender equality, he was focused on fender quality," she quipped.

"Very nice," I said.

"Thank you."

"Anyway, for quite a while, I think my dad thought I was gay, or a communist, or perhaps a gay communist. I don't quite fathom the logic in that. But my father has never been known for his logic."

"What did you do after you decided on your cause?"

"I borrowed and bought books and started reading up on the history of sexism and the women's movement. I knew that not being a woman left me unable to truly experience the injustice

I was fighting, so I tried to compensate by reading everything I could get my hands on. I read Wollstonecraft, de Beauvoir, Friedan, Millet, Dworkin, Jong, Brownmiller, MacKinnon, Steinem, you. I read *you*. I read them all, including the emerging Canadian feminist writers. In fact, *Women and Children First* by Michele Landsberg was as influential as almost anything else I read, back then."

"My goodness, aren't we earnest. I'm impressed. And you actually read their books? I mean, really read them?"

"Of course! Cover to cover. Most of them were great. The good ones made the issues so simple and straightforward. I remember thinking that if every man on earth could read one or two of those books, we might make significant progress in a very short time," I said. "Anyway, in the longer term, my goal was to graduate and begin a career as a crusading freelance journalist, exposing injustice, righting wrongs, of course with a focus on women's issues. Yeah, right. That worked out well."

"Let me guess," she said. "The world was not ready for a young man with the feminist bit between his teeth who wanted to write about women's equality. You were an anomaly, an aberration, a freak."

"Well, let's go with anomaly, shall we?"

"Certainly," she agreed. "So, however committed and informed you were, no one would hire you or assign you stories on the women's beat because it just wasn't credible. Some news outlets were skeptical. Some feminist editors might even have thought of you as fifth columnist, an undercover agent from the male species, bent on keeping women in their place."

"Wow, you are good," I said. "It's like you were there with me."

"I know that world. It was my world, a long time ago."

"Anyway, I ended up taking any writing gigs I could get, just to put food on the table and pay the rent. I've written very compelling newsletter stories for the Artificial Joint Manufacturers Association – think orthopedic, not narcotic – the Septic Tank Cleaners Association, the Canadian Society of Spiritualists, and the North American Broomball Federation. Surely you've read some of my work. I get all the big stories."

"Not exactly Woodward and Bernstein, I know, but you're surviving as a writer. That's saying something," she replied.

"Thanks, but it gets worse," I said. "In the last five years, I've gained a reputation as the 'go-to' writer for the cosmetics and make-up trade journals. The money is good and I've just kept doing it, despite the self-loathing and sense of betrayal."

"And the aging student activist slice of your soul is dying a little with each mascara article. Am I right?"

"I like to think of it as the slow but steady hollowing out of my principles. I'm now supporting the multibillion-dollar cosmetic machine that enslaves women and girls in the bonds of the beauty myth. It's pathetic, depressing, and demoralizing."

"Very poetic. You should write that down," she teased.

"I'm being paid by the very forces I worked against, while in the movement."

"And you're not happy."

"I am not happy."

"And discovering a certain old woman in a rehab hospital in Orlando only makes it worse," she suggested.

"Beverley, if I can call you Beverley, meeting you is an incredible thrill. But I guess it's reminded me of who I once was and who I seem to be now. It's as if my life peaked in university when, at the time, I thought I was just getting started. Instead, it's been a steady decline ever since."

"Calm yourself, young Everett," she soothed. "You're an unusual man, I'll grant you that. But you're young, and your heart and head seem to be in the right place. You've got a lot of time yet to make the mark you always wanted to make."

I was so focused on Beverley and my own wallowing that I hadn't noticed him until he was nearly upon us.

"I let down my guard for one minute and my own son is out here trying to put the moves on my girl," Dad said as he pushed his walker close and dropped onto the bench.

"Woman, Dad, she's a full-grown woman, and she certainly doesn't belong to you," I said evenly.

"Thank you, Everett, but I'm sure your father wasn't being serious," Beverley said.

I just looked at her with tilted head and elevated eyebrows.

"The hell I wasn't," Dad snapped.

I nodded.

"Oh dear" was all she said.

CHAPTER 3

After a five-minute, sometimes heated, debate, I finally persuaded Dad that my intentions with Beverley were honourable and wholly platonic. I then lectured him again on his near constant use of the word "girl" when he really meant "woman." You'd think I might have learned by then that lecturing my father was not exactly a high-percentage exercise. Let's just say he was very adept at missing the point, over and over again. I'm almost certain he was just messing with me, but he sure didn't make it obvious. Besides, I was still on the lookout for a stroke-related decline in his already limited powers of "perception and judgment." Finally, after practically stalking Beverley for the preceding few weeks, I thought it time to formally introduce Billy Kane, diehard boorish man's man, circa 1950, to Beverley Tanner, aging, iconic, witty feminist writer. Oil, I'd like you to meet water. Matter, say hello to anti-matter.

Dad didn't seem put off by her pioneering feminist background and beliefs, which I dutifully presented in some detail. Although, he might not have had a solid handle on what a feminist actually believes. I say that because he simply continued his shameless and thinly veiled sexual overtures, genuine or not. She parried his advances with patience, good humour, and the odd barb that may or may not have registered with Dad. It was painful to witness. He was clearly impressed that she'd written a book. He stared at her cover photo for an unduly long time before turning to Beverley, smiling, and nodding his head.

"Nice. Very nice," he said. "But I gotta say, as God is my witness, I think you look even hotter now."

"Dad, please don't do this," I said, eyeing the heavens.

"It's fine, Everett, he's not being serious," she said.

"The hell I'm not."

"And there you have it, my father has once again crashed right through the good-taste barrier, in record time."

This banter carried on for another few minutes until I could take it no more.

"Okay, that's it." I stood up and pulled Dad back to his feet.

"Whoa! Calm down, son, I'm just having a bit of fun," he protested.

"Dad, trust me when I say this. It's only fun for you."

"Ouch," Beverley said with a wince and a wink.

We left her on the bench and walked all the way to the end of the Yellow path. Then we tried a section of the Blue path until he was too tired to talk. Mission accomplished. We rested for a few minutes and then headed back inside.

Chevrolet was where he always seemed to be – directly between us and the door. Dad went right up beside him.

"Okay, look, Chevy, this is getting boring. I think we gotta bury the hatchet if we're going to be living under the same roof, don't you?"

Chevrolet looked wary but said nothing.

"Okay, me first," Dad said. "I'm Billy Kane and I worked the line at Ford for nearly forty years."

"Where?" Chevrolet asked with apparent disdain.

"Dearborn, then Oakville, up in Canada, then back to Dearborn till I got packaged out. You?"

Chevrolet paused for moment as if deciding whether to accept the olive branch Dad had extended.

"Kenny Jenkins. Forty-six years at GM in Flint, till they shut it all down. I started out making cars but in the end was only turning out generators and fuckin' fuel filters. Sad. Broke my heart."

"Okay, so we did the same goddamn thing on different sides of the fence. We got plenty of stuff to talk about."

Kenny just stared out at the walking paths as if Dad wasn't leaning over him.

"Okay, I'll start the wheel a turnin'," my dad said. "It's hard to get this out, but I'm prepared to say that the Corvette is an American classic. Okay, Chevy, you're up."

Finally, Kenny Jenkins turned slowly to look at Dad. He sighed.

"All right, Ford man, all right. You're goddamned right about the Vette. But I guess the Stang wasn't a bad car either, but only with the 351 Cleveland under the hood. The Windsor engine was pure shit."

"Well, the Cleveland was definitely better, but the Windsor wasn't that bad."

They circled one another for a few more minutes before Dad got tired standing and we headed back inside. They seemed to have paved enough common ground to park their respective cars on the same lot. That was a good sign.

"Good on you, Dad," I said, as I armed him back to his room.

"Life is short, son, even if you've spent most of it building cars."

He'd been doing a lot of walking. But even though I tried, I had difficulty seeing any measurable improvement in his gait. He still seemed to be dragging his left leg as if he had absolutely no control over it.

We made it back to his room, where he tipped himself onto his bed. I helped him swing his bad leg up. He closed his eyes for a time and sighed.

"Dad, does your left side feel any different, now that we've spent a week or so walking the equivalent of the Boston Marathon?"

He thought for a moment.

"I can't say it does," he replied. "You know, I thought I'd be down twenty pounds and out of this joint by now, or at least dancing the tango with a nurse with my hand on her ass."

For once, I bit, rather than unleashed, my tongue. Letting it go seemed wrong. It always seemed wrong. But another rebuke from me would hardly accomplish the desired outcome.

"Dad, this is a long-term thing. It's going to take time. And everyone recovers at a different pace. But you'll get there if you just keep doing what you're doing – and I'm only talking about the walking part."

"Blah, blah, blah" was all he said.

Right on cue, Beverley appeared at the door.

"Everett, if you can pop down to my room, it's two down and across the hall, I've got something I think you'd like to see."

"Of course," I replied.

"Jesus Murphy! There it is, right out in the open! Shameless. And while I'm lying right here, too," Dad piped up in mock indignation. "This is moving a little too fast. Just what exactly are your intentions, ma'am?"

"Well, Billy boy, based on your reaction, I'd say I've already fulfilled my intentions," she said, and promptly disappeared from view down the hall.

Dad just looked at me and smirked.

"Hell, she is a real pistol, that one," he said, shaking his head.

She was more than a pistol. At one time, Beverley Tanner was a leader among the most prominent and recognizable feminists in North America. She was part of the small group of activists who helped Gloria Steinem launch *Ms.* magazine back in 1971. But by the early eighties, she had left *Ms.*, receded from the public eye, and was now largely forgotten (except by amateur feminist historians, like me).

A few minutes later, I knocked, though her door was already open.

If I'd surfaced from a coma in her room, I'd have had difficulty deciding if I were in a home with hospital equipment or a hospital with homey touches. She was sitting in a distinctly non-hospital easy chair by her window. She waved me in and I took the more institutional and uncomfortable chair across from her. A weathered wooden trunk with a kind of fringed tablecloth draped over it sat on the floor between us, impersonating a coffee table. In my limited experience, hospitals don't usually provide antique wooden trunks, so I assumed it belonged to her. Her pen and paper rested on it, always within reach.

"It looks like you've settled in here," I said. "How long do you think you'll be staying?"

"I've been in here, on and off, for months at a time, for the last four years. They're watching me pretty closely. My last stroke hit my left side quite hard. Two months ago, I was walking like your father is now. I expect I'll be here for another month or so, unless I'm struck again. And frankly, that's probably what will happen. I'm a big old stroke waiting to happen. It's sort of what it must be like to live in San Francisco, waiting for the quake to end all quakes. But I'm still here and I'm still waiting."

She smiled and raised her hands, as if to say "Ta-daaa!"

"How do you know it'll happen again? How do the doctors know?"

"They're smart folks. They look at my history, my blood, my circulatory system, and my damned propensity to throw clots, and they just know. There's not much mystery to my situation. So I wait."

I didn't know what to say to that, so I handed her my copy of her memoirs.

"I forgot to ask when we were outside, but I'd be thrilled if you would inscribe this."

"Well, you thrill mighty easily," she replied, reaching for the pen on her coffee table/trunk. "Of course, I'll sign it."

"Two Ts?" she asked.

"Yep, two Ts."

"Well, I haven't done this for more than a few years, now."

She finished and handed it back to me.

It said: "From one ardent but unusual warrior to another. Keep the faith. On the eve of equality, Beverley Tanner."

"Thank you. That means a lot," I said. I paused. "What was it like, I mean, really like, back at the very beginning?"

"I must look older than I am," she quipped. "But if we're talking about a woman's place in the world, you're dead right. I believe it did start, as you say, right back at the very beginning."

"Well, *Ms.* magazine started in '71, didn't it?"

"Ha! A common misconception," she replied. "In my

sometimes addled mind, *Ms.* magazine started much, much earlier. In fact, I've always thought the die was cast even before humans had language. In the earliest stirrings of human civilization, when survival often depended on physical strength, men found themselves at the top of the food chain by default, despite their obvious cerebral shortcomings. Add in the physical reality of pregnancy, childbirth, and child-rearing, and the deal was done. The subjugation of women was etched in stone alongside the cave paintings that celebrated man as the great hunter. Not everyone agrees with me on that score, but I've had a lot of time to think about it."

I nodded, thinking.

"If you don't mind me asking, why did you kind of fade from the feminist scene? The book mentioned a rift of some kind, as I recall."

"Like most social movements, anger was the founding fuel. Without it, I doubt anything would have happened. But anger has its poisonous side. It can stop you from seeing things clearly. That worried me, because eventually, the media and the people stopped listening. After a while, the rage that caught their attention in the early days just seemed to wash over them. It was like we'd somehow inoculated them against anger even though we were all still banging the angry drum. That's when the phrase 'feminists have no sense of humour' seemed to take hold. And it stuck. It's been a millstone hanging around the movement's neck ever since."

"And you were 'the funny one,'" I said.

"That's what they called me. I always believed humour could be a trenchant instrument of change, even social change, if wielded carefully. But most of the activists around me thought it would trivialize what was a very serious issue."

"Right. Hence the rift," I said.

"Hence the rift," she agreed. "I think when you take aim at an injustice armed not just with rage, but with humour, you stand a better shot at winning. And I have always loved to laugh, especially at whatever I'm fighting. It shows the movement has confidence. When you laugh at patriarchy, you weaken it. You take away some of its power."

"So what do you think of the movement today?" I asked.

"It was certainly much simpler back in the seventies. You were either a feminist or you weren't. It was a binary decision. There were no hyphenated-feminists," she said.

She paused in thought for a moment before continuing.

"You know, one of the benefits of a movement that has grown so much and gained at least some ground in the last forty years is that it's now mature enough to support divergent views. We can sustain differing opinions within the feminist tribe without threatening the whole. So we now have hardcore feminists disagreeing on pornography, and affirmative action, equal pay laws, and any number of other related issues. Having so much internal debate and even dissent is fresh and invigorating and vital. But it can also be challenging."

"And a little confusing," I added. "How do you now define the term 'feminist'?"

"The same as I always have. To me, a feminist is anyone who believes that women should have equal rights and equal opportunity in society. It's as simple and clear as that."

"Exactly! I feel the same way," I replied. "Then what's with the recent backlash against the term? There's even a #notafeminist Twitter hashtag going around, often promoted by young women. It's crazy."

"I've read about that and it's very dismaying. Perhaps they don't realize they're reaping today what we sowed on their behalf thirty and forty years ago. I think they'll come around. Perspective often comes with time. But it is troubling."

"But on the bright side, we have made some progress. Look at all the laws that have changed," I said.

"Agreed. But changing laws is the easy part. The real goal must be to change minds and change attitudes. New legislation helps, but we need people, men and women, to think and act differently before we can truly claim victory."

"Amen to that."

We went on like this for quite a while, though I can't tell you how long. I found it fascinating. I found her fascinating. It was amazing to talk with her. She was a time machine. She took me back to my student movement days, eighteen years behind me. She took me back to how it felt to be part of something larger than yourself. I liked being back.

She folded the fringed cloth and lifted the lid of the trunk between us.

"Having met so few men feminists as informed and dedicated as you, I don't think I've ever shown this to another man," she said.

She pulled out a slim and very old book, bound in faded red cloth, and handed it to me. I cradled it in my hands as if I were holding a baby bird and looked at her.

"It's okay, you can open it, gently," she said. "It's survived nearly 150 years, and it's meant to be read. In fact, the world would be a much better place if more people read this short volume."

I opened the pages gingerly and made my way to the age-stained title page where I read: *The Subjection of Women* by John Stuart Mill, 1869.

"Is this a first edition?" I asked.

"It surely is."

"I've never heard of this book. I've read Mill's *On Liberty*, but I've never come across this."

"Who hasn't read *On Liberty*? We've all read *On Liberty*. It overshadows the rest of his writing. It's undoubtedly a great work. But so is this, in its own way," she said, pointing to the faded red book in my hands. "Just read the very first paragraph."

I started reading it to myself.

"Aloud, if you please," she said. "I never tire of it."

I read aloud.

The object of this Essay is to explain as clearly as I am able, the grounds of an opinion which I have held from the very earliest period when I had formed any opinions at all on social or political matters, and which, instead of being weakened or modified, has been constantly growing stronger by the progress of reflection and the experience of life: That the principle which regulates the existing social relations between the two sexes – the legal subordination of one sex to the other – is wrong in itself, and now one of the chief hindrances to human improvement; and that it ought to be replaced by a principle of perfect equality, admitting no power or privilege on the one side, nor disability on the other.

"Wow. That perfectly sums it up in one paragraph, doesn't it? And from 1869!"

"Indeed, back in a time when it would have been a Herculean task for any woman writer to have published such a book," she replied.

"Could I borrow this?" I asked, without thinking.

She winced. So I winced.

"Alas, that is a prized possession that I just don't think I can lend, not just to you, but to anybody," she started. "However, all is not lost. Do you have a computer or an iPad?"

She reached in the trunk again and held up her iPad.

"I do," I replied. "Both."

"That Mill treatise is, by now of course, in the public domain and may be downloaded for free from multiple sources, including the diabolical behemoth, Amazon. When I read Mill, I do so now on my iPad. It's lovely to be able to enlarge the font."

"I'll download it as soon as I'm home tonight."

"Mill is not perfect in his message. He remains a creature of his time. But his central thesis captured in that very first paragraph of ornamented, Victorian prose is very nearly perfect."

Yolanda peeked into the room holding a translucent plastic cup bearing what appeared to be several pills.

"If I could interrupt you two hippie activists, it's time for Ms. Tanner's dessert." She shook the plastic cup so it sounded like maracas.

"Olé" was all Beverley said and took the cup Yolanda offered.

———

When I arrived back at my apartment, the noise from the renovations in the space below me was fearsome. As I sat in my new living room reading the *New York Times* on my iPad, I watched as my kitchen table shimmied across the floor, riding the vibrations from below. There was a symphony of sounds coming from downstairs. Hammering, a circular saw, a pneumatic drill, workers arguing, and a powerful percussive noise that made me think of blasting caps. What was going on down there?

I tried to ignore the noise. I was reading an article that immediately made me think again of Beverley Tanner. It was a piece headlined "Mason Bennington: The Future of Men's Entertainment?" It was about a chain of high-end gentlemen's clubs that this guy, Bennington, was opening across the country.

It was a new take on the neighbourhood strip joint where women had been exploited, and men entertained, for generations. Instead of rundown establishments located in seedy low-rent districts where vagrants, drunks, and drug addicts were the prevailing demographic, this new incarnation of the strip club was usually nestled in a ritzy part of town. High-end furnishings, mahogany bar, mood lighting, nicely dressed security staff, and good food gave it the feel of an upper-crust men's club. The only difference was that stunningly beautiful women would dance on stage, eventually wearing nothing at all.

Known simply as XY, presumably after the male chromosome, Mason Bennington's clubs seemed to be raking in the members and raking in the dough. There was lots of security to enforce the strict "no-touching" rule. The dancers were highly paid and were therefore never tempted to offer customers any additional services beyond exotic dancing. If they ever did, they'd be fired. They were also offered health benefits and even had the opportunity to participate in a retirement plan funded in part by XY.

Men had to join as members and observe strict rules of behaviour or their membership would be revoked with no refund.

So far, XY clubs in New York, Washington, Chicago, Boston, Dallas, Los Angeles, and San Francisco were all flourishing. The article went on to note Bennington's plans to expand to Seattle, Houston, New Orleans, and other undisclosed markets.

I wondered what Beverley would think about XY. I fired up my laptop, and my good friend Google quickly provided lots of opinions on Mason Bennington. Many thought he was a hero for cleaning up the strip scene. He was lauded for paying the dancers a top-notch wage and for keeping them off the streets where they'd be more vulnerable to violence and poverty. Others thought he was just another greedy misogynist exploiting women to make money, but with plusher seating and better lighting. There were also rumours of ties to organized crime. It was an easy call for me, and I suspect for Beverley Tanner. I finished the *Times* and turned off my iPad.

I was just moving my kitchen table back to its normal position when the heavy vibrations started up again from below. It felt and sounded like something was coming right up through the floor, directly below the table. Just then, something came right up through the floor, directly below the table. As the whirling object ground to a stop, apparently stuck in my kitchen floor, even I could identify the business end of an electric drill. Well, I assume it was electric. Then again, given the noise, vibration, and the ease with which it entered my kitchen right through the floor, it could have been a nuclear drill for all I knew. A moment later, the drill receded, leaving me an obscured view of the room below, through a veil of sawdust.

"Hello?" I shouted through the hole in my floor. "Maybe you shouldn't have taken that left at Albuquerque because you just drilled right into my apartment!"

"Oh shit!" a voice said from below. "You weren't home when I checked a while ago. Hang on a sec."

A minute or two later, I could hear someone climbing the stairs, followed by a knock at my door. I opened it to find a big guy dressed either for construction or demolition, I wasn't sure which.

"Uh, hi. Peter Blackwell. Yeah, ah, sorry about this. We've been rushing to finish the place downstairs on time. Anyway, we had to install this, ah, fixture just below here, but you weren't home earlier. So we put it off as long as we could, but you still weren't home."

"Yeah, I was visiting my dad in the hospital."

"Oh geez, sorry about that. Anyway, we decided we couldn't wait any longer and were just going to get the hole drilled and leave you a note on your door to let us in to finish the job tomorrow. But here you are, home. You must have just come in."

"About fifteen or twenty minutes ago," I replied. "Did you really mean to drill right through my floor?"

"Yep. The fixture is going to be under a lot of stress when the place opens up, so the engineer told us we had to bolt it right through the floor, rather than just screwing it into the ceiling below."

"Yeah, well, it would have been nice to hear about in advance so I could, you know, prepare for a drill coming up through my floor."

"Look, I'm sorry, we didn't think you were home," he said. "Just give me a minute to finish the job and then we'll be out of your hair for good."

"Fine, but I'm more interested in when you'll be out of my *ears* for good. The noise is a bit of a problem."

I stepped out of his way so he could move the kitchen table and crouch down.

"I know. I'm sorry. It won't be long now. The place is supposed to open in the next couple of weeks."

He bent down close to the hole and shouted.

"Okay, Anthony, you know what to do. Let's go!"

A few seconds later, a fat threaded bolt came right up through the floor.

"Okay, hold it there."

Peter reached into his pocket and pulled out a plastic package. He ripped it open and took out a very large nut (at least I'm pretty sure it's called a nut).

"Shit, there's no lock washer," he said before moving closer to the hole again.

"Anthony, there's no lock washer. Where is it?" he shouted.

A muffled response seeped into the room around the threaded bolt.

"I told you yesterday, they're fuckin' backordered! You gotta go without for now."

"Shit. Sorry about the language. But this fixture really should have a lock washer. Anyway, I guess we gotta go with just the nut, for now."

Peter threaded the nut and then pulled a giant honking wrench from some secret pocket in his work pants. I wondered what other gargantuan tools of the trade he might have secreted in his clothes. Using the wrench, he tightened the nut, punctuated by two loud grunts and a very heavy exhalation. Then he took a rag from his back pocket and buffed up the nut so it looked better than nuts usually look when protruding from kitchen floors.

"That must be one honking heavy chandelier you're hanging," I said.

"Well, actually. . ." he stopped. "Okay, yeah, it's a very heavy chandelier."

"So what's the big secret going in downstairs, anyway?" I asked. "Restaurant? Bar? Bowling alley? CIA headquarters? The Riddler's lair? What?"

"You're asking the wrong guy. I got nothing for you. The boss is a little, yeah, a little concerned about security and secrecy. We get fired if we say anything about the job we're on. I lost a good guy last week who blabbed to the dude delivering drywall. So you'll get nothing from me. Sorry."

"Even though you just drilled a big-ass hole in my kitchen floor?"

"Yep. Sorry."

The din continued after Peter returned downstairs and didn't stop for the day, er night, until just after 10 p.m. Man, it was quiet when the compressor and pneumatic drill were finally shut down. It was so still you could almost hear a spoon drop. In fact, when I dropped a spoon onto the kitchen floor, the noise was almost deafening. I was about to head to bed when my cellphone chirped. I looked at the call-display screen before answering.

"Hi, Mom."

"Hi, Ev. Where are you?"

"I'm standing in the kitchen of my new apartment here in Orlando, or should I call it *our* new apartment?"

"Good, so that means you got the money I transferred."

"Well, if I hadn't, there's no way I'd be standing in the kitchen of *our* new apartment."

"Good, I'm glad. So bring me up to date. How's your father?"

"If you were only listening to him you'd think nothing happened. He's just the same crusty, off-colour, sexist. . ."

"I know what's he like, Ev, I was married to him," she interrupted.

"Right. Well, mentally he's just as socially stunted as he always was, but physically, he's kind of in rough shape."

"How rough?"

"Right now, his left leg is really just dead weight. He just drags it along behind him. I'm sure his right leg is getting nicely toned because it's working harder than it should be to compensate. And his left hand is not what it used to be. He'll never be able to cut the cards with that hand alone. His fine motor control is virtually nonexistent at this stage. So his dream of learning the violin and playing at Carnegie Hall is out the window."

"Oh, God."

"Mom, he's going to be okay by the end of all this. We're working on his walking every day. And he spends the rest of his time in physio and squeezing these two little black balls in his left hand to regain his strength and control. It's going to take some time, but he can and will recover from this. He can do it. We can do it."

"How much has he improved in the last week or so?"

"Like I said, it's going to take some time, but he'll get there."

"So, there's been no improvement? None at all?"

"I've lost four pounds if that counts, and Dad is able to drag his left leg faster than he could before," I said. "Mom, we're going to get there."

"Well, you'll be pleased to know that I'm moving down for a while, so I can help out, too," she said.

"Mom, you don't need to do that. I've got it under control. You've got a company to run."

"Relax, Ev. It's really company business that's bringing me down. We're finally breaking ground on a big new resort across from Disney. I've been working on the deal for the last two years, and it's time to put shovels in the ground. So I'm coming down. I don't trust our jackasses down there to get it right. So I'm doing it myself."

"I didn't know your duties included putting shovels in the ground."

"I'm supervising. I'll be the one wearing the white hard hat. The white hats do a lot of standing around and issuing orders. It's right up my alley."

"I see."

"And when I'm there, I'll drop in on your father, now and then. And you and I can see more of one another, too."

"That would be great, Mom. But be prepared for a less than effusive reaction from Dad. You might be cramping his style at the hospital. He's been on the prowl since he got there, if you can prowl with only one good leg. There seem to be more women patients than men."

"Just the way your father likes it. Don't worry, I won't be staying long."

"By the way, Mom, have you ever heard of a guy named Mason Bennington?"

"I was hoping never to hear that name again," she replied. "Yes, regrettably, I have come across him."

"How? Why?"

"We had some discussions with him about locating one of his fancy clubs in one of our adult-oriented resorts. I found him to be ruthless, conceited, and of questionable moral fibre. But we turned him down in the end, so who cares."

"Good for you, Mom. You made the right call," I said. "Thanks for saying no to an exercise in misogyny."

"I couldn't care less about misogyny. We turned him down because the numbers weren't there for us. We said no to an exercise in losing money."

"I'm so proud."

"Pardon?"

"Nothing," I said. "Regardless, you still made the right call."

———————

I tried to sleep, but my mind was still whirring from my talk with Beverley. I downloaded *The Subjection of Women* and read a good chunk of it. Beautiful, if ornate, writing, but with a real mission. I set it aside to try again to sleep. I tossed and turned for a while. Then I switched it up and tried turning and then tossing for a while, to no avail. I tried to identify what I was feeling, why I couldn't sleep. Eventually I decided I was excited. Yes, excited. Talking with Beverley had rekindled feelings that had been submerged since my days in student politics. I realized, in hindsight, that I had never felt more alive, never felt more needed, never felt more focused, than I had while working in the student movement, particularly on gender equality issues. I'd also never felt more angry than when I realized the extent to which society favoured men over women, and always had. I remember being utterly outraged when the full force of the history and ubiquity of women's inequality sank in. Yes, I was a serious young man back then. I was lots of fun to be around in those days.

I was mad because I began to see my chosen injustice everywhere around me, every day. In advertising, media stories, TV shows, movies, and books. I heard it in daily conversations with my own family, friends, colleagues, professors, and perfect strangers. It was everywhere. I was immersed in it. Society was immersed in it. I perhaps became a little too invested in the cause. Friends started avoiding me or censoring what they said around me, lest they offend my precious principles. My male friends stopped commenting on attractive women when we were together. In hindsight, I was not great company for a time back then. Come to think of it, my three most recent girlfriends might suggest that all these years later, I'm still not much fun to be around.

I know this all seems a little strange, a little weird. I know it seems far too earnest – that I'm far too earnest. It often feels that way to me, too. But that's how I felt back then, how I still feel today. I can't help it. I can't just turn off anger over an inequality that is so insidious and pervasive yet is accepted by so many. And it bothers me that society considers a man's feminism to be so strange, to be so aberrant. If I were as deeply committed to environmental protection, or nuclear disarmament, or animal rights, it would not be weird at all. But a man who feels deeply about women's equality is immediately suspect – "He must have ulterior motives." "He must be trying to meet women." A staunchly feminist man simply does not fit within the accepted order of the universe. But there you have it.

I still couldn't believe I'd met and spoken with Beverley Tanner in a rehab hospital in Orlando. I replayed our conversations in my mind. She seemed to have tapped a spring of beliefs and emotions that, while not exactly dormant, had not been this close to the surface for some years. (I had botched three relationships in the last two years with women who certainly wouldn't consider my opinions on the topic to have been anywhere near dormant. But everything is relative. On the other hand, I'd spent the last few years writing stories for cosmetic magazines. Go figure.) One seldom has an awakening like the one I had while at university. Having a second, eighteen years later, seemed even rarer.

I lay in bed, not sleeping. It was close to three in the morning and I was unable to shut down my brain. I couldn't stop thinking about the aging feminist icon rehabbing quietly and trading barbs with my sophomoric father in an Orlando hospital. I thought it must be a sign – meeting Beverley, I mean, not my sophomoric father. As unusual as it was for a youngish man like me to have gravitated toward women's equality as a cause so many years ago, I liked the feeling that came with this renewed sense of purpose, this renewed sense of mission. But I was no longer in the student movement, surrounded by equally committed people who could muster a protest rally and devise creative chants in the perfect marching cadence, all on a moment's notice. Those days were gone. That was years ago. I'm on my own now.

So how to seize this moment before it slips away, and act on the interest and energy Beverley seemed to have reignited? How can I capitalize on it? How can I contribute, now? What can I do? Those were the questions swirling in my head as I closed my eyes and tried to sleep.

And when I snapped awake again just a few minutes later, I found the answers sitting right there, waiting for me. Only one question remained unanswered: Why the hell was there a giant nut and bolt coming up through my kitchen floor?

CHAPTER 4

I'm a writer. So I'll write. That was the answer. Simple and clear. Still, it took me a while to figure out what it actually meant. I cycled through the possibilities. I could write articles and submit them to newspapers and magazines where they would surely be rejected and never run. A feminist man writing about women's equality was kind of a "man bites dog" story, but still a little too strange to yield much traction in the mainstream media. No. I guess I could write a collection of essays or even a book on the issues as I saw them and then join the ranks of millions searching in vain for a literary agent or publisher. No. Wait, I could always self-publish it. Yes, I suppose I could, but then what? Selling self-published books is extremely difficult, even one as captivating and scintillating as the tome I would write about gender equality. No bookstores would stock it. No one would know about it. I'm pretty sure my parents would enjoy the book. Hang on, come to think of it, I'm really not sure my parents would even read the book, let alone enjoy it. So, no. What else have I got?

It took some web surfing for the idea to land. I probably should have thought of it sooner. I turned it over in my mind, considering the opportunity, examining it from various angles. Hmmm, it might just work. Why not a blog? Yes, a blog. I could write a blog exploring women's equality. Blogs are increasingly popular and influential, drawing a growing number of subscribers. It was a nimble platform that would allow me to make timely comment on current events and related issues in the news. A blog. Yes, that might be just the ticket.

You might be wondering what made me think I could write blog posts that would be of interest to anyone. There were other feminist bloggers out there. Lots of them. Lots of really good ones. What could I contribute that was different, more compelling, more meaningful, more effective, more powerful than what already existed in the online world? Well, the obvious short answer was, I had no freakin' idea. I really didn't. I certainly wasn't convinced I had anything more or anything different to offer than that which was already out there. But I wanted to try. I felt I needed to try. I was eager to recapture the passion of my university years, when I felt I belonged to something. And I wanted to staunch the feeling of drift and ennui that accompanied a career that had not panned out the way I'd wanted. I was motivated again. I feared that if I didn't leap now, my rekindled ardour might flag. I needed to act. In the end, the idea was rooted in my desire to get off the sidelines and do something. It was really to satisfy me. I had no expectations that anyone would read my blog, let alone consider it a worthy contribution to the feminist ferment. I just wanted to do it, to do something, even if it were just for me.

My mind turned again to Beverley Tanner as the digits on my bedside clock approached 4:30. I decided to try to take a page from her playbook. I liked the notion of humour as a weapon in the fight. I would try to leaven anger with humour. There still wasn't a great deal of "funny" in the women's movement. I'd try to laugh at patriarchy to weaken it. I'd write short, thoughtful, bal-anced, reasonable, readable posts about a range of equality issues in the hopes of building support among men and women who perhaps didn't think of themselves as feminists, even though they probably were. The idea would be to motivate the silent majority of feminists to do more than privately support equal rights. So in each post, I'd try to have some kind of a simple, personal call to action. In my wildest dreams, I wanted my writing to spur even a modest behavioural change in my readers, or at least cause them to think, if only for a moment or two. That was the extent of the plan. It was clearly an "easier said than done" moment, or perhaps even an "are you crazy, you'll be crucified" moment.

But do I sign my name to it? Do I shove myself forward as the blogger? This wasn't easy. I went back and forth on it. I knew that in the blogosphere – yes, that's what they call it – the idea of transparency was important. On the other hand, I didn't want the fact that I was a man writing a feminist blog to overshadow what I was writing. Without going all Marshall McLuhan on you, as the medium, I didn't want to become the message. Besides, the anatomy of the blogger shouldn't be important or even relevant. Rather, it's all about the words, the message, the cause. Secondly, I truly believed that a man should not be seen to be out front on feminism. That would be just like a man to try to take over the women's movement. We'd taken over everything else in history, in society, in the world, why not feminism, too? No, I don't think so.

So I made the call. It would be an anonymous blog. No one would know I was the author. I wasn't after recognition. I just wanted back that feeling I'd had years earlier. I just wanted to help move the yardsticks toward the goal of gender equality. Oops, check that. I wanted to help "make some gains" toward the goal of gender equality. I was obviously rusty after my fifteen-year hiatus from the movement. Never, ever, should one employ football metaphors in the service of women's equality, particularly when the Lingerie Football League is still with us (I'm not kidding). Never.

I finally fell asleep around 5:00 and didn't open my eyes until 10:30. The name for the blog presented itself shortly thereafter. It was staring at me in Beverley's inscription in my book. I wanted something optimistic and forward-looking. And even though it was to be an anonymous blog, I liked that my own name would be buried in the blog's moniker. No one would ever know. I waited for an hour to see if I still liked the name I'd lifted from

Beverley. I did. And I liked that she was somehow part of it, now. So I signed in to Wordpress.com using a fake name and newly minted Gmail address and created a blog with a simple, clean look. The masthead read *Eve of Equality*. I liked it. It spoke of positive change in the past, but also clearly indicated that we hadn't yet made it to the promised land. Yeah, I liked it. On the blog's "About" page, I simply wrote *"Eve of Equality* is a feminist blog offering thoughts and observations on a spectrum of issues that touch women's equality." Broad enough. Bland enough. Anonymous.

I decided to host the blog separately and privately from Wordpress.com. It just made me feel like I had more control over it. So I arranged for hosting services locally with a smallish firm creatively called OrlandoHosting. I did it all online and by email using the same fake name and Gmail address I'd used with WordPress to create the blog in the first place. It did require a phone number, which left me a little uneasy. But after some hemming and hawing, I provided my cell number. The hosting fees were reasonable, and the blogger reviews I read on the Internet spoke well of OrlandoHosting. Good enough for me. Twenty minutes later, the online infrastructure was ready. I had only to write a blog post, hit the big blue Publish button, and it would be live.

I spent what was left of the morning browsing through the top-ranked feminist blogs on the Internet. I found a wide variety of bloggers representing women academics, man-hating extreme feminists, countless women's advocacy groups, young women, older women, straight women, LGBT women, women homemakers, women entrepreneurs, women athletes, women lawyers, women politicians, women teachers, women of science, women of medicine, women chefs, women union leaders, women civil servants, women against porn, women for porn, and many, many more. (I've just barely scratched the surface here.) And they all, every last one of these women bloggers, considered themselves feminists. It was a very crowded space reflecting not just the urgency of the need, but also the breadth and complexity of today's women's movement. And I found all these in just the first few pages of a standard Google search.

However, even after digging deeper and switching to other search engines, nowhere, and I mean nowhere, did I find an anonymous feminist blog featuring thoughtful, informed, occasionally amusing, but still serious posts, written by a youngish feminist man pining for his days in the student movement. Against all odds, there was nothing that even faintly resembled my vision for *Eve of Equality*. Great! There was obviously a gargantuan hole in the anonymous feminist blogosphere that needed filling. The particular audience seeking just such a perspective demanded and deserved satisfaction. Well, I'm your man, er, blogger.

———

When I left my apartment later in the afternoon to head back to the hospital, I noticed two workers varnishing the beautiful

newly installed wooden front door to the establishment downstairs. Green garbage bags enveloped and protected what seemed
to be oversized door handles. They were making progress. It
wouldn't be long now. A line of young people, mainly women,
okay, almost all women, snaked out of the side alley and curled
onto the sidewalk in front of the building. They were all holding forms of some kind in their hands. I figured secret job
interviews were underway in the secret business below my
apartment. Kitchen staff? Waiters? Okay, a bar or restaurant,
perhaps? Pounding music seeped out of the establishment.

A big guy, a really big black guy, in a black suit with an earphone stood off to the side where the line ended. I couldn't
help but stare at the last young woman in the line. She was
quite stunning. Beautiful face, short auburn hair, and a body
that actually conformed to the unrealistic standards fashion
magazines have been setting for decades. And there it was,
another sneak attack of what I've come to call my "principle-
personal paradox."

No matter how committed I am to women's rights, no matter
how deeply I feel about gender equality in my head and in my
heart, still I couldn't help but be struck by the sight of what society considered an attractive woman. I don't know whether it's
purely visceral, hormonal, or instinctive, but it happens, quite
often. I'd catch myself staring, and force myself to look away.
Sometimes I'd weaken and sneak another peek while she was
still in my field of view. It made the high-minded progressive

liberal in me cringe and complain. But it was difficult not to look sometimes, not to appreciate physical beauty. I sometimes wondered whether it was an offshoot of aestheticism, the noble search for true beauty. But just as often I thought there might be a more primal sexual angle to it. Who the hell knows?

The principle-personal paradox. *My* principle-personal paradox. My brain hurt thinking about it. I felt guilty and conflicted, but I don't want to overstate it. It wasn't exactly like the monk who flayed himself and bled over impure thoughts. But still, I didn't feel good about it when it happened.

She raised her eyes and caught my lingering look.

"Job interviews?" I asked.

"You could say that," she replied.

"Keep walking, please," commanded big black suit earphone guy. "Nothing to see here."

I was about to make a crack about the CIA or the movie *Men in Black* but decided against it. I had serious reservations about this guy's sense of humour. So I just walked on by, slipped into my father's car, and pulled into traffic.

Dad and I made our way slowly along the Red path until we found her, as usual, writing, sitting alone on one of the benches spaced along the walking trail. It was a beautiful day. Cotton ball clouds hung in a cobalt sky. Thankfully, it was not overly hot for Florida.

"Looking good, *Mrs.* Tanner," Dad said, enjoying his little jibe as he continued up the path.

"Now, Billy, I think we can dispense with that archaic, outmoded, value-burdened prefix. You can call me Beverley, the way Everett does. I'd say we're now on a first-name basis. Wouldn't you?"

Dad kept shuffling but aimed a strained smile back at her as he passed.

"Whatever you say, little lady," he wheezed.

"Dad, don't you think it's time to retire 'little lady' from your repertoire?" I asked.

"Ha. There's more where that came from. I've got a million lines like that" was all he said in reply.

"You say that as if might be an attractive attribute," Bev said, almost, but not quite, under her breath.

Dad just laughed and continued walking. As we'd negotiated, I sat down with Beverley. We'd agreed that if Dad walked two more benches up the path, he could turn around and drag himself and his walker back to join us.

"He's incorrigible, unrepentant, and unreconstructable, if that's even a word," I said.

"He's your father," she replied. "In my experience, many men of his generation, perhaps most men his age, hold similar views."

"Yeah, but I doubt many of them seem to be quite so proud of them as Dad."

"Everett, the stroke has already dealt a blow to what he perceives to be his own power and masculinity. Perhaps he's overcompensating with his mouth."

"His post-stroke mouth seems just about the same to me. I'm more concerned about the brain that's sending the words to it."

"He clearly loves you. I can see deep down that he's a good person. I see him helping others around here and doing his part. I know he sent a cheque the other day to the Florida Hospital for Children. And he's clearly not an imbecile. Look how he's brought Chevrolet Jenkins out of his embittered shell. That took some doing. Besides, I've had some interesting conversations with your father when you've not been around," she said. "The foundations are strong. We can work with that. He'll come around, in time."

"The operative phrase being 'in time,'" I replied.

We sat in silence for a while as I pondered her assessment of my dad. She might well have been right. But did he have to make it so difficult?

"You sure write a lot of letters," I said.

"I try to write one a day. Lord knows I've got the time," Bev replied. "At least until, you know. . ."

"Until what?"

"You know, until I throw that final big clot."

"Beverley, please," I protested.

She closed out her letter and slipped it, and her pen, back into her canvas bag.

"You must have a lot of friends and fans," I said gesturing to the letter as it disappeared from view.

"Don't I wish. No, I'm long forgotten, and happy to be," she said. "I only ever write to my son."

"I didn't know you had a son. Wikipedia doesn't even know you have a son," I said.

"There's a lot Wikipedia doesn't know about me."

"So you really do have a son?"

"It's a little-known fact I'd like to keep little known."

"Right. Does he visit often? Will we get to meet him? How old is he? What does he do?"

"These questions and more on the next Jerry Springer show!" she intoned in her best TV announcer voice. "Everett, please. Let's return to my earlier statement that my son is a little-known fact that I'd like to keep little known. Period. Full stop. End of story. Next topic?"

"Okay. Got it. He's off limits. I hear you. I feel you. I can take a hint," I replied.

"Well, it was hardly a hint – more like a sledgehammer declaration – but I do appreciate your powers of perception and discretion."

"Those are my strong suits."

We sat in silence for a few moments.

"Um, I do have a favour to ask," I said.

She released a very big sigh.

"Everybody wants a piece of me." She threw her hands up. "It never stops."

"Oh, um, well. . ." I stammered.

She looked at me, puzzled.

"Everett, I'm kidding! I'm the funny one. Remember? Where are the vaunted powers of perception I just commended?" she chided me. "I will always say yes when committed men feminists ask for my help. So ask already."

"Oh, okay," I said, shaking my head. "You really got me there."

"Yes. Yes, I did. More than I intended. Now how can I help you?"

"It's nothing, but if I were to start writing short essays, would you look at them, and tell me if you think I'm on the wrong planet?"

"And are you going to write these little missives on a topic that might be described as in my wheelhouse?" she asked.

"That's certainly the plan. If they're not in your wheelhouse, I'll be badly missing my mark."

"What prompted all this?" she asked.

"Let's just say that I recently met someone who rekindled my interest in the issues that, um, reside in your particular wheelhouse. And I want to do something about it for a change and not just think about it. For the last fifteen years or so I've been doing far too little *thinking* and even less *doing*."

"That sounds quite serious. This person sounds like she's had a real impact on you. You're very lucky to have met her. She must be extraordinarily gifted and wonderful in every way."

"Oh, but she is, she is. Every other relationship I've had has ended because of my feminism. But this one is different. I've really fallen for her, hard. I'm not sure I can live without her," I said dreamily, looking at the sky.

Her head snapped my way as she shot me a look of – well, let's call it a look of concern tending toward horror.

"Gotcha," I said, winking and smiling. "Speaking of vaunted powers of perception."

"Touché," she replied, shaking her head.

"When I was caught up in the student movement, I was very rarely writing about the issues. That seemed too passive. I was running around organizing marches, and leading workshops, and booking school buses, making placards, and getting parade permits. There was so much to do. But I never really wrote about what we were fighting for. There wasn't time," I explained. "Well, now I have time. So I'm going to write."

"I like that idea. I like it a lot."

We sat in silence a bit longer.

She broke the silence to ask "The young women you dated just couldn't live up to your views on equality? Is that why they bailed out?"

"They didn't always put it that directly, but I'm pretty sure that's what happened," I replied. "My last girlfriend, um, well, woman friend – although that just sounds weird – broke it off just when we were starting to get serious."

"What happened? If you don't mind me asking."

"Well, it seemed like a minor disagreement at the time, but the issue was clearly standing in for a whole bunch of baggage I was carrying," I explained. "We were talking about marriage, in a remote, oblique kind of way. But I mentioned that even if my eventual spouse wanted to take my name, I wouldn't *let* her take it. It was a concession to patriarchal tradition I wasn't prepared to make."

"And that led to a lengthy and heated discussion?"

"Well, yes, you could say that. She didn't consider that particular tradition to be another small cog in the malevolent misogyny machine, the way I did."

"Did you really refer to it as a malevolent misogyny machine?" Beverley asked.

"I might have. I'm a writer. And I have a weakness for alliteration."

"I see."

"Yes, well, she didn't. She ended a two-year relationship the next day," I said. "The fact that her last name was Higginbottom might also have been a contributing factor."

"Yes, perhaps."

I fell into a routine over the next two weeks or so. I'd rise in the morning with the hammering, sawing, drilling, and yelling that always ensued as the construction below hurtled toward completion. To be clear, I didn't really rise *with* all that noise but rather *because* of it. And then I'd write. Then in the afternoon, I'd head to the hospital to coach my father around the walking paths and meet with Beverley about the latest essay. Then in the evenings, I'd revise, based on her comments. I was studiously ignoring the bio piece I owed *Make-Up Artist* magazine that I should have been working on. But the guy I was supposed to profile was not responding to my emails and phone calls to set up a time to interview him. What was I to do, fly to LA and camp out on his doorstep?

So I wrote thirteen six- to eight-hundred-word blog posts for my *Eve of Equality* blog – a baker's dozen. I was strictly blogging behind the firewall, still finding my voice. The posts weren't yet live. I still hadn't hit the Publish button. But I was feeling good about them. In the posts, I was riding the rail between substantive and rhetorical, serious and light, but always with the goal of making the reader think, and feel, a certain way by the end. I also tried to leave readers with something they could actually do, or in some cases, stop doing. Sometimes the "ask" was easy. Start using gender-neutral language, for instance. Words are powerful. They shape our way of thinking and reinforce damaging stereotypes, etc., etc. Other times, there wasn't anything concrete to require of my still nonexistent readers beyond simply having them think differently or believe something. If nothing else, it was an intellectually stimulating and fulfilling exercise in refining my own views on an increasingly complex set of social issues.

I researched and wrote blog posts on:

- Gender streaming in the education system;
- The lack of women in government;
- The impact of Internet porn;
- The glass ceiling for women in business;
- How few women served on corporate boards;
- The power game of sexual assault on university campuses;
- Whether affirmative action programs really worked;
- The insidious, enslaving power of words and language;
- The continued stereotyping of women and men in advertising;
- Gender roles in current TV dramas and sitcoms;
- Accessible feminist authors and their books;
- John Stuart Mill's *The Subjection of Women*; and
- Everyday unintentional acts of misogyny.

I'm not suggesting that I was in any way qualified to write about these sensitive subjects with any expertise and authority. But I could write about them with enthusiasm, energy, and conviction, because I did feel strongly about all of this. I also worked very hard to present a clear, balanced, thoughtful, and reasonable viewpoint without being in any way incendiary, divisive, and insulting. I wanted to take that club out of the hands of the opposition.

It was very difficult to keep the posts within the eight-hundred-word limit I had set for myself. And even eight hundred words seemed a trifle long for the online reader's attention span. But it forced me to hone my arguments and focus on clarity, brevity, and the pure force of words. I had no idea whether I'd been successful. After labouring for days over the same thirteen blog posts, phrase by phrase, sentence by sentence, sometimes word by word, my sense of perspective on what I'd written had pretty well abandoned me. That's where Beverley came in.

I don't mind saying that I took great satisfaction from her surprise at the power of the writing. She kept saying things like "Did you really write this?" as she waved around the printout of the latest post. She made a few suggestions, usually when she believed I either wasn't giving the reader enough credit or was assuming too much knowledge on their part. She also offered some interesting anecdotes that brought some of my positions to life and made them more compelling. Often, a true story has much more impact than yet another rhetorical flight. Storytelling is a powerful tool in advocacy.

In one post, she wondered whether affirmative action programs might set back the cause of equality by prompting doubts about how some high-flying women in business and government came to be high-flying. I argued that until equality is achieved, we need programs in some sectors to hasten the pendulum's return to the middle, to equilibrium. I'm not sure I convinced her, but she seemed more comfortable after I'd toned down my conclusions. We had great discussions that always left me feeling very much alive and utterly exhausted at the same time. After each visit, I was more and more comfortable in my humble endeavour. My father even sat with us for some of our discussions, as even that fate was preferred to yet more walking. He scoffed often and openly at the beginning, prompting the occasional "Oh hush, Billy" from Beverley. But by the end, he registered his views less frequently and often only by rolling his eyes.

I still hadn't explained the blog idea to Beverley. I'm not sure why I hadn't beyond a faint need to keep *Eve of Equality* anonymous in the strictest sense of the word. So she still thought I was just writing essays that I might gather into a collection at some point. I allowed her to carry on under that misconception but felt a little duplicitous about it.

We'd just finished reviewing the final few blog posts I'd written by then. I could see Dad labouring up the Blue path across the verdant hospital grounds, making his way toward us. Beverley handed me her marked-up copies of my "essays" on John Stuart Mill's book and on a selection of seemingly innocuous daily acts of misogyny.

"I like the Mill piece," she said.

By that stage, I'd read the slim Mill volume three times and researched it as well. I liked my Mill piece, too.

"I'm glad you gave Harriet some credit, even if her name doesn't appear on the cover."

"Clearly the book was a joint effort, and I thought his wife ought to get the credit she deserved. In fact, I'm surprised he didn't insist on equal billing on the front."

"Men ran the publishing world then, and now, so I'm just happy the treatise was published at all," she said. Then she turned to the final essay. "Provocative title. Perhaps a little too provocative?"

"How do you mean?" I asked.

"Well, 'misogyny' is a very strong and politically loaded term."

"Yes, it certainly is. That's precisely why I used it in the title, to draw people in."

"Yes, but do you deliver on 'misogyny' in the piece, or is it more about the inherent 'sexism' of our daily lives?"

"I'm not sure I distinguish between the two. Do you?"

"Not really, but 'misogyny' always seems the more bellicose term to me. More Machiavellian. More cruel."

"Agreed, but I like the power of the word in the title. I was going for provocative."

"It's your piece," she replied. "Other than that, I think you've written another compelling essay that deserves a broader audience."

"Thanks," I said. "I'm thinking about writing one more piece. Are you familiar with a guy name Mason Bennington?"

"Everett, I might be somewhat isolated in a Florida rehab hospital, but I am not living under a rock. Of course I've heard of that reprobate. He's a degenerate of the first order, set on returning women to what he thinks is their rightful place – naked and writhing on a pole for the collective entertainment of boors and louts."

"I see. So you're still wrestling with your views about him."

She smiled. I continued.

"I was thinking about writing a piece that challenges all the positive press he somehow seems to generate. Some stories even call him a saviour to all those women working in seedy, dangerous strip clubs across the continent. It's offensive."

"More than offensive," she said.

My father reached our bench and dropped onto the end of it as far away from Beverley and me as possible.

"Hello, ladies," he said, huffing and puffing. "Have you saved the world yet?"

"We're getting closer, Billy boy, we're getting closer," said Beverley. "The question is, when the day of reckoning comes, will there be a place for you in the new order."

"Can I still watch the NFL in the new world?" he asked.

We both ignored him.

"So you think I should do it? Write a piece on Bennington?"

She looked at me and narrowed her eyes. She looked almost fierce for just a second.

"Get your ass home, and get writing."

I skipped dinner and sat down at my laptop on the kitchen table. The music was pounding below again, as it had been for most of the last week. Out my kitchen window, I could see the alley below and the loading dock for whatever enterprise was about to open below me. Several woman were smoking out on the concrete outcropping where trucks had been unloading equipment and supplies earlier in the day. I rested my foot on the big nut and bolt below the table. I could feel them vibrating to the pulsating beat of the music. Once in a while, I heard a metallic click, almost like a tiny squeak, as the whole unit shifted microscopically. Were they swinging on the chandelier? After a time, I could have sworn the nut and bolt felt warm. I wasn't sure whether I'd warmed it with my foot or if it were getting hot one floor below. It was almost comforting to cup the nut and bolt with my two feet as I wrote. Strange, I know.

I focused and wrote about Mason Bennington that night. It stretched to 875 words. I suspended my eight-hundred-word limit for this piece alone, as I wanted to get it right. I think it warranted the extra few paragraphs. I liked it. I really did. But what did I know? Beverley and I had become so immersed in this stuff in those two weeks that I'm not sure I could be impartial about the essay. In fact, I'm certain I couldn't be. I read it one more time and then went to bed. Not to sleep, just to bed. It took a few hours to get to sleep. Tina Turner's "Private Dancer" drifted up from below as I finally drifted off.

I spent the next morning taking a final read-through of all the posts. I then decided on some kind of order for them so that one theme more naturally flowed into the next, taking the reader on a kind of a journey – perhaps not an enjoyable journey, or even an enlightening journey, but a journey nevertheless. As it worked out, the Mason Bennington post seemed to work best as the last essay in the series, at least until I wrote the next one. The plan was to contribute one post each week after the blog was up and running with these initial essays.

I couldn't think of a reason not to, so I spent an hour copying and pasting the posts into the back end of my WordPress blog. I carefully and comprehensively tagged all the posts with appropriate keywords to try to draw like-minded readers to the blog. If someone were searching for a feminist blog that tackled the issues I'd already written about, they would find *Eve of Equality*, if they knew their way around an Internet search engine.

Then, to spread the word further, I launched TweetDeck on my laptop and, before I could lose my nerve, opened an @EveofEquality Twitter account using the same phony email address I'd employed to create the blog. I made sure to list the blog's URL in the new Twitter account profile so the curious could easily find it. Then I spent an hour or so following several dozen leading feminists, including celebrities, activists, writers, bloggers, and academics, as well as those who led the major feminist think-tanks and advocacy organizations. I spent some time retweeting all their tweets to try to kick-start my own following. It worked, a little. By the evening, I had managed to attract exactly fourteen Twitter followers. I still hadn't issued a single tweet of my own. But the infrastructure was coming together.

I decided against creating an EofE Facebook page, LinkedIn profile, or Pinterest account. One step at a time. Besides, I thought Twitter would suffice for promoting the blog. I checked again. I was up to sixteen followers even though I still had yet to hit the button to release my inaugural tweet. Clearly I was tearing up the social media space.

It was time. I toggled back to the EofE blog site. Rather than publishing all fourteen blog posts at once, and to try to drive a little more Google juice out of the exercise, I scheduled them to be published on the blog, one by one, every three hours until they were all up. This would herald a blog with lots of new and frequently refreshed content. That might help my search engine optimization and perhaps push traffic to the blog in, well, perhaps even in double digits, if I were lucky. My expectations were low.

The publishing order I'd determined for my fourteen missives would leave the Bennington essay as the last one to be posted. As a consequence, it was the newest, and therefore, most visible post. After I'd loaded and scheduled them all, my finger hovered over the Publish button. I thought of Beverley's final words to me the day before. My stomach felt tight but I'm pretty sure it was excitement or anticipation, rather than constipation. There was no reason to hold off any longer. I hit the button and *Eve of Equality* went live – just another personal blog among millions on the Internet. But it somehow made me feel alive again.

CHAPTER 5

A couple of days later, when I woke up, I grabbed my iPad from my nightstand and called up *Eve of Equality*. In the night, the last of the fourteen blog posts had been published. There it was, the Bennington post, leading the pack. I thought it looked pretty good. I'd added some photos, and even some charts and graphs, all just lifted from Google images, to illustrate the blog posts. I checked my analytics. Exactly no one had visited the blog yet. Not a single reader had stumbled upon it, beyond its author. My Twitter following had inched up to nineteen. Off to a great start. Gaining traction. Moving the needle. Making progress.

Not so much. Viral, it wasn't. But it was early days. Eventually, the tagging I'd done on each post would attract at least a few readers. It was inevitable. The power of search engine optimization. But it would take some time. The more pressing question was when readers found my blog, would they stay? Would they read my offerings? Would they point people toward it? Would they think differently about the issues? Would they wonder who actually wrote the pieces?

I used my newly minted EofE Twitter account to tweet links to a few of the EofE posts, including the Mason Bennington piece. It was time to start spreading the word.

As I walked downstairs to the street later that morning, what I didn't hear was any construction noise. The din of power tools and generators and arguments had slackened in the previous few days and become more sporadic. Now it seemed to have stopped altogether. As I left the building, I noticed there still wasn't a sign installed on the front of the building that might yield some idea of what would soon open. In fact, I saw no indication that a sign was even planned. The gleaming wooden doors, still accessorized by the green garbage bags covering the handles, gave the only suggestion that a business might soon be operating in that space. Strange.

"Hello, Everett," Yolanda greeted me.

"Hi, Yolanda. How's the patient this morning?" I asked.

"You're just in time for the fun, honey. I looked in a minute ago and our star physios are about to tag-team your father. I don't think he's quite used to it yet. Come to think of it, I doubt Mike and Liz are used to your father, either."

I seemed to have arrived in time to witness my father in physiotherapy. I kind of wished I'd arrived a little later. Mike and Liz, the two young physios on duty that day, were working him over. And work it was. I watched from the doorway as they stretched out his left leg at various angles while Dad did his part by grimacing and groaning. Then Liz moved down to work on his lower leg, kneading his calf, ankle, and foot in what I would describe as a turbocharged massage. At the same time, Mike moved up to work Dad's upper thigh, digging in deep on his quadriceps, glutes, and groin. I'm not sure whether the expression on Dad's face reflected physical pain or the garden-variety homophobe's discomfort at having another man's hands anywhere near his groin.

"Hey, Mikey, great job there, but you did such nice work on my ankle yesterday, let's not mess with success, eh?" said Dad. "Howzabout switching up with Liz?"

"My groin is just fine, Mr. Kane," Liz cut in. "It's your groin that needs the attention."

"You're a laugh riot, Liz, but you know that's not what I meant by 'switching up.'"

"Nice try, Mr. Kane, but your groin is all mine this morning," Mike replied.

"Yeah, I can see that, and feel that." Dad sighed. "Why don't we let the beautiful and talented Liz decide what part of my body she'd like to be working on?"

Just then Dad yelped as Liz pushed his ankle in a direction ankles generally aren't designed to go.

"Oh, gee, I'm so sorry, Mr. Kane," Liz said in mock surprise. "Did you feel a little twinge there?"

"Okay, okay, you two. Have it your way. Just don't enjoy your-self too much down there, eh Mike?"

"I won't if you won't," he replied.

"I guess I could be *squeezing my balls* while you're doing that," Dad said straight-faced but carefully enunciating and emphasizing the wrong words in the sentence.

"Good idea, Mr. Kane," Mike replied. "That'll save you some time this afternoon. Physio multi-tasking. I like it."

"All right, all right. But I'm so bored with *squeezing my balls*." Dad reached with his right hand for the two black rubber balls resting on the tray mounted on the physio table. "But I know my day is not complete without spending at least a couple hours *squeezing my balls*."

Thanks for that, Dad. Neither Mike nor Liz reacted in any way to my father's juvenile comments. No eye-rolling, no looking at one another, no deep sighing. They just kept their magic hands working on his inert left leg. I guess context is everything.

It probably goes without saying that my father's sense of humour stopped developing in adolescence. It was trapped in high school like an insect in amber. He pushed the two black balls into his compromised left hand and did a fair impersonation of the human squeezing action.

Only then did Dad look over and see me standing in the doorway.

"Ev! Hey son, thanks for coming."

"Dad, I come every day. You don't have to thank me. It's what sons do when their fathers are in sick bay."

"I know. But, well, thanks anyway," he said before nodding to his two physios. "I get this every morning. I feel like a NASCAR stock car in for an hour-long pit stop."

"Except in a NASCAR pit stop, there's no flirting with the pit crew, or keeping up an endless stream of off-colour banter," I replied.

"Well, if you're going to be like that, you'll have to excuse me, as I must *squeeze my balls* for a while longer."

"On behalf of the patients, family, and staff of this hospital, that line is getting very tired, Dad."

"Bullshit, it's a classic. It never seems old to me."

"Clearly."

———

We'd just "enjoyed" lunch in Dad's room when she arrived. I didn't mind the food at the rehab hospital, but Dad was sick of it by then. He was propped up in his funky, multi-positional, Swiss Army knife of a bed that seemed to have a mind of its own. I'm no expert, but I suspect it could do everything from folding Dad in half to catapulting him across the room, depending on the mood – the bed's mood, not Dad's. Fortunately, at that moment, its mood was sedate.

"Hello, boys."

We both looked up from our lime-green Jell-O to see her standing in the doorway. She looked amazing, dressed to the nines, not for a night on the town, but for an executive suite boardroom. Business chic all the way. Now I'm not sure about the terminology here, but my mother was standing there wearing what I think is called a power suit, in a striking shade of blue. Her stiletto heels added another four inches of altitude to her already above-average height. She was accompanied by a young nervous-looking man in a business suit who carried what I assumed was my mother's purse and a shiny metallic briefcase. She turned to him.

"Nathan, you can wait for me down the hall in the reception area."

He nodded, turned on his heel, and headed back down the corridor.

Through all of this, my father was staring at her, slack-jawed. One of the black balls escaped his grip, hit the floor, and bounced over to Mom. She caught it on the second hop and handed it back to him.

"I think this belongs to you."

"Christ, Evelyn, will you look at you!" Dad exclaimed. "It's like you just stepped out of some magazine."

"Hello, Billy," she replied. "It's just another day at the office. But it's Florida, so I thought azure was the right shade."

"You got that right! Zowie," Dad said, still staring her up and down. "Did you drop a few pounds?"

"I might have lost a bit of weight. Who knows? I just don't have time to check."

"Well, maybe your little bag-carrier, Nathan, can schedule a weigh-in," Dad replied.

She leaned down toward Dad and whispered. "I'm not sure he could handle that yet. I'm still working him in."

For the first time, she turned to me.

"Ev dear. You look good."

"Hi, Mom. You look great. When did you get in?" I stood up to hug her.

"I arrived a couple of days ago but have been locked in meetings till now. We've got a big sod-turning with the mayor and a bunch of other hotshots tomorrow at the building site, so it's been a little crazy," she explained. "You can't imagine the petty politics wrapped up in a stupid little groundbreaking ceremony. They drive me insane. If everyone doesn't get a goddamn shovel to hold while they preen for the photo op, their noses are out of joint. Well, I'll friggin' give them a shovel and put more than their noses out of joint. It's so infuriating. I just can't believe. . ."

"Helloooo!" Dad cut in. "It's okay, honey, I'm fine here flat on my back in a rehab hospital, you know, major stroke and all. But don't worry, I'm going to be okay. . ."

She stopped her tirade and reached for his hand.

"I'm sorry, Billy, I've just a few things going on right now. I'm a bit preoccupied."

"Really! You don't say," he replied. "Well, I can sure see what is *not* preoccupying you."

"Billy, don't be like that. I'm here. And things should calm down a bit after tomorrow," she soothed. "Hey, you look great. In fact, you look just the same."

"Yeah, well, you haven't seen me on the walking paths out back. I look like the goddamned elephant man."

"I'm sure you don't," she said.

Dad just looked at me. Then Mom looked at me.

"Well, the elephant man is a little harsh. I'd say he gives off more of a Quasimodo vibe, but not as scary."

"There, you see, Billy," Mom chirped.

Surprisingly, we had quite a nice visit. It was strange seeing them together. They were civil to one another, and Dad was clearly pleased that she'd come. I suggested the three of us tackle a walk on the grounds, but Dad begged off saying he'd rather do it on his own later on. I think he just didn't want to put his full disability on display in front his ex-wife. I understood. So we just talked for a while. After a few minutes, Mom seemed to stop obsessing about her job, at least for a while. But about an hour later, she suddenly turned antsy and started looking at her watch. She summoned Nathan the purse-bearer, and the two of them left shortly thereafter. He trailed a few steps behind her. She promised to come back.

Before leaving, she leaned down and gave Dad a big hug and kissed his cheek. He was caught a little off-guard, but recovered to hug her back. I got the same treatment and she was out the door.

"Well, what the goddamn hell was that?" Dad asked when she had gone.

"That was your ex-wife coming to check in on her ex-husband. It's what families do, Dad," I replied.

"She looks amazing. Doesn't she look amazing?" he asked.

"She does, Dad. She really does."

"Shit, I'm late," Dad said, checking his watch.

"Late for what?"

"Late for scoring a few more points for Ford against that evil upstart Chevrolet."

———

I watched from just inside the doors. Dad parked his walker off to the side, next to the wheelchair of Kenny Jenkins. They nodded to one another in grudging acceptance of their mutual existence. Kenny lifted his good hand to signal he was ready to go. Then Dad, gripping the handles of the wheelchair, started pushing Kenny down the path. I took in the strange scene for a while. They were both talking and gesturing. Well, Kenny was gesticulating wildly, undoubtedly extolling the virtues of General Motors products. Whenever Dad took his right hand off the handgrip to return fire on Ford's behalf, the wheelchair drifted to the right and threatened to collide with one of the benches stationed along the path. Dad almost always got it back under control before hitting the bench. I felt someone standing next to me. It was Yolanda.

"He's done a good thing, your father," she said. "Kenny hasn't moved from that spot out there or said boo to anyone since he arrived. Now look at them out there talking up a storm."

"Let's hope the storm isn't too violent," I replied.

She smiled and patted my back.

I headed back to my apartment. Three burly workers seemed to be putting the final touches on the front door. It was a little hard to see, but they seemed to be buffing the door handles with some fluffy cloths. Another guy was working very hard at sweeping the sidewalk, as if he planned to eat his dinner off the concrete. There were plenty of cars parked around the building but two new Valet Parking signs ensured an open space right in front of the doors. Something was up. When I made it upstairs, I surveyed the scene in the alley below my kitchen. Three trucks were lined up waiting their turn while a team of muscle-bound guys was hand-bombing boxes from a fourth truck backed up to the loading dock. Something was definitely up.

I sat down at my kitchen table to see what activity there might have been on the blog in my absence and then to start drafting my next post. I planned to write about the steady growth in women enrolled in medical school and law school, to the extent that they now equalled, and sometimes surpassed, the number of men students. But the news was not all good. The number of women enrolled in university engineering programs still lagged. Two steps forward, one step back. But progress nevertheless. I was eager to get to work on another post. I had to feed the beast, as they say.

I turned on my laptop and first checked my personal email account. There was another email from my cosmetic mag client asking about my profile piece and when she could see it. I ignored it and was about to check the blog when my cellphone rang.

"Hello?"

"Thank Christ you picked up!" snapped the youngish man's voice. "I've been trying to reach you for the last hour. Don't you answer your phone?"

"Calm down. I've been at a hospital and they like us to switch to airplane mode when we're there. Who is this, anyway?" I asked.

"First things, first. Do you manage the, what the hell's it called again, oh yeah, the *Eve of Equality* blog?"

Uh-oh. That didn't sound good.

"Well, um, maybe. Why? What's going on? Who is this?"

"It's Aaron from your ISP. We're hosting your blog."

"Well, I wouldn't necessarily call it *my* blog. I'm just, um, peripherally involved, you know, in the back-end technical stuff."

"What you do with your back end is totally up to you, but when your fucking blog crashes our system, that's when I get upset. So what the hell is up with your blog?"

"What are you talking about? My fucking blog, er, I mean *the* fucking blog is fine, I think. At least it was fine this morning when I last checked it. What's going on?"

"Well, exactly sixty-seven minutes ago, your blog's big-ass traffic crashed our servers and knocked us completely offline!"

In an instant, I clicked the shortcut on my desktop to take me to *Eve of Equality*. Error. Grey screen. Nothing.

"Hey, no site," I said.

"Hey, no shit," he said.

"That makes no sense! I only have about two readers and I'm one of them. What do you mean, my blog crashed your servers? I don't get it."

"I promise you, you've got more than two readers, now. Never seen a spike in hits like that in such a short time. I don't know what triggered it, but at 2:56 this afternoon, the tsunami started. We crashed out at 3:39. No one noticed around here until we went dark."

"I have no idea what you're talking about. There must be some mistake. It must be someone else's blog. I just went live yesterday. I don't have traffic. I have a trickle."

"Look, you're not listening. It's your fucking blog, all right," he snapped. "I'm looking at the analytics right now. They're off the charts. At 2:56, you hit the big time. Shit, I would never have agreed to host you if I'd known you were going to pull this many clicks. You said you expected light to moderate traffic at best. You were wrong by a pretty fucking big margin and we were down for twenty minutes. Twenty fucking minutes is a lifetime when you're a hosting service."

"I've got nothing for you. I'm stumped. I have no idea what happened. Must be some kind of coding error," I said. "Hey, if you were only down for twenty minutes, why isn't my blog back up?"

"If I'd put you back up, we'd have crashed out again. I've put everyone else back up except you. And I'm done with you. You're way too much for my shop. I don't have near the capacity to carry you. You're out."

"So what do I have to do get back up?"

"I'll have to migrate you to a big-boy hosting service. The sooner the better. Like right now."

At that stage, I still didn't know what the hell had happened, but I focused on getting the blog back up as it might hold the answer. It took two hours on a three-way call with my disgruntled mom-and-pop-shop ISP and the largest web-hosting operation in the southern U.S. I took great pains to preserve my anonymity. That was critical. I never once gave my name, and I constantly referred to my specific role as just an intermediary between the ISP and the actual blogger. Had it been possible, I would have done the call from a pay phone. But even if I could have found an aging and forgotten phone booth somewhere in Orlando, it certainly would not have provided Wi-Fi or even a flat surface on which to rest my laptop, and both were necessary as we managed the migration of the blog from one hosting service to another. So I used my cellphone for the lengthy three-way call. I had no other option.

Just after eleven that night, *Eve of Equality* flickered to life again on my laptop, supported by a much more robust network of servers. Five minutes later, I knew what had happened. I could hardly believe it, but I could see the entire chronology playing out online before my eyes, as I surfed among Google, Twitter, YouTube, Facebook, several other social media platforms, and my own blog. Holy shit. Holy shit. And thrice times, holy shit. My hand was trembling as it worked my mouse.

I don't know where or how to begin to explain it. I'd been so certain the guy hosting my blog had been wrong. He had to have been wrong. I was convinced there was another explanation. There had to be. What he'd claimed had happened that afternoon seemed utterly impossible. But he was right. He'd been right all along. It had unfolded just as he had reported. It took me a while to restore normal respiration and manage the nausea.

So here goes. Looking back, it all started with one of my many innocent clicks earlier that morning. I had hit my mouse button to follow the Twitter feeds of the big three network daytime TV talk shows hosted by Candace Sharpe, Oprah Winfrey, and Ellen DeGeneres. I hoped that they might automatically follow the EofE Twitter stream in return. Following Candace was my undoing. Had I not followed her that morning, everything probably would have been fine. I'd still have fewer than twenty Twitter followers, and at most, a handful of people would have read my humble blog posts. But some higher authority clearly had other plans.

Candace Sharpe was quite a story all on her own. I think she's very good and I love her meteoric rise to stardom. She is one of the very few to successfully make the jump from big-time digital/social media star to network TV talk show icon, and all in two years flat. Her wild ride started in Vancouver. She was just another nameless producer at a popular radio station when she started a weekly podcast about current events and pop culture. She recorded it afterhours at the station so the sound quality was perfect. She released the podcast through iTunes, and a few of her DJ friends plugged it now and then on their shows. Young, hip, liberal, and smart, she offered a thoughtful, newsy, funny half-hour take on what she saw happening in the world that week. She always had a guest to play off when tackling a hot topic. Sometimes they agreed. Sometimes they didn't. And it worked. It worked better than she or anyone else ever dreamed.

Word-of-mouth, and then the media coverage her show somehow earned drove up subscriptions to the free online podcast at a remarkable rate. It all happened so fast. One day she had a few hundred listeners, then a few thousand. Within eight weeks, she had hundreds of thousands of listeners around the world. The Internet's great pyramid scheme flexed its muscles, and she went viral. By this stage, I was already a devoted listener.

Knowing a good thing when they saw it, major mainstream radio stations called offering her buckets of money and prime-time slots if she would just bring her podcast to the traditional airwaves. She was about to sign a big syndication deal with a New York–based radio network when cable TV came calling. No wonder. She had never been accused of having a face for radio. Candace Sharpe looked like a ready-made TV star. So she bypassed radio all together and went straight to the bright lights of a leading cable station in LA. *Candace Conversations* started in a late-night time slot and was an instant success. Within two months she was moved to the lucrative afternoon market to compete directly with *Oprah* and *Ellen*.

Many critics predicted she would fall on her face trying to make the move from the looser, "anything goes" world of podcasting to the more restrictive, heavily formatted and formulaic demands of mainstream television. They were wrong. She defied the odds mainly on the strength of her intelligence, personality, seemingly boundless knowledge, and voice. I think she succeeded because she truly understands and has mastered the lost art of conversation, a staple of the social media world.

Most talk shows are conversation-free zones powered by a strict Q&A format. For Candace Sharpe, talk shows are never about "interviewing" celebrities and experts. Rather, it's all about "conversation." And she does conversation very, very well. She is so smart, knowledgable, and engaging that it never feels like an interview, but a true conversation where she is an active participant rather than a passive moderator. She just strikes that rare and elusive perfect tone that has attracted a huge slice of the talk show television audience. In case it's not yet clear, I'm kind of a Candace Sharpe fanboy.

Six months after *Candace Conversations* debuted on cable, she made the jump to network television with a show simply called *Candace*. You know you've made it when your first name is all you need. Ever since, she's been swapping top spot in the afternoon Nielsen ratings with *Ellen* and *Oprah*. Candace Sharpe was big. And now, somehow, I was on her radar. As far as I can tell, here's how it all went down.

Around noon, while I was offline, hanging out at the rehab hospital as my mother and father circled one another in a rare post-divorce encounter, whoever was managing Candace Sharpe's official Twitter stream and her 25,678,369 followers (not kidding) retweeted my tweet promoting my Mason Bennington post on the *Eve of Equality* blog. Let me run that by you again in case, for some reason, you missed it or tuned out for a moment. Not to put too fine a point on it, Candace retweeted the link to the lead post on my new anonymous feminist blog to every one of her 25,678,369 ardent, devoted, crazed followers. That's when things kind of got out of hand.

I clicked through to the blog and logged into the administrator's back end. (Yes, I know, there's something mildly suggestive about that last phrase.) Because I was never expecting much traffic, I hadn't turned on "comment moderation" on the blog. This meant that whenever a reader left a comment, it appeared on the blog directly without having to await my approval. That was probably a minor oversight on my part, or maybe even a humungous oversight. I activated the comment-moderation function. There were already several hundred comments appearing on the Mason Bennington post, and fewer but still plenty of comments on each of the other thirteen posts. I had a following, and it was massive, very vocal, and overwhelmingly supportive. For every forty or fifty supportive reader comments, there lurked messages that were crude, suggestive, sometimes anatomically impossible (or at least very difficult), and occasionally violent. It was clear that men had written most of these horrible comments, dwarfed by the deluge of encouraging ones from women. I stopped reading and closed my laptop.

Then I flipped out for a few minutes and walked around the apartment at a brisk pace, hyperventilating, largely because I didn't know what else to do. I briefly prayed for a time machine. But when nothing materialized, I gave up on that plan. After a final deep breath, I sat back down, lifted the laptop lid, and opened my Twitter profile. And there it was, staring me in the face and clenching my bowels. It was worse than I thought. Having started out that morning with nineteen followers, I was a little unnerved, okay I was just a few synapses short of a complete mental meltdown, when I saw the modest little increase to 237,453 followers. I immediately refreshed my screen and the number jumped to 237,602 followers. Shit. There was an endless stream of retweets from thousands of Candace Sharpe's acolytes. There were hundreds of tweets directed specifically at me. When I say that, I mean they were directed at the blogger behind EofE. Most of the tweets were from women who had read the Bennington blog post. But there were plenty more from those who had clearly read some or all of my other posts, too. By eyeballing the stream, I'd estimate that over ninety per cent of the tweets were positive, even laudatory. I stopped counting how many used the shopworn phrase "You go girl!"

I left Twitter and went to Facebook. Mistake. A big one. A basic search of the *Eve of Equality* name generated literally thousands of Facebook posts, each one driving even more traffic to the blog. I feared my index finger might be headed for a repetitive stress injury from endlessly scrolling the wheel on my mouse. Enough Facebook. I wanted to stop this online torture trip, but I really needed to assess what had happened, how big it had gone, and what the hell I was going to do about it. So I kept working my mouse.

YouTube was my next port of call. That might also have been a mistake, though it did clarify matters. I pumped "Eve of Equality" into the search bar and was greeted by dozens of the very same clip. Every one of them had been uploaded that afternoon. So here's the deal. It seemed that Candace Sharpe had not only retweeted one of my tweets, but she'd singled out my blog on her show that afternoon. You know, on the air! On TV! I kid you not. Through a coincidence of monumental proportions, my blog went live the very same day that Candace's show was dedicated to examining "the current state of feminism in America." Great. Just great. I played the brief clip, oh, I don't know, about twenty-seven times, just to allow the full significance of it to wash over me.

I then hit Play a twenty-eighth time and watched as the familiar and beautiful face of Candace Sharpe filled the screen. One of the most powerful women on television wore a smile a mile wide as she looked directly into the camera.

"And just before we go, I was grazing on the Internet this morning, as I'm wont to do, when I stumbled upon a new and fantastic site that has officially become my favourite feminist blog. In light of today's show, I took it as a good omen, as a sign. So I paid attention. The address is on your screen. Check out *Eve of Equality* if you want a clear and thoughtful take on a whole range of issues affecting women and our continuing fight for equality. I particularly liked her post taking down Mason Bennington. She captured my thoughts precisely, and maybe yours, too. Definitely worth a read. We don't know who's behind *Eve of Equality*, but she is one smart cookie who knows how to write. Find out for yourself, and we'll see you back here the same time tomorrow."

The clip I was watching ran for another thirty seconds or so as the credits scrolled up the screen, with the *Eve of Equality* URL anchored in the bottom right-hand corner for all to see.

I felt a little sick to my stomach. No, that's not quite true. It felt more like I was about two-thirds of the way through my own autopsy. Then I realized there was one more piece to the puzzle I was forgetting. It suddenly occurred to me that my phony EofE Gmail email address was provided on the Contact section of the blog. Shit. I zipped over to Gmail and watched as several hundred emails loaded before my eyes. I started reading but stopped after the first dozen or so. Most of them were remarkably similar. A snippet sampling:

"Love this blog!"

"Where have you been all my life?"

"Eve, whoever you are, you just put my own mixed-up feelings into words and made sense of them. Thank you, thank you, thank you."

"For the first time I feel like I can be a feminist without having to carry the giant coat-hanger in the Women's Day protest march. (Not that there's anything wrong with that!)"

"Please, please, please, keep writing. This is great stuff. I need it."

Then, occasionally, there would be more militant expressions:

"You were way too soft on that asshole Bennington. He should be strung up in the public square by the balls, and thrashed."

"It's time to accept that women have no future in a world run by men."

"We need to answer violence against women with violence against men."

There were also many anti-feminist comments, most of them, perhaps nearly all of them, obviously from men. I won't bore you with their imbecilic and profane sentiments.

Finally, there were several emails that suggested new topics for me to write about, including LGBT issues, women and gun control, gay marriage, just to cite a few. I scrolled down to the bottom end of my Gmail inbox. It took a while to make it all the way down to the first email. It had arrived at 2:58 p.m. I was done. There were too many emails to read. It was overwhelming. I stopped when I thought I had a handle on the general categories and the proportions of emails in each. By this time it was well after midnight.

So I shut everything down in surrender and climbed into bed. It probably goes without saying, but I pulled the comforter right up over my head. For the first time I noticed the music pounding from below me. Perhaps it was opening night downstairs. I just lay there in the pitch black, thinking, trying to take it all in. It took twenty minutes for the pinprick of light to cut through the darkness of my jumbled thoughts. The glow was barely discernible at first, but it slowly and steadily grew and brightened. A question circled my mind, flitting from the shadows to cut through the edges of the light. It took a while for the query to land, fully illuminated. It then evolved into a cascade of questions.

- Wasn't this a good thing?
- Wasn't this exactly what, in my wildest dreams, I wanted?
- Wasn't I incredibly lucky to have been graced by Candace Sharpe's viral touch?
- What the hell was I complaining about?
- Would I tell Beverley any of this, and if I did, what would she think?
- If I pulled my comforter back down and uncovered my head, would it be easier to breathe?

By two o'clock in the morning, I'd nearly fully recovered my faculties. Sure, it was shocking to go, in the span of about four hours, from a tiny blog with no visitors to what Google's search algorithm now ranked as the world's most authoritative and popular feminist blog. But after I thought about it for what seemed like a very long time – first in a crazed and psychotic way, and then eventually in a more thoughtful and logical fashion – I came to a place of peace and calm. While this unbelievable turn of events was certainly unexpected, it was undeniably a precious gift, and a rare opportunity. To squander it would be a crime against the very principles that spawned *Eve of Equality* in the first place. I would not waste this chance. I could not waste this chance.

By half-past-two in the morning, the fear, anxiety, and, yes, abject terror ebbed, as reason, confidence, and even a little of the old excitement, flowed back in. I was starting to feel myself again. Of course, it could also have been throwing up twice that settled my nerves and restored my resolve. Regardless, I was too wired for sleep. Besides, I doubt anyone could sleep with the music pulsating below. My chest buzzed with the bass line. So with a "no time like the present" attitude, I pushed back the covers and returned to the kitchen table. I avoided the Internet and simply opened a new document in Word to start the women and post-secondary education essay for the *Eve of Equality* blog. It was time to feed the beast again.

I started by reviewing the notes I'd already made. Then I reworked my outline to heighten the impact of the message. Finally, I started to write. The words were flowing reasonably well as I typed in time to the beat downstairs. I'd gotten into the habit of resting both feet around the nut and bolt emerging from my kitchen floor. The vibration was very faint at first. The soles of one's feet are quite sensitive. I wondered at first if my legs had fallen asleep, leading to that pins and needles sensation. But it soon became clear that the nut-and-bolt assembly was in fact vibrating. Ten minutes later, I could not only feel it in my feet but also in my calves and thighs as the tremor grew. Soon, metal-on-metal squeaking sounds in time with the music escaped from under the kitchen table. Finally, the vibrations morphed into straight-up shaking. The whole fixture was moving beneath my feet.

Shit. I feared the chandelier was about to crash onto hundreds of happy, dancing, drunk, opening-night patrons in the bar downstairs, assuming it was a bar. Not an auspicious beginning. I got down on my hands and knees to take a closer look at the large, polished nut and bolt sticking up through my kitchen floor. Uh-oh. That was not good. I could now see it moving. I watched the nut slowly coming loose, as visions of missing lock washers danced in my head.

I'm not very handy. My knowledge of tools hit the wall after hammer, saw, drill, wrench, and screwdriver. But I was pretty sure when that nut finished unscrewing itself from the bolt in my floor, something bad was going to happen. I tried to tighten it with my hand. I could turn it a bit, but it seemed to reverse itself and loosen again each time I stopped. I looked at my watch. It was ten to three in morning. Why was the place still open, anyway? I knew that last call in Florida bars was 2 a.m. I didn't want to go down there, but what choice did I have? I was the only one who knew that a heavy light fixture would soon have its Phantom of the Opera moment and crash to the floor below.

I pulled a sweater over my head and slipped on my running shoes. I went downstairs and out the door at the front of the building. Fancy cars were still parked up and down the street. A silver Audi R8 pulled in between the Valet Parking signs and stopped. I watched as an older, nattily suited man got out and handed the car key to an attractive young woman in a rather skimpy red vest. She slid into the driver's seat, started the car, and pulled away, presumably to a parking spot nearby. I just stood there off to the side, my eyes following the man as he spoke to the same big security guy I'd encountered the other day. The muscle-bound bouncer was wearing a black suit and tie, accessorized by an earphone. He referred to his clipboard, nodded to the stylishly dressed man, and then pushed a button on the small black remote control that hung around his neck like a pendant. Instantly, the beautifully polished and lacquered wooden double doors behind him opened automatically to admit the owner of the silver R8.

Believe it or not, it didn't strike me when I first looked at the great doors moving on their own. But it hit me like a sledge to the head three seconds later when they closed. The two large and shiny brass door handles met again in the middle when the doors swung shut. I'd already had one serious shock that night.

Having a second was almost physically painful. I stood there transfixed, wrapping my arms around my chest as if to prevent my lungs from escaping. I couldn't take my eyes off those two big lustrous metallic door handles. There they were, in all their polished glare and glory – a big brass **X** on the left door, a big brass **Y** on the right. Oh shit.

PART TWO

CHAPTER 6

The big black burly security guy broke my trance.

"Hey, dude, move along. You're blocking the way."

"Um, I live here" was all I could muster.

"I know where the fuck you live," he replied. "But you're still clogging up the entrance. I got cars lined up. Go on back upstairs or take a long fuckin' walk. Your choice."

I was pretty sure he was not the guy I wanted to talk to about my loose-nut issue, and my name was certainly not on his gold-plated invitation list, so I started toward the alley. But one step later, grasping at a teeny-tiny straw, I turned back to the man in black.

"Hey. Those door handles. It's no coincidence, right? I mean, it's no fluke, you know, choosing those particular letters and putting them in that order?"

He smirked and shook his head.

"Man, the only fuckin' fluke is that you're still standing here. Now walk!"

I held up my hands in surrender.

"I'm walking, I'm walking," I said, and hustled around the side of the building.

I passed by the fire escape up to my kitchen door and continued on to the loading dock. The big bay door was open. Light from inside and from two powerful security lamps mounted on the outside wall illuminated the elevated concrete outcropping. I stopped in the alley and looked up. There, bathed in light, was an absolutely gorgeous, tall, and shapely young woman, dressed in a Wonder Woman costume. Well, "dressed" might not be the right verb. Her suit looked as if it had been applied with a spray gun. To me, most people are tall. But I could see that even leaning on the railing, smoking, and reading a paperback, she was tall – easily taller than I. All that was missing was her golden lariat and invisible plane. (Well, for all I knew, her invisible plane could well have been parked right next to me.) Knowing now exactly what enterprise had moved in below my apartment, encountering Wonder Woman didn't really surprise me at all.

Having written for cosmetic magazines for the preceding five years or so, I knew a professional job when I saw one. Her face was stunning, framed perfectly by flowing black hair. Her make-up seemed to light up her eyes, cheekbones, and lips from within. I just stood there, paralyzed by the art and beauty of her face. It's also possible that what was revealed and concealed by her skimpy, skin-tight superhero suit may have played a minor role in my paralysis. I'm not proud of that. I was reminded yet again of the conflict between my intellectual commitment to feminism and the more reflexive hormonal response of the primitive man still lurking somewhere inside me. It was troubling. I zeroed my eyes in tightly on hers and looked nowhere else.

"Um, excuse me. Sorry to interrupt your reading, but I live just upstairs, there." I pointed up. "And I really need to speak to someone in charge."

She sighed, lowered her book, and lifted her eyes to mine. She was even more striking when looking directly at me.

"Look, if you're here to complain about the music, don't even bother. Our psycho leader had it written into the lease that he could blast that mindless, relentless, soul-destroying, electronic shit, twenty-four seven. Sorry, you're SOL."

"Well, I can't say I love the music, but there's a more, um, immediate issue," I explained. "That big honking light fixture of yours is about to plummet to the floor."

She pushed off from the railing, flicked her cigarette into the alley, and stood up. She must have been nearly six feet tall. In my mind, I recited the mantra. Focus on her eyes. Focus on her eyes.

"What are you talking about? What light fixture?" she asked.

I pointed up to my apartment window.

"It's mounted up through my kitchen floor with a massive nut and bolt. But it's coming loose, and squeaking and shaking. The thing's going to come down if we don't tighten it up. I just don't want anyone to get hurt."

TERRY FALLIS

She moved her hand through her hair and then pulled her ebony mane right off her head. She hung the flowing black wig over the metal rail and then raked her own short, shiny, chestnut brown hair. She stopped, looked up at my kitchen door, then lowered her eyes along the wall of the building.

"Uh-oh. Is that bolt-thingy right up there, say, about eight feet in from that wall?"

I just nodded.

"Holy fuck!" she said. "And it's coming loose?"

I nodded again. It was a little jarring to hear an F-bomb burst from the mouth of a bona fide superhero.

"Holy fuck!"

Still jarring the second time.

She turned and ran through the big loading-bay door. I hustled up the concrete steps and joined her in what turned out to be the kitchen. An open door off to the side revealed a long counter and a wall of rectangular mirrors, each with perimeter lighting. Three more scantily attired women were leaning forward in the chairs facing the mirror working on their faces. Next to the dressing room were double push doors, one with *In* stencilled on it, and the other with, as you might expect, *Out*. Several attractive women bearing trays of food were walking through the *Out* door while still more attractive women with trays of dirty dishes and empty glasses barrelled through the *In* door. Each time either door opened, the sound of a very large crowd and the infernal music spilled in.

Wonder Woman walked to the *Out* door and peered through its round porthole of a window. She motioned me over and pointed through the glass.

"That's where the bolt goes up, right?"

I looked through but could see no heavy light fixture hanging from the ceiling.

"Where?" I asked.

She pointed again.

"Right there! Right in front of you."

She was pointing directly at a polished chrome pole anchored at one end to the floor and at the other to the ceiling, around which gyrated, not one, but two of the most beautiful women I'd ever seen. They both had long blond hair and were dressed in nothing but come-hither smiles, dangly earrings, and glowing perspiration. All was revealed in an instant. Literally. It all suddenly made sense. I finally understood. Despite all evidence to the contrary, I'm actually a quick study.

Just be calm, I told myself. Don't react. Just relax. We're all adults here. Just be calm.

"Holy shit!" I shouted. "There's a stripper's pole bolted to my kitchen floor!"

"Hey, we call it a dance pole."

"Right. Sorry. Holy shit!" I shouted. "There's a dance pole bolted to my kitchen floor!"

"Calm down!" she ordered. "We got to get it tightened before the Boobsey twins get hurt."

"They call themselves the Boobsey twins?" I asked.

"Nah, that's just what I call them." She looked again through the porthole, then quickly swung open the *Out* door.

"Lewis!" she called over the music. "Lewis!"

She then waved her hand frantically and closed the door again.

Another gigantic black man stepped through the *In* door nearly knocking me back out onto the loading dock.

"So sorry, man. Are you okay?" he asked, helping me to my feet.

"Yeah, I'm fine," I lied, massaging my shoulder. "Serves me right, standing right behind the *In* door."

"No time for this!" Wonder Woman snapped.

"Right," I said.

"Lewis kind of has a few roles around here. Mainly security, but also a little maintenance, a little unloading, and, um, some other services," she explained to me. "Sorry, I don't even know your name."

"Everett. Everett Kane."

"Shawna Hawkins. Nice to meet you." Wonder Woman shook my hand before turning to Lewis. "So, Lewis, Everett lives upstairs. The dance pole goes up through his kitchen floor, and it's coming loose. We need to tighten it up fast. Can you help?"

"Can I help?" he repeated, breaking into a broad smile. "That's what I do! I help! That's why I'm here."

"Well, it's got to happen now or Suzy and Tammy might end up impaled on the pole."

"I'm not too sure what 'impaled' means, but I think I get the idea," Lewis replied. "Is it a big nut on a bolt?"

I nodded.

"Hang on a sec."

Lewis trotted over to the far side of the kitchen where a dark blue plastic toolbox rested on a low shelf. He flipped it open, grabbed a very large wrench, and headed for the loading dock.

"I'm on in ten, so over to you, boys." Shawna waved as she disappeared into the mirrored dressing room.

I led Lewis up the fire escape and into the kitchen. The racket made by the loose pole was now much louder than it had been when I'd left the apartment ten minutes earlier. We didn't have much time. I pushed the kitchen table out of the way, revealing the nut and bolt assembly. It was wobbling and hopping around almost as if two well-toned sisters might be swinging on the pole one floor below.

Lewis immediately sized up the situation and dropped to the floor, wrench poised.

"That nut only had a few turns left on it," he said, as he cranked the wrench.

With each turn, the rattling and metallic squeaks softened until only the percussive beat of the music was left. He leaned into the wrench, straining. The nut and bolt were fused into one solid unit again.

"Crisis averted," I said, as this giant pulled himself back to his feet.

"We didn't meet formally downstairs," I said. "I'm Everett Kane."

"Great to meet the man upstairs," he replied as he beamed. "I'm Lewis Small."

"Your name is Lewis Small?" I said before thinking. "You don't exactly live up to your name."

"Yep, that's my God-given name," he said, the smile still fracturing his face. "I think it'd be way worse if I was a little tiny guy. No one really bugs me about my name."

"I can't imagine anyone bugs you about anything," I said. "Just how big are you?"

He had the grace to laugh.

"Six-ten, 275."

"Wow."

"What about you?" he asked.

"You mean, how big am I?" I clarified.

"Yeah."

"Well, um, I'm five-nine – you know, average height – and 160."

"Yep. Just about what I figured," Lewis said. "When you work security, you learn to size people up pretty quickly. You look taller, by the way."

"You think?" I brightened. "Thanks. That's what I've always thought, too."

Although, when standing next to him, on tippy-toes, it felt like I was just tall enough to carry on an intelligent conversation with his navel.

Lewis, still smiling, was eyeing the rest of the apartment.

"Can I take a peek around?" he asked. "I've never been up here."

"Sure. Help yourself." You can go wherever you like, do whatever you want, I thought to myself. Stay as long as you like. It's all entirely up to you.

He wandered around a bit.

"Hey, this is really nice, man. You've done a nice job up here."

"Thanks. I've only been in a few weeks, so I'm still sorting out a few things," I said. "So what exactly do you do for, you know, XY?"

"My real job is security."

"Really? I can't imagine why they'd put someone like you on security."

He looked perplexed for a second or two before he started chuckling and pointing at me.

"You're a funny guy, Mr. Kane. I like you."

I smiled and shrugged.

"Call me Everett, please," I said.

"So, anyhow, Everett, I make sure nobody gets too out of control when it comes to booze and beer, and the girls. You know."

"The women," I interjected.

I must stop blurting things out without thinking them through, particularly when directed to a six-foot-ten, 275-pound giant, smiling or not.

"What?"

"Nothing. Just ignore me," I replied. "Have you had to throw anyone out yet?"

"Nope. Most of them are pretty well behaved. I handed out a few warnings, but Mr. B screens members pretty good before letting them in. So everyone's been cool so far."

"Mr. B?" I said. "You mean Mason Bennington?"

"I just call him Mr. B."

"Um, what's he like?"

"Well, he can get a bit cranky. Sometimes a lot cranky, like tonight. But he's been good to me. I got a job and that's something. So I just roll with it. No skin off my nose."

"What do you think he's upset about tonight?" I asked.

"Who knows, man? He doesn't say much to me, but something crawled up his ass this afternoon and really pissed him off."

"You don't say," I said, wondering if I looked and sounded as casual as I hoped to.

He reached over and picked up the current issue of *Make-Up Artist* magazine from the coffee table in the living room.

"Hey, why do you have this?" he said, as he started to leaf through it. "Your girlfriend leave it here?"

"I wish I could tell you that my girlfriend had left it here, but that would presuppose the existence of a girlfriend."

He looked a little puzzled again.

"Forget it. I mean I'm very single right now. And I write for that magazine, sometimes. Check out the story about the Broadway make-up guy toward the back."

Lewis flipped through it and then stopped to read.

"Yeah, I wrote that piece."

"No shit! So are you some kind of make-up hotshot?" he asked.

"Are you kidding? I can barely tell eyeliner from a sharpie. But I know how to string words together. I'm a freelance writer. I write for quite a few different, um, publications."

"That is so cool, Ever-man! Wish I could write," he said. "Hey, you don't mind if I call you Ever-man, do you? I'm always making up nicknames for people. It's kind of a thing of mine."

"Lewis, has anyone in your entire life ever complained about a nickname you've given them?"

He looked at the ceiling for a few seconds with his brow furrowed.

"Nope. I don't think so."

"Right. I'd say you can call me whatever you like, whenever you like, and I'll always answer in a polite and timely fashion."

He laughed.

"You're a funny guy, Ever-man," he repeated. "Do you mind if I borrow this mag? Um, there might be some useful tips and stuff, you know, for the girls."

"Wome–" I started, but caught myself and covered it with a cough. "I mean, no worries, of course. I've got quite a few cosmetics zines lying around. Help yourself."

"Thanks, man," he said as he pumped my hand and headed for the fire escape. "I better get back down there. It's almost closing time."

My hand tingled when he released it. I flexed my fingers to make sure I still had full mobility.

"By the way, I thought last call in Florida was 2 a.m.," I said.

"It is. But Mr. B set us up as a private men's club. We don't have to follow the same liquor rules as bars. Works out pretty well for us," he said. "Let me know, Ever-man, if the nut starts to come loose again, and I'll zip back up and crank her tight."

"Deal."

Just as he reached the fire-escape landing, a young woman's voice drifted up from the alley.

"Hey, Lewis! I need you to work some magic on me before I go on. I really need you. Can you come down?"

Lewis looked at me, grinning. He shrugged in an "it's a tough job, but someone's got to do it" kind of way.

"On my way down, Miss."

———

I guess it made sense. Orlando was a perfect location for Mason Bennington's XY enterprise. Think of all the well-off golfers. Think of all the well-off widowers. Think of all the well-off men, married or not. In light of Orlando's demographics, there might not have been a better market in the U.S. for an exclusive club like XY. I just wished I wasn't living right over top of it. I began to think of my apartment as Irony Manor. The idea that I was writing what had suddenly become the most popular feminist blog on the Internet, while resting my feet atop the so-called dance pole of the X-rated men's club below, seemed like irony on steroids. If you were to read such a scene in a novel, or see it in a movie, you'd call it far-fetched and never believe it. Yet there I was, sitting at my own kitchen table, working on a post for the *Eve of Equality* blog, soon to be seen by hundreds of thousands of readers, while the big nut pulsed in the floor below my feet. The words began to flow. Life is very strange, and certainly much stranger than fiction.

———————

When I arrived at the hospital late the next morning, I spied Beverley and Dad walking the paths together. Kenny Jenkins was eyeing them from his regular spot. He didn't look too happy. Then again, I'd never seen him look any other way. Kenny and I just watched Dad and Beverley for quite a long time. They were yakking away with one another and occasionally laughing at something the other had said. She was genuinely funny, so I was not surprised to see Dad laugh. But she might well have been manufacturing polite laughter in the face of my father's twisted, archaic sense of humour. They made quite an unlikely pair. I didn't approach them until they finally sat down on a bench.

I decided not to stay for lunch as I had another stop to make on the way home. The Orlando offices of the Pearson Group were located in a high-end building in the downtown business district. The understated logo of the company my mother led was emblazoned at the very top of the greenish-blue-tinged glass skyscraper. The tower was not unlike those found in every other major city on the continent, except for the fact that my mother had a palatial corner office in this one.

"I'm here to see Evelyn Kane," I said to the receptionist. The young, well-groomed man was seated behind a curved and streamlined marble-and-glass counter with a computer screen built into the surface. His name tag said Edmund.

"Do you have an appointment? I know she's extremely busy today," he said in a tone that lowered the temperature between us.

"No, I don't have an appointment, but she told me to drop by anytime, and this seemed like the right time."

"I see. I'm not certain that Mrs. Kane would agree," he replied, pursing his lips.

"Did she ask you to refer to her as Mrs. Kane?" I asked.

"Only when she objected to the initial use of Ms. Kane. But that's neither here nor there. The point is, she has a full slate of meetings this morning, and I doubt very much that we can fit you in." He paused for a moment before adding, "What did you say your name was, again?"

"You hadn't asked, but I'm Everett Kane."

This might be kind of fun. I watched as his eyebrows arched, his spine stiffened, and the air around us seemed to warm up a few degrees.

"I see. Are you related to Mrs. Kane?" he asked, smiling now.

"You could say that. I'm her only son."

"Well, then Mr. Kane, I'm sure we can accommodate your

request. If you could just have a seat over there, I'll contact one of her assistants," he said, now in full retreat.

"How many assistants does she have?"

"Well, quite a few. Just have a seat if you would. Can I get you a coffee, latte, espresso, cappuccino, tea, chai, or spiced cider while you're waiting?"

"Could you do a Flaming Sambuca?" I said. He blanched. "I'm kidding. I'm just fine, but thank you, Edmund."

I dropped into a sleek leather chair, a few paces away, while he worked his keypad and headset. He turned away from me and spoke in hushed tones, presumably to one of my mother's multitude of assistants. In time, he swung around and resumed his original front-facing posture at his station. He caught my eye and held up three fingers before mouthing a silent countdown – three, two, one. . .

"Ev honey, why didn't you tell me you were coming, I would have cleared my schedule," my mother said as she swept out from the corridor beyond the reception counter. And "swept" was definitely the right word.

She was dressed in another perfectly tailored "don't mess with me" suit of deep dark red. And when I say deep dark red, I mean it in the true hematological sense of the word. A blazing white blouse and some kind of white and red patterned scarf thingy led one's eyes up to her very attractive face and perfectly coiffed hair. Red pumps – at least I think that's what you would call these high-heeled power shoes – completed the ensemble.

"Hi Mom, or should I say *Mrs.* Kane?"

She sighed.

"Here we go. Is it a crime that I just prefer the terminology Mrs.? Margaret Thatcher, Britain's first woman prime minister insisted on it. Why can't I?"

"Mom, it's fine," I replied. "It just seems a rather strange concession to patriarchy for a powerful woman CEO to make. Besides, Maggie Thatcher, for all her groundbreaking and trailblazing, was still a supremely conservative woman."

"So, nothing wrong with that," she replied. "And she was also smart, tough, and powerful, and took no shit from anyone, man or woman."

"Yes, all true," I agreed. "Okay, well that was fun."

"Yes, it was. Let's move on," my mother said. "Come on in. I've got a few minutes before my world comes crashing down on me."

She took my hand and we walked down the corridor. It took me back to when she'd grab my hand when crossing the street. As we sauntered by, Edmund tried and failed to pretend we weren't there.

"Wow!" I exclaimed as we entered the largest and most beautiful office I'd ever seen. If you pushed the board table off to the side, I'm sure there was room for a regulation tennis court, or at least badminton. Her wraparound desk was at the far corner, next to the floor-to-ceiling windows overlooking downtown Orlando. I remembered we were on the forty-third floor.

"Breathtaking, Mom. Just amazing."

We both sat down on a white leather couch resting off the perimeter of a white shag carpet. Not the brutal shag carpet of the seventies. This was more like sheep's fleece or perhaps a polar bear pelt.

"Yes, it's quite nice," she conceded, taking in the expanse and luxury of her office. "I confess, I prefer my Toronto suite to this. But this will do while I'm down here."

"Where are you staying while you're down here?"

"I've got a condo in that building over there," she said as she pointed to another glass tower a few blocks away. "It's the penthouse."

"Of course it's the penthouse," I said. "As it should be."

"It's very convenient. Sometimes I even walk to the office."

"Settle down, Mom. It's a good four blocks away," I joked. "How else would you get here if not on foot?"

"There are many demands on my schedule," she replied. "A car usually picks me up. It saves time."

There was a knock at the door.

"Come!" she intoned.

Two middle-aged men stood there, looking unhappy and a little frightened.

"Gentlemen, meet my son, Everett. Ev, this is George and Liam from Finance."

I nodded. Then they nodded and looked from my mother to me.

"You may speak freely in front of my son," Mom said. "What's up?"

"Sorry to interrupt, Evelyn, but we've hit a snag on the financing," George said.

"Yeah, Citibank is dicking us around on the rate. They've bumped it up a half point," Liam added.

"Jesus Christ, boys, we had an agreement with them," my mother started off semi-calmly but through a clenched jaw. "I negotiated that rate and it was a done deal. The rest of our financing depends on it. We're not paying another half point. That is not on. Just tell them to forget it. We had a deal."

"That's what we've been telling them," George whined. "But they seem quite insistent."

"Holy shit, you two, get your heads out of your asses and grow some balls, for Christ sakes," she exploded. She had jumped to her feet and the two finance guys took a step backward and huddled closer together. "We had a fucking deal! If they aren't willing to honour it, you tell them First National offered us an even better rate, and we're going to walk across the street and jump in bed with them. Citibank will be left with sweet fuck all. If that's what they want, we're happy to oblige. Just tell them that, and stop tiptoeing around those assholes. We hold the cards on this one. We are in the power seat. They need us."

"Okay, okay. Leave it with us. We're on it," Liam said, as the two of them inched toward the door.

"And if they give you any more shit, tell them the next call will be from me to their chairman. Tell them that!"

"Will do, Evelyn. We're on it."

They both slunk out, bumping in to each other in the doorway and immediately started arguing in the corridor.

"Keep walking boys, I can still hear you," she shouted, before turning back to me. "Jesus, it's hard to get good help around here. I have to do everything my goddamn self."

"That was quite a display, Mom," I said, still reeling from the encounter.

"Why, thank you, Ev."

"It wasn't really intended as a compliment."

She snapped her eyes onto me.

"What do you mean by that?"

"Well, you were kind of mean to them, weren't you?"

"Look, Everett, I didn't make it all the way to the corner office by being nice, and touchy-feely, and tolerant of idiots. You have to be tough. This is how business gets done in the real world."

"I get the need to be tough. And I'm proud of what you've achieved. You're a big-deal CEO. But can't you get there without being rude?"

She smiled.

"Would you say that to your father, if he were CEO of this company?"

I thought about it. Good question.

"I hope I would, but, to be honest, I don't know," I said. "It just seems that men CEOs are often megalomaniacal assholes. It's almost a stereotype. But I don't remember you being like this when I was a kid. So I guess I'm wrestling with whether you're just masquerading as a male CEO or if treating those two finance guys like you just did is who you really are, now."

"You're getting too Freudian for me. But there's no masquerade. I'm just trying to do the best job I can. And that sometimes means raising my voice, stomping my feet, and reminding people that I'm the CEO."

I nodded.

The silence hung between us for a few beats.

"Is your father getting any better at all?" she asked, at last mercifully changing the subject.

"I think he has improved in the last week," I started. "The physios told me it would happen like this. He'd struggle for the first several weeks, and then we'd start to see some modest gains. I'd say we've just started to see those modest gains. He's faster on his feet. He's able to lift his foot higher off the ground when he walks. And he seems to be gaining some control over his left knee. And that news is hot off the presses."

"Good. Because he still looks like he's struggling, to me."

"Mom, he *is* struggling. And a month from now, he'll still be struggling. But he is getting better. And he seems pretty dedicated to his recovery. He'll get there. Plus, the mobility and fine motor control in his left hand is ahead of schedule thanks to how much time he spends. . ."

"Please don't make another balls joke. Your father has milked that one well past its expiry date."

"Mom, please. Give me some credit," I complained. "I was

about to say 'thanks to how much time he spends exercising his hand muscles.' I was just going to leave the rest to your imagination, without getting into specifics."

"Thank you, honey."

We talked for another fifteen minutes or so, but the CEO side of her life would not sit idly by for an extended visit. She had work to do, decisions to make, employees to berate, and a company to run. I gave her a hug and headed back home.

Inspired by my mother, I sat at my kitchen table and kicked around a new blog post idea. I thought I might write about the women who climb to the top of the corporate ladder by adopting, and then turbocharging, the same despicable behaviour employed by so many men CEOs. After more than a century of business hegemony, men become the role model for many businesswomen on their way up. To compensate for not being men, they crank up their own man-o-meter to eleven and, go figure, immediately start raking in the promotions. Sure, they avoid the glass ceiling but at what cost? I quickly realized I was enmeshed in a very tricky subject, nestled in a minefield, surrounded by a moat of piranhas and poisonous snakes.

I certainly didn't want to impugn the success of women who have reached the top in a man's world. Such achievements should be celebrated, not challenged. But a small part of me wondered whether their victories might be somewhat hollow, perhaps even pyrrhic, in some cases. Shouldn't true equality mean that women can rise to the top as women, and not only as nastier clones of men? But really, who the hell am I to make such an argument? It was fraught. I sat there holding my head, trying to think it all through. Eventually, defeated by the complexity of the issue, I erased what I'd written. By that stage, my brain hurt. I decided there were plenty of other, more pressing, issues to tackle without questioning the tactics of the few women CEOs we have. Despite her performance that afternoon, I also felt some loyalty to my mother. Or perhaps I was just scared of her. That could also have explained it.

I grabbed a beer from the fridge and stepped out onto my fire escape to clear my head in the late afternoon sunshine.

"Hey, Everett, you're blocking my rays."

I looked down to see a young woman in sweats leaning on the loading-dock railing, reading a book. There was something familiar about her.

"Oh, sorry," I said, and descended the fire escape stairs until she was again awash in sunlight. "Um, have we met?"

"Ahhhh, how soon they forget. It's Shawna, Shawna Hawkins. You know, we met last night? Just a few short hours ago."

I squinted as if that might help me remember her face. I realized the only part of the scene that was familiar was the book she was holding.

"Wow, um, you look so, well, different."

"Gee, thanks. You know just what lines to roll out."

Shit.

"Sorry, but I've just never seen Wonder Woman dressed, um, quite so casually."

"Point taken."

"What are you reading?"

She looked at the thin volume in her hand and then held it up so I could see the cover."

"No kidding! *A Room of One's Own*," I said failing miserably to conceal my surprise. "Um, that's a classic."

"So what's with the shock in your voice?"

Shit.

"Um, well, I don't know. I guess I just didn't expect you to be, um, reading Virginia Woolf," I stammered, as one foot slipped into my mouth and started the journey down my throat.

"You were thinking I should be reading, what, *G-String Quarterly*, or *Strippers' Digest*."

"No, no, of course not. That's not what I meant at all," I babbled. "Is there actually a *G-String Quarterly*?"

"Not that I know of," she conceded. "I was just messing with you."

My cellphone rang in my hand. I looked at the number and didn't recognize it so I just sent it to voice mail.

"So you're working tonight?" I asked her.

"No, I just have a thing for loading docks. There's no place I'd rather read. I come here all the time."

"You're messing with me again, right?"

"You're a brainy one," she said. "I work most nights."

"Does he pay you well?"

"Who? The nut-bar?"

"Mason Bennington."

"Right, the nut-bar whack-job," she replied. "He pays us more than any other exotic dancing operation in the country. In fact, the boys at the National Association of Sleazy, Dirty, and Dangerous Strip Joints are all pissed at him for raising the bar so high."

"I'm not surprised they're upset," I said. "You can always count on the NAS-double-DSJ. They're nothing if not predictable."

She just looked at me with brow furrowed.

"I'm just messing with you," I said.

She smiled in a way that transformed her face.

"Yeah, well, no one is more pissed right now than the whack-job himself." She nodded her head toward the door as she said this.

"Mason Bennington is in there right now?" I asked.

"Yep, and he's been on the warpath since he arrived."

"What's his problem? Everything seems to be going very well for him," I replied. "The luxury cars were lined up around the block, each one disgorging yet another hormonally supercharged jerk. I'm ashamed of my species."

"Hey, those jerks are paying for my education," she said. "The club is doing great. He's happy about that."

"Then what's eating his shorts?" I asked.

"He's mega-pissed at some blogger. There's been talk of contract killings or at least a severe beat-down."

Shit. Contract killing? Severe beat-down? Surely just a figure of speech. Yes, just a figure of speech. Uh-huh. I just stood there, taking in her statement, trying to process it. I always thought "knee-knocking fear" was just a clichéd exaggeration. I reassessed my opinion on the spot.

The silence reigned for a bit too long, and she looked up to see if I was still there on the fire escape.

"Hellooooo! Earth to Everett."

"Right. So what blogger? Do you know?" I said this badly feigning a nonchalance I certainly was not feeling.

"No idea. But he was bordering on apoplectic," she said. "Oh, and he also wants to knock off Candace Sharpe."

And once more, shit.

"Well, I think I hear my phone ringing," I said turning to head back up the stairs.

"You're holding your phone," she replied.

"Right. Well, I hear something. I'll see you around."

"Whatever."

She waved at me before turning back to her book, and I bounded up the last few steps.

Most of my heart and my mind were consumed with the news that Mason Bennington would like to end my all too brief run in the human race. But a tiny part of my brain also registered that Shawna had used the word "apoplectic."

After closing the fire escape door, I checked my voice mail and heard the unmistakable voice of Beverley Tanner. She always sounded energized, but I thought I detected an extra zip in her voice.

"Hello there, young one. I talked Billy, your dear stegosaurus of a father, into handing over your number. He gave it up, eventually. Well, Everett Kane, I gotta say, you are one interesting man. Now get your ass over here! We need to talk, now."

CHAPTER 7

I had no idea what Beverley was talking about but felt compelled to heed her rather pointed call and head back to the hospital. Unfortunately, it looked as if I'd make it in plenty of time for what they called dinner. I dumped the remaining half of my beer in the sink. Just before heading out, I decided to check my Twitter numbers and the stats on the EofE blog. That might not have been my best decision of the day. I was soon awash in swirling, conflicting feelings of pride, excitement, anxiety, and something approaching terror. The already astronomical numbers were still in steep ascent. I had thought that my fifteen minutes of fame might already be on the wane, yet the viral spike had clearly not abated. Literally, by the second, more and more people were visiting the blog and following me on Twitter.

I checked the blog and noted 279 new comments awaiting moderation. Yes, 279 new comments. Okay. Calm down. Why the fear and anxiety? I forced logic and reason into my brainpan, and eventually, a more thoughtful pride at what I'd created eased into my mind. I reminded myself that, however unlikely this all was, this was what, in my wildest dreams, I'd hoped might happen. Right? I wanted to use my ideas, my words, my writing, to make an impression, didn't I? That was the whole point, wasn't it? Who really knows what impact I was actually having, but one point was indisputable. People, many, many people, tens of thousands of people, were reading my words. I shuddered, in a good way.

I sat there at my kitchen table for a few minutes with my eyes closed to try to centre myself, come to ground, as it were. I felt a little better afterwards and immediately scrolled through all 279 comments waiting to be blessed or rejected with the click of my all-powerful mouse. It didn't take as long as you might expect. Twenty minutes later, I'd approved 198 comments, mainly supportive but not all, tagged 51 as spam, largely, no pun intended, from male potency evangelists, and rejected 30 offensive missives laced with enough profanity to offend even the most openminded and tolerant web-surfer. Finally, I checked Technorati, a site that, through proprietary algorithmic alchemy, somehow measures the "authority" of blogs. It seemed that at that precise moment, *Eve of Equality* was the most trusted, most popular, most widely read feminist blog on the Internet. I closed my eyes again for a few minutes.

While I was at it, I logged into my EofE Gmail account. I decided I didn't have time to scroll through all the email that had arrived since my last check-in. I was just about to close out of Gmail when one of the most recent emails caught my eye bearing the subject line: *An invitation to appear on the show.* Uh-oh. I clicked it open.

Dear Eve,

Love your new blog. So fresh, thoughtful, and well-argued. Love the humor, too. I think that's what makes it seem so hip and different. Anyway, Candace loves it, too, as you've probably discovered. She'd like to have you on the show sometime soon, before everyone else gets their claws into you. We don't even know where you live in the world, but that doesn't matter. We'll fly you in from wherever you are and put you up here in LA. Can you let us know if we can make this happen? The sooner, the better. We'd love to have you first.

Sandi Jacobs
Senior Producer
Candace

Shit. I closed my laptop without responding, I mean, other than the anguished guttural moan that escaped from somewhere deep within me. I'd never heard that noise before and had no idea I could produce it. I grabbed the car keys and walked out the door.

———

I scanned the grounds. I saw my father's familiar crustacean-like gait, as he hobbled and wobbled his way along the Red path, pushing Kenny Jenkins in his wheelchair. I watched him for a moment. He was working hard. The previous week, he had retired the walker and had graduated to the cane Kenny held in his lap. Dad was still struggling but had come a long way from our first faltering steps together weeks before. He could cover so much more distance now between breaks and was faster, too. And what had started out looking like an entirely new mode of locomotion, barely resembling walking, now looked like no more than a very pronounced rolling limp. He'd made real progress. Kudos to him. He'd done everything asked of him. He'd dragged himself around those colour-coded paths with orderlies, with me, lately with Beverley or Kenny, and sometimes on his own. But he'd stuck to it. An unexpected shot of pride swelled my chest.

They were at the far end of the property, heading away from me. I saw Beverley stationed on a bench in the sunshine a little way along the Yellow path, working on yet another letter. I had just started toward her when she looked up and saw me. Instantly, she stowed her pad and pen, stood up, and started waving maniacally at me, or to me, I'm not sure which. She had an almost crazed look on her face. She was gesticulating wildly with her arms jerking around in a kind of spasmodic semaphore. She might simply have been exhorting me to run to her, rather than walk. But she could also have been frantically signalling a Search and Rescue chopper for all I knew. I waved back and picked up my pace in the hopes she wouldn't dislocate a shoulder. As I came closer, I heard a high-pitched squeal that could only be coming from the nearly unrecognizable mass of geriatric energy formerly known as Beverley Tanner.

"My boy, my boy, my sweet boy!" she said as she grabbed me in a bear hug and bounced us up and down like a possessed pogo stick. I confess it felt a little odd.

I hugged back but looked furtively for an orderly in case I needed help to restrain the patient.

"Whoa, Beverley. Let's sit down, shall we," I said as I lowered her to the bench. "I'm not sure your doctor would approve of your, um, frenetic calisthenics."

She sat but wouldn't let go of my hands. I speculated that perhaps she'd won the Florida Lottery. I'd never seen her like this and I was at a loss explain her odd behaviour.

"Everett, you are a man of action, you are," she said. "I can't believe it! I can't believe you!"

"Beverley, calm down," I said. "Breathe! That's it, breathe."

She relaxed a bit so that she was simply beaming and rocking, still holding my hands.

"Better. Now what's going on? What are you all, um, exercised about?" I asked.

"As if you don't know. You have to know," she started. "You asked me to read every one of your little essays. And I read them all. Every one. They're wonderful. Perhaps even better for my suggestions. Did you really think I wouldn't notice? Did you think I wouldn't recognize them? Not to mention the title you chose. I'm deeply honoured."

Understanding dawned. Shit. This wasn't part of the plan.

"Um, Beverley, have you been dipping into the Internet again?" I scolded. "I've warned you before about what lurks there. It's a cesspool of, well, of very bad things."

She didn't appear to be listening.

"I can't believe what's happened. I was watching the show when she talked about it. Always curious about the next big feminist thing, of course I whipped out my iPad and, hello *Eve of Equality!*"

And there it was. Right out in the open. This wasn't part of the plan.

"Ah yes, it may be Shark Week on the Discovery Channel, but it's Feminist Week on *Candace*. Just my luck," I said.

"Now, why didn't you tell me you intended to publish your pieces on a blog? I could have been promoting it all this time."

"Beverley, I didn't really know what I was doing. I still don't. I just wanted to get them out there to see what would happen. I'm flying by the seat of my pants here."

"Well, you sure know how to take off!" she replied. "Hell, you're famous!"

"Whoa, Beverley, keep your voice down!" I hissed. "You, and possibly a small, independent and now frazzled Internet service provider, are the only other living souls who know I'm the Eve in *Eve of Equality*. And that's how it's got to stay. That's how it must stay. No one else can know," I said, narrowing my eyes to slits as I stared her down. And believe me, it's hard to stare someone down when you narrow your eyes to slits. But I managed.

"But why the secrecy? Why don't you take a bow and all the accolades? You've earned them. You deserve them."

"Beverley, I think you know why," I said. "You know very well why."

"What? Some misplaced belief about who should speak about gender equality? Who has the right to expound on feminism? Is that what you're worried about?" she asked.

"I just don't think a relatively privileged youngish white man should all of a sudden become the new face of feminism. It's not right. It would rightly trigger a huge backlash. It would be a distraction. It would be a disaster," I replied. "If we're ever going to achieve real equality, women have to lead the movement, and be seen to lead the movement, as they always have, and as you yourself argued in your own book."

"Everett, if we're ever going to achieve true equality, and the way things are going, I have my doubts we ever will, men need to be part of the discussion. Real equality means that men are going to lose a big chunk of the power and privilege you've enjoyed for, well, for the goddamned whole of recorded history. So men bloody well better be part of the conversation," Beverley said. "Look, you, my boy, are in a rare position to push men to the table. If you have the balls to ride it out."

"Wait a second! Don't hang all of that on me," I said. "I just want to contribute to the debate. I just want to be a loyal foot soldier back in the middle ranks, doing what I can to help us gain some ground. It's a long haul. And I'm just a small cog in a big wheel. That's all I ever wanted to be."

"Hello! Lowly foot soldiers, small cogs, and whatever other lame metaphors you choose to employ don't prompt Candace Sharpe to sing their praises and promote their platform. This is big! This is huge! Hell, you might even get to be on the show!"

I looked down and let the silence hang. She swivelled her head toward me.

"No, no way!" she said.

I nodded in resignation.

"I received an email invitation this afternoon." I sighed.

"Jesus Christ!"

"No, not quite, it was from the senior producer, actually."

She slapped my arm.

"I'm not doing the show. I'll never do the show. And no one will ever know the writer behind the blog. You have to promise me you'll never rat me out, ever, not to anyone, not even to my father."

Beverley repatriated her hands and then folded her arms across her chest. She looked down for a time, I assumed in thought.

"The two faces of Eve, eh?" she said eventually, looking up at me.

"I'm serious, Beverley. I never would have created the blog in

166

the first place if I thought I'd ever be outed. I took a raft of precautions to prevent my identity from ever being revealed. It's important to me," I pleaded. "I want the blog posts to speak for themselves. I want my writing to help persuade, and cajole, and encourage those quiet, middle-of-the-road feminists, women and men alike, to step up a bit more, to raise their voices a bit more. That's all I signed up for. I just wanted to capture that feeling I had when I was at university. That's what this is about. Nothing more."

She nodded, listening intently. But she held her peace.

"But nothing, I repeat, nothing can be gained by the world knowing that I am the writer behind the blog. Nothing. It'll just blow up in my face, and any good that has come from those modest essays will be permanently undone."

I looked up.

"Uh-oh," I said. "My father and Chevrolet are coming in hot, twelve o'clock high."

Beverley glanced up.

"Not a word, Beverley. I'm serious," I said. "Promise me."

She smiled and nodded.

"I promise. For now."

"Make room! I'm about to drop," Dad said as he shambled up to the bench.

He let go of Kenny's wheelchair so he coasted to a stop a few more yards up the path. Kenny craned his neck behind him to see why his joyride had ended.

I shifted over to create a spot big enough to accommodate at least two of my father. Somehow he managed to use all the space as he slid in for a landing.

"Phew! I'm freakin' beat! I must have walked fifteen miles," he said.

"More like fifteen minutes," countered Beverley. "I've been watching you two out there since you came out. The way Kenny waves his arms around, he might have gotten the superior workout."

"That's just what I was telling him," Kenny said from his chair up the path a ways.

"Anyway, Billy, you're doing very well. But that was not fifteen miles."

"Well, I know it's hard to take your eyes off me when I'm out here breaking a sweat, but I didn't think you were keeping track of my distance."

"Ha!" she snorted. "You are twisted and deluded, Billy, even for a man."

"I'll take that as compliment," he replied, with a smug smile.

"I'm not surprised you thought that was a compliment," she said. "It speaks to the deluded part of your character."

That round seemed to be over and we sat there in the sunshine for a time.

"So what revolution were you two plotting over here while Kenny and I were dragging our sorry asses and my lame left leg around these paved pathways to hell?"

I looked over and noticed that Kenny had nodded off in the sun's warmth. At least I hoped he was only dozing.

"We were just catching up, Dad," I said. "Absolutely nothing to see here. You can just break it up, go on about your business, and move along."

"What your son is so inelegantly positing is that it's nearly dinner, and you know what night it is."

"Damn right I do," Dad said as he checked his watch. "Geez, will you look at the time." Dad hauled himself back to his feet. "Fried chicken comes once a week. And I aim to be there, on time. Kenny! Wake up!"

Dad shuffled over to the wheelchair and spun Kenny around with enough centrifugal force to tip the chair up on the outside wheel for a split second.

"Jesus Christ, man, do you hate Chevys that much that you'd try to kill me?"

"Settle down, Kenny, and buckle up. We've got fried chicken waiting for us."

"Save us two seats. We're right behind you," I said.

We watched as Dad and Kenny rolled toward the dining room.

"Okay, Everett, have it your way," Beverley said. "You created the blog and wrote the pieces. I guess that earns you the right to control who knows how much, and when. I'll follow your lead."

I squeezed her hand.

"Thank you, Beverley. Thanks for understanding."

"Oh, I'm not sure I understand just yet. But it's your show, so it's your call," she replied. "I just want you to keep the bigger picture and the broader good in mind. You're riding a rocket and that gives you some power that not many have."

"I hear you."

"By the way, what did you think of that jackass Bennington's tweet?"

"What are you talking about? Wait, Mason Bennington?"

"Hmmm. You were probably already on your way over here by then," she said as she pulled her iPad from her bag. "I signed up to the *Eve of Equality* Twitter stream this afternoon as soon as I discovered the blog. A nice touch, Everett."

This did not sound good. She fiddled a bit with her iPad and then handed it to me. I was looking at the @EveofEquality Twitter stream. I recognized the tweets I'd composed and published earlier. Close to the top was a recent tweet from one @XYMasonB. It said:

"Hey @EveofEquality. Stop hiding & show yourself! I've cleaned up men's entertainment & made it safe for women. What have you done? #coward"

"What a jerk!" I said.

"Well, I think your epithet is remarkably restrained."

Since Beverley was already halfway in the tent, I decided to pull her the rest of the way in.

"Just before we head in, there's a little more to the story," I started. She nodded and gave me her full attention. "You might have heard that Mason Bennington is expanding his xy Club operations."

She nodded again.

"I read a squib about it in the paper," she replied.

"Yeah, well, guess where the newest xy just opened?"

It didn't take me long to explain it all, including the precise location of the dance pole. But it took a very long time before her laughter subsided enough to allow me to walk her into the dining room. We had to pause at two other benches on the path to allow waves two and three of her hysterics to pass. I imagine her stroke risk briefly shot off the charts during our little walk in for dinner. She eventually composed herself enough to appear semi-normal in the dining room, though every few minutes or so, she just shook her head and gripped my knee under the table.

It was about 8:30 when I finally made it home. The fried chicken was, well, extremely fried. And now the clump of congealed chicken and grease was sitting heavy in my gut. Dad loved it and shoved down most of Beverley's, too. It seemed to be a busy night at xy so I had to park quite a distance from my apartment. I was walking past the main entrance to the club toward my separate entrance when I recognized Lewis Small standing out front wearing the company uniform – black suit and earphone. He stood stock still with his legs somewhat spread and his hands clenched behind his back. The man was a giant. The cliché "he was built like a brick shithouse" was wholly inadequate and mildly insulting to Lewis's solidity. He stared straight ahead with a look of pure, unalloyed menace. At least I thought it was Lewis. I stopped in front of him and looked more closely at him.

"Lewis?"

His face started to vibrate, then quiver, before it collapsed in a broad and toothy laugh. He grabbed me by the shoulders in what seemed like an affectionate gesture. I sure hope it was an affectionate gesture.

"Damn, Ever-man! I am just not cut out for this fierce-face security shit," he warbled in mid-snicker. "Mr. B says I got to kill my smile and dial up my asshole index, but it's hard. It just ain't me, man!"

"Don't be too hard on yourself. You scared the shit out of me."

"Thanks, man," he said, patting my shoulder. "So is that big pole nut of yours giving you any more trouble?"

"So far, it's all quiet and tight. But I'll let you know when Shawna and the twins start swinging on it later on."

Shit. I honestly hadn't meant to extend the sexual innuendo in the exchange. I didn't even realize how it sounded until it passed my lips.

"Yes, sir. They surely do know how to work that pole. I can tell you that."

I just nodded.

"So just let me know if it starts squeaking or moving again, and I can be upstairs in a flash with the wrench. You just say the word, bro."

"Will do," I replied. "So what are you doing out here? I thought you mainly worked inside."

"I do, but Mr. B's about to pull up, so he always insists we beef up security when he's here. You know, the man has some enemies," he said, before leaning in closer to me. "It's because he's so damn good at making enemies."

"Well, you look good and, um, stern, in that finely tailored su–"

He cut me off and gently steered me out of the way, over toward my apartment entrance.

"Just slide over there for a sec, Ever-man. The big B is just pulling up."

I leaned against my stairwell door and watched as a big, black, and painfully shiny Bentley eased up to the curb. The regular behemoth of a security guy I'd spoken to before got out of the driver's seat and zipped around to open the rear passenger door. Mason Bennington oozed out of the car wearing a grey three-piece pinstripe suit with an open-necked purple, yes, purple, shirt. A black cape of some kind was slung over his shoulders. It looked ridiculous, utterly ridiculous. He was actually shorter than I was. Not by much, maybe just an inch shorter. His black hair was slicked straight back aided by enough product that had he been anywhere near an open flame, he would have burned like a patio torch for hours. His anemic moustache rounded out the weaselly figure he cut. I'm not even sure "weaselly" is a legitimate word, but it seemed the right one in this case. Mason Bennington smiled as if he were strutting up the red carpet at a movie premiere, stopping periodically to pose. Clearly he was overcompensating for something.

The big brass x and y split as the two beautiful wooden doors opened automatically to reveal two beautiful women. They approached Mason Bennington and each took an arm to escort him into the club. Lewis put on his intimidating security face again and presumably amped up his asshole index to impress the boss.

"Evening, Mr. B," Lewis said while keep his eyes roaming for any peripheral threats.

"Hello, Lurch. You're looking particularly mean tonight," Bennington said. "Let's keep that up all night and keep that smile of yours under wraps."

"Yes, sir, Mr. B."

It only took about eight seconds for Mason Bennington to disembark from his Bentley, demonstrate that he's an incredible jerk, insult Lewis, and enter the club, with two shapely women and the other gargantuan suit in tow. It was quite a performance. He looked over my way just before he reached the door, but I had no desire to make eye contact with him, so I looked elsewhere, possibly at my shoes or my fingernails or the sky. I don't remember which.

The doors closed again, reuniting the shiny x and y.

I saw Lewis exhale and both sides of his mouth start to twitch upwards, despite his efforts to keep them grounded.

"Lurch? From the *Addams Family*?" I said to Lewis. "He calls you Lurch? What a dick."

"Mr. B pays me good coin. He can call me whatever he wants," Lewis said, smiling.

"Why don't you just put your hand gently on his shoulder, press down lightly, and ask him to call you Lewis?"

Lewis burst out laughing, even doubling over to hold his stomach. I can report that this suddenly and severely lowered his asshole index. He had to work on that.

"Bro, you are one funny dude, Ever-man. And you obviously don't know Mason Bennington."

"Who's the other massive guy with him?" I asked.

"That's Brawn."

"Brawn?" I replied, incredulous. "His name is Brawn?"

"Yep. Brawn."

"Brawn what?" I persisted.

"Just Brawn. He don't need a surname."

"No, I guess he don't," I agreed. "Well, he seems very nice and pleasant."

"Ever-man, you should plan on staying far, far away from Brawn. He is the real thing. And he'd take on a charging bull to protect Mr. B."

"Well, that's hardly a fair fight."

"You're right. A single charging bull wouldn't stand a chance."

"Point taken," I said. "Note to self, stay the hell away from Brawn."

"Right."

The music was pounding through the floor when I made it up to my apartment. I was getting used to it by then and found that it wasn't nearly the distraction it had been in the early days. I guess you can learn to live with almost anything.

———————

As I'd grown accustomed to doing, I cupped my feet around the big nut and bolt beneath the kitchen table as I wrote. There was no squeaking, or rattling, or movement. But I could feel the whole assembly pulsating. And as the hours passed, the bolt became warmer. Strangely enough, my writing seemed to come easier, smoother, and faster when the pole was doing its thing beneath my feet. I'd noticed this on two earlier occasions but refused to acknowledge it. How bizarre that the pole's vibrations, energy, and temperature seemed somehow to inspire my best writing. On the other hand, I guess it was no stranger than any other aspect of this surreal situation.

Building on one of my original posts – the one about the power of words – I crafted a follow-up post specifically on the use of gender-neutral language to combat gender stereotypes. I'm a big believer in the unintended impact of words and how they shape our thinking. With the pole working its magic underfoot, or under feet, as it were, it only took about an hour or so to get it to where I thought my argument worked but also captured the desired spirit and tone of the blog. I hit Publish and up it went, live.

On a whim, I popped out onto the fire escape. She was there below me, reading by the rail of the loading dock. I didn't recognize her directly, just the book in her hand. I casually descended the stairs until I was just a little above her and sat down on the metal steps.

"Oh, hi, Shawna, fancy meeting you here."

She was dressed like a noble woman from the days of the French Revolution. I might not have the history or country right, but she reminded me of the Uma Thurman character in the *Dangerous Liaisons* movie, complete with a severely up-thrusting bustier. Again, stunning.

"Hey, Everett."

It didn't feel at all strange to be conversing with a beautiful woman wearing a ball gown that looked like it might require a two-week training course to don. I can't explain why it didn't feel strange. It just didn't. Although I'm sure it looked strange.

"I see you're working tonight," I offered.

"No, I was just feeling all Marie Antoinette today so I hauled this old number out of my closet," she replied, straight-faced. "We're having cake later."

I laughed.

"Yes, Everett, I'm working tonight."

"Looks like you're nearly finished," I said, nodding toward the Woolf book.

"It's an avoidance strategy," she replied.

I must have looked puzzled.

"Every waking hour I'm not on stage, I should be spending on my dissertation. But I can't seem to get focused, lately. I just read Woolf, instead."

"You did say 'dissertation,' right?"

"Yeah, so."

"Ph.D.?"

"Yeah, so."

"In what?" I asked, again trying hard to disguise my surprise.

"History, but with heavy sociology underpinnings. At the University of Central Florida."

"No kidding. In what, specifically?"

"I'm examining the early history of burlesque through a feminist lens."

"I didn't know you could view burlesque through a feminist lens."

"Most men don't because you tend to use the brain between your legs instead of the one between your ears," she replied.

"Right."

"I'm looking at a small corner of the early world of burlesque that was owned and operated by women, for women, as an expression of power, as a way to shed the strictures imposed by patriarchal society."

"Fascinating," I said, and meant it. "And there's the feminist lens."

"Right."

"And your job here is, what, research?"

"It started out that way, but I've become addicted to the money," she said. "I have a little daughter at home, so money is something I greatly need."

"And you make more here than you do as a TA in the classroom."

"Sad, but true."

"Do you feel 'powerful' when you, you know, dance?"

"In this place, I do. I know I'm safe. I'm in control. I'm in the position of power. And I can see it in the eyes of those watching me."

"What about Mason Bennington? Isn't he really the one with the power?"

I don't know why I couldn't stop myself from going there.

"Everett, you're going all deep on me, here," she said, smiling up at me. "Yes, you're right, the psycho-nut-job ultimately has the power. But in the moment, when I'm out there on stage, I feel a certain power over those pathetic sex-craved vessels of testosterone. An illusory power, perhaps, but I feel something."

"So I guess you would not describe yourself as a charter member of the Andrea Dworkin/Catherine Mackinnon/Robin Morgan feminist clan," I said.

She just stared at me with her mouth open.

It's not the first time I've shocked a woman with my deeper-than-expected knowledge of feminism. But it might have been the first time I actually intended to. Shame on me.

"Wow, Everett. That is one impressive party trick," she said. "Where did you pull those names from, Wikipedia? Is this a strategy for picking up girls?"

"Women," I said involuntarily. "I mean, of course not. It's a long story. Just think of me as a refugee from the student movement. Or as my father describes me, a pinko, whacko, commie, feminazi. And he loves me. No, I'm legit. Done all my reading, marched in the rallies, led the workshops, know the secret handshake. And as for picking up women, I can tell you that a commitment to feminism has cost me more relationships than it's ever delivered."

"Really. You must have it bad," she said. "And to answer your question, I'm more from the Susie Bright/Naomi Wolf school of feminism."

"Hmmm, interesting," I replied. "I'd say they represent two slightly different schools, but in the same general sphere, I suppose."

"Now, you're just showing off," she said, smiling and pointing.

"Guilty. But I don't often get the chance to strut my stuff with a fellow feminist scholar."

"Well, I prefer to avoid male-loaded terms like 'fellow,' but I take your point."

I laughed.

"So, how old is your daughter?" I asked after a pause.

"Chloe is four years old, going on eighteen," Shawna said. "She is, quite simply, the most amazing creature I've ever encountered and the best thing I've ever created in my short life."

"Does she, um, stay with her father when you're here?"

She laughed.

"Her father, whomever he might be, is not in the picture, never has been, and never will be," she replied. "My mother stays with her at night, till I get home. Then I'm with her most of the day, except for her nursery school in the mornings. This arrangement gives us lots of time together, so it's nice."

"You're lucky to have your mother."

"I'm more than lucky. I'm truly blessed."

"How close are you to finishing the Ph.D.?"

"If I can get my shit together, there's not much more to do. My dissertation is essentially written. I'm just going through final editing and polishing. And then I have to defend it."

She shuddered.

"Well, that shouldn't be so bad, should it? You wrote it, after all."

"That's what I keep telling myself. But for some reason, I find it easier to confront that rabble inside here than to face my dissertation panel."

"Well, in case there's any confusion, a tried-and-true strategy to calm your nerves is to just think of the panelists without their clothes on," I suggested. "Just make sure, in the heat of the moment, you don't fall into old habits and take off yours."

She had the decency to chuckle, though that line didn't deserve it. I tried to salvage something.

"Well, if I can ever help you as you try to keep all the balls in the air, I'm just upstairs. I'm a freelance writer, so I'm supposed to be good at proofreading and editing. Always happy to help another Virginia Woolf fan."

"Why, thank you, Everett. That's a very sweet offer that I might well accept," she said.

"Speaking of feminist authors, have you ever read *The Subjection of Women* by John Stuart Mill?" I asked. "A friend just turned me on to it. I can't believe I hadn't heard of it before."

"Yep. I have a dog-eared copy at home. He was one radical thinker for his time," she replied. "I know very few men who think the way JSM thought."

"Well, now you know one more," I said.

"Yes, I guess I do," she agreed, nodding. "Now I know one more."

She smiled as she glanced at her phone.

"Oops! I'm five minutes from hitting the stage. I gotta go," she said as she handed me the Woolf novel. "Hold that for one sec, if you don't mind."

I didn't mind. I didn't mind at all.

She gathered the flowing gown around her, taming the wild folds into some semblance of order. Then she placed a hand below each breast and shoved them upwards into what I can only assume must have been the performance-ready position. She offered me her hand. On instinct I reached out to take it.

"Virginia, Everett," she said. "Virginia."

"Oh, right. Sorry. Here you go," I said, handing her *A Room of One's Own*.

She took it and carefully turned toward the open loading-dock door. She was just about inside when she stopped.

"Hey, it was really nice hanging out and talking with you, Everett. You were not what I was expecting. I don't meet a lot of men with your interests."

"Occupational hazard, I guess," I replied. "I enjoyed our talk, too. Don't forget my offer of help on the dissertation. You're so close."

She was stalled at the door. I think she was listening to the music leaking through the kitchen doors, perhaps waiting for the song she had chosen to bring her on stage.

"How did a feminist come to live overtop of such a classy and well-appointed den of iniquity?"

"I've been asking myself that question ever since I saw the xy door handles," I replied. "Just my good fortune."

She turned her ear to the open doorway again, listening.

"Okay, I'm up. See you around."

And she was gone.

Upstairs, I discovered two more emails from Sandi Jacobs, each more plaintive than the last. Candace really wanted to be the first to introduce to the world the writer behind *Eve of Equality*. After three emails, I figured I owed her a reply.

Dear Sandi,

I'm grateful for Ms. Sharpe's interest in the blog and in having me on the show, but I'm afraid that won't be possible. I write this blog anonymously so that my words stand on their own, alone. Who I am simply doesn't matter. Only the message matters.

Eve of Equality

CHAPTER 8

It was a good idea. In fact it was so good, I should have thought of it sooner. When I got up the next morning, I researched and then signed up for Google Adsense to introduce online advertising to the blog. *Eve of Equality* had such massive traffic that I thought I might as well earn some dough on the side to offset the hosting charges. As I investigated the model more closely, I discovered that I could earn an obscene amount of money if my humble blog continued to attract as many eyeballs and drive as many mouse clicks as it had in the past few days. I'd passed up some serious coin by waiting until now to sign on. Candace probably had no idea what she'd created.

But before I locked in, I made sure that the ads that were about to start discreetly appearing on the site would generally reflect the sensibilities and views of the majority of my readers, whom I would describe as mainstream feminists. No, I'm not certain what that means. But I made sure there'd be no penile enhancement ads appearing on EofE. I also decided I would donate half the ad revenue to the National Organization for Women (NOW). Not only was it was the right thing to do, but it was also a hedge against any backlash from readers who might not be happy that *Eve of Equality* was to be "sullied" by online advertising. Finally, I wrote a blog post outlining the decision to accept appropriate ads on the site and announcing the NOW donation. I accepted the Google Adsense contract and hit Publish on the blog post before I could change my mind.

I spent the next several minutes hyperventilating, holding my stomach with crossed arms, and gently rocking. When my vital signs appeared to have returned, as the paramedics say, to normal sinus rhythm, I got back to work.

I researched and composed a couple of dozen thoughtful, witty tweets, all with links to interesting and timely content from around the feminist web and shamelessly included a few nods back to *Eve of Equality*. Then I programmed the tweets to publish over the course of the next few days, suggesting that the blog had a team of community managers hard at work spreading the EofE gospel. The @EveofEquality Twitter stream now boasted more than 403,000 followers. So I had a following to satisfy – a large, steadily growing, and hungry following.

It took me another hour to wade through the mass of comments stuck in the blog's moderation queue from yesterday's post on inclusive language – the good, the bad, and the ugly. There were plenty of each, but the good won the day. As well, there were still more comments stacked up on every other post. This suggested that visitors were not just reading one post, commenting, and bolting for greener online pastures. Rather, they were staying and grazing on the other mini-essays on offer. Even the very first post I wrote was still pulling big numbers. But my Mason Bennington screed still led the popularity pack.

By then, it was noon, and I was wiped from the hours spent tending my online garden. I ignored the emails piling up in the EofE Gmail account. They could wait.

A Twitter Direct Message bonged in my cellphone. I picked it up to check it and nearly dropped it. The private DM was from Candace Sharpe's own Twitter account. She was reaching out to me personally. What the hell was happening? The earth seemed to have shifted just a bit on its axis.

@EveofEquality Really dig what you're writing. It just works &
it resonates with real power. Please, please, come on the show.

I could see the scene playing out before a live studio audience. That is, if Candace would even agree to talk to me after discovering who and what was pulling the levers behind the blog's curtain. What a disaster. What a cataclysm. The impact of the blog would instantly erode to nothing, as the smoke of the controversy obscured everything. Three small steps forward, fifteen giant leaps backward. I ignored her DM. I ignored Candace Sharpe. Rude, but safe.

I passed the afternoon at the hospital. I had planned to walk Dad until he or I dropped, but that didn't happen. When I arrived just after lunch, I once again found Dad and Beverley arm in arm, going around the Red path with jilted Kenny looking on from the sidelines. Even from a distance you could see they were deep in conversation. Beverley's right hand was gripping Dad's left arm while her left hand carried on an animated aerial routine, no doubt synchronized to the point she was making. Dad's right hand worked the cane as he eased his left leg forward with a far less pronounced body-roll than I'd yet seen. As usual, he was working hard, but I could also see he was listening intently, deep in thought, nodding and grunting occasionally. I couldn't tell from where I stood whether he was nodding in agreement or opposition. It was a very strange scene. Brought together by errant blood clots, there was the irredeemable, unapologetic man's man with a rouge-tinged neck, walking, arm in arm, with one of the founders of the modern women's movement. Very strange.

"So what were you two discussing in such an animated fashion while promenading?" I asked when I joined them on the bench. They were both breathing heavily from their exertions. I thought Beverley's eyes were wider than usual.

"Well, although I promised I'd never attempt it, given your father's blind but rock-solid support for all things patriarchal, he does represent a formidable challenge," she began. "And some-how, I guess he just got my competitive juices flowing. So I'm now in full Pygmalion mode."

My father turned to me and offered a sheepish smile while Beverley barrelled on.

"My mission is to turn this apparently unreconstructed mass of male ego into someone who, if he looks very far in the distance just might envision a time when women have more to offer this world than cleaning, cooking, sewing, child care, and the free and frequent use of the anatomical parts that always precede the need for the aforementioned child care."

Dad looked at me again and smiled, but this time there was some tension beneath the bonhomie.

"Wow, Beverley. That is one great line. Don't anyone say any-thing. I want to write it down before I forget it," I said patting my pockets for some kind of a writing utensil. "I'm serious. Can I borrow your pen and pad for a moment?"

She didn't move.

"Beverley, I mean it. It was a brilliant one-line summation of the stone-age man's mind, and I can use that. I mean I know someone who can use it, somewhere."

She reached into her bag and handed me her pad and pen. I wrote down what I could remember, with Beverley looking over my shoulder.

"You forgot 'sewing' right there, and add 'and frequent' right there," she said, pointing.

"Right. That strengthens it."

I ripped the page from the pad, folded it up, and slipped it in my pocket before returning the pen and paper to Beverley.

"Thanks," I said. "So, um, where were we?"

"Beverley was in the middle of taking all the fun out of courting," Dad replied. "I think I'm closer to making it to first base with Kenny than with her."

"Billy, we're not courting," she snapped. "You and I are simply engaged in intellectual discourse about an age-old question. And no matter what everyone else says, I *do* think you're capable of rational thought and rudimentary reasoning."

"I like the way you say 'intellectual discourse,'" Dad teased. "It reminds me of another word."

She rolled her eyes. Then she turned to me.

"You see what I'm up against?"

"Well, I sure know what I want to be *up against*," Dad cut in.

"So now you're resorting to ribald double entendres?" she asked. "Unbelievable."

"I have no idea what those words mean, ma'am, but what I do know is you can't fight biology," Dad said.

"Christ. That's the best you can do? Trot out biology?" She sighed. "Billy boy, we have a long way to go. But we'll get there. You could not have turned out this boy without harbouring somewhere deep inside a closeted feminist just waiting to burst forth."

"Ma'am, I can assure you, I have always only had eyes, and

other parts of my body, for women. There's no closet anywhere inside me. On the hetero gauge, I'm an eleven," Dad
protested.

Beverley looked up and exhaled in a way that startled the
sparrows in the trees above us. I reached over and held her
hand.

"Are you starting to get a sense of the magnitude of this
challenge?"

Dad smiled and promptly stood up.

"Well, ladies, my work here is done," he said. "I need a drink,
and Kenny needs to back up his stupid idea that the first
Camaro was better than the first Mustang. Yeah, good luck
with that."

He shuffled off down the path toward Kenny's wheelchair.

"That man is incorrigible," Beverley said when Dad had moved
out of earshot.

"Yes. Yes, he is," I replied. "So what's your strategy?"

"Well, I was hoping to let the power of logic and reason
prevail, but he's been somewhat impervious to that approach
thus far."

"I tried to tell you. He's locked in a very different time. He's
Ozzie and Harriet, Leave It to Beaver, and *Father Knows Best,* all
rolled into one. And that show plays in his head 24-7."

"I might have to bring out the big gun sooner than expected,"
she said.

"What's the big gun?"

"It's hard to fire it with fathers who only have sons, or in this case, son. But I might have to try to get him to imagine what it would be like to have a daughter. He'd really have to dig deep to think of himself as the father of a daughter. Then I'd hit him hard with what she would surely encounter – the obstacles placed in her way – over the course of her life."

"Hmmm. That sounds serious."

We sat in silence for a time.

"If I can get him to imagine what it would be like to love a daughter, I might be able to nudge him along the path toward a very modest state of enlightenment."

"I concluded years ago that he's a lost cause. And his performance today does little to change my view. But never has he confronted a motivated and energized Beverley Tanner. I wouldn't bet against you."

"Thank you, Everett," she replied, squeezing my hand. "Now, if my enunciation suffers in the coming weeks, blame the bit between my teeth."

From my window, I could see them gathering in twos and threes across the street. There weren't many of them initially, but in time, the crowd was quite impressive. I watched from my second-floor window. It became clear soon enough what was happening. Many of them brought signs to hold aloft – shorthand for their thoughts and voices.

POLES APART

XY NOT IN MY BACKYARD!

THERE ARE CHILDREN IN THIS HOOD!

SILVER SPOON MISOGYNY IS STILL MISOGYNY.

MISOGYNY WITH SECURITY IS STILL MISOGYNY.

MASON BENNINGTON IS NO SAVIOR.

Some protestors even pushed strollers bearing cute occupants in various states of consciousness, with juice boxes and Cheerios stowed beneath their seats. The community had come together. The neighbourhood was speaking out.

Wisely, they stayed on the far side of the street, creating a kind of demilitarized zone between them and Brawn, patrolling his beat on this side. As dusk faded into evening, placards started pumping, and voices started chanting. A fuzzy-buzzy megaphone made it feel authentic, with a real sixties protest rally vibe. It was fascinating to watch. I wanted to rush across the street and embrace each one of them. But I wasn't sure it was wise to reveal publicly that the person who shared a building with Mason Bennington was out to bring him down. So I stayed where I was and cheered them on privately.

The chants were simple and to the point:

"One, two, three, four, let's show Mason B the door!"

"Five, six, seven, eight, close the doors and leave the state!"

What they lacked in creativity, they made up for in clarity.

The group started marching up the sidewalk until they were beyond the front door of XY, before turning and marching right back again. As darkness fell, I heard the music start up through the floor below me. Fancy cars started to arrive for the night's festivities. The protest group employed another interesting tactic whenever a Jaguar or a Benz pulled up to the front door and disgorged more wealthy and fashionably attired men. Immediately, the chanting would stop. The placards were flipped to reveal different slogans on the other side:

SHOULDN'T YOU BE HOME WITH YOUR WIFE?
WHAT WOULD YOUR KIDS THINK?
THINK AGAIN, AND GO HOME.

At the same time, a dozen cameras would emerge from protestors' pockets, and a new refrain would echo across the street.

"Smile, you're on *Candid Camera!*"

"And on YouTube, Facebook, Twitter, and Instagram."

"Great shot! Looking good!"

Welcome to Shame-apalooza. The effect was quite startling. On several occasions, men ducked back into their cars and peeled away. Some others pulled their suit jackets up over their heads for what looked like a classic perp walk into the club. Still others didn't even stop their cars. They would slow down, see the protestors and placards, and speed on by. Brawn was getting visibly steamed. Business was slower than usual, due in no small part to the effective antics of this neighbourhood group. By this time, there was a police cruiser there to keep the peace and to keep Brawn from going completely ballistic.

At nine, a local news station satellite truck pulled up. Ten minutes later, a rival station arrived. This was getting interesting. I had a perfect, front-row seat for all the action. If I craned my neck, I could just see Brawn below me talking into his sleeve and pressing his earphone a little deeper into his ear canal to block out the boisterous chants. I figured he was in touch with the big man himself. Twenty minutes later, that suspicion was confirmed when the big black Bentley eased up to the curb. I couldn't see who was driving, but the back door opened and a young, attractive, well-dressed woman, with tied-back dark brown hair, emerged, followed almost immediately by Mason Bennington himself. He turned to face the protestors and held his hand up to quiet them. He took a step forward so that he was standing right at the curb.

"Give me five minutes to set up a microphone here and then I'll be out to respond formally to your concerns," he shouted across the street.

With that, he turned and walked into the club. The Bentley pulled away and was gone.

This momentarily flummoxed the protestors, but they soon renewed their marching and chanting, and even seemed to kick it up a notch. I was supposed to be writing a new blog post and responding to emails but I was glued to my front window. A few minutes later, a smiling Lewis Small carried out two PA speakers and mounted them on tripods to give them some elevation. Finally, he wheeled out a handcart bearing a small PA board and a microphone and stand. In a matter of moments, he had the microphone and the two speakers plugged into the board. He plugged the whole thing into the exterior wall outlet and the red light on the board lit up.

"Test, test," he said into the mike, adjusting the volume until he was satisfied. Then he disappeared back into the club. Another police cruiser had pulled up. Three police officers stayed with the protestors to make sure no one got out of hand and started across the street. A fourth officer stood on the XY side of the street, but well out of reach of Brawn. Probably wise. There were now three camera operators and several reporters with microphones and digital recorders gathered around the microphone in a tight semicircle. To get that kind of a media response, I suspect Mason Bennington's publicity team had swung into action hoping to make a silk purse out of a sow's ear.

Right on cue the big double doors opened and out walked Mason Bennington, as usual dressed for an awards gala, the young woman by his side. She looked a little like a deer in the headlights. But she stepped smartly up to the microphone. I slid my window open a little more to ensure I heard everything.

"Hello, hello. Is this thing on?" she asked.

For some reason, I liked her immediately.

"We can hear you just fine," someone shouted from across the street.

"Oh, right. Okay, then. Well, I'm Megan Cook. I'm on Mr. Bennington's legal team. And Mr. Bennington would like to say a few words."

She then lowered the microphone slightly and stepped aside with some alacrity. Mason Bennington took his place. The bright lights mounted on the cameras all clicked on, blinding anyone in a two-mile radius, including yours truly. Mason Bennington raised his hands in front of his face until he grew somewhat accustomed to the lasers shining in his eyes. Then he lowered them and tried to smile. The reporters pushed in to seize the prime real estate around the microphone.

"Good evening. I want to address this to the people who have assembled across the street, I assume to protest the recent opening of the newest private, members-only xy Club. I know you're concerned that we're located just across the way from a residential neighbourhood, your neighbourhood. I want to assure you that we will never give you cause for concern."

"We're already concerned! You've opened a sleazy smut shack in my backyard!" a voice shouted.

"With these lights in my eyes, I can't see who said that, but let me address your concern. The only part of xy that will ever be visible to anyone who is not a member is this beautiful hand-carved wooden door. There are no windows. The employee entrance is at the back of the building. I've invested nearly $2.5 million in this property, employing dozens of local tradespeople and creating more than a hundred permanent jobs. I'm committed to cleaning up what has been a notoriously corrupt and immoral industry and replacing it with a clean, well-managed, safe, and secure operation that I hope will see the end of the sleazy strip clubs that have dominated the business for decades. The young women who perform within these walls are paid, on average, thirty per cent more than the industry standard. They have access to financial planning counsel, a jointly managed retirement fund, full health benefits, and many other perks, including tuition support if they pursue higher education. No one touches anybody in this club. The performers are separated from the club members at all times. This, my friends, is the future of men's entertainment."

"You don't fool us for a second!" a woman's voice shouted. "You can dress it up all you want, but women are still undressing for men's pleasure, right in our neighbourhood!"

"I admire you all for coming to express your concern and promote your community," Bennington said, trying to regain the floor.

"Don't give us all that crap about community. You're only after more money, made on the backs of women who have nowhere else to turn. It's a disgrace! You're a disgrace!"

I'm not sure I'd have phrased it quite that way, but the protestor's point was valid.

Bennington held his hand up for silence. It looked to me like he was working hard to maintain his civil exterior.

"Please, could I just finish?" he started again. "I can see you're upset. But I want you to know that you do not have a monopoly on concern for this neighbourhood. This is now my community, too, and I'm going to invest in it and make it even better. Jackson Park, a few blocks north of here, will soon have all-new state-of-the-art playground equipment, and the pool will be refurbished within the month. The in-line skating trails will also be repaved. I'm trying to do my part."

"You can't buy us!" a man shouted. "We'll be here every night. We're not going away until you do!"

Bennington seemed about to lose it then. He turned his back on the crowd, looked to the sky, and clenched his fists and his jaw. Then he relaxed and turned back to the microphone. The reporters were getting edgy, positioning themselves to hurl the first question.

"Thank you again for coming. We'll keep you all updated as our community investment program progresses. I hope I've assuaged your fears, a least a bit, tonight. My attorney will handle any reporters' questions. Good night."

"Why don't you say goodbye instead, you reprobate!"

Bennington waved, stepped back, and then leaned in to Brawn. I was so close, just above him, that I heard him say, "Shut down the PA. We're done."

Bennington then brushed past Megan Cook and back into the security of the club, the heavy doors closing silently behind him. She was clearly caught off-guard when he threw her to the media scrum. She looked around, I'm not sure for what – perhaps deliverance – but then inched back up to the microphone. I know nerves when I see them.

Just as she was about to open her mouth, Brawn snatched the microphone and unplugged the board, leaving her facing just the array of reporters' microphones. My window was just above where she stood, so I could easily hear what she was saying.

"Um, yes, are there any questions I can try to answer for you?"

"Does Bennington always travel with a lawyer?"

"Of course not," she replied. "I flew in from Washington for meetings with Mr. Bennington on other matters unrelated to this XY location."

"Are there local bylaws being contravened by this so-called private men's club? You can't just open any kind of business wherever you want, can you?"

"I can assure you that all local, county, state, and federal rules, regulations, laws, bylaws, legislation, and statutes have been scrupulously observed in choosing all XY locations. Moreover, as Mr. Bennington himself stated, this operation has created dozens of new and lasting jobs, caused a significant increase in business for local contractors and suppliers, and cleaned up what was a moribund block of real estate."

I thought she was doing pretty well, under the circumstances.

"Yeah, but there are still naked women shaking their money-makers inside," a reporter noted.

"Be that as it may, this business is completely legal, has secured all of the appropriate approvals, respects all laws, and exceeds all legislative employment standards. And he's investing in this community in ways that really only benefit this neighbourhood and have no real return on his own balance sheet."

As the questions flowed, Megan seemed to find her feet, in a strictly legal way. I wouldn't say she was comfortable with everything she was saying, but she knew her stuff and spoke well.

By this time, the protestors had started to disperse. There were kids to bathe and put to bed.

"How long have you been Mason Bennington's lawyer?" an older woman reporter asked. "You can't have been practising that long."

"I'm just one of a team of lawyers at Mackenzie Martin serving Mason Bennington's legal needs. I just happened to be here in Orlando today."

A few of the reporters drifted away then to make sure they snagged a few interviews with the protestors. As the final reporter withdrew her microphone, Megan Cook turned around and bolted through the big wooden doors that Brawn had just opened for her.

I thought about Mason Bennington's bold move to step into the fray and address the protestors directly, however briefly. Wise move? Not sure. I decided that Mason Bennington was accustomed to being the most persuasive guy in the room. He was used to getting his own way. He had a nearly spotless track record of convincing people to agree with him, to do it his way, to succumb to his charms, or his money, or his "Brawn," as the case may be. What he was most certainly not accustomed to, if he'd ever experienced it at all, was a group of protestors who ignored his rhetoric, rejected his vision, and saw right through his grand gestures. This night had not unfolded as he had expected, so he bailed and left his lawyer to mop up after him. I think this knocked him for a loop. Maybe what made it doubly troubling for him was that fewer than fifty savvy protestors, armed only with handwritten signs, some rhythmic chants, and their cellphone cameras, had managed to dampen his business, at least for this one night.

I made myself a box of macaroni and cheese, grabbed a beer, and sat on my couch. My beer was sitting on the coffee table. If I looked closely through the glass of the beer bottle, I could see ripples appearing and disappearing on the surface in time to the incessant beat of electronic music below. I snagged my laptop from its usual spot on the kitchen table and brought it with me back to the couch. Taking its name all too literally, I rested the computer on my lap, opened it, and turned it on. It was a bit of a risk eating Kraft Dinner and guzzling a beer while trying to compose a new blog post on the laptop, but only one spoonful ended up on the keyboard. No harm done. I finished dinner but stayed on the couch to write.

I was working on a post about how influential parents can be in leading their children to embrace or reject traditional gender roles. I'd already reviewed some academic studies on the topic. Even those parents who were committed to creating a completely gender-neutral environment for their kids reported on how stubborn and tenacious the old roles seem to be. Many families banned toy guns of any kind, particularly with young boys in the house. Yet so ubiquitous is gun imagery and the traditional connection between little boys and toy guns that even those boys who had never ever seen or held a plastic water pistol would instinctively pick up sticks in the backyard and mimic gunplay. Similarly, there were lots of reports of little boys and girls from scrupulously gender-neutral homes being ushered into a focus-group room, with researchers watching from behind two-way mirrors. The room was filled with toys of all descriptions. Almost without fail, within five minutes, left on their own, the little boys were vroom-vrooming Hotwheels around the carpet and wrestling over Nerf guns, while the little girls were burping dolls and playing house. How does one explain it?

Some researchers believe this kind of gender-specific behaviour has always been, or has somehow become, written into our DNA. Others still believe that even in the most gender-neutral households, children cannot be completely isolated from the daily onslaught of stereotypes in books, in music, on television, on the radio, on iPads, online, and in countless other aspects of their daily lives. Snippets and glimpses of traditional gender roles are all around us. They're insidious and propelled by centuries of social inertia. They are so deeply rooted in our society and culture that we often don't even notice. They no longer register. No matter how dedicated a parent you might be, it's a steep and treacherous mountain to climb, and few ever reach the summit.

I wanted to summarize this research and explore this idea with some thoughts about what we might do to extinguish these gender stereotypes in our children. Isn't that the most effective path to true equality? Start very young? I thought I'd write the piece as a narrative from two points of view: a child in a family with traditional gender roles, and a child raised by parents in a gender-neutral setting. Well, it might work.

I opened a new document, my fingers poised over the keyboard. Okay, *go*! Nothing. Right, then, *begin*! Hmmm. I couldn't seem to get started, even though I had a mental map of pretty well the entire blog post in my mind. I tried a few different opening lines, but backspaced through them. I tried to write the conclusion first. No dice. I sat there for half an hour, utterly blocked. It was so strange. I'd written more than twenty posts by that stage and had never experienced this. Something was different, I mean beyond my arrested words. Something felt different. I thought about it a little longer until the mist suddenly cleared and an idea magically resolved in front of me. Surely not! But it was worth a try, wasn't it?

I carried my laptop back to the kitchen table, where perhaps it belonged. I sat down. My socked feet instinctively cupped the bolt and nut protruding from the floor. I felt the pole's pulse and warmth. I sat there for a few minutes taking it in. Then I wrote that seven-hundred-word post in twenty-three minutes flat. My fingers never left the keyboard, not once. They flew from one key to the next until I was done. I read it over several times, making minor word substitutions and sometimes shifting the back half of the sentence to the front. After thirty minutes, I hit Publish.

It was quite late by this time, which was why I was a little surprised when my cellphone rang. I was even more surprised to see "Billy Kane" displayed on the screen.

"Dad? Is everything okay? Are you okay?"

"Sure, Ev, I'm fine, Why wouldn't I be?"

"Well, it's just that I don't think you've ever called me this late. I was just crawling into bed."

"Yeah, sorry about that. I went to bed two hours ago, and still can't sleep," he said.

"And you thought if you can't sleep, I shouldn't be able to either," I replied. "I'm kidding, Dad. I'm not sure I can sleep either. What's up?"

"Nothing much. Beverley and I had another turn around the grounds after dinner. She is like a dog with a bone, now that she thinks I can be saved."

"Dad, you're very lucky to have one of the real pioneers of the women's movement taking an interest in this little experiment. You should try to free your mind up and really try to hear what she's saying."

"You think I have a choice in the matter?" he replied. "She just won't stop. If I didn't like her so much, I'd have bailed on her long before now."

"But are you taking in the points she's making? Are you truly giving it a chance?"

"Look, son. I'm an old dog and this is a new trick. But I think I'm trying. I hope I'm trying. She sure is something else."

"Please, Dad. Try. It would mean a lot to me. And I know it would mean a lot to Beverley. But don't mess with her mind and tell her you're buying in to it all if you're really not."

There was silence between us for a few seconds. I just let it ride.

"Hey, Ev, did your Mom and I ever tell you that for most of her pregnancy we truly thought you were going to be a girl, that is until we caught a glimpse of your minuscule block and tackle."

"Um, no Dad. You've never mentioned that."

"Yep, it was all kind of strange. For the last four months of Mom's pregnancy, until you were born, we thought we were having a daughter."

CHAPTER 9

It snuck up on me. In moments when my mind was occupied with other, more pressing matters, Shawna Hawkins seemed to materialize in my thoughts. I wasn't thinking about her on purpose. She would just pop into my consciousness and hang around, being smart and beautiful and funny. I couldn't really explain it. I think it might have been one of those head-heart dichotomy things.

Intellectually, I don't think I'd ever considered Shawna as a viable relationship candidate, not that she'd be interested in me, anyway. Why? I suspect my brain couldn't get past the fact that she was an exotic dancer. That other fact, that she had a daughter, might also have played a part in my reflexive, thought-free, reluctance to ask her out. When I identified and analyzed this instinctive reaction, I felt narrow-minded and small. After all, she seemed very nice. She was obviously intelligent. Hell, she was just a dissertation shy of a Ph.D. She shared my interest in feminism and my taste in books. So what if she took her clothes off in front of wealthy men to earn money? Should that matter? Should that be a deal-breaker? My heart seemed to be leaning toward no, while my head was firmly in the "be careful, it's complicated" camp. Of course, I had no idea what her relationship status was or if she might even consider saying yes if I ever asked her out. My brain hurt from the exertion of it all. I tried to get my mind to change the subject, but she continued to loiter in my thoughts, hovering somewhere between my head and my heart.

Revenue from EofE's online advertising was starting to roll in. The amount was quite shocking. My writing had never earned this much money before, and probably never would again. I kept reminding myself that Candace Sharpe's blessing, a lightning strike, a fluke, was responsible, at least for this initial stratospheric spike in the blog's popularity. But I also recognized that my massive Candace-induced following would only stay with me if they continued to feel nourished, satisfied, and fulfilled by the content I provided. Candace might have led the horse to water, but I would have to make it drink, and keep on drinking.

In short, the ad money would dry up fast if my audience stopped coming back. Only I, and the blog posts I wrote, could keep them here. That responsibility weighed on me but also excited me. I certainly did not start the blog to become rich. But I confess this recent and significant financial incentive to keep my newfound following aboard the *Eve of Equality* train, did keep me very focused.

That afternoon, I received an email to my EofE address from the *Huffington Post*, one of the most popular news sites on the Internet. It invited me to cross-post to their site, thereby giving me access to a much broader audience. No money would change hands. I thought about it for a bit before responding. Eventually I agreed, but only after insisting that the EofE URL be prominently displayed at the top and bottom of each post I sent them, with at least one link to the site embedded near the top of each post. I didn't want the *Huffington Post* to siphon visitors from my site but rather help to spread the word and increase traffic on the EofE blog. It took about an hour of email exchanges to nail it down after I declined an invitation to talk about it over the phone. Half an hour later, the most recent of my blog posts appeared on the main page of the *Huffington Post* site. They also issued a news release and made a big online announcement about Eve of Equality's availability on their site. The net was spreading ever wider.

———

Again that night, I watched it all from the front-row seat of my living room window. The neighbourhood protestors were back. But this time, Mason Bennington was ready for them. As soon as their numbers reached a critical mass and the marching and chanting started across the street, the big wooden doors of XY opened and out streamed about fifty supporters, also bearing placards and a passable sense of vocal rhythm. The pro-XY contingent all carried signs mounted on five-foot-long polished chrome mini-dance poles. Clever. I recognized some of the dancers, but Shawna was not among them. Perhaps she had the night off. But Lewis Small and Brawn, good soldiers both, were also marching and chanting. This was getting interesting.

A selection of the pro-XY signs:

XY CLEANS UP AN INDUSTRY!

PENSION PLANS FOR DANCERS!

WOMEN DESERVE HIGH WAGES!

WOMEN DESERVE SECURITY!

XY INVESTS IN THE COMMUNITY!

XY CREATES 150 NEW JOBS!

Their chants were not particularly original, but in a two-party rally, it was more about volume than content. With both sides trying their best to drown out the other, I had some difficulty discerning the words of the pro-XY chants, but I did catch these few lame little gems:

"Keeping women off the streets. That's what Mason B believes."

"More jobs, better pay. Mason, Mason, wins the day."

"His dancers come, his dancers stay, 'cause he protects them every day."

To add some visual flair – and probably to ensure that the pro-XY side of the rally snared the lion's share of the media coverage – the dancers donned their performance costumes. It made for quite a sight. It was hard for middle-aged local residents in casual clothes to compete visually with provocatively dressed versions of, among others, Little Bo-Peep, Cat Woman, Amelia Earhart, I think, and possibly Sappho from the Island of Lesbos. As expected, the several news station vidcams on site were largely focused on the smaller, but more arresting, group of marchers on xy's side of the street. Speaking of arresting, this time there were four police cruisers on the scene. I'm not sure it was a coincidence that more of the women police officers seemed to be patrolling the neighbourhood protestors' side of the street, while the men in blue were clustered around the scantily clad xy contingent. Lewis Small and Brawn were stationed almost as sentries it seemed, at either end of the xy line of marchers.

Mason Bennington didn't seem to be at the club tonight. Probably wise. But I did catch a glimpse of Megan Cook, below me, near the front door of the club, watching the scene with considerable concentration. She was wringing her hands a bit and then stopping abruptly when she noticed what she was doing. From her dour demeanour, it was quite obvious she'd rather have been just about anywhere else at that precise moment, including, but not limited to, at a dentist's appointment, at her nine-year-old nephew's bassoon recital, or perhaps even in the midst of her own alien abduction.

For a while, the two sides of the rally kept it pretty civil, even courteous. For a time they took turns, letting one another chant unopposed. But around 10 p.m., the antiphonal chanting ended and things started to get ugly. The forces on the other side of the street suddenly swelled with the addition of what appeared to be a gang of young thugs looking for trouble. They were spoiling for a fight and didn't seem to have any connection to the neighbourhood group. But you could just feel the animosity spike in a matter of moments. One of the young hoodlums from this new group, who also happened to have an absolutely booming voice, started hurling insults and epithets. I watched as the original community protestors backed away from the scene. It was pretty clear to me that they were as surprised as anyone with the violent turn the situation seemed about to take. They beat a hasty retreat.

The XY troop responded by marching and chanting faster and louder. I watched as Lewis and Brawn started bobbing from one foot to the other as they surveyed the scene. Lewis no longer looked happy. And Lewis almost always looked happy.

At about 10:05, the first projectile arced over the road and landed just beside Megan Cook. This did not make her happy. It turned out to be a smoke bomb, and a very effective one at that. Just before Megan disappeared in the smoke, she wrapped her arms around her head in anticipation of what might fly by next. It was a rotten tomato that hit the wall above the door and showered everyone within a twenty-foot radius with seeds and foul juice that I could smell through my open window. I had a feeling the other side of the street would have come armed with more than one smoke bomb and one rotten

tomato. I was right. In the next few seconds, a veritable veg-
etable patch of rotten organic grenades landed on the XY side
of the street, pretty well on target, with several direct hits.

The vegetables were just the appetizers, as it were. The gang
of thugs then charged across the street and the hand-to-hand
combat began. I saw Little Bo-Peep swinging her shepherd's
crook at one leather-jacketed youth, while Amelia Earhart lowered her goggles over her eyes and started kicking anyone who
came near her. Brawn was in the middle of the melee subduing
about six opponents at once. Lewis was trying to separate two
groups of combatants. The police were wading in with billy clubs
a-swinging, but they were vastly outnumbered.

I looked for Megan Cook in the riot and finally located her in
the middle of the road, inching around various battles and trying
to make it back to the door. But the smoke bomb was still spewing its eponymous contents just in front of the main entrance.
She looked scared and still carried her arms up around her head,
frantically turning one way, then the other. Without thinking
about it, I flew out my front door and dashed down the stairs to
my separate entrance. I carefully pushed open my door and there
stood Megan Cook having made her way back at least as far as
the sidewalk in front of XY. I waved to her from my open door.

"Megan! This way!" I shouted above the din. "You'll be safe
in here."

I held open the door and motioned. She didn't even hesitate
but ran past me and up the carpeted stairs. I slammed the door,

making sure the lock engaged, and followed her up. When I entered my apartment, she was standing just inside the door, still hugging herself and looking very anxious. Her charcoal-grey business suit was smeared with the aromatic entrails of various vegetables. Her hair, no longer tied back, flew madly off in all directions about her shoulders. Overall, she looked as if she'd just escaped from the middle of a violent confrontation with plenty of smoke and compostable organic missiles. I stood in the kitchen, giving her space as she started to calm down.

"Who are you? Have we met? Do you work for Bennington?" she asked, her eyes wide.

Maybe she hadn't yet started to calm down.

"Hello. I'm Everett Kane, freelance riot chaperone at your service," I said, hoping to break the ice.

She looked puzzled. No ice was broken.

"Um, just kidding. And no I don't work for XY. I just live above it. This is my apartment," I explained calmly, keeping my distance from her. "I just saw from my window that things were getting a little out of hand down there, and that you didn't seem to be too comfortable in the middle of a chaotic clash of protestors."

"But how did you know my name?" she asked, her eyes narrowing. "You called me Megan."

"Ah. Good question. Well, you see, I was home last night when you spoke to the reporters outside, and you said your name when you introduced yourself – which I understand is common practice when introducing oneself," I fumbled. "Anyway, I'm pretty good at remembering names. Um, I'm friends with Lewis Small and Shawna Hawkins, who both work downstairs, if that eases your mind. I was just trying to help," I added, in my most trustworthy voice.

She seemed to accept what I was saying and that being in a stranger's apartment high above a riot was somewhat preferable to being back on the street in the middle of it.

"Okay. I guess that kind of fits together," she replied. "Well, thanks. It was insane out there."

I just nodded.

"Can I get you something to drink?"

"A mickey of vodka with a tequila chaser would be a start, right about now," she said.

"Sorry, no vodka. But I do have beer."

"I'll take one, maybe even two. Thank you."

By this stage she was no longer gripping herself but had wandered over to the window to see that the mayhem was still in full bloom down below. I handed her a beer I'd poured it into a glass that at least looked semi-clean. Then I stepped back again.

"Thanks," she said.

"Cheers," I said, raising my beer, still in the bottle. "If you like, I can walk you down my fire escape into the side alley and then in the loading-bay doors of the club."

As I said that, I glanced out my kitchen window and saw that the riot had now spilled into the alley. One pair of protestors was exchanging blows on the bottom step of my fire escape.

"Check that," I said. "That route is, um, not yet available. I guess you'd better sit tight here for a while. I'm sure the police will send reinforcements soon."

I maintained a fair distance between us in case she was nervous about being here in, you know, a strange man's apartment. She sat down on the couch while I half-sat, half-leaned on the kitchen table.

"Thanks for helping me out. I haven't been to too many riots," she said with a weak smile that still warmed up the room.

"No worries," I replied. "It looked pretty tense from up here."

"This is not exactly what I signed up for," she said.

"Is Mason Bennington downstairs right now?"

"No. He had meetings in New York, but wanted someone here to monitor the so-called community unrest."

"And you drew the short straw?"

She nodded.

"I seem to be drawing the short straw quite often lately." She sighed.

"Really, how so?" I asked.

"Never mind. It's fine," she replied.

"No, no. Go on. I'm interested," I said, sneaking a peek out the window again. "It looks like we've got some time to kill until the coast is clear."

"It's nothing. It's just that I'm a junior lawyer. It's my first year of practice. I really shouldn't be out on my own, acting as a media spokesperson for my client. It's obvious to me I'm not ready for that, and I can't figure out why it's not obvious to my bosses."

"I thought junior lawyers always drew the short straws."

"Well, we do. But that usually means I'm locked in the law library catacombs every day, spelunking for precedents and citations," she replied. "Not dodging smoke bombs and facing a phalanx of microphones."

"Wow. That's quite impressive," I said.

"What?"

"Well, I don't know too many people who could correctly use both 'spelunking' and 'phalanx' in the same comment."

"You like words," she observed, nodding.

"Yes, I like words," I agreed. "I'm a freelance writer. Words are what I do."

"I like words, too."

"Clearly."

"Anyway, that aside, I shouldn't be out on my own, dealing with reporters and speaking for the client. That's what a partner should be doing, not a first-year associate."

"What firm are you with again?"

"Mackenzie Martin, in Washington."

I grabbed my iPad and Googled the firm.

"What are you doing?"

"Just a little quick research."

I scanned the website, reviewing the "history of the firm" page and the listing of partners.

"Sounds like a respected shop," I said. "Been around since 1905. Small to mid-sized well-established, blue-chip firm."

"Yeah, I guess so," she replied.

"Forty lawyers. Twelve partners," I said.

"Yeah?"

"Just a stab in the dark here," I started, with caution. "I see that only one of the partners is a woman."

"I know, I know. But they've committed to fast-tracking some of the other senior associates so that there'll be more balance in the coming years."

"Does the woman partner work on the XY file?" I asked.

"No. She's a trademark and copyright lawyer. That's not what we need on the Bennington account."

"So is the senior partner on the file really busy and has to delegate all this stuff to you because he's got too much on his plate?"

Her wheels were turning, now.

"No. I wouldn't say so. He's still taking long Washington lunches," she said. "He just explains it by claiming he's giving me a prime opportunity to gain a ton of experience in a very short time."

"Right. By any chance, are you the only, um, woman lawyer working on the Bennington file?"

This could go south in a hurry. She tilted her head and looked up to the ceiling.

I was about to say something else, but she held her hand up to stop me as she thought a bit more. I left her in silence. She stood up and walked to the other side of the room, her back to me. After a brief pause, she turned to face me.

"Okay, smart guy. So you're suggesting that I'm all of sudden being asked to punch above my weight on this file because it looks better in public to have a youngish woman defending Mason Bennington? That the 'optics' are a lot better than having an old white-haired white man lawyer standing next to the infamous founder of a chain of classy strip clubs. Is that where you're going with this?"

"I'm not going anywhere with this," I said, stepping back with my hands raised in surrender. "I was just trying to help you, um, draw some conclusions on the question you, yourself, posed about the kind of work you've been assigned lately, you know, by your old white-haired white man lawyer boss."

She looked at me, hard.

"What's going on here?" she asked.

"Nothing." I said. "Nothing. I was just making polite conversation to pass the time until it's safe to venture downstairs. That's it."

She didn't say anything for a while. But she sat back down and took a few long draws on her beer.

"So what kind of freelance writer are you?"

"A struggling one, I guess you could say," I admitted. "I write for some rather obscure trade magazines that are well-read by a devoted but tiny audience. I wanted to do more serious, hard-hitting journalism, you know, for major news outlets, but I've just never been able to break into that as a freelancer, or land a full-time reporting gig. Newspapers, as you might have heard, are struggling. Jobs are scarce."

"What did you say your name was again?"

"Everett Kane."

"How did you come to live upstairs from, you know, what's going on down below?"

"I had no idea what was going on down below when I took the apartment a few weeks ago. It was just a construction site then. Not sure I'd have taken it if I'd known. On the other hand, it is a great apartment. I really like it."

"It's not bad," she agreed, turning her head to take it all in.

Her wandering gaze stopped in the kitchen and she stared for quite a long time at the big nut and bolt protruding from my kitchen floor.

"Don't ask," I preempted.

I looked outside to see more police than protestors. Two police vans were being loaded, apparently one for each side of the riot. I saw Little Bo-Peep and Amelia Earhart handcuffed together, stepping into the back of one, while several young hoodlums, their wrists secured in plastic tie-wraps, were stepping up into the other. It was all over but the paperwork at the station.

A few minutes later I walked Megan Cook down the stairs.

"Are you staying in town long?" I asked on the landing.

"I'm giving the wait staff a briefing in the morning on recent changes to the liquor code in Florida, but then I'm on my way back to DC."

I pushed open the door.

"There you are, Miss Cook!" said Lewis pacing about the sidewalk. "I've been worried. I thought we lost you. Mr. B would not have been happy with me if I'd lost his star lawyer!"

Lewis was smiling in relief.

"Sorry, Lewis. It got a little wild there and Mr. Kane, here, came to my rescue. We've been waiting it out, upstairs."

"Hey, mucho thanks, Ever-man," Lewis said, pumping my hand.

Lewis took her arm and headed through the big wooden doors as they opened.

"See you around, sometime," I said.

She looked back, smiled, and nodded.

"Thanks for saving me, and for the career counselling," she said. "I owe you one."

I nodded once, waved, and headed back up to my apartment. I sat down and after gathering some stats and other information that were readily available online, I wrote a new blog post, my feet massaged by the big vibrating nut below the kitchen table. The words came fast and free. I wrote about women in the workplace. I hit Publish.

———

The email arrived the next morning at 9:34.

TO: Eve of Equality
FROM: Sally Gifford, Random House, New York
RE: Possible book deal?

Dear Eve of Equality,

My colleagues and I have been following your blog ever since it started some weeks ago. We are very impressed with the writing and the reasoning. Very few feminist blogs, or feminist books, for that matter, seem to be able to strike a tone that is as balanced, nuanced, researched, thoughtful, humorous, yet still serious and substantive, as yours. We also like very much the narrative storytelling you use to breathe life into the well-researched positions you advance. Finally, the broad range of issues you've covered thus far, and seem committed to addressing, means that your audience, mainly women of course, cuts across social, political, socioeconomic, and other demographic lines. In other words, your writing has very broad appeal. That's something we're always looking for, but seldom find, in a new and emerging writer.

To get to the point, we'd like you to consider taking the best of your current and future blog posts, reworking them a bit, and turning them into a book. You have a very large following online, but a book can open up new opportunities for you and help you reach an even larger audience. We assume you're being courted by other publishers, so we'd like to short-circuit any kind of auction and put something on the table that makes you comfortable signing on with Random House directly.

We know you don't yet have enough content on the blog for an entire book, but at the pace you're posting, it might not be long. Are you open to a discussion about a book deal? Do you have an agent with whom we should be speaking? We're eager to move this forward quickly, to strike while your iron is hot, so to speak. Could we set up a meeting depending on your location in the coming days, or at least a call in the next twenty-four hours?

We're excited about this project and its support of women's equality, a cause about which my colleagues and I here at Random House feel deeply.

Regards,
Sally Gifford

I read it over twice. Actually, I read it over about a dozen times. A book. A *book*! What the hell was happening? I've always dreamed of writing a book one day. I think it's the goal, implicit or explicit, of most writers. I was no different. My only regret, should I decide to proceed, was that my name would not appear on the cover. It could not. I sat very still, thinking, for what seemed like a very long time. I turned it over in my mind. I assessed the risks. I contemplated the rewards. I weighed my options. I wondered what she meant by "put something on the table." I vibrated with excitement. I raked my hair, sneezed twice, and burped once. Then I replied.

TO: Sally Gifford, Random House
FROM: Eve of Equality
RE: Possible book deal?

Dear Sally,

Thank you for your intriguing email. As I think it through, a book does seem like a logical and constructive extension to the blog that would bring the Eve of Equality message to a broader audience. I don't think it would take me very long to develop enough content to complete a book-length manuscript.

There are a couple of caveats Random House would have to accept or I'm afraid we would not be able to proceed. Firstly, I'm afraid I am simply not prepared to reveal my identity. I write the *Eve of Equality* blog anonymously and I would have to write the *Eve of Equality* book anonymously, as well. I'm happy to authenticate my ownership and authorship of the blog somehow, but I will not identify myself to anyone. I'm afraid this is non-negotiable. I realize this might compromise promotion efforts for the book as I'll be unable to make appearances, do media interviews, or take off on a book tour (if authors still do book tours). Of course, I'm prepared to do as many live chats online, Facebook Q&As, and Tweetups as you might suggest.

Secondly, I'm afraid all discussions, negotiations, and the entire editing and publishing process would have to be undertaken via email. I'm not able to conduct any of this business, or discuss anything at all, over the phone. I pledge to respond to your emails in a timely and thorough manner (as I think I have with this first one). Does this change matters from your perspective?

As for the offer, in principle I confess I quite like the notion of an auction, with several publishers competing for the book. I imagine the advance (if that's what you call it) would be highest in the case of a hotly contested auction. With this in mind, I'm certainly prepared to consider a sole-source offer, but it would need to be attractive enough to preempt the excitement of an auction. What did you have in mind?

Thank you,
Eve of Equality

I hit Send. My stomach was tight, and little tingles radiated across my chest. I briefly felt as if I were occupying someone else's body. A book. I had no idea what the offer might be. I knew a little about the book world courtesy of a few friends who were authors. But I didn't even know how many figures might be involved in an auction-avoiding offer. But I was cool. I was calm. I could wait. I kept one eye on my email inbox and one eye . . . ah, who am I kidding? I fixed both eyes on my laptop screen waiting for Sally Gifford's response. It didn't take long, though eight minutes staring hard at my screen left my eyes tearing up just a bit.

TO: Eve of Equality
FROM: Sally Gifford, Random House, New York
RE: Possible book deal?

Dear Eve (may I call you Eve?),

Thanks so much for your very encouraging email. We're all doing handsprings around the office. What you're doing for your sisters in the world is truly inspiring. We hope we can help spread your message even further. I know we've yet to agree on anything but we're very excited at the prospect of putting an offer in front of you.

As for your two caveats, we have no concerns with what you have outlined. We have often worked with anonymous and pseudonymous authors. While it is a little unusual for us not to know your true identity, we're comfortable moving forward. Should we enter a contract, we will require from you what I would describe as modest assurances that you are not a convicted serial killer, fugitive megalomaniacal dictator, or escaped convict. But those are just formalities as far as we're concerned.

While this is not the actual contract, replete with indecipherable legalese, here are the major elements in plain language:

- *Random House to hold worldwide ebook/print/audio publishing rights;*
- *The author to be paid an advance against royalties of $250,000;*
- *Standard royalty rates of 10% on print copies and 25% on ebooks;*

These are the principal parameters, with the rest of the details to be covered in the actual contract.

We would count on you to participate actively in the marketing and promotion of the book to the extent that you're able to as an anonymous author.

How does this sit with you? We're standing by to start cranking out the paperwork if you can give us your agreement in principle to these terms. As well, we'll need to be assured that you are the true and sole author of the blog posts, but our IT people have some thoughts on how we can make that happen to our satisfaction without either of us leaving our computers.

Yours in anticipation,
Sally Gifford

It seems that six figures are required to forestall a publishers' auction. I was paralyzed for about seven minutes. Eventually feeling was restored to my extremities. But I let her wait. I took a shower – a long one. The trick of it is not to think too hard about it, not to dwell on the gigantic payday that seemed to be coming my way. Just calm down. Apply shampoo, rinse, repeat. Don't forget the conditioner, now. Okay, towel off, just as you have so many times before. Muscle memory kicked in and I dried myself off without straining any ligaments. Even though my bathroom was not equipped with grab bars, I managed to maintain my balance and stay upright even though I was at least mentally hoisting a briefcase bearing $250,000 high above my head like it was the World Series trophy.

I reached for my razor and then quickly put it back on the marble vanity. I just didn't think wielding any kind of sharp object at that particular moment made much sense. But I did feel comfortable working my hairbrush and spent a few minutes coiffing my do. I sustained no injuries in the process other than a stinging eye courtesy of a small stray dollop of styling gel that got away from me.

My instinct of course was to reply to the email offer with something reserved and restrained like *"Sally, you have a DEAL!!!"* typed in 85-point font. But I decided I owed it myself to think it through and negotiate aggressively. This opportunity was unlikely to be coming my way again any time soon. Clearly, Sally was keen to ink some kind of a deal before the other houses leapt into the play. So I figured I had a bit of latitude on the advance. It took only two more emails to agree to the terms in principle. I squeezed an additional $25,000 out of Random House on the advance. We agreed on $275,000 and a deadline for the manuscript in four months. Holy shit.

I spent the next hour with their IT people leading me through some linked computer wizardry that seemed to satisfy the Random House leadership team that I was in fact Eve from the *Eve of Equality* blog.

Sally sent me a formal contract between "the *Eve of Equality* blogger" and Random House. I read it and understood the first sentence and the last, but had some difficulty fully understanding what the hell the middle twenty-three pages said or meant. I did my best not to look like an idiot as Sally and I exchanged three more emails that afternoon to clarify a few points (or really, a lot of points). By 1:30 p.m., I was reasonably satisfied with the offer – read, I was nearly overcome with excitement and spent several minutes jumping in my living room trying to touch the ceiling with my head. I couldn't quite get the altitude I needed, but my head did hit the overhead light fixture once.

I printed off the final version of the offer and headed downstairs. If my stars were holding in the aligned position, she would still be there. The big doors were locked, so I knocked. I heard footfalls inside and the deadbolt slide across. Brawn opened the door and pretty well filled the entire space. I don't think he was ecstatic to see me. The feeling was mutual.

"Yes, hello, um, Brawn, I think it is, isn't it?"

"What do you want?" he snapped. "We're busy in here."

"Yes, well, I know Megan Cook was running a training session this morning for the wait staff, and if it's over, and she's still here, I really need to see her."

"Everett?"

Brawn was doing to the doorway what the moon does to the sun in a total lunar eclipse.

"Megan?" I said. "I can hear you in there, but I can't see you. Can we chat for just a minute?"

Mercifully, Brawn stepped aside and there stood Megan, dressed slightly more casually the morning after her first riot.

"Oh, hello. It is you," she said. "I thought I recognized the voice."

"Hi, Megan. I thought you might already be gone."

"I'm off in about twenty minutes. We just finished the session."

"How'd it go?"

"Fine. I probably didn't even need to meet with them. They're all pros and already knew about the new regs."

"Um, I wonder if you might be able to do me a very quick favour? I swear it'll only take a few minutes."

"And here I thought 'I owe you one' was just a harmless, meaning-less figure of speech," she replied, but she smiled when she said it.

She waved me into the big room and over to a table on the edge of the dance floor. Brawn didn't exactly look welcoming but he made room for me to slip by him. Megan and I sat down.

"Okay, what have you got?" she asked.

I'd brought with me just the actual clauses of the contract and not any of the up-front pieces that named the book or out-lined the advance and royalty structure. I already understood that part of it.

"Well, it looks like I'm about to sign my first book deal," I started. "It's all still very confidential at this stage, but I wondered if you would mind casting your legal eye over the contract. It's supposed to be a standard, boilerplate publishing contract, but I just want to be sure."

"A book deal! That's fantastic! Congratulations."

"Thanks. Thanks a lot. It's a little overwhelming."

"What's the book about? Is it a novel or nonfiction? What's the title?"

"Oh, geez, I'm sorry Megan, but I signed an NDA, so I'm bound to keep all of that confidential. Sorry. When the book comes out, you'll have one of the first copies."

She looked skeptical. I wasn't surprised.

"Please, just have a look at these pages and tell me if anything seems out of place. I'd really be grateful."

She took the pages and started reading. I found myself watching her closely. Her hair was tied back in a rather severe, ultra-professional-looking arrangement. Even amidst all the truly beautiful women moving about the interior of XY, she held her own. And then I chastised myself for making that observation in the first place.

"Random House. Big name," she said without looking up, and kept reading.

It took her about five minutes to scan the contract provisions.

"Where's the rest of it?" she asked.

"I'm not permitted to share those sections under my non-disclosure agreement. But I understood the other passages."

"Okay, then," she said, putting the papers back into their proper order and laying them down on the table. "Look, I'm no contract law expert, nor have I ever advised on a book deal. But this seems quite straightforward. Random House gets worldwide ebook and print publishing rights, not just in North America. They also have the audio book rights. But you retain the film, TV, and stage rights. You get an accounting of sales and royalty payments each year in November and in May. They also get first right of refusal on your next book. They owe you ten copies of the book when it's printed. Other than that, it all looks rather run-of-the-mill. Congratulations."

She handed the paperwork back to me.

"What a relief it is to know that I've retained the stage rights," I said. "Broadway beckons."

She smiled.

"I've got a flight to catch." She rose from the table.

"Megan, thanks so much for helping me with this. I appreciate it," I said as I stood up, too.

She handed me the contract.

"No worries. Thanks for getting me safely off the street last night," she replied. "By the way, I was up a good part of the night thinking about what you said, you know, about my job."

"I didn't say anything about your job," I protested.

"Yes – yes, you did."

"I have no memory of that," I said. "Um, I was wondering if maybe you might want to get together again some time when you're back this way? Maybe have dinner or coffee, or dinner and coffee?"

She looked at me for a few seconds, thinking it through, I guess. She might have been a tad surprised at my overture – a reasonable conclusion given that I was downright shocked I'd just asked her out.

"Hmmm, interesting," she replied, still holding my eyes with hers. "Why not? I'll be back early next week – Monday afternoon, in fact."

"Monday night it is," I said. "Thanks again for the once-over on the contract."

I slipped out the big front door and back up the stairs to my apartment.

No, I don't know what came over me, what possessed me – perhaps some kind of a stroke, or maybe a minor aneurism. It's a mystery I cannot fathom. Clearly, it was not enough that I'd written an incendiary post casting wholly justified aspersions on Mason Bennington. It was not enough that Candace Sharpe had pushed tens of thousands of her fans to read said negative post about Mason Bennington. It was not even enough that the very powerful and dangerous Mason Bennington – you know, the guy with ties to organized crime – was royally pissed at whomever had written the post in question. No, all of that was not enough. I had to go and ask Mason Bennington's attorney out on a date. Good thinking. Made total sense. Brilliant idea. I made a mental note to donate my brain to science when I died – which might be sooner than I'd like – so that we might learn why my normally well-functioning mind would simply shut down and permit such inexplicable decision-making.

Then I remembered that I was holding a book contract in my hand. I hit Reply on Sally's last email and in an impressive display of dignified restraint, I typed:

Sally, you have a DEAL!!!

But I limited the font size to 40-point.

CHAPTER 10

The next morning, as I'd almost come to expect, Shawna was lurking about in the back of my thoughts. But she wasn't alone. Megan was also there. Great. Like I didn't already have enough going on in my head. They hung around on different sides of my mind, ignoring one another, but each drawing my attention in turn.

I was doing some research for a new blog post I'd been considering comparing men's and women's professional sports. I was going to try to look at a range of measures, including salaries, TV time, column inches in sports sections, public popularity, and even team attire (like the uniforms in women's beach volleyball, which are required to be skimpy – even at the Olympics – versus men's). I wasn't sure yet where it was going but it felt like a storyline was starting to emerge. To ensure I could concentrate on the new blog post, I did not check Twitter, email, or the ever-growing balance in my online advertising account. Focus.

———

Have I mentioned just how consistently beautiful and temperate the weather seems to be in Orlando? I couldn't remember it raining since I'd arrived. Not once. As I walked from the car into the hospital that afternoon, again, it was warm and sunny. Kenny Jenkins was sitting in his spot with a tabletop of sorts balanced across the arms of his wheelchair and secured by Velcro straps. A checkerboard was set up. Only an opponent was missing.

"Hi, Kenny," I said as I approached. "Do you want a quick game?"

"Thanks, but no thanks. Your dad is coming to play so I can hand him his Ford-loving ass on a scorched Pinto hubcap," he replied. "Inside car joke. Before your time."

"Kenny, please. I grew up in a Ford family. I'm well aware of the explosive history of the Pinto." I pointed to the checkerboard. "But, beware. My dad's actually pretty good at checkers. Watch out for the Catalonian-Abramowicz Modified opening. He leans on it a bit too much, in my mind."

Kenny stared at me with an unusual expression – he furrowed just one of his eyebrows. As I left him and walked along the Blue path, I tried to furrow just one brow. It's hard. I couldn't do it. I could elevate one eyebrow. But when furrowing, both of mine only worked in lockstep. I wondered if Kenny's ability was another consequence of his stroke.

I found Dad resting and reading on one of the outside benches. Wait. I'm pretty sure I just said "reading." I'd seen my father resting often enough – quite often. But I could not recall ever seeing him reading. When he leafs through his magazine collection – cars or carnal – the prose is clearly secondary. I don't count it as reading.

"Are you actually reading that book or just airing out the pages?" I asked.

He looked up, closed the book, and shoved it under his right leg.

"Have you ever heard of knocking?"

I sat down beside him on the bench.

"Hi, Dad," I started over. "So what were you reading?"

"Nothing."

"Come on. I love that you were reading. What book?"

He sighed and then, without looking at me, reached under his leg and handed me Beverley's autobiography.

"Nice, Dad. Nice," I said. "So, what do you think?"

"Hell, I don't know. I guess it's kind of neat to read a book by someone I know. I can sort of hear her voice reading it to me, even though I'm the one doing the reading."

"But what about what she's saying in the book? Do you like what you're reading? Do you agree with her?"

"I don't friggin' know! I'm just trying to understand who the hell she is and what the hell she wants with me!"

"Dad, maybe she just wants you to start thinking of her, and maybe even thinking of women in general, a little differently. You know?"

"Yeah, well, it's too early to say for sure. I just started and I'm kind of a slow reader."

"Have you laughed yet?" I asked him.

"Coupla times. She does have a mouth on her, that's for sure."

"But are you thinking about what you're reading? Or are you just scanning the words and missing the story, or worse, the point?"

"Jesus, I don't know. I'm just reading one page after the other, like you're supposed to. That's all," he said. "I can't figure it all out, but what's strange is, I keep thinking of your mom. It's weird."

"Actually, Dad, that doesn't strike me as strange at all. In fact, I bet Beverley would be pleased to hear you say that."

"Well, that ain't happening anytime soon. She doesn't even know I have a copy."

"Oh. Where did you get it?"

"There's this little mom-and-pop company I sometimes deal with when I feel like buying stuff. They call themselves Amazon, I think it is. You should check them out, sometime. Anyway, Yolanda helped me order it on the computer at the nurses' station."

"Nice," I said. "So, you want to walk for a bit?"

"No. But I guess we'd better. But we don't have much time," he said, consulting his watch. "I'm going to knock Kenny Chevy around the checkerboard before his afternoon nap."

He lifted himself up off the bench, grabbed his cane, and headed off down the path. I followed, carrying *The Funny One*, by Beverley Tanner. My father was walking quite well. The limp was still quite pronounced. But he seemed to have absorbed it into his gait so that it almost took on a feeling of normalcy. He seemed in complete control of his limbs, even if there was a dip-and-roll vibe to every step. He settled on a bench closer to where his opponent waited.

I pushed Kenny's wheelchair and checkerboard over to Dad. I left them just as they started arguing about who would play red, and whether the F-150 or the Silverado was the better pickup. They resolved the former, but I think the latter was left as a stalemate. Apparently, there was an endless supply of intractable Ford versus Chevy questions to resolve, or rather, to debate, at full volume, replete with automotive invective.

I walked back into the building.

"Thanks for helping my dad satisfy his newfound interests in books – or rather, book," I said to Yolanda in the corridor.

"Honey, I was happy to help, after I recovered from the shock of it all," she replied. "Is he enjoying it?"

"It's kind of hard to tell. But at least he's actually reading it," I said. "Did you know that you had one of the great feminist pioneers in the house?"

"I knew it the minute I laid eyes on her – even before I saw her chart. But that was a few years ago now. She and Angela Davis were heroes of mine back in the day. I love having Bev around. We've had some good chats. But since she's taken on Project Billy Kane, I don't see as much of her."

"There's a name for it?"

"Oh, just among the staff."

"I haven't seen Beverley today. Is she around?"

"They bumped her physio to this afternoon. Liz is working on her now."

"She seems to walk very well. I didn't know she had regular physio."

"She walks so well *because* she has regular physio. It's just part of our all-inclusive spa service," Yolanda said, sounding briefly like a radio ad.

———

I spent a couple of hours that afternoon monitoring and managing the EofE social media feeds to keep the masses engaged. There was continued growth on all fronts –Twitter followers, visits, and RSS subscriptions to the blog, comments left on the blog, emails to the Gmail account. I replied to a sampling of the blog comments and emails. There was another email from Candace along with invitations from several other major network talk shows, including *Oprah* and *Ellen*. By this stage, I was unfazed by it all, though quietly thrilled. I politely but firmly declined all invitations.

On a whim, I Googled "Eve of Equality" and refined the search to "News." I was a little taken aback by how many newspapers and radio stations were interested in identifying the author of the blog. Beyond the talk show invitations, I hadn't appreciated that I was the subject of considerable speculation in the mainstream media. A sampling of headlines from various daily newspapers around the country:

"Mystery feminist blog has massive following"
"Who is Eve?"
"Eve staying Mum"
"Who writes hugely popular blog?"
"Eve of Anonymity?"

These were not small publications. We're talking the *Detroit Free Press*, the *Los Angeles Times*, the *Chicago Tribune*, the *Washington Post*, and several others. This was a little unnerving. I quickly reviewed my arsenal of anonymity measures and satisfied myself that it would be very difficult for even the most enterprising reporter or accomplished computer hacker to discover Eve's true identity. Still, it was disquieting, though somewhat offset by the online advertising revenue amassing in my account. Breathe.

Rather than continuing my work on the new sports blog post, I spent a couple of hours trying to assemble the existing posts in some kind of order with a semi-logical narrative flow for the book. I was on a deadline, after all. I started by writing a preface to the collection of mini-essays, outlining the goals of the blog and of the book. Then I tried to write introductions to each post that placed them in a broader and less time-dependent context, so they would still make sense if read three years from now (which I hoped they would be). That wasn't easy, but it felt like I was making some headway. I also considered where the narrative strand would logically take me next. I came up with several more post ideas to sustain the blog (and the book, for that matter). As usual, I'd need to do some research, but I felt as if I now had some semblance of a path before me.

I found that time just slipped away when I was writing. The nut beneath my feet was not yet "alive," for it was only 8:30, early in the evening but still, the words seemed to be flowing. But it wouldn't be long before I'd start to feel the warmth and vibrations on the soles of my feet. That's when the writing, for some strange reason, seemed to come most easily.

I got up and took a quick peek out the front window of my apartment. The nightly protest was taking shape. There were not nearly as many protestors as there'd been earlier. But a small, stalwart contingent, many of whom I recognized from earlier assemblies, was gathered. The leather-jacketed young agitators were nowhere to be seen. As well, there appeared to be no counter-protest from XY. I wondered if Megan Cook had advised her client that nothing was to be gained by tele- vised clashes in front of the club. Sound advice. I went back to my laptop.

A few minutes later, outside my kitchen door, there arose such a clatter, I sprang from my chair to see what was the mat- ter. (I couldn't resist.) Someone was climbing up my fire escape in a very big hurry. When the footsteps stopped at my door, the urgent knocking started.

"Everett, are you in there?"

It sounded like Shawna, but I wasn't certain.

"Coming," I shouted, and swung the door open.

It wasn't Wonder Woman or Marie Antoinette, just Shawna. Man, she was tall. She was not made up at all, or anywhere near ready for her stint downstairs, which, by my watch, started very soon. She was huffing and puffing.

"Thank goodness, you're here," she said stepping by me into the kitchen and looking around. She dropped a big blue canvas bag on the floor. "Hey, nice place you have."

It is perhaps a measure of how much Shawna had been on my mind that it wasn't until she was standing in my apartment that I noticed the very little person she held in her arms.

"Shawna! Hi, um, welcome. Ah, is everything okay?" I stammered, shifting my gaze from her beautiful face to that of the child resting in the crook of her right arm. She was one of the cutest little girls I think I'd ever seen. With hair the same rich auburn as her mother's, she wore denim overalls, a red striped shirt, and perfect little blue running shoes. A pint-sized plastic Wonder Woman backpack was slung over her tiny shoulders. She looked at me, expressionless.

"No, everything is very much not okay, except that you are right here," Shawna said, bringing me back. "I need to ask you a big favour. A very big favour. And it's only because of your clear feminist bona fides that you could not have faked, and have already demonstrated on more than one occasion, that I'm even standing here. But I'm so out of options. Can you help me? You are my last, faint hope."

"Of course. I'm your man, so to speak. I'll do whatever I can to help, unless it's 'open pole night' downstairs and you're looking for volunteers."

"Nothing quite so demanding," she assured me. "This is the brilliant and talented Chloe Hawkins, my daughter."

We both looked at Chloe.

"Say hello to Everett, honey."

Chloe looked directly at me.

"Hello Everett honey," she chirped and smiled at the same time. She also held out her hand to me. I very nearly melted.

We shook.

"Hi there, Chloe," I said. "I see you're a Wonder Woman fan."

"Yes. She's a suggorate for powerful women everywhere."

"Sorry?" I said.

"Surrogate, honey," Shawna said. "Surrogate."

"That's what I said. Suggorate."

Shawna smiled at Chloe and gave her a little squeeze before turning back to me.

"So here's today's crisis, Everett. My mother has just started spewing with the flu, and if Chloe catches it, the next several days will be even crazier than they already promise to be. So I can't have my mom look after her tonight. I'm hoping she'll be in better shape tomorrow. Then, my usual emergency backup plan fell through."

"So you want me to watch Chloe?"

"Would you? I really don't want her downstairs awash in that sea of testosterone."

"Terostero, terosteronie, tesostaroni," Chloe mimicked.

"Tes-tos-te-rone, honey."

"Tes-tos-te-rone," Chloe repeated, and nodded.

"Right. Good," Shawna said, turning back to me. "It's almost her bedtime. I brought her blanket and she could just stretch out on your couch until I'm finished. She won't be any trouble. And I'll slip up between sets to check on her."

"Um, sure. I'm kind of new to the whole taking care of young children thing, but I'm up for it, if you're sure. Do you want to have Lewis up here, too?"

She smiled and squeezed my hand.

"He's tied up trying to fix one of the draught beer taps. He loves Chloe, so he might pop up to see her, but I have faith in you, Everett. I trust you." She smiled. "Lewis has vetted and approved you and he's a solid judge of character."

"I'm honoured," I replied. "And he can also tell you exactly how tall you are and how much you weigh, just by looking at you."

Five minutes later, the couch was set up with Chloe's blanket and her stuffed rabbit, oddly named Saffo. Shawna had taken her daughter into my, thankfully, reasonably clean bathroom to brush her teeth and get her into her flannel pajamas, which featured, yes, Wonder Woman. Shawna also set up a baby monitor on the coffee table. Chloe was sitting on her blanket flipping through a

Dr. Seuss classic, *The Sneetches*, when Shawna noticed the time on the oven clock.

"Okay, honey, I have to go to work now. I'll be just downstairs. You're going to go to sleep here, and then when you wake up, we'll be at home, and you'll be in your own bed."

"Is Lewis coming up to say night-night?" Chloe asked.

"He's going to try, but he's stuck downstairs trying to fix something."

"I'm good at fixing things," Chloe said, still looking at her book.

"Yes, you are, honey," Shawna said. "I'll try to get Lewis to come up, okay?"

"That would be good. Lewis is much bigger than Evet, isn't he."

"Yes, I guess he is, honey. And it's Ever-ett," Shawna said. "Will you be good for Everett? He's really nice, too."

"Can he read stories?"

"Can I read stories?" I jumped in. "I don't just read stories, I write stories!"

"Can you make one up with me in it?"

"I already have," I said holding my hands up as if it were a foregone conclusion. "I'm going to tell you the story when your mom is at work. Okay?"

"That's good. That's nice," Chloe replied. "I'll be waiting right here on this couch when you're ready."

Shawna leaned down to give her a hug and kissed her on the cheek.

"See you later, Chloe. You be good, now. I still want to be friends with Everett, tomorrow."

Chloe looked completely happy sitting on her blanket, Saffo in her lap, turning the pages of her book. I walked Shawna to the kitchen door.

"I'm on in seven minutes and I'm not nearly ready," she said as she reached for the door. "Luckily, I'm doing Princess Leia tonight, from the Jabba the Hutt scene. So it doesn't take long to get ready."

"Right," I said, as the image involuntarily sprung to mind.

Just before stepping out the door onto the landing, she stopped, turned to me, and grabbed both my hands. Though we were both standing, facing one another, she leaned down, brought her face quite close to mine, and made what I would describe as rather intense eye contact.

"Everett, I really, really appreciate this. I'm sorry to drop this on you but my other options dried up. I'll put my end of the baby monitor in the dressing room. If things get hairy, just talk into the monitor. Someone will be listening and we'll come running."

"Sounds like a plan. No worries. I've got this," I said with much more confidence than an only child with absolutely no toddler experience could possibly possess.

Then she leaned a little lower and kissed my cheek, as if it were the most natural and expected gesture.

"See you in a bit," she said as she dashed down the fire escape.

I wobbled for a moment in my kitchen, processing. She'd kissed me. On the cheek, but it was definitely a kiss. I looked over at Chloe and saw that she was staring at me.

"My mom likes kissing."

"I can see that."

"She kisses me all the time. A real lot."

"Well, I can understand that. She loves you a real lot."

"Okay, so I'm ready for my story," Chloe said as she patted the spot next to her on the couch.

"Um, right! Your story. Coming right up."

I joined her on the couch. I didn't want to sit too close to her in case she was nervous. I turned sideways from my end of the couch so I could face her.

"Okay, Chloe, before I tell you the story, I want to make sure the Chloe in my story is really you. Okay?"

"Okay."

"So tell me a little bit about you."

"I'm Chloe. Chloe Hawkins. I live in an apartment with Mommy and Saffo."

She held up the stuffed rabbit for me to see before continuing.

"I like pancakes most of all. And this book." She held up the dog-eared copy of *The Sneetches*.

"What else? Do you sing? Can you dance? What do you like to play?"

"You ask a lot of questions."

"I just want to make sure that you are the Chloe in my story. I think you are, but I want to be sure."

My story-spinning wheels were, well, spinning.

"Of course I can sing. I sing all the time. My mom sings with me, but I don't think she's a very good singer. But she can dance."

"Really? Does she dance at home?"

"Yes. She does shows for me. Just for me."

"I bet she's pretty good."

"Yeah, pretty good. I can dance, too."

"Okay, what's it like at nursery school?"

"It's good. Kevin and Susannah are my friends."

"And do you like rabbits?"

"Of course I like rabbits," she said, holding up Saffo for me to see, again. "I love rabbits."

"Then you must be the Chloe in my story, because she has a giant pet rabbit in the story. And the rabbit can fly."

And I was off, skating my way through a rather convoluted but, I hope, entertaining, story. Part way in I had a brainwave and conflated my swashbuckling tale of Chloe flying around the forest on her giant pet rabbit with the feminist classic, *The Paper Bag Princess*. I droned on for a good fifteen minutes. Chloe was transfixed, spellbound, on the edge of her seat. I looked at her after a particularly exciting segment about the heroine's narrow escape from an evil squadron of flying aardvarks, and she had fallen into a deep coma. Edge of her seat? Not so much. Edge of her sleep? Closer. Well, I liked the story and kept talking until the climactic scene where Princess Chloe tells the Prince to take a long walk on a short pier.

I gathered the blanket around her and just looked at her for a while. I'm not sure I'd ever seen anything quite so innocent, beautiful, and serene as Chloe Hawkins, fast asleep.

Eventually, I tore myself away from the couch and spent some more time on the professional sports blog post. Below me, the nut and bolt in the floor were doing their thing. It was odd to think that Shawna was likely responsible for the big steel nut's warmth and vibrations massaging the soles of my feet.

A knock at the kitchen door startled me. You could tell by the way I kind of shrieked and bounced off my chair, nearly knocking over the table. A quick glance at the couch told me that Chloe was still down deep. I opened the door and Lewis Small filled my entire field of view.

"Sorry, Ever-man. Did I scare you?"

"Not at all. Why?"

"Oh. Well, it sounded like you screamed and kicked over some furniture."

"Oh, that. Right. Well, I can usually hear when someone is climbing the metal fire escape. But you just seemed to materialize outside my door. It might have caught me a little off-guard," I said.

"Ever-man, remember I'm a security guy. I move like a puma – all stealthy-like. I have to," he said, his broad smile compromising the menace I normally associate with stealthy pumas.

"Good to know."

"Now where's the wonder-Chloe?"

I nodded toward the living room. Lewis stealthily crept over on his haunches and settled on the floor next to the couch where she lay curled up.

"Have you ever seen anything like her?" Lewis whispered without taking his eyes off Chloe.

"No, I don't think I have."

"Just lying there, asleep, she has the power to make me forget who I am, where I am, and what I do," Lewis said almost in a whisper. "She is damn-near perfect, isn't she?"

"She surely is. She comes from good stock."

"You got that right. Shawna is good people, all the way. She's got some big brain, too."

We chatted for a while as we both watched Chloe sleep, her shoulders rising slightly with each breath.

"Well, Ever-man, I just told Brawn I was going to the can, so I'd better get my ass back onto the floor."

"I dug out a few more make-up mags if you want to take them for the women downstairs. I don't need them anymore," I said, lifting the magazines from the shelf under the coffee table.

"Serious?" Lewis said. "That's awesome, man. Thanks so much. I appreciate it, um, on behalf of the dancers, I mean."

He took the stack I offered and quickly rifled through it.

"These look great. Thanks again, Ever-man. You're good people, too, you know that?"

"Thanks, Lewis. I'm happy that someone of, um, your stature, likes me. I'd be worried, perhaps even terrified, if you didn't."

He clapped me on the shoulder and was out the door and down the stairs in a flash, and in silence. He really could move like a puma. I briefly contemplated fetching some ice for the shoulder Lewis had just clapped, but decided I'd survive. I took another long look at the sleeping Chloe and returned to the kitchen table to write.

———

I must have fallen asleep. I realized that when something woke me up. I could see on my laptop screen that my forehead had typed several lines of gibberish as I nodded off. I'd rubbernecked all the way down to the keyboard. Then I heard the noise again. It was a man and woman arguing in the alley below. I looked out the window and saw a shiny Lexus with the driver's door open. The man, about my age, maybe a bit taller, and wearing a grey suit, was standing a few yards away with his right arm outstretched. In his hand, he held the hand of Shawna Hawkins, who clearly did not want her hand held. She was trying to pull it out of his grip, without success.

I opened my door and stepped out on the veranda but hesitated. What was I going to do?

"Get your tight little ass in the car," he snapped at her. "You knew how this was going to end when you gave me that look in there. Don't back out now."

"If you value your ability to procreate, you'll let the fuck go of my hand, right now!" she said in a low and slow voice.

"Hey!" I shouted. Apparently, I wasn't hesitating anymore. I tore down the stairs and within about three seconds was standing between them, though their hands were still linked.

"It's okay, Everett, I can handle this jerk."

"I got this, Shawna," I said in my Power Ranger voice, before turning to the jerk. "Let go of her hand, right now. Get in your car, and leave."

"Shut the fuck up and mind your own fuckin' business. This is between me and her. So blow."

"Seriously, Everett, I can clean this up, on my own. But thanks," Shawna said.

"Listen to the Amazon, little man. This doesn't fuckin' concern you."

I kind of lost it then, as happens often in those rare fight-or-flight moments, at least according to psychologists. I turned toward the jerk, holding my hands up in a rather unusual claw-like configuration I made up on the spot. I imagine it looked like a cross between the talons of a large bird of prey and chronic arthritis.

"Look, asshole," I growled. "I've been waiting a long time for this. Ten years of Tsing Tao training and two years as an instructor, and not once have I been able to use it in a real-life situation on someone who really deserves it. Not once. Until right now. Your number just came up. Please don't disappoint me. Let's do this."

His expression changed only slightly, but enough to let me know he was rethinking his options.

"So let's go," I pushed, bouncing up and down on the balls of my feet, waving my talons around in intricate patterns. "There are a hundred different moves in my Tsing Tao repertoire and they all lead to pain. Some of them yield blood, and two of them have been known to cause paralysis. So what do you want first? It's up to you. Extremities, head, face, or midsection? Your choice."

I moved a little closer to him, jerking my head forward toward him, and feigning right, then left, still with my claw hands slicing through the air in ways even I couldn't predict.

He blinked. Or rather, he let go of Shawna's hand. Then he smirked – the last refuge of the humiliated bully. (I just made that up, but I like how it sounds.)

"Yeah, well, fuck you and your pansy martial arts, too," he sneered as he slipped back into his car and slammed the door.

I stepped forward, now that it was safe, and smacked my hand hard onto the car roof. It made a very loud noise and hurt my hand so much, my eyes watered.

He gave me the finger and squealed out of the alley.

I took Shawna's elbow and led her up the fire escape to my still-open kitchen door.

"Are you all right? Did he hurt you?"

"Everett, I'm fine. I had the situation completely under control. I didn't need a Bruce Lee intervention."

I confess, this caught me a little by surprise. Where was the gratitude, the fawning over my bravery, the marvelling at my take-charge resolution of a potentially dangerous situation?

"Shawna, I looked out my kitchen window, and see this guy, this asshole, trying to kidnap you. I kind of just acted on instinct."

We stood facing each other. Well, I came up to her neck. She was still in full make-up. The pure beauty of her face very nearly took my breath away, which was quite an achievement as I was already hyperventilating from the alley altercation. Then, without warning, I started to tremble uncontrollably. Out of nowhere, my body was behaving as if I were standing on the shore of the Arctic Ocean in January, in nothing but a Speedo.

"Everett, what's wrong? You're shaking like a leaf."

"Um, I'm aware of that."

She took hold of me and tried to stop my shaking by squeezing me in a bear hug.

"You're scared?" she asked. "It's all over now. The time to be frightened was about three minutes ago. You're a little late."

"I think it's some kind of delayed reaction to the, er, the trauma," I said, my teeth chattering. "I wouldn't exactly call it fear. Perhaps it's early onset Parkinson's. Or maybe it's just nervous energy, since I didn't have to fight the guy."

She wasn't buying it. My trembling calmed down a bit. She rubbed my back.

"But you have ten years of training in Tsing Tao. You're a Tsing Tao instructor. That jackass was terrified of you. You could see the fear in his eyes. It looked kind of like what's in your eyes now."

The trembling picked up again. Still hugging me, she led me over to the couch where Chloe remained asleep at the far end and lowered us both down onto it. We sat there, huddled, for a few minutes until my tremors subsided.

"Tsing Tao is a chicken dish I order from that Chinese restaurant down the street," I confessed in a voice so sheepish it had fleece.

"I know, Everett," she said, and chuckled. "I order it too. It's so good, but not good for you."

"You knew I was bluffing the whole time?" I asked.

"I liked the gnarled wavy hand action you added. That made it seem all the more authentic," she said, pausing before continuing. "Everett, it was sweet of you to come to my rescue. But I really did have it under control, though it might not have looked like it at the time."

"I really thought he was going to do something to you."

"And you thought you'd charge in on your white steed and save me."

"No. Not really. Maybe."

"And if matters had escalated, well, I'm bigger than you, sweet Everett, and bigger than the jerk in the Lexus. I probably could have taken the both of you and I don't even have your deep knowledge of the ancient and sacred martial art of Tsing Tao."

"Okay, so maybe I didn't think it through. Maybe I was running on adrenaline and instinct."

"And millions of years of gender stereotyping," she chimed in.

"Ouch. That hurt."

She hugged me a little tighter.

"I mean it. It was sweet and brave of you to step in between us like that. I know you were doing what you thought was right. You were trying to protect me. I'm grateful for that. You put yourself out there for me. You were kind and courageous, and I love you for it," she said in quiet, intoxicating voice.

I thought I detected a subtle change in her tone. She leaned forward, face-on to me, and looked in my eyes, her hands holding my upper arms. Then it seemed to me that she started to move in. Based on millions of years of highly developed, acutely sensitive, male instinct, I moved in, too. I closed my eyes, and configured my lips in what I thought would be the most enticing position. I then felt my lips press up against her, um, against something that didn't feel much like her lips. I opened my eyes and saw that I was in the act of kissing the palm of her right hand. I liked her hands, but I wasn't expecting that. With lightning speed, she had thrust her hand up between our faces. As a talented dancer, she clearly has extraordinary powers of physical coordination and kinesthetic awareness. There was not much room or time to complete that particular manoeuvre without her fingers winding up in my nostrils. But she somehow pulled it off.

"Sorry, I'm pretty sure that was my fault," Shawna said. "I thought you knew."

"Thought I knew what, that you might be into palm-kissing?"

She laughed. She had a really nice laugh.

"No, that I bat for the other team, all the way, one hundred per cent of the time, no exceptions," she explained. "Always have."

I must have looked as puzzled as I felt.

"I'm gay. I'm a lesbian. I'm sure you've heard of us. You know, the Island of Lesbos, Ellen DeGeneres, Melissa Etheridge, Martina Navratilova, to name just a few of the tribe."

Apparently, I still looked befuddled.

"Come on, Everett, you got to lose the crewcut, chunky, no-make-up, women's-prison stereotype you're carrying around with you. We come in all shapes and sizes."

"I know that," I whined, feeling like an idiot. "I just misread the situation. It happens. I swear I had no idea you hailed from the Island of Lesbos. Besides, Chloe reported that you liked kissing."

"That's because I kiss her all the time. I can't help it."

My eyes darted over to Chloe again and then back to Shawna. I must have still been displaying my puzzled look.

"I assume you've heard of turkey basters," she said.

"You impregnated yourself with a turkey baster?" I said, wrinkling my brow.

"Of course not. It's a metaphor. I had artificial insemination, in a real clinic. No turkeys were harmed in the making of this sweet child," she said, stroking Chloe's back next to us.

"And the father? Did you know him?"

"I only know him as #7802478. He was an anonymous donor, and that's just fine with me."

We just stared at Chloe, who it seemed could sleep through a Metallica concert.

"She really is amazing," I said.

"Yes, she is. But so are you," Shawna said. "I loved the story you told her. It was perfect."

I dusted off my perplexed look for about the fourth time in the preceding ten minutes. She merely pointed to the baby monitor still on the coffee table, its red light glowing.

"Shit, I forgot about that," I replied. "Just give me a moment to review everything I said in the last five hours."

She laughed.

"You said all the right things."

She gathered up all the paraphernalia that comes with being the mother of a beautiful four-year-old girl and stowed it in the canvas bag. I picked up Chloe's rabbit from the floor where it had fallen and looked at it.

"Oh, okay. That makes more sense," I said, nodding to Shawna and holding out the stuffed animal. "I will immediately stop spelling the bunny's name with a double 'f'."

She nodded in return, smiling.

"I might have saved myself that whole hand-kissing humiliation thing if I'd only figured that out earlier," I sighed.

I walked them to her car. Shawna carried the big blue bag and I carried Chloe. Still sound asleep, she was pure warm weight against my chest and shoulders. Her head fit perfectly against my neck. I could feel her breath on my skin. I slid her into her car seat, and Shawna buckled the straps. Still, Chloe slept.

"Thank you for everything you did for me tonight. And I mean everything," she said, kissing my cheek. "If only you had breasts, this could have been a magical night."

"Well, at this precise moment, believe me, I wish I had breasts, too."

She laughed, slid into her car, and pulled away.

CHAPTER 11

When I arrived, Dad was pushing Kenny Chevy all around the paths. Even from a distance, it was easy to tell they were both in full rhetorical flight. I spied Beverley sitting in one of her usual spots.

"Greetings, young Everett, or should I say, Eve?" said Beverley when she saw me approaching.

"You definitely should not say Eve," I whispered, as I sat down beside her.

She put her pad and pen back in her bag.

"So what's the latest? Your last post was very strong. A multitude of comments, too," she said.

"Thanks, Beverley," I started. "I'm just trying to keep all the balls in the air. It's kind of stressful. I thought the furor might have died down by now, but it keeps on coming. I turned down interviews on *Good Morning America, The Today Show, The Daily Show*, the Canadian Broadcasting Corporation, and dozens of others."

"Oh, what a waste of precious media time. Are you sure you don't want to step forward? You might be able to get even more eyes on your essays."

"Oh, I'm sure, all right. If I came clean now, it would shift the entire focus of the debate onto the youngish man who writes a feminist blog. The message would be lost and the medium would take centre stage. No thank you. Not now. Not ever."

"Didn't someone once claim that the medium was the message?" she asked.

"Marshall McLuhan. But that doesn't apply here. The message is everything in this case. I know it."

"Well then, how long before the mystery of who writes the essays starts to overshadow the all-powerful message in the essays?" she asked.

Good question. I thought about it for a moment.

"I don't think we'll ever get to that point," I said. "I have to believe the message will always prevail."

She looked at me for a moment and then patted my knee.

"Well, who said earnest altruism was dead?" she asked.

"I don't think anyone's ever said that."

We sat in silence for a few moments.

"Oh, during breakfast, I had a thought for another essay topic you might consider," she offered.

"I'm all ears. I've got several more ideas for posts, but I'll be running out soon, and I need more. What have you got?"

"How about taking a look at what constitutes 'consent' between couples before they have sex? I've read so many troubling stories lately about university students and what they call 'campus hook-ups.' So many young women are claiming to have had sex when they weren't sure they wanted to. It's like the line between consensual sex and sexual assault has blurred, not that it's ever been that distinct."

"Serious stuff. I remember when I was at university, the phrase 'No Means No' was big. We had a whole campaign, with buttons and posters and pamphlets. I think it helped, but it clearly didn't solve the problem. I don't think the incidence of sexual assault on campuses, reported or not, has declined."

"It doesn't seem to have. The issue keeps coming up."

"Let me kick it around a bit, and do some research. But I like the idea. It's an important issue. Thanks."

"Have you thought yet about writing a book? I could probably arrange a meeting with my publisher. I think they'd still remember me."

"Beverley, I'm sure they still remember you," I said. "You were with Random House, right?"

"I was."

"Well, it's a very kind offer, Beverley, but, well. . ." I paused. She turned toward me with a puzzled look on her face.

"Everett?"

"Well – and I've been meaning to tell you – but believe it or not, I signed a book deal with Random House two days ago."

"You're kidding! That is fantastic! When were you going to tell me? I can't believe how fast this is all moving," she exclaimed. "So Random House came to you? Directly?"

"Yep. Through the blog's email."

Beverley was now leaning forward, her eyes, face, and entire body, alive, energized, almost quivering. She was rubbing her hands together as if trying to start a fire between them.

"Do they know who you are and what you are?"

"Of course not. I refused to meet with them or speak to them over the phone, claiming that anonymity in all dealings was imperative or there could and would be no deal."

"And they agreed?"

"They did," I replied. "We conducted the entire negotiation and inked the deal via email. They said they'd done several books over the years with anonymous authors. They usually know the identity of the anonymous author, even if the public doesn't. But publishing a book where even the publisher doesn't know the author's identity is not unprecedented."

"And that was it? They just sent you a contract?"

"Well, no. They undertook some serious due diligence to satisfy themselves that I am, in fact, the writer of the blog. Their IT staff showed me how to provide them with time-coded drafts of each blog post from my hard drive to prove I had written them *before* they were posted on the blog. As well, they showed me how to connect online so that I could share my laptop screen with the head of Random House on her computer. Then they watched as I gained access to the back end of my blog. I'm the only person in the world who could do that. In the end, they were satisfied I was legit. It was kind of a cool process."

"Amazing. Wonderful, I'm so proud of you," she said. "So what's the book to be?"

"Well, in essence, it'll be a collection of the mini-essays on the blog, with some other stuff added. I obviously need more content before there's enough for a whole book. So your continuing support on topics to tackle is welcome, even mandatory."

"I'll keep them coming," she said, before pausing. "This is all so utterly extraordinary."

We sat in silence for a few minutes.

"So how goes the Billy Kane enlightenment initiative?" I asked.

We both looked up to see my father and Kenny at the far end of the grounds. I noticed again that Dad was walking very well. He continued to limp a bit, but it was almost fully assimilated into his gait. And his left and right hands looked the same as they both gripped the handles of the wheelchair.

"I can see some progress. It's slow, but he's coming around. I really think he is. It'll be a while before a lifetime of patriarchal brainwashing can be reversed. But the patient seems more willing, more compliant, now than he's ever been," she said.

"How do you mean?" I asked.

"It's all in the pacing and intensity of our discussions. I've learned that if I try to go at him too hard, with too much, he shuts down and regresses into his 1960s adolescent boy's boy. It's not pretty. So I have to watch for the telltale signs that I'm overstimulating his brain and trying too hard to rewire his belief system."

"There are telltale signs?"

"Oh, yes. The back of his neck turns a shade of crimson, tiny wisps of smoke issue from his ears, his eyes bug out, and if we're walking at the time, he starts to pull to the right."

I just stared at her.

"All right. Let's just say I can just sense from his monosyllabic responses that I've gone too far, too fast. So I slow down and come back to where I left him. We reconnect and move forward together, a little slower."

"I assume you've already played the 'daughter card,'" I said.

"I ended up throwing that down in our first session. He's a tough nut to crack. I was hoping to hold it in reserve, but I clearly needed it early. It's usually a dependable play."

"My hat's off to you. Let me know what I can do to help."

"You're helping already. Your father has read every single one of your blog posts."

I snapped around to face her.

"Relax, young Everett. He has no idea who wrote them."

We sat a while longer in silence. The sun felt so good. After a time, she pulled out her pad again and resumed her letter.

"So about your son," I started. "Why doesn't he ever visit you? Does he live that far away?"

She sighed and looked a little annoyed.

"He lives very, very far away. I haven't spoken to him for a very, very long time. And that's my very, very last word on the subject."

"But. . ."

"Very, very last word. End of story."

———

She was late, but at least she'd left Nathan in the car. I was seated in the corner of a Starbucks about halfway between her office and the rehab hospital. She was wearing some kind of a pantsuit thing that would not have looked out of place on the set of a science fiction movie. It was grey and red and very sleek.

"Mom," I said, standing to give her a hug, "you're looking very Gene Rodenberry today."

"I'm afraid I don't have time to keep up with fashion designers. I'm surprised you do."

"Right. So how are you?" I asked.

"I'm fine, honey. But so fu—, so friggin' busy I don't know which end is up."

"That's the life of a powerful CEO. That's the role," I said. "I'm very proud of you, Mom. You are a corporate, hardcore business rock star. And I really think you were made for it."

"I just wish I hadn't waited so long to get started. I lost half a career vacuuming and ironing."

"Well, you weren't just doing housework. I was there, too, if you'll recall."

"Yes, and that was what made it all tolerable, honey. Thank you."

"So what did you want to chat about?"

"Can't a mother just spend time with her only son without having an agenda?"

"Of course, any time you like. That would be nice. But you said you wanted to discuss something, remember?"

"Oh, right, yes, I guess I did. But I do just like spending time with you," she backfilled, holding both my hands across the table.

"Mom, it's fine. I've got a full plate these days with Dad, and, well, a few other things, too."

"Of course, dear. So anyway, what is with your father? What's gotten into him?"

"What do you mean? If he's not defending Ford's honour in the face of a diehard Chevy evangelist, he's either trying to pick up his physiotherapist, who's twenty-five years younger, or the regrettably forgotten feminist pioneer who's a decade older. So I don't know what you mean."

"He's been calling me and leaving me these weird voice-mail messages."

"Really? Like what?"

"Well, stuff about being so proud of what I've accomplished in a man's world and that he's sorry he wasn't more. . ."

She stopped and opened her purse and pulled out her cellphone.

"You can hear it for yourself. I saved the last one."

She cued it up and handed the phone to me.

"Hiya Evie, honey. How's the big business typhoon doing? Listen, I was hoping to talk with you a bit, maybe even get together. I can get a day-pass from this joint, and maybe we could have lunch. Anyway, I just want you to know that I think what you've done since, you know, the split, is just incredible. I'm so proud. And I'm sorry I was such a dick about it all, way back when. I didn't know what I was doing. I was scared everything would change. It changed anyway, I guess, didn't it? Anyway, I'm an idiot. So how about calling me?"

"Wow. That really is Dad's voice."

"Of course it is. Each time I listen to it, it's still Billy Kane. Who else would call me a 'business typhoon?'" she said. "Although that was kind of sweet. But that's not all. He's started mailing me clippings from the paper whenever I'm mentioned in a business story or my picture appears. He even printed a *Forbes* online bio piece from two years ago and sent it to me. That means he's been pumping my name into Google and checking me out."

"He's just proud of you, Mom. We all are. And I think he's just starting to realize, way too late, mind you, that he was – as he just admitted – an idiot. Maybe our little boy is growing up."

"Easy, Ev. He's still your father," Mom scolded.

"Mom, please. We both know he's a man from a different era, maybe a different geological period," I said. "Perhaps living with a diverse group of stroke patients and hanging out with them everyday as they all get better has exposed him to some ideas and ways of thinking that aren't rooted in the 1950s. This is a good thing, isn't it?"

"Well, I guess so. If he'd been like that when I wanted to do my MBA, we'd probably still be together. But it's just so odd. I don't know how I feel about it."

We didn't talk for much longer. Mom's phone buzzed.

"Shit. That's Nathan in the car. I gotta go, Ev."

"No problem, Mom. Go forth and build resorts," I said, standing up to give her a parting hug. "And keep me posted about Dad's, you know, evolving behaviour."

I wore my best jeans, a white button-down-collared shirt, and a casual blue blazer-type jacket. I pulled on my brown Blundstone boots to give me an extra inch. I fussed and mussed with my hair for an embarrassingly long time until it fell just the way I wanted it to. This was a little unusual. Normally, I was fine with my hair falling however it wanted to, as long as it wasn't falling out. Strange. Then I checked my coif in every reflective surface in my apartment as I paced the place. My hair looked best in the toaster, where the curved stainless steel edges somehow made my locks look fuller, more luxuriant. At least I thought so. Plus, if I positioned my face square-on to the toaster at close range, and at just the right time, the toast appeared to pop directly out the top of my head. Finally, thankfully, it was time to go. I grabbed my car keys, checked my hair one last time in the lustrous bowl of a serving spoon I'd left in the dish drainer, and headed down the fire escape.

We'd agreed to meet on the loading dock so as to avoid any of the early-bird demonstrators who might soon be gathering out front. I'd parked my dad's car in the alley before jumping into the shower. As I turned on the landing of the steel staircase, I saw that they were both there, Megan and Shawna, leaning on the railing and talking. Last time I'd seen them together, they'd been in my head. Now, they were actually together, laughing. I wondered about what. Despite Lewis's skill, I found it hard to descend a metal fire escape with anything approaching stealth. They both looked up as I tried to look casual and cool coming down.

"Here comes trouble," Shawna said, leaning toward Megan. But she was smiling. They both were.

There was more than an hour till show time, so Shawna was still in her sweats and her face was as free of make-up as mine. To be clear, that means utterly bereft of any cosmetic assist. Her face looked lovely *au naturel*. Megan was dressed a little more casually than the last time I'd seen her, but could still pass for a lawyer. She had donned some make-up – when you write about cosmetics, you tend to notice them – and clearly knew how. I'm not that skilled in the art of women's fashion, but I think you would call what she was wearing a blue dress, though I'm probably not doing it or her justice. She looked great.

"You haven't been filling her head with stories that might be prejudicial to my reputation, have you?" I asked, more concerned than I dared let on.

"Not at all," Shawna replied. "Would I do that? In fact, I've been pumping you up. Right?" She looked at Megan, who nodded vigorously.

"Oh yes. I've never met a babysitting Tsing Tao master," Megan said. "It's a great honour."

"Fantastic," I moaned. "It's going to be like that, is it?"

They both laughed. Then Shawna stepped forward, pressed her hands against my arms, not unlike the move she'd made in my apartment, and planted one on my cheek.

"My hero," she said, before turning to head back into the club. "Have fun, you two."

Megan and I watched her disappear through the loading-bay door.

"I didn't expect to connect so easily with people who take their clothes off professionally. But she is very cool," Megan said as we walked down the steps to the alley and my dad's Ford Focus.

"I know what you mean," I replied. "But I guess they're not much different from us in many ways. You know, they take their pants off one leg at a time, too."

"Yeah, but when we do it, there's no pole and no people," she noted.

"Yes, and that's a good thing, in my case," I admitted.

"For you or for the people?"

"Both. And the pole for that matter."

"Right," Megan said. "You know, Shawna said some really nice things about you."

I opened her door for her and she slid in. I dashed around to the driver's side as fast as I could to try to stay on this agreeable topic. Then I calmly lowered myself into the seat.

"That was kind of her. Unless she's just messing with us both, you know, by setting unrealistically high standards that no mortal man could ever achieve."

"Oh, I think she was giving me the straight goods."

"Speaking of *straight* goods, did she happen to mention that she and I are just, you know. . ."

"Good friends?" Megan filled in the blank.

"Right. Good friends. That's it exactly."

"No, she didn't really mention that."

"Oh, well, it's true," I said. "And I got to say, her daughter, Chloe, is a little miracle. When I babysat her for a few hours the other night, I couldn't tear my eyes away from her perfectly innocent face as she slept."

———

Our drive to the Capital Grille over on International was nice. We chatted about lots of things. Megan was far more relaxed than at our first meeting. Then again, the absence of smoke, flying dropkicks, fists and rotten vegetables, and the police might have been a factor. But she seemed comfortable. We seemed comfortable. It all seemed comfortable.

My mother had recommended the Capital Grille as a reasonably priced but classy and quiet restaurant. She was right. We were seated in a private corner in high wingback chairs. The chef was clearly gunning for membership in the Cholesterol Hall of Fame in his first year of eligibility. That was okay with me. I ordered a crock of French onion soup, followed by seared tenderloin with butter-poached lobster tails – you know, lobster tails poached in butter – followed by chocolate hazelnut cake accompanied by a trio of handcrafted ice creams. Megan skipped the appetizer and went directly for the pan-seared scallops and wild mushroom risotto leading directly to a flourless chocolate espresso cake. I didn't plan to eat again until the weekend.

"So how goes the book, whatever it's about?" Megan asked when the waiter had taken our order.

"Oh, you know, it's coming along. Still a long way to go, but I've got it pretty well outlined and about a third written. I just have to put my ass in the chair and get the rest of the writing done."

"You're really still not able to tell me what it's about? It'll be public soon enough anyway, won't it?"

"As an attorney, I'm sure you're not counselling me to abrogate my contractual obligations to secrecy and confidentiality, are you?"

I made sure to say this with a smile.

"It's going to be like that, is it?"

"I'm afraid so. My own mother doesn't even know about this.

In fact, you're one of just a handful of people who know. But I appreciated your legal eagle eyes on the contract."

"It's nothing weird like erotica or porn, is it?"

"Of course not! It is so not like that at all," I stammered. "If you only knew how off the mark that suggestion is."

"You are a mysterious one, Mr. Kane," she replied. "What else do you do around here?"

"I moved here for a while so I could help my dad recover from a stroke he had a couple of months ago. He's at the Orlando Health Rehab Institute learning how to reuse the left side of his body."

"Oh, I'm sorry to hear that," she said. "So, ever the good son, you drop everything and come to take care of your father. Impressive. Commendable. Shawna might be right."

"What do you mean?"

"Well, she initially thought you might be masquerading as a truly enlightened man just as a ploy to meet women. And looking as she does, Shawna has had lots of opportunity to practise judging men, and women for that matter. But she declared you legit pretty soon after meeting you."

"I'm honoured to have passed Shawna's scrutiny. I think she's an impeccable judge of character," I said.

A few minutes later, the waiter delivered my onion soup with a flourish. I was then forced to carry on an adult conversation while trying to wrangle the cheese strands that always seem to making eating onion soup a trial. But it tasted so good.

"So what's it like working alongside Mason Bennington?" I asked before shoving home a spoonful of soup.

"Every day is a new adventure. He's about as mercurial as they come. But like every other American, he deserves, and is entitled to, legal representation."

"If you were a sole practitioner, would you have him as a client?" I asked.

She narrowed her eyes a tad.

I had promised myself before the date that I wouldn't lead her down the same path that had ended my previous three relationships. I'm either not very good at keeping promises or I have a problem recognizing which path I'm on until it's too late to turn around.

"I'm a first-year lawyer, fresh out of law school, fresh off the bar exam. I'm with a good firm, a respected firm. But I have no power in the firm yet. I'm not in a position to decide which clients I work on. So I'm doing what I have to do to get by until I *can* decide."

"Sorry, sorry, my question came out sounding far more judgmental than I intended," I said. "I'm sorry. I was just trying to discover how you really feel about Bennington and his little enterprise. I know your firm has tied your hands professionally. I was more interested in how you felt personally."

"I'm a bit conflicted. Personally, as you might imagine, I'm not thrilled to be serving the legal and business needs of the owner of a chain of strip clubs, however progressive they might be.

They're still strip clubs. But professionally, I've been exposed to so many different areas of the law, and gained so much more experience than I ever would have had chasing down precedents in the law library for the tax partner. Bennington's legal needs are so deep and wide, I'm basically getting five years of experience in a matter of months."

"Is he good to work with?"

"Without violating attorney-client privilege, he's a nightmare. The people who work for him, Lewis, Shawna, the other dancers, they're great. But Mason is, shall we say, challenging. And if he's in a bad mood, get out of the way. And he's been in a bad mood quite a bit lately."

"What's eating him? He seems to be the toast of business pages."

"Yeah, well, the business pages haven't yet picked up on the fact that for Mason Bennington to succeed, members have to join XY, and then come often to eat, drink, and ogle. The members aren't exactly breaking down the doors here in Orlando."

"I guess the demonstrations and the protestors' GoPro cameras have put a damper on walk-in traffic."

"Yes, but Mason thinks it runs deeper than that. He thinks it all started when Candace Sharpe made that unknown feminist blogger famous overnight. Her post about *him* is a very painful thorn in Mason's side. And it makes him crazy that she can hide behind this veil of anonymity and yet command such popularity."

In the ensuing few minutes, I like to think I proved that it's possible to descend into a full-on panic attack, complete with the threatened loss of most bodily functions, while maintaining at least a viable impression of a cool and calm exterior. It's a gift. I could feel my legs trembling beneath the table. I lifted my feet off the centre pedestal support of the table so I wouldn't set off resonant frequency vibrations and topple our dinners into our laps.

"Why is he so fixated on a no-name – a literally no-name – brand-new, flash-in-the-pan feminist blogger? It seems like an overreaction, doesn't it?"

I worked hard to keep my breathing and the timbre of my voice under control. It wasn't easy. It didn't sound like my normal voice, but Megan didn't seem to notice.

"I have no idea. It's like that post wounded him, publicly humiliated him, and he's out for revenge."

"Let's not talk about Mason Bennington," I suggested, through my ably disguised hyperventilation. "What's the future for you? What do you want to be doing in five years?"

"Who knows? I guess I'd like to be established in my legal career and in a position to work on cases that would mean a lot more to me than defending the likes of Mason Bennington."

"Like what cases?"

"I worked as a researcher at a big legal aid clinic right in the heart of Anacostia, a pretty rough part of Washington, while I was at law school. I really liked the people who work there. They work hard. They care about their clients. And when they win, it usually means that something good happens to someone who hasn't had many breaks in their lives. I miss that feeling. I don't get that feeling when we score a legal victory on behalf of the XY Club."

"What do your parents think about it all?"

"Both my parents are lawyers in DC. My mother works at the State Department and my father is chief legal officer for a big NGO that builds hospitals in sub-Saharan Africa."

"Following in the family footsteps. They must be pleased and proud you went into the law."

"They know and like the firm I joined. But I doubt they're enamoured of my principal client – not that I had any say in it."

By then, our entrées had arrived and we went on to other things. Our conversation lightened considerably as we covered a whole range of topics that might have seemed superficial – movies, television, books – but really help shape an impression of another person. I liked this other person. She had her head screwed on right. I found her to be thoughtful, deliberate, confident, gentle, and kind. At one point, she looked up and noticed that the couple at a table farther along the wall from us was trying to take a selfie, with limited success.

"Be right back," Megan said, as she pushed her chair back and walked over to the neighbouring table.

"Why don't I take the shot?" she offered, holding out her hand.

"Would you?" the man said. "I can't get us both into the photo."

"Happy to. Ready?" She pulled back so she could squeeze them both into the frame. "Done."

"Thanks so much."

"No worries."

Megan slid back into her seat and resumed our conversation without missing a beat, as if she'd never left to deliver a good deed. By dessert, I was pretty well sucked into her orbit. I could feel myself being drawn in and could do nothing about it. I was powerless. It was like opposing gravity. Gravity always won. I'm not saying I fell in love at the Capital Grille. I'm just saying I was having difficulty looking anywhere else, or listening to anyone else, or thinking about anyone else, when we were together. I don't know if she was feeling the same way. But it felt like she might be. I just wasn't sure.

I could feel the pressure building. It didn't seem right not to tell her. It felt like the kind of revelation that, if not made early, might not end well when discovered later. But it was scary to ponder the potential range of her reactions. It could all be fine and might even endear me to her more. Conversely, I might soon be wearing her flourless chocolate espresso cake.

"Um, I think there's something I should be probably tell you about me. Better to do it early," I said, putting my fork down on my plate and looking directly at her.

"That doesn't sound all that good to me," she replied, setting down her own fork and returning my gaze. "Let me guess. You're married?"

"Ha! No, I'm not married."

"Gay?"

"Nope. Not that there's anything wrong with that."

"Of course not," she agreed. "Okay, you keep pet snakes?"

"Nothing like that. I hate snakes," I said.

"You're a convicted criminal on the lam using various pseudonyms."

"No!"

"Okay, I'm tapped out."

"It's, um, well, I should tell you that . . . well, I don't know where to begin with this. It's kind of a funny story. Well, sort of, I guess. Er, you see there's something about me that you really ought to know that might, um, or possibly could, influence, how you feel about me, about us, I mean if there's even an 'us' or and chance of an 'us'."

"Okay, now I get it. You're indecisive? Prone to vacillation? Anxiety attacks when you have to break important news? Can't get your words out?"

"No, despite how I just sounded," I said. "Okay, here goes. You see, Megan, I mentioned earlier that I'm a writer. And, well, it just so happens, that I'm. . ."

She looked at me just then with the most innocent, wonderful, warm, and inviting countenance, her lovely face turned slightly upwards in anticipation.

". . . *Canadian*. I'm a Canadian. There I said it. I'm Canadian, born and raised in Oakville, Ontario, a bedroom community of Toronto. I'm Canadian."

Her face crumpled. She recoiled in horror, then placed her hands on top of her head, her eyes wild and wide.

"No! No! Not that! Not Canadian. Why does it always have to be this way?"

She said this in a rather loud voice. Diners four tables over looked our way.

She promptly resumed her normal appearance, lowered her hands to the table, and returned her eyes to their normal aperture.

"That's it? That's the big reveal?"

"Well, I actually have dual citizenship," I replied.

"Why you two-timing skink!"

"Skink? That doesn't sound good. What exactly is a skink?" I asked.

"I'm not sure, but it's bad," she replied shaking her head with impressive gravitas. "I think it's a lizard of some kind."

Turns out she loves Canada. Ever since she'd heard about the Canadian ambassador to Iran who helped spirit American diplomats out of Tehran, she'd had a very soft spot in her heart for all things Canadian. Growing up in DC helped engender an interest in foreign affairs. Lucky me. She'd visited Toronto and Halifax on a couple of occasions, and even made it to Vancouver, once. She'd also gained a strong preference for pure maple syrup, not the maple-flavoured confection most Americans pour over their pancakes at Denny's.

After my big Canadian confession, things seemed to progress quite quickly from there. The conversation flowed almost as effortlessly as the wine. We had a wonderful time. We talked for so long that the head waiter finally approached somewhat apologetically and mentioned that they would be closing soon – like right then. We hadn't even noticed. We'd had enough wine that when our long, leisurely dinner finally ended, we hailed a cab. Whether it was the wine, fatigue, or something else, she leaned against my shoulder in the back seat. It felt good. I said good night to her in the lobby of her hotel while the cab idled in the driveway. She kissed me on the cheek and thanked me for a lovely evening that was much better than she'd expected. My cheek had been getting a workout, lately. She was due to fly back to Washington early the next morning. We agreed to have dinner again on Friday when she had to return for late afternoon meetings with zoning officials at the City of Orlando. We decided to meet right there in the lobby at seven. Could I make it through four days of anticipation? She smiled and waved as the elevator doors closed. I arrived at my front door ten minutes later, still aglow.

Still with a lovely buzz on from the wine, I sat down at the kitchen table, turned on my laptop, and began a long-overdue scroll through my email accounts. In my personal email there wasn't much of interest beyond two more increasingly plaintive requests from my editor at *Make-up Artist* magazine for that profile piece I'd been contracted to write. Despite a stream of emails and phone calls to the hotshot who was to be the subject of the interview, he still hadn't responded. I hit Reply and suggested I write about someone else and that I'd give some thought to who the replacement might be.

Then I started wading through the hundreds of emails that had arrived in the previous few days to the EofE mailbox. Most of the messages were from supporters applauding the blog in general or commenting on particular posts. A much smaller complement was from right-wing anti-feminist whackos and Bible-thumpers on whom even Beverley's "daughter card" would surely fail. Finally, there were dozens and dozens of media inquiries, mostly intent on speaking with me. Buried in the email stream from midafternoon was a message from my blog-hosting service.

TO: Eve of Equality

FROM: Jessica Blythe, Customer Relations, OrlandoHosting

RE: Inquiry

Congratulations on how much traffic the blog you represent is pulling! The *Eve of Equality* numbers are staggering and still growing. And I really dig the content, too.

According to our account files, you've gone to great lengths to protect the identity of the blogger, so I just thought you should know that we had a very insistent inquiry today about the blog, and more to the point, the blogger. This man really really wanted to know the identity of the blogger and how he could reach her. I pointed him to the email address on the blog as the only appropriate way to contact the blogger and that we were prevented, by law, from providing any additional information. But he was not satisfied – not at all. In fact, he got quite rude and belligerent, and demanded the blog owner's phone number and address. Of course, I refused politely, and then not so politely. We would never reveal this kind of personal information.

But here's the thing, in the course of our "conversation," I happened to mention the date you had joined OrlandoHosting, which is of course public information posted on our site. He · reacted strangely. He asked me to repeat the date, so I did. He stopped talking for a moment, though I could hear him breathing, and then he hung up without saying another word. It was all very strange.

I don't normally reach out to our customers about an inquiry, but this one was so off the wall I thought I'd better let you know about it.

Congrats again on the blog.

Jessica

Okay, that was weird. I had no idea what it was all about. I pulled out my cellphone. I'd had it set to silent mode for my dinner with Megan and hadn't missed it once. There was one voicemail message waiting from about five hours earlier, around the same time I met Megan. I punched in my code and hit play.

"Hi, ah, this is Aaron, you know, your ex-blog-hosting service. Yeah, I, you know, just wanted to let you know that I kind of might have just passed your cellphone number over to someone who was very, very keen to get it. Actually, to be honest, I did just do that. Look, I'm really sorry, but he offered up a lot of money for it, and if I hadn't given it to him, he promised to beat the crap out of me. And I believed him. He looked very, let's say believable. He was big enough, and mean enough that I could imagine him breaking my legs without breaking a sweat. You see, I'm very much into self-preservation, and I could sure use the dough. So, anyway, I'm sorry, dude. I really am. But it is what it is. Please don't call me. Just wanted to give you a heads up."

PART THREE

CHAPTER 12

The text was waiting on my phone when I woke up the next morning. The sender's number was blocked. All it said was:

"Gotcha! Won't be long now."

Things went south from there, literally. An hour later a second text:

"Ha! Florida! Makes sense. Getting warmer. Yes I am."

I ignored it. It was probably a wrong number or just another spammer. It happens all the time, right? I ignored it. Yes, that's right. Those weren't alarm bells I was hearing, they were doorbells, and school bells, and those bells that sound every hour on the hour in church steeples everywhere. Right.

So I dedicated myself to living a normal day as if the texts had never arrived. As if they weren't real. That didn't really work. I did not possess the mental discipline to pull that off. So I existed in a bicameral haze that day. Part of the time I was replaying in my mind the previous evening with Megan, and enjoying the anticipation of seeing her again on Friday. Then I'd snap out of it and break into a cold sweat at the realization that someone out there, probably deluded and deranged and almost certainly bigger than I – because, after all, most everyone is – might be on the verge of finding me. Could you secure an address for someone if you only had a cellphone number? In spy movies you just had to plug the number into some hand-held electronic gizmo and instantly on the screen would flash the unsuspecting victim's address, birthday, food allergies, shoe size, astrological sign, and colour preferences. I wonder how long it would take in the real world.

I pulled out my phone and texted Megan.

"Good morning. Just wanted to say I had a great time last night. The time just flew. Who said conversation is a lost art? So looking forward to Friday. Thanks again. Ev"

Within seconds, the little indicator on my phone told me she was texting in return. Eventually, her message materialized on my screen. Magic.

"Well hello. You're up early. I'm sitting in the departure lounge waiting to board. My head is a bit heavy from the wine, but I remember enough to know how nice an evening it was. Thank you. See you Friday in the lobby at 7:00."

Yes! That was just the kind of morning-after-the-night-before message I needed. It wasn't weird, or cold, or needy, or passive-aggressive. It struck just the right tone, conveying that our first encounter had gone well and we could try it again. I liked this woman. Then again, it was likely that some crazed wing-nut was already stalking me. But think how much worse it would be to contemplate that potentially violent confrontation without the offsetting pleasure of anticipating dinner with Megan. I considered it a wash.

I couldn't think of anything else to do, I mean beyond stewing in my own anxieties, so I sat down and started working on the research for the blog post Beverley had suggested about sexual consent. After all, I needed a whole book's worth of content, fast, so there was no time to waste. I found a few academic papers from a small Midwestern college, and UCLA, and the University of Michigan. There were several magazine articles and some newspaper stories that touched on the subject, including news reports about the all-too-many date-rape campus stories Beverley had mentioned. But I was just gathering information at this stage. I took a half-hearted stab at outlining a post, but the words weren't there. Not yet. Too much on my mind, I figured. Besides, the big nut and bolt were cold and still beneath my feet. I was staring at my screen, not writing, when my cellphone chimed with a newly arrived text. I hoped it was another from Megan.

Nope.

"Orlando! Unbelievable. How con-fucking-venient!"

That was not good. I resisted the temptation to respond. What would I say? What would that accomplish anyway, except perhaps to inflame him further? I wondered if I should call the police. But on what grounds? Again, what would I say? I could hear the call unspooling in my mind:

"You've reached 911, the emergency operator. What is your emergency?"

"Oh, hello. Yes, um, I've just received three strange texts from someone I don't know, using a blocked number."

"Are they of a violent, sexual, or threatening nature? Are you in danger right now?"

"Well, no, not really. But it is a little unnerving."

"I'm not following." A note of testiness enters her voice. "You've called 911. Do you need the police, fire department, ambulance, or other first responders at this time?"

"Well, no, I think that would be an overreaction at this stage, don't you? I just feel uneasy about these unexpected texts. . . Hello? Operator? Hello? Hello?"

No, I wouldn't be calling the police. At least not yet. Instead, I shut down my computer and left the building. I didn't really know where I was going. It was a little early to head over to visit Dad, and much too late to connect with Mom. Her high-powered day would already be in full flight. So I walked for twenty minutes and discovered a major mall. To be fair, you don't need to walk twenty minutes in Florida to find a major mall. Five to ten minutes in any direction and you should bump into one. I'd chosen an unlucky route.

You know the kind of mall I mean. They all sort of look the same to me. Large skylights welcomed light into the huge structure. It was almost as if you were strolling outside down a sunlit boulevard, yet you were inside with thousands of shoppers in climate-controlled comfort, with your choice of about 150 retail outlets.

I told myself I just needed some time and space to process what had happened, what was happening, what might happen. The word "process" suggests I already enjoyed a basic understanding of the situation. But I really didn't. Not by a long shot. So I just walked up and down the air-conditioned avenues of this mall, my brain straining with confusion, speculation, and conjecture. Every ten minutes or so, Megan would push herself centre stage in my head and remind me that last night had gone very well, and that perhaps Friday night might even be better. Then the evil, violent texter, who seemed to be getting warmer and warmer in his quest for my location, would shove Megan offstage and command the spotlight again. Occasionally, I would come to my senses when jostled by another shopper. Turned out I had a tendency to stop walking when I descended too deeply into my thoughts. Several times I would snap out of it when bumped and resume walking.

I don't think I made much headway toward resolving my plight. As a first step, I decided to list in my mind the knowns and the unknowns.

Knowns:
- The EofE blog was wildly popular and read by, conservatively, tens of thousands of readers.

- The EofE blog enraged a small but intimidating portion of the population.
- EofE's most widely read post was a tirade against business magnate Mason Bennington.
- Mason Bennington was known to associate with thugs, hoods, and criminals.
- Mason Bennington had very large security guards.
- Someone had used bribery and threats of violence to obtain my cell number.
- That someone was now texting me, apparently getting closer to finding me.
- I liked Megan, perhaps a lot.
- I have a very low pain threshold as the family dentist discovered the hard way when I was a kid . . . and again two months ago when I had an emergency root canal.

Unknowns:
- How long could I protect my anonymity as the writer of the *Eve of Equality* blog?
- Who was this potentially violent texter, and what did he want?
- What would the potentially violent texter do to me when he found me?
- Just how low is my pain threshold?

"Hey buddy, have you studied it long enough?" said the security guard. "Come on, dream somewhere else. Move along."

I had stopped again, deep in contemplation, and was looking off into space, lost in my troubled thoughts. It just so happened that I had stopped directly in front of Victoria's Secret, and the space in front of my eyes was occupied by a larger than life plasma screen in the front window, playing the rather revealing runway show of their most recent collection on an endless loop. I shuffled off.

I circumnavigated the mall a half dozen times, turning my predicament over and over in my mind, examining it from multiple perspectives, probing it from various angles, really going deep into it. I was exhausted from the pure intellectual exertion of it all. But I did draw an important conclusion – I had absolutely no idea what was happening or what I was doing. Yes, I know, that's two conclusions.

I was walking along the sidewalk, nearly back at my apartment, when my cell rang. I stopped and reached for my phone with considerable trepidation. It was another blocked number.

"Hello," I croaked.

"Jackpot," the voice said. "Gotcha." Then he hung up.

I swivelled my head back and forth like a hopped-up sprinkler, in search of . . . I don't know, somebody on a phone, maybe crouching behind a pole, or slouching in a parked car, or even lounging on a nearby rooftop next to a tripod-mounted sniper rifle. I looked for that police drama staple, the unmarked, nondescript, white stakeout van. But I saw nothing and no one suspicious. Not a soul was looking at me. Everyone had their heads down, getting on with their own lives, and clearly didn't care about mine. Then I stared across the street at the Chinese restaurant, you know, where I had gained my Tsing Tao Master designation, and I knew. I could just sense it. I was convinced that behind the reflective barrier of the mirrored front window sat my mystery man, staring back at me, perhaps even waving at me, taunting me.

I decided right then I was going to march across the street, barge through the front door, and face him down. I was going to throw down the gauntlet, step into the fire, walk into the lion's den, go toe to toe in the centre of the ring, and otherwise summon up every other confrontation cliché from the depths of the metaphorical well. Whatever *this* was, it was going to end right now. Still holding my phone, I stood there staring at the restaurant window, breathing heavily, rage building, steeling myself for the clash to come.

No, I don't think so. Instead, I sprinted to the front entrance of my apartment, climbed the stairs, and locked myself in. This isn't a movie, and I'm not a complete idiot. As soon as I slid home the deadbolt on my front door and pushed the couch up against it, he texted me again.

"You gotta be kidding me! That's really where you live? Unbe-fucking-lievable."

I didn't respond, again.

I holed up in my apartment until lunchtime. After cooking, and then not eating, a cheese omelette, I decided I would try to act normally and attempt to make it to the rehab hospital without soiling myself. I called a cab. It pulled into the alley a few minutes later, as I'd instructed. I slipped out the kitchen door, down the fire escape, and into the cab, keeping my head down. I had the driver take a rather circuitous route back to the restaurant to pick up my car, I mean Dad's car. I slipped behind the wheel as discreetly as I could, and pulled into traffic. I then drove around in a rather haphazard fashion, doing my best to throw my pursuer off my trail, if he was indeed following me. I kept my eyes glued to the rear-view mirror trying to see if I was being tailed. It's hard to drive forward competently when your eyes are glued to the rear-view mirror. After two missed stop signs, three honking horns, a monodigital gesture, one hurled epithet, and a near miss with a motorized wheelchair and its elderly occupant, it was a miracle the police didn't show up in my rear-view mirror. After about fifteen minutes of this, I was pretty sure I was not being followed. Or as sure as my vast experience in advanced countersurveillance measures would permit.

Damn. I needed gas. I pulled into an Exxon self-serve, pumped a tank of unleaded into my dad's car, and then, with my head down, slipped inside the store to pay. Standing there, waiting for my change, I realized I needed to use the local facilities. The cashier pointed to the hallway at the back of the store. I saw the familiar stick figure emblazoned on the door. I entered the stall and latched the door, as I tend to do in gas station bathroom stalls. I heard someone enter the washroom, approach the sink, and wash his hands. He was humming a happy little tune. The hand dryer was not quite loud enough to drown out the door opening and closing again as the guy left. I sat there for a while, as one does. I heard not a sound, beyond the ones I was making. I stood up, buckled up, and slid back the simple latch to release the stall door. It flew into my forehead, knocking me back onto the toilet. A big guy grabbed the front of my shirt with his club of a right hand and hoisted me up off the toilet to press me against the back wall of the stall. The flushing handle was now rather uncomfortably lodged between my butt cheeks.

I'm sure I made some kind of a noise when this was happening, but I either can't remember what it was or am too embarrassed to note its pitch.

"Gotcha. We meet at fucking last," he said in a calm, American voice.

He was a big, blond-haired, defensive lineman-type, with a swagger and a smirk that made him seem even more sinister. Did I mention he was big? The entire wholesome beach-boy bodybuilder look was somewhat sullied by the telltale faintly yellow-tinged eyes of a heavy steroid user. Rather than fighting my way out of the bathroom and making good my escape, I thought it would be prudent to listen to what he had to say and, you know, see what he wanted.

"What are you doing?" I managed to gurgle through the

pressure of his pile-driver fist pushed against my throat. "What do you want?"

"Don't talk, Everett. Just listen," he said evenly. "You've made someone very angry. That was not smart. Not fucking smart at all."

"What are you talking about?" I said. "Are you threatening me?"

He laughed at me, right in my face. He came in so close I could feel the air currents of his guffaw against my cheek.

"Am I threatening you, he asks? I can see this is your first rodeo," he sighed, shaking his head. "So just to clarify, if I were threatening you, I'd be holding you upside down right now. I'd be gripping your ankle in my right hand, and your head would be partially submerged in this here toilet. I might even flush a few times to reinforce my point. Now Everett, with all your powers of deduction, do you think I could suspend you upside down by my right hand only, with your head in this here toilet bowl?"

I thought about it briefly.

"Yes, I would have to say you probably could."

"Right. Good answer."

He then pulled me forward and lowered me back onto the toilet so that his right fist, still clenching the front of my shirt and propped under my jaw, no longer supported my entire body weight. Again, he leaned in close, very close.

"To be fucking clear, no, I'm not threatening you. I merely offering you some friendly advice that really, and I do fucking mean, *really*, you should take, and embrace fucking fully. In case you hadn't noticed, I quite like the word 'fucking.' It's helpful when I'm trying to be serious, or in your case, fucking serious."

It was an unexpected relief that his breath was quite minty and fresh.

"You're going to have a visitor in the not-too-distant future. Now I'm telling you this straight up. You should do what he asks of you. Really, you should. You're going to want to fucking trust me on this point."

"And if I don't?" I asked, totally taking leave of my senses, my mind rooted in all those TV shows where the victim says stuff like this and always comes out okay in the end.

"You really did not just fucking ask me that. Do you really want to let that stand, or should we just forget it ever slipped out?"

"I withdraw the question."

"Okay, then, I think we're done here," he said, as if we'd just cut the lawn together. "Oh, by the way, I understand your father is recovering nicely from a stroke. Glad to hear it. He's got quite the nice fucking view from his room over at, you know, the Orlando Fucking Health Rehabilitation Institute."

"What does that mean?" I asked.

"Ah, ah, ah, now. Remember?" He wagged his finger at me so it stroked the tip of my nose.

"I withdraw the question."

"Fucking right, you do."

After he left, I felt the need to make use of the facilities a second time. He was nowhere in sight when I emerged from the bathroom twenty minutes later.

The cashier didn't even look up when I wobbled out the door and back to the car. I raced over to the hospital, still spending more time than was safe with my eyes on the rear-view mirror.

Just like almost every other day, Yolanda was at the nurses' station. But it didn't really feel like every other day.

"Yolanda, is everything okay around here? Is my dad okay?"

"Hello, Master Everett. Everything is just fine now, but you did miss some excitement this morning. We had what we call a Code 22 mini-lockdown."

"A Code 22 mini-lockdown? That doesn't sound good. What does it mean?"

"We had an unauthorized visitor cruising the hallways, looking for someone."

"Who was he looking for?" I asked, feeling a little queasy.

"Well, we're still not sure, but he did spend some time with your father. Your dad pulled the patient alarm string."

"Oh my gosh. Is Dad okay? Did the guy do anything to him?" I asked.

"If I've learned anything since your father arrived, it's that you don't mess with Billy Kane. Your dad had it all well in hand," she explained. "Anyway, before security could get there, the guy was smiling and sauntering back out the front door like he owned the place, still humming to his big self, like nothing had happened. I tried to speak to him, but he wasn't in the mood for conversation."

I hadn't heard much after the two words "big self."

"What did he look like?"

"He kind of looked a little like that guy who played the Joker in that Batman show?"

"Cesar Romero?"

"No, not the TV show, the movie."

"Jack Nicholson?"

"No, not that movie. One of the newer ones."

"Danny DeVito?"

"No, no. He was the Penguin, I think."

"Right! Oh, was it Heath Ledger?"

"Bingo. That's the one," she said. "Hey, you're pretty good. You should get yourself on *Jeopardy*."

"One of the few benefits of a misspent youth in front of the TV," I conceded. "So this intruder guy looked like the late, great Heath Ledger?"

"Pretty much. Except this guy was about three times the size and had a dirty mouth on him, to boot."

"Pardon my language, Yolanda, but did he happen to say 'fucking' a lot?"

"Now how could you possibly know that?" Yolanda looked at me with arms crossed over her not insubstantial chest. "He didn't say much to me, but he did use that particular word quite a bit in our brief encounter. Do you know this dude?"

"Of course not. Does he sound like the kind of guy I would be hanging out with?" I protested. "You said yourself he had a dirty mouth. I just put two and two together. Anyway, I guess I'd better check in on my father."

She kept her eyes on me for a minute longer before uncrossing her arms.

"He's still in his room, hon."

I found him propped up in his bed, flipping through the latest *Car and Driver* magazine.

"Dad! Are you okay?" I said, perhaps with a little too much concern in my voice.

"Whaddya mean, am I okay? Why wouldn't I be? The new *C and D* just came through. The meatloaf at lunch tasted a little less like sawdust than the last batch, and I get to have a nap soon. Of course I'm okay. I'm fine."

"Dad, I mean that big guy, that intruder, did he touch you?"

"What are you yammerin' about? Some juiced-up Charles Atlas comes in to look around and everyone blows a head gasket," Dad replied, returning to his magazine. "That happened like four hours ago. I've already moved on, and it'd be great if you would, too."

"Well, just before we move on, what did he want? What did he say?"

"He just asked me my name, so I told him. That was about it."

"Then what happened?"

"Well, he started moving around the room, picking up stuff, and looking at it. When he grabbed the photo of you and your mother there, and stared at it with this funny look on his face, well, that's when I told him to shove off."

"Dad, the guy's huge. Why would you say something like that to him?"

"He was taking liberties and I didn't appreciate it. So I did what I always do when people take liberties. I called him on it."

"What did he do?"

"He just smiled and put the photo back, all gentle-like, and said 'Whatever you say, old man.' That kind of pissed me off so I asked him to kindly take his muscle-bound ass out of here. That's when I pulled the call-stringy thingy."

"And he walked out? Just like that?"

"He gave me a smirk and said we might be seeing more of each other.

"'Not if I see you first,' I told him."

Just then, Yolanda came into the room with Beverley on her arm.

"Nobody tells me anything around here. I just heard the news. Are you all right, Billy?" Beverley asked. "Or is the more appropriate question, is the intruder all right?"

"Oh jeez, here we go again. I'm just fine. Top drawer. Couldn't be better," he said. "Look, nothing happened. And it's over. I can't tell the story again. Let's change the subject."

"Come on, Billy, I don't have a lot of excitement in my life these days, not counting the pool on the timing of my own impending superstroke royale, of course. So how about cutting an old gal some slack and spilling some details."

"Beverley, there's nothing to tell," Dad started. "Some cocky jerk dragged his big-ass muscles in here to rattle my cage a bit. So I just sent him and his big-ass muscles on their way. End of story."

"That's not nearly as exciting as Yolanda made it out to be."

"I just calls them like I sees them," Yolanda replied.

She settled Beverley in one of the guest chairs at the foot of the bed and stepped out of the room. I sat down in the chair nearer the head of the bed and fidgeted a bit.

"Okay, what's going on, young Ev?" Beverley asked. "What's happened?"

I took a deep breath and let it out slowly.

"Is it that obvious?"

"Not to your father, because you don't have a steering wheel and a turbocharged engine. But it's obvious to me something is rotten in Denmark. How about you tell us?"

I sat there in silence for a minute or two, assessing my options. I didn't like any of them.

"Okay, well, since I'm apparently an open book, you're right, I have a bit of a situation on my hands. And I think it's time I let you both in on it. I could use your help. Dad, Beverley knows part of this story already, but not the whole picture, or what's happened in the last twenty-four hours."

Beverley looked worried and leaned forward a little. Dad looked at his magazine and leaned back a little. Beverley slapped his right foot.

"Look alive, Billy, your son is about to tell us a story. And I think you're going to want to hear it. I know I do."

"Cripes, can't an old car guy just read his new mag in peace?" Beverley answered by shaking her head.

So he closed the magazine, folded his hands across his chest, and nodded to me.

It took me about twenty minutes to get it all out. I held my hand up twice to quell questions from Dad that I was about to answer with the next part of the story. I covered everything from stem to stern – the club, the pole, the blog, the Candace Sharpe plug, the tidal wave of readers, the money I was making from online advertising, the invitations to do major network talk shows, the book deal, Lewis, Shawna and Chloe, the protest rallies, Megan, the mysterious texts, and finally my washroom waltz with the bulked-up beach boy on the way over, who had apparently tangled with my father earlier in the day.

For the most part, neither Dad nor Beverley interrupted me, but I could tell by the way their eyes widened at certain points and Beverley's hand shot to her mouth during the bathroom bully scene that I'd been able to hold their attention.

"Let me get this straight. The dance pole is actually in your apartment?" Dad asked.

"Your son is terrorized in a public bathroom by a blond behemoth and you ask about the dance pole?" Beverley asked him, shooting him a look of thinly veiled contempt. "That's the part of the story you want to clarify?"

"What? He's fine. Look at him," Dad replied. "I'm just trying to visualize the sweet setup he's got in his bachelor pad, that's all."

"Dad, the pole isn't in my apartment. So you can dial back the mental picture of naked women swinging around my kitchen. It's only the nut that anchors the very top of the pole to my floor that's in my kitchen."

He looked down and shook his head.

"Too bad."

Beverley slapped his foot again.

"Focus, Billy. No backsliding," she scolded. "You've come too far to relapse now."

"Geez, can't a guy just be a goddamned guy for even a couple of seconds anymore?" he complained. "Okay, so you think the jackass who joined you in the bathroom stall is the same guy who paid me a visit this morning?"

"Sounds like the same guy to me. And it clearly was no coincidence."

"Thanks, Columbo," Dad replied.

———————

Both Beverley and my father suggested I stay at my dad's condo that night. Why would I go back to the apartment? I could see the logic in their proposal, but in my state of mind, logic wasn't necessarily the dominant actor. Frankly, looking back across a lifetime of decisions, logic has seldom enjoyed the influence it so clearly deserves. My computer, the source of my currently inflated income, was at the apartment. All my clothes, my toothbrush, all my other stuff, and a six-pack of Corona were all back at my apartment. No steroid-addled bronzed blond muscle for hire was going to keep me from my own apartment. Of course, it was easier to make such a bold decision when the pumped-up enforcer wasn't holding me up against the wall of a stall with one hand. I headed home, anyway.

I drove the wrong way for a while, turning every couple of blocks, then corkscrewing through a labyrinth of residential side streets before finally meandering my way back toward my apartment on lesser populated roads running parallel to the major thoroughfares. I'm not sure why I took these precautions given that my muscular friend already knew where I lived. But I was a little foggy-headed. I remembered along the way that I needed groceries, so I stopped at a supermarket when I was almost home.

I pushed my cart around the aisles, doubling back in the middle of frozen foods and again in canned goods to make sure no other shopping cart was shadowing me. All clear, I thought. I picked up enough provisions to get me through the next several days, including a nice New York strip loin from the butcher's counter that I figured I'd earned. As I turned to push my groceries to the checkout, I caught a flash of movement in the corner of my eye. A young man on a mission was moving my way. I took off down the cereal aisle, my shopping cart fishtailing in front of me.

"Hey!" the man said as I sprinted ahead of him. "Hey, buddy! Wait!"

I wasn't sticking around for round two of "Let's Bully Everett."

"Wait, your phone! Your phone!" he shouted as I skidded into the juice and pop aisle.

Yeah, right. There was no way I was going to fall for the old "You left your phone on the butcher counter" gambit. No way. I'm no greenhorn. Then I slowed down and finally stopped. I'd left my phone on the butcher counter. The young man finally caught up, breathing hard.

"You left your phone. . ."

"I know, on the butcher counter," I interrupted, accepting the phone from him. "Thanks so much, I'd forget my head if it weren't attached."

"Hey, are you okay? You look a little spooked."

"Yeah, I'm fine. Rough day. Sorry about bolting on you there. I, um, thought you were someone else."

"No worries," he said. "You're fast. Glad I caught you."

"Me too. Thanks again."

———————

I'd been home for about half an hour. It wasn't until after I'd loaded my groceries into the fridge and cupboards that I noticed it. Now that I'd spied it, I wondered why I hadn't seen it sooner. A small yellow Post-it note stuck to the closed lid of my laptop. I hadn't put it there. I didn't even have any yellow Post-it notes. I felt queasy all of a sudden. Everything went quiet in the apartment. I was too far away to read what it said on the little yellow square. I just stood there, frozen at the fridge, my steak half in the meat drawer and half out. I let go of the steak and it slid the rest of the way in. I closed the drawer and then the fridge. I stayed where I was, listening. I could hear the kitchen crew downstairs getting ready for the night ahead, but there was not a sound in the apartment. From my spot by the fridge, I scanned every inch of my space for other telltale signs of a home invasion. Nothing looked out of place. Nothing seemed amiss.

I then forced myself to tiptoe over to my bedroom door. The room was empty. With a level of stealth I didn't know I possessed, I eased over to my closet and yanked open the door with considerable force. Nothing. Good thing. What would I have done if bulging beach boy had been in there waiting for me? I mean, after changing my pants, what would I have done? I clearly wasn't thinking straight. After checking everywhere, from under my living room couch to under my kitchen sink, I concluded that there was no longer an intruder in my apartment. There were no signs of forced entry. Both my front and fire escape doors were locked.

Finally, I inched over to my laptop and focused on the little yellow note stuck to the middle of the lid.

"Do what he wants."

That's all it said in relatively neat capital letters. I don't know why I delicately flicked at the note with my finger. Maybe I thought it was a trigger of some kind, a tripwire for an explosive device inside. Ridiculous, I know. I came to my senses and opened the laptop. A larger yellow Post-it note graced the touchpad inside.

"So this is where you make the magic. Well, get ready to make some more."

I was beginning to rethink the "sleepover at Dad's condo" idea. I did another thorough search of the apartment. Again, I found nothing out of the ordinary, except perhaps for the two-week-old slice of pizza I discovered under my bed. Over the last couple of days, I'd wondered about that faint oregano scent in the room.

To calm my nerves, I drank three beers in quick succession. It almost met the definition of chugging. After unleashing a window-rattling burp, I sat down on the couch and hauled out my cellphone. I'd texted Megan earlier in the afternoon just to let her know I was thinking of her. I figured she'd want to know such important news. I know she's a busy lawyer and all, but I was a little surprised that I still hadn't heard back from her. I texted her again, reiterating what a wonderful time I'd had last night – though it felt to me like a very long time ago. I noted again how happy I was that we'd be seeing each other again on Friday night. I signed off with "Good night, Ev." Half an hour later, there was still no reply. She was probably already asleep. I could wait until tomorrow.

Taking a page from the *Hardy Boys' Detective Handbook*, I then dumped half a box of corn flakes onto the kitchen floor, near the front door and over by the fire escape door. I carefully spread the cereal around, covering the floor as evenly as three guzzled beers would permit. I thought it was all quite ingenious. No uninvited guest could ever make it to my bedroom without waking me up with a cacophony of crackling corn flakes underfoot. Think of it as my own Distant Early Warning System. Feeling good, I then downed the remaining three beers to calm my nerves and went to bed.

Eight hours later, I awoke to a violent pounding in my head. It took me a moment or two more to realize there was also a violent pounding on my front door.

CHAPTER 13

I can attest to the cacophony made by walking through corn flakes scattered carefully on the floor. It definitely woke me up. What I had not anticipated was how awful it would feel on my bare feet as I shuffled to answer the front door. Given the violence of the blows raining on the door, I wondered if the building were on fire and this was the firefighters' evacuation notice. I know it seems strange, but this was the only possible explanation I could come up with while half-asleep, walking through corn flakes. I opened the door.

Lewis was raising his fist to take another shot at punching his way through my front door. He looked angry. Really angry.

"Lewis! What gives? It's only. . ."

He stepped back for the big reveal. Mason Bennington, dressed in a black pinstriped suit looking like the quintessential Chicago mobster, was standing behind him. And "reveal" is the right word. Lewis is so gargantuan that Mason Bennington's immediate family could have been back there with him and I'd never have known.

"Sure we'd like to come in," Mason Bennington said. "Thanks for asking."

He pushed past me into my apartment.

"Hey, you can't just barge into my apartment. This is private property," I protested, as I opened the door a little wider to admit Lewis, his rage face still in place.

"Oh really? Is that so? Well, I'm standing in your apartment, numbnuts. So it looks like I *can* actually barge into your apartment," Bennington said, leaning in, his index finger tapping my sternum.

Standing so close, I could smell his hair product. Or maybe it was his aftershave. No. No aftershave could be that bad. I looked at Lewis, but he just stood there with his legs spread, his hands clasped beyond his back in what looked like the security guards classic "ready" position. Lewis seemed to have finally gained control over his asshole index.

I decided it was in my interest to dial down the hostility and amp up the hospitality.

"Yes, well, be that as it may, I'm always happy to have visitors in the morning," I said.

"Looks like we interrupted your breakfast," Bennington said, taking in the corn flakes strewn about the kitchen floor. "They have these things now called bowls. You should get yourself one. Makes eating cereal much easier."

"Thanks for the tip. Now what can I do for you gentlemen?"
I asked.

"We haven't met formally. I'm Mason Bennington, and it's a
good thing I wasn't able to buy this building or you'd be out on
your ass by now."

This felt different from being roughed up in a gas station bathroom stall by the blond Hulk. I knew Lewis Small, and I was
standing in my own apartment – home field advantage. Plus, Mason
Bennington is not that intimidating a physical presence. After all,
I could make direct eye contact with him without looking up.

"Oh. I see. Have there been noise complaints? Have I been
playing my Gordon Lightfoot too loud? Has it been drowning
out the European electro-crap that's been shaking me awake
since you opened? Sorry about that."

"So you're a smart ass as well as a wordsmith, are you?" he said.

"What?"

Intellectually, I'd of course already made the link between
yesterday's bloated beach-boy bouncer and Mason Bennington.
But it didn't feel real until that moment, as I shifted uneasily
from one foot to the next, making corn flake crunching sounds.

"Look Kane, let's lose the preliminaries and cut to the main
event. I have now determined beyond the shadow of a doubt that
you are the sole author of a little blog known as *Eve of Equality*.
I also know that you have gone to great lengths to protect your
anonymity. I don't know why you don't want your name on it,
but you clearly don't."

"I don't have a clue what you're talking about. I'm a freelance writer. I write stories for trade magazines. That's what I do."

"He's right on that score, Mr. B. I seen a few of his articles," Lewis chimed in, breaking character for just a second.

"Shut up, Lurch!" Bennington snapped, turning to Lewis. "You're supposed to be the strong silent type. How about a little more of the silent part!"

Lewis nodded once, reset his face into a malevolent scowl, and looked straight ahead.

"Hold that thought," I said, holding up my hand like a Stop sign. "I'll be right back."

I zipped back into my bedroom, conferred with my cellphone, pocketed it, and returned to my guests in the kitchen.

"You were saying?" I said to Mason Bennington.

"You can cut the innocent-ignorant act, Kane. You're our guy. I've got enough computer geeks on the payroll to break into the Pentagon. We've got you. All electronic roads lead directly to that laptop computer, right there. There's no point in denying it. Why waste the time. We're going to end up in the same place."

"So you're the guy who strong-armed my blog-hosting service," I said, as it all fell into place.

"I didn't strong-arm anybody. I have people to do my strong-arming for me. Besides, money works better than muscle. That guy sang like a baby when we flashed a few Benjamins in his face. He rolled over fast. After that, it was just a matter of time till my boys could tighten the noose around your neck."

"I think the phrase is 'sang like a bird' but I get your point," I said. "And do your boys include the Californian bodybuilder you sicced on me yesterday?"

"His name is Derek, and believe it or not, he's more than just a body builder from Wisconsin. He's also a grade-A computer nerd."

"Well, that's weird," I said. "Anyway, the point is, it's perfectly legal to create and write an anonymous blog to help redress an extreme historical social inequity. There's no law against it."

"Listen, Everett Luther King, if there were a law against it, my lawyers would already be so far up your ass they'd be counting your teeth as they shut down your precious little blog. But the law can't help us much in this case. Believe me, I tried," Bennington said. "So a little more creativity is required before I can get the justice I require. You see, you wrote a piece about me that made me stark-raving crazy. It made me insane. I'm minding my own business, trying like hell to clean up a very dirty and dangerous business for dancing girls in this country, and you, you little shit, start taking shots at me, insulting me, and questioning my motives. It drove me nuts, didn't it, Lurch?"

"Yes sir, it surely did, Mr. B," Lewis replied, still looking straight ahead.

"Well, I'm sorry to hear that," I said. "But what you're doing is fair game for reporters or bloggers, or for anyone to comment on. Why don't you just start your own blog if you want to refute something I've written on mine? Or why don't you write a guest post presenting your side? If it's any good, I'll run it. That's what reasonable, law-abiding adults would do."

"I thought of that. But I think it would be better if you wrote a second post, taking back what you wrote the first time. You know, after sober second thought, and learning more about XY and more about me, and what we're doing for girls in the trade, you've decided it's a good thing, and the girls are in a better and safer place."

"Women."

"What?"

"Never mind."

"Whatever," Bennington said. "How about you write a post like that, put it up there on your little blog, we'll call it square, and that'll be the end of it?"

"What? You want me to say what you're doing with this little chain of strip joints, where rich men buy the chance to see women take off their clothes, is good for women? Why would I do that? It runs counter to everything I believe in. Wait, I get it. You're going to have Lewis or Derek or Brawn 'persuade' me to write it. Is that the plan?"

"I thought you'd never ask," Bennington replied. "But that is not my plan, though I do have one. We don't need to resort to violence, or not much violence, anyway. I'm hoping we don't need to go there at all. There's another reason for you to warm up your fingers and start writing the 'Mason Bennington is a great American' article. You see, if you don't, I'll blow your cover. The entire world will know that the ever-popular *Eve of Equality* blog, this beacon of social justice, is written by a smart-ass writer with a dick in his pants, named Everett Kane, who uses his so-called feminism to get laid. There's no law against using all of my considerable resources to push out that story far and wide."

"You know that's not true. You can't just make stuff up and call it the truth," I said.

"You mean there's stuff on the Internet that's not true? I'm horrified." Bennington recoiled with his hands in front of his mouth.

"This isn't how the world works. We have free speech in this country. You can't just threaten people into doing your bidding."

"Actually, I've found that threats can be a very effective strategy. Right, Lurch?"

"Right, Mr. B."

"Now you listen very carefully to me, Everett fucking Kane. I'm only going to say this one more time. I always get what I want. Always. It'd be much cleaner and less painful for you, in every way, if you just whipped up a nice puff piece about me, and what I'm doing to support good American girls in the exotic dancing trade. And then it's done. We're done. You can go on with your little crusade and write your precious little blog for all I care. Just don't ever mention my name again, or I'll be back. You have five days to post the positive piece about me or the world will know that Eve is really Everett."

He stepped close, very close, so we were quite literally toe to toe and eye to eye. Then he again pressed his finger onto my sternum. I pushed my chest forward to hold my ground.

"Five days. That's it. And the blog post better be nice and positive, because I'm still holding all the cards. And every last one of them says 'Hey everybody, Everett Kane is actually *Eve of Equality*.' I'll be watching for your post every day, for the next five days. I'd better see it, or we're nowhere near done."

He stepped back and turned toward the door.

"Give him a little something to help him remember our visit, will you, Lurch?"

"I've got my implements of persuasion right here, Mr. B," Lewis said, as he whipped out from behind his back what looked like a roll of fabric secured with a tie. He must have had it stashed in the waistband of his pants.

"Don't show me your tools, you vacuous gronk!" Bennington snapped. "Leave me the hell out of it. I pay you to leave me out of it. Remember?"

Lewis quickly concealed the fabric roll behind his back again. "Yes sir, Mr. B. Sorry, Mr. B."

Mason Bennington shook his head, walked out of my apartment, and slammed the door behind him.

"Okay, Ever-man, have a seat and let's get this over with," Lewis said in his enforcer voice while still redlining on the asshole index.

He put a hand on my shoulder and pushed me down into a kitchen chair. I had no choice in the matter. I suddenly felt as I did in the bathroom stall the day before – scared, and wondering about the odds of bumping into so many really, really large people, lately.

"Hey, Lewis, friend. Where's the happy-go-lucky giant I've come to know and love?"

"Shut up!" Lewis shouted, the ferocity of his command making me twitch in the chair.

He slammed the fabric cylinder onto the kitchen table in front of me, loosened the tie, and unrolled it. With visions of the *Marathon Man* torture scene in my head, I expected to see an array of dental instruments designed to inflict maximum pain but leave no visible marks. Instead, I saw lots of fabric sleeves holding various brushes, powders, mascara, eye shadow, and a few tubes of what, I don't know. This was a make-up artist's portable cosmetics kit.

"I got you good, didn't I?" Lewis said, bursting out laughing.

He immediately pressed his hand to his mouth and looked toward the door. He darted over, opened the door a crack, peeked out, and then closed it again.

"All clear," he reported. "Man, I had you going but good. Admit it. You were about to start begging for your life, right?"

Lewis was holding his stomach and laughing. I was still staring at the make-up kit with my mouth open. I don't think I looked too happy.

"I'm so sorry, Ever-man, but I had to play my part when Mr. B was in the room. I had no choice. My ass was on the line."

"Well, you played it pretty well. You were very, um, convincing," I said, finally finding my voice. Then I reached into my pocket, pulled out my cellphone, and stopped the digital recording I'd made of the entire encounter.

"Man, just be glad I was the guy in the room today. Brawn is usually Mr. B's go-to muscle, but he's up in New Jersey at his sister's wedding. So I got the nod today. Lucky for you."

Lewis slapped the table, hard, and knocked over another kitchen chair, making a big noise. Then he started banging the floor with his foot.

"What are you doing?" I asked.

"Putting on a good show in case Mr. B is still downstairs. I've got a reputation to uphold and a job to keep," he replied. "Okay, Ever-man, let's get this down, dusted, and done."

"What? What do you mean?"

"I mean that Mr. B likes to see evidence that his orders have been filled. I owe him an iPhone photo of my handiwork. So let's get started. Lift up your shirt. This is a rib job. He didn't want anything visible on the face."

"What are you talking about?"

"Trust me, Ev. We got to do this or we're both in trouble," he said as he pulled a chair over to sit directly in front of me.

He motioned for me to lift up my shirt. I finally understood. I did as I was told, hoisting the hem of my shirt. He immediately grabbed a selection of powders in a variety of shades and got to work. I couldn't see what he was doing, but I could feel his brushes, creams, powders, and eye shadow being applied, shaded, even sculpted. He actually tickled me a few times as he worked his magic. It took him about fifteen minutes before he pulled back and admired his handiwork. He leaned in again to put on the finishing touches, before pushing back his chair and standing up.

"Okay, Ever-man, you can check it out now."

I looked down and almost doubled over in pain, because it looked liked I'd suffered a serious thoracic injury. This could hardly be called handiwork. No, this was pure, unadulterated artistry. Two large multicoloured contusions, with shades of red, purple, yellow, and a little blue, graced the left side of my rib cage. They almost looked 3-D in their standout perfection. I touched the skin around the "bruises" to make sure that the 3-D swelling I was seeing was just an optical illusion. It was. There was even the shiny liquid slickness of bleeding, yet it was all dry to the touch. I swear my "wounds" started to hurt as I stared at them.

"Lewis, that is amazing! Stunning. Looking at it makes it hurt to breathe. You need to do this on YouTube. You'd be a viral star in no time," I said. "Where did you learn to do that?"

"I've been painting people for years. I used to work in film and TV out in LA, but there didn't seem to be enough work for a big black guy with make-up skills. So I caught on at the XY in Hollywood. Now I help out whenever a new club opens. Plus I get to make up the dancers. That's really what gets me up in the morning. And that's why they look so smokin' hot out there on stage."

"You're their make-up man? You make Shawna look like that every night?"

"Shawna and the rest of them, too. I couldn't handle the other parts of my job if I couldn't do their faces every night. Keeps me sane."

"You are one interesting dude, Lewis Small."

"Okay, say cheese," Lewis said, as he unholstered his iPhone. "Don't worry, your face won't be in the shot. I just want to capture my rib work for Mr. B."

"Of course," I replied. "I'd like one, too. Just email it to me. Why not put it in your portfolio, too? It's truly a work of art. I just had no idea the big security dude was also a talented make-up artist."

"Yeah, well I had no idea the guy who was making Mr. B so mad was living in the apartment right upstairs. How strange is that?"

I held up my shirt and he snapped a few photos.

"I guess we all have our secrets," I said. "So, Lewis. Is Bennington really serious about his threat? It's blackmail, you know."

"Ever-man, I've never known Mr. B to be anything but serious when he threatens people. Trust me. Blackmail is just the first step. You don't want to know what comes next."

"How can you work for him?"

"Look, man, I told you before, I got to earn a living. It's not always fun. But I got a job. And it's tough for guys like to me to get jobs. I got limited options. For now, I got this gig."

"Do you know this Derek guy, too?"

"Sure, I know Derek. He specializes in finding people who don't want to be found. He's a whiz with a computer. You ought to see his fingers flying over that keyboard. It's a blur, man. And when he finds whoever he's been hired to find, it sure helps that he's big. He usually gets his way."

"No shit."

"He's gone home, now. Left this morning after giving his report to the B-man. He did his job. He won't be bothering you no more."

"And I was just getting to know him. We were quite close there for a bit yesterday."

We sat there in silence for a moment or two, until Lewis looked at me, hard. He pointed his finger at me to hold my attention.

"Hey, Ever-man, you're going to want to write what Mr. B's telling you to write. Really, I'm telling you straight. Just swallow it, and do it. Then we can all go back to living our lives."

He gathered his cosmetics, brushes, and applicators, rolled it all back up, and secured the fabric tie. Then he stood up and moved to the door. I stood up, too, and met him there.

"I'll think it over, Lewis," I said, my hand disappearing into his as we shook. "And thanks, you know, for not breaking my ribs for real, but making it look like you did a really serious number on them."

"You're welcome. Thanks for sitting still when I was working."

I pulled up my shirt again to survey his masterpiece.

"That is true art, my friend. Hey, how do I get it off?"

"Leave it for a few days, just to be sure. Then just use some cold cream to lift it. I'll bring some up later."

"Thanks, Lewis."

While I was thinking it all through, I made myself useful by sweeping up the corn flakes. Then I ate the one small bowl full that was still left in the box. I wasn't sure what I was going to do. Would it be so bad to draft a lukewarm, semi-positive post pointing out the innovations Mason Bennington had introduced? One could argue that he had made the lives of those young working women better than if they'd still been stuck dancing in sleazy dives where the rough clientele expected more than stripping. The security measures, the no-touching rules, the better pay, the retirement plans could all be positioned as significant improvements in working conditions over historical norms. I even started crafting the kinds of lines I'd use to introduce and carry the post. I'd need to lean on phrases like "It's possible I was a bit hasty and narrow-minded in an earlier post," or "upon further reflection," or "giving credit where credit is due." You know, words by which to backpedal, backfill, um, reverse one's self.

If I made this one little concession, I could be free of all this unpleasantness, keep the blog, and most importantly, preserve my anonymity. Under these unusual circumstances, and keeping my longer-term goals in mind, it seemed like the right call. By that, I mean it *sounded* like the right call, and it *looked* like the right call. The real problem that emerged from my deliberations was that it just never, not for one instant, *felt* like the right call.

He was back sitting in his original spot, not doing much of anything.

"Hi, Kenny. How come you're not roaming the range with your personal chauffeur?"

"Cuz your old man has thrown me over for someone else. Just like the fickle Ford man he is."

He lifted a finger and pointed out to the paved paths. There was my dad guiding someone else down the Blue path. I didn't think it was Beverley. Because of the angle, it took me a second or two to see that it was my mother walking beside him. I looked at the other end of the path and spied Beverley, pad and pen in hand, ensconced on a bench bathed in sunlight. I set off along the Yellow path that looped around to join the Red one just about where Beverley was writing. My timing was perfect. As I closed the distance to her at a brisk pace, it seemed I'd arrive at almost the same time as my mother and father.

"Young Everett, you're back," Beverley greeted me, stowing her letter in her bag as usual. "And just in time for a family reunion." She winked when she said it.

"Hi, Beverley. Hi, Dad. And hello, Mom. Fancy meeting you here."

Dad dropped onto the bench beside Beverley, and Mom sat beside him. With not much room left on the bench, I stood before them as if auditioning for something.

"Hello, Everett," Mom started. "Yes, your father has been promenading me around the grounds for a good half-hour now. I think I'm more tuckered out from it than he is. That speaks well of his recovery, don't you think?"

Dad had his arms resting on the back of the bench, his left, behind Beverley, his right, behind his ex-wife. He looked quite pleased with himself.

"You looked pretty spry out there, Dad," I commented.

"I wasn't sure how many more laps your mother had in her, so I thought we'd better take a break."

Mom said nothing but rolled her eyes just ever so slightly.

"Okay, what's going on now?" Beverley asked. "You're looking jumpy again. What's happened?"

"I guess I failed the audition. Remind me never to take up acting," I said. "I clearly suck at affecting nonchalance."

I stood facing what I now considered to be my war cabinet.

"Okay, let me start by bringing Mom up to date in case Dad hasn't yet briefed her fully."

And I was off again. I spent the first twenty minutes or so bringing Mom completely into the circle. She was dutifully flabbergasted at what I'd been up to. I think she might have been a little disappointed that I was obviously still in the throes of what she'd always called my feminist phase. But in deference to Beverley, five-star feminist royalty, she held her tongue. Then I brought them all up to speed on my visit that morning from five-star misogynist royalty, Mason Bennington. Beverley's jaw dropped when I described the scene and Bennington's unmitigated temerity. I held up my hand to hold the floor until I'd described exactly what had happened. There was much head shaking when I covered the cosmetic virtuosity of Lewis Small. I detected skepticism, so with great fanfare, I lifted my shirt to reveal my two perfect rib contusions. I got the response I wanted.

"Geez, that looks painful. How are you walking around? In fact, how the hell are you breathing?" Dad asked.

"Dad, weren't you listening? These aren't real. It's make-up," I said, tapping the middle of the larger wound with my index finger.

"Sorry, Ev, after you said cosmetics, I kind of tuned out," Dad confessed. "Those sure look real. That guy is a wizard."

"Let's not get hung up on the least important element in the story, shall we?" Beverley suggested. "I'm certainly glad you weren't injured, but the more pressing matter is the blackmail blog post. Are you going to buckle under and write it?"

"Of course you are," my mother piped up. "I know this Bennington snake, and he isn't going to stop until he gets what he wants, even if he has to break a few bones to get it. Just give him his little pump-me-up piece and it'll be over."

I held up my hand again to get on the speakers' list.

"Believe me, I've thought this whole thing over from every angle in the last few hours. I've done the analysis, I've listed the pros and cons, I've examined it up, down, and sideways. I have no desire to tangle with Mason Bennington any more than I already have. But I just can't sing his praises in a post and put it up on *Eve of Equality*. It would cripple the blog's credibility in one stroke and lose us legions of followers. The life of the *Eve of Equality* would essentially be over. So who cares if we can protect my anonymity if the blog no longer has a meaningful voice? It would be over."

"I'm with you, Ev. You can't let that grade-A asshole and patriarchy-loving misogynist win," my father said, leaning forward and resting his clenched fists on his thighs.

Nobody said anything for a moment. There was dead silence. My mother and I filled it by looking at Dad with both our jaws, not just dropped, but dislocated. Only Beverley was smiling and nodding. Dad wasn't happy that we were staring at him as if he'd just materialized from another galaxy.

"What?" Dad snapped. "Can't I call someone a grade-A asshole without offending your tender ears? We're all adults here."

"Dad, there's no debate he's a grade-A asshole. It was the

'patriarchy-loving misogynist' line that, well, kind of threw us for a loop."

"Wake up, son. Of course Bennington's a patriarchy-loving misogynist. For Christ sakes, he makes money when his girls . . . when his women take off their goddamned clothes for the enter-tainment of asshole men. What else would you call him?"

"Who are you, and what have you done with my ex-husband?" Mom said when she eventually found her voice.

"Aw geez, here we go," Dad sighed. "Evelyn, honey, can't a guy grow a little bit in his old age? Come on, give me a break. People can change, you know."

Mom looked over at me and then at Beverley. The funny feminist just shrugged but said nothing. Then leaned over and patted Dad's arm.

"Okay, so we're agreed that you're not going to bow down and write some obsequious codswallop to pump up Mason Bennington's already overly inflated ego. So we need a Plan B that won't have young Everett joining us here as he rehabs from two broken legs. And I think I have an idea."

I scrunched onto the bench beside my mother as Beverley took over. She presented her idea in a thoughtful and measured way. She covered off all the possible outcomes and how we'd handle each one. Then she discussed the benefits and drawbacks of the plan. All of us had questions. We all kicked around the answers. It was a true case of collaborative thinking. And when I could separate myself from the very real physical implications that might befall me, it was an interesting and intellectually satisfying exercise.

It wasn't an ideal plan. But it was the best one we had.

"And you think she'll go for it?" I asked Beverley.

"I think I still have some pull around there. But we'll have to move quickly. Can you make it there tomorrow? We don't have much time."

"Well, I had signed up for an all-day salsa-dancing workshop at the Forbidden Dance Clinic tomorrow, but I suppose I can put that off to another day."

"That would be good," Beverley said, nodding and patting my knee. "That would be good."

I figured I was safe for the next five days. By then my ribs would have "healed," and the plan, such as it was, would have worked, or crashed and burned, trapping me in the wreckage. I sat down at my kitchen table that night, wrapped my feet around the big, warm, and pulsating nut in my floor, and composed the most explosive blog post I'd yet written. It didn't take me much time to write it, though it was my longest post yet. The words fairly poured out of me. I did not hit the Publish button. It wasn't yet time. But when it was, I'd be ready.

I did publish another post I had in draft form from the previous week. If I didn't post content regularly, ideally twice a week, my readership would decline. I couldn't afford that. So I touched up a post I'd written about the number of women political candidates in federal elections across the G20 countries. It was a sad litany of under-representation with few programs in place to encourage more women to run. The Scandinavian countries fared reasonably well, but there wasn't much good news beyond that.

I took a quick look out my front window to check on the status of our friendly nightly neighbourhood protest. It was late by then, so the rather small group of stalwart demonstrators was just breaking up. There weren't too many cars pulling up in front of XY. The protestors and cameras were doing their job and having their desired effect.

In the rush of the day's events, I realized I still hadn't heard from Megan, despite several texts. I checked my email. Nothing from her there, either. I texted her again, in a pseudo-romantic tone, about counting the days until our Friday night dinner.

My cellphone rang. "Orlando rehab" appeared on my screen.

"Hello?"

"The bright star shone over Istanbul just after midnight."

"Beverley, we're not in a spy novel."

"Indulge me, young Everett. There's not much room for fun and excitement in my life. So this is it."

"I hear you. But it's a little too much excitement for my blood," I replied. "So are we all systems go?"

"We're on! Or at least you're on for 11:30 tomorrow morning. So you'll have to catch an early shuttle. I used up most of my political capital to get the meeting. I did not give her any details, so she doesn't know *why* you're coming, just *that* you're coming. And I think that's the right way to handle it. She'll see you at 11:30."

"Okay, I guess we're on! I can't thank you enough, Beverley. I mean it. If we pull this off, it'll be because of you. I'm grateful."

"Stop it! You're going to jinx it. Just get your fanny on that plane in the morning and make your meeting."

We talked for a few more minutes. After thinking about it for a week or so, I finally asked Beverley if she'd write a guest post, under her own byline, for the blog. I suggested she could write about the women's movement then and now. She was reluctant, but I pushed. She said she'd think about it. She hadn't said yes. But neither had she said no.

I hung up shortly thereafter and booked my flights online. I knew approximately what time it was by what song was pounding below me. I'd come to know the dance program by heart, or rather by ear. It was almost time for Shawna's second turn on the runway. I'd never seen her perform. In the battle between my hormones and my feminism, my feminism had always won out. But, I confess, it was close sometimes.

I scanned Twitter for a few minutes, something I'd neglected in the previous day or so. There were still hundreds of new followers piling up each day. The EofE Twitter stream was still growing. One tweet in particular caught my eye before I shut down my laptop for the night. It was from Candace Sharpe's personal account:

"Haven't given up on having *Eve of Equality* blogger on show. We still don't know who she is. But we're relentless. Stay tuned. #Stilltrying"

I took a shower and crawled into bed. Just as I turned out my light, a text bonged in my phone.

"Please stop texting me. I know who you are. We are not having dinner on Friday night. You betrayed me. You put me in a very difficult position. You used me to gain information about my client for your own benefit. You made me look stupid in front of my client and my employers. Don't try to contact me again."

Against all hope, and all logic, I checked the number to see if perhaps it might not be from Megan. Yeah, right. I didn't respond. I didn't try to contact her again. I'm generally pretty good at following instructions when they're as explicit as hers were. I rolled over, exhausted, and then lay awake for the next five hours.

CHAPTER 14

I'd never flown into Reagan National Airport before. For a few moments, as we were descending, it felt like we were going to land in the middle of downtown Washington. Then, just as we were about to touch down, it felt like we were going to belly-flop in the middle of the Potomac River. Mercifully, we landed where we were supposed to, right on the runway. If I'd arrived at the larger and busier Dulles Airport, it would have taken quite a while to make my way into the city. But Reagan Airport, the old Washington National Airport, is just three miles from downtown DC. Even with the tighter security imposed at an airport so close to the White House, I was still in a cab and on my way to my meeting in under twenty-five minutes from landing. Not bad.

My destination was on H Street NW, not that far from the White House and the National Mall. The National Organization for Women (NOW) was created in 1966 over the course of two seminal meetings in Washington, DC. The forty-nine women and men – the vast majority were women – who attended those two gatherings, including the groundbreaking author of *The Feminine Mystique*, Betty Friedan, are considered the founders of the organization. Over the years, NOW has emerged as the leading voice for women in America. I was about to meet with the president of NOW, that is, if I didn't throw up in the back of the cab from the squadron of butterflies locked in aerial mixed martial arts combat in my stomach.

NOW was headquartered in a rather nondescript, ten-storey building with architecture best forgotten from the middle of the last century. Save for a couple of modest architectural grace notes around the front entrance, and I do mean modest, and just two, the most generous physical description one could offer before entering the realm of hyperbole and exaggeration was "concrete quadrilateral." I paid the driver and stepped out, my breakfast still where it belonged, but my butterflies agitating for eviction if not ejection.

I was right on time as I stepped into the elevator and punched the button for the third floor. The receptionist looked up as I entered suite 300.

"Good morning. May I help you?"

"Um, yes, thanks. I believe I have a meeting with Shelley Hunter at 11:30."

"You must be Everett Kane," she said after consulting her computer screen.

"I am, indeed."

"I'll take you down to her office."

I followed her through a massive array of open-concept cubicles, bordered by offices along the windows. It was a seriously hopping and happening place. It would have been obvious to even the most cynical observer that there was a lot of work going on in that office. Made sense. There was a lot of work to do.

Her office door was open at the far end of the third floor. The receptionist stuck in her head.

"Your 11:30 is here. Everett Kane?"

"Thank you, Susan," the voice said. "Come on in, Mr. Kane."

I nodded thanks to Susan as she made her way back to the front, and I walked into the corner suite. Shelley Hunter had been head of NOW for the preceding five years. A lawyer by training, she is widely considered to be brilliant, tough, relentless, and an outstanding communicator when protecting, pursuing, and promoting equal rights for women. She wore a grey business suit, the kind with pants, and an open-necked white shirt. She had shortish, sandy-coloured hair and classy black-framed glasses that deepened her intellectual vibe. She wore a slight smile, almost as if she was not sure what to make of all of this – probably because she was not sure what to make of all of this.

"Hi, I'm Everett Kane. An honour to meet you, and very good of you to see me on such short notice," I began.

"Shelley Hunter. My pleasure. I'm glad I was in town. I've been on the road a bit lately. Anyway, you come with the blessings of Beverley Tanner, one of my favourite forebears, one of my heroes. I'm sorry her health is a little fragile."

"Yes, but her spirit and mind are as vibrant as ever. I feel very fortunate to have met her, and now to count her among my friends. In a way, we've become co-conspirators in a little initiative of mine."

"Please, have a seat," she said, waving me into a chair before her large desk. "Coffee? Water?"

"Neither, thanks. I'm fine."

"Well, now that we're settled, how can I help you?"

"Did Beverley give you any indication as to what I wanted to see you about?" I asked, even though I knew the answer.

"None. Despite my best efforts to pry it out of her, she was insistent that you were the only one to enlighten me. So I have no idea what this is all about, just that someone I respect greatly has asked that I meet with you."

"That's what I thought. Okay, then. Well, here goes," I said, taking in and then releasing a big breath. "Are you familiar with a relatively new feminist blog known as *Eve of Equality*?"

"Are you kidding? I think there are very few feminists in the world with high-speed Internet connections who do not know about that particular blog. I read it religiously. It's great stuff."

Then she seemed to catch herself.

"Wait. Are you about to tell me that Beverley Tanner is the author of that blog? It makes perfect sense now."

She looked up and shook her head as if she should have guessed long ago.

"Um, no, that's not it. What I was about to tell you is something slightly more difficult to believe. I was about to say that . . . okay, here we go . . . that, um, I am actually the author of the blog. I guess you could say that *Eve of Equality* is short for *Everett of Equality*," I said, letting it hang there for a moment, between us. I wanted to give her a chance to mull it over. She didn't mull for long.

"Look, Mr. Kane, you're the fourth person this week and the second man to claim to be the author of the *Eve of Equality* blog."

"You're kidding? Others have come forward? That's outrageous. I'm offended. I'm sure Beverley would be offended, too. I can assure you that while others may claim to have written those posts, I'm the only one who has."

"Well, it sure helps that you've arrived here bearing Bev Tanner's stamp of approval, but I'm afraid I can't just accept your word on it, especially when she said nothing to me about the blog."

"Okay. I get that. I can understand your skepticism, given that I'm, you know, a man, and all. And that, as a species, we do have some baggage when it comes to equality issues."

"A little baggage, yes," she replied.

"Right. I know it seems a little far-fetched. But bear with me and I'll try to make my case. Would you mind if I used your computer for just a moment?" I asked. "You can watch everything I do."

She thought about it for a moment and then rotated her laptop so I could reach it, but we both could still see it. I immediately called up the blog and logged into the back end of WordPress, revealing all the posts and the comment moderation mechanism.

"Okay. So you've gotten into the blog. How do I know you haven't just hacked your way in? It's happened before. Other sites have been compromised. Maybe you're an ace hacker?"

"Believe me, I'm not nearly geeky enough to hack into anything more complicated than a wet paper bag. Maybe this will help."

I proceeded to log into the EofE Gmail account and Twitter stream. It was unlikely that I could have hacked into all of these relatively secure platforms. Then I moved back into WordPress and showed her the draft post waiting to be finished and posted. I turned the screen toward her and described the draft post in considerable detail, including phrasing I could remember as I'd agonized over portions of it.

She sat looking at the screen, nodding her head slowly. The pause between us lengthened almost to the point of discomfort.

"Okay, I'm starting to feel more comfortable that you are who you say you are, but I'm not sure we're quite there yet. Where did this all start and what else can you do to establish your feminist bona fides?"

"Well, it started at university in Ontario. I'm Canadian. Well, I have dual citizenship. It started when I was active in the national student movement. As you probably know, there's a strong feminist strand in the student movement."

I thought for a moment, and it paid off. I then turned back to her keyboard and typed in the URL for the *Globe and Mail* archives.

"As I'm sure you know, this is Canada's national newspaper," I said as I navigated through the archives, using the site's search engine and filters.

I soon found what I was looking for and clicked on it. A photo opened on the screen from an International Women's Day rally on Parliament Hill in Ottawa from all those years ago when I'd been heavily involved with the Canadian Federation of Students. There I was, on the riser, in front of the microphone, my fist in the air, my mouth open in the midst of exhorting my brothers and sisters. I was surrounded by fellow activists, all of them women.

"There I am at the annual Women's Day demo calling out the government on reproductive rights."

"It sure looks like you," she said.

"I'm glad you think so. I was afraid you'd ask me to recreate that demented expression on my face to convince you. It's really not a good look."

"I know that look. I've been to my fair share of demos. Just looks like passion, to me," she said, looking from the photo, to me, and then back again. "You haven't changed that much."

"Well, it wasn't all that long ago."

I then opened a new window and worked Google to pull up a few more photos and an article about me in the *Sudbury Star* from around the same time. It was a story about a women's issues workshop for men I had just led at Laurentian University. The guy in the photo did not have his face scrunched up in rage, so it looked quite a bit like me, only younger. I think Shelley was impressed. But I had one more card to play.

I opened my Google Adsense account on her laptop and scrolled through to my revenue summary page for the *Eve of Equality* blog. Again, only the blog owner could gain access to this very secure site.

"Because the blog has been so popular, thanks largely to Candace Sharpe's lightning strike, I'm earning more money from online ads than I've ever earned as a freelance writer." I moved the cursor so that it was directly under the big dollar amount paid out for the previous month.

"You might have seen my post a while back when I announced there would be a modest level of advertising on the EofE site to help offset the not inconsiderable and still-growing hosting fees."

"I do remember that. And I also remember what else was written in that post," she noted.

"Right. You mean my pledge to donate half the Google Adsense revenue to NOW."

She nodded. I reached into my pocket, pulled out my wallet, and extracted a cheque I'd already written for the first month's donation. It was not a small cheque. I handed it to her.

"I didn't have time to certify the cheque," I explained. "I don't even have a bank down here in the U.S. yet, so it's on my Canadian account. But if you deposit it, I guarantee the cheque will clear."

"Holy Hannah," she gasped. "Well, I must say, this is very generous, but. . ."

"Ms. Hunter. . ."

"Shelley, please," she said.

"Shelley, this contribution and the donations I've pledged in the future are not tied to any help you may be able to offer after I explain my current dilemma. If nothing comes of our conversation this morning, the cheques will still arrive for however long the blog continues to generate ad revenue."

"Again, that's very generous," she said. "Okay, so let's assume that I now believe I'm sitting in front of the youngish man who just happens to be the anonymous creator of one of the most popular feminist blogs on earth – and I'd say I'm feeling pretty secure about that now, based on what you've shown me – just what exactly is your so-called dilemma, and how can we help? As you can imagine, we'd sure like you to continue blogging. We don't come across many men holding your views, let alone promoting them so effectively to such a large audience."

I told her my tale of woe. I spoke for the next nineteen minutes straight, without interruption. I was getting better at telling the story. I took her through the whole thing, from the time I'd arrived in Orlando to help with Dad's recovery, right up to that moment sitting in her corner office at NOW. I covered it all. I left nothing out. I probably told her far more than I needed to, including my short-lived relationship – if you could call it that – with

Megan Cook. I spilled everything. It felt quite cathartic to have the whole adventure rush from me like a whitewater torrent, even if it was before a complete stranger.

We sat in silence for a few seconds again when I'd finally stopped talking. She was shaking her head slowly as she processed my little odyssey.

"Mr. Kane. . ."

"Everett, please. My father is Mr. Kane, and it doesn't even suit him."

"Everett, I'm flabbergasted. I don't know what to say. That is one extraordinary story. Did you call the police?"

"I thought about it. I even reached for the phone a few times. But in the end, it just felt like it would degenerate into a simple case of my word against Bennington's. And I didn't think that would get me very far."

"Probably not," she agreed. "Tell me again why it's so important for you to remain anonymous as the blog's author?"

"Well, it might be a moot point now, but I just don't think it's right for a man to be at the pointy end of the women's movement. It's not a man's place."

"Why? We need men on board if we're ever going to achieve *real* equality and not just *legislated* equality."

"Yes, I know. That's what Beverley says, too. But men run everything else in the world. That's the whole problem. Men should not have a prominent role in the women's movement. It should always only be supportive, ancillary, secondary. Besides, when it

345

comes out that a man is – that I am – the Eve in *Eve of Equality*, the driving message in the blog posts will be lost."

"Maybe for a short time. But that can be managed. And while I understand your point about a man on the front lines of the women's movement – believe me, I do – I think that can be managed, too. When it becomes known that you write the blog, you could shift your focus to that all-important space where men and the women's movement come together – and they must come together. You can then write freely as a man committed to gender equality, concentrating on what supportive men can do to serve the cause. Do you understand what I'm saying?"

"You mean I could shift gears on the blog to embrace my membership in the male species, begin to write for men, but still focus on gender equality."

"Precisely. So there's no longer any masquerade, pretence or obfuscation. Then it's all above board, but still staunchly feminist."

I turned this over in my mind. It might just resolve my central concern, provided we survived the initial revelation and transition.

"But I now seem to have tens of thousands, even hundreds of thousands, of subscribers to the blog, and I suspect that all but a handful are women. Won't they feel betrayed, or at least offended, when they discover the truth? Won't a lot of them just stop reading?" I asked.

"Some might. But if we, and I mean *we*, handle it all skillfully and sensitively, I bet your readers would understand, and many would stay on board."

"Hmmmm. I just wish I knew how this was all going to play out," I sighed.

Shelley seemed to be getting into it now. She was leaning forward, moving her hands about as she spoke, a plan formulating.

"Everett, this is a tremendous communications opportunity. There's still plenty of media speculation about who is behind your blog. We have the chance here to control the message and turn this into a big win-win."

"That's just what Beverley told me you'd say,," I admitted. "But how?"

"Look, if we take Mason Bennington at his word, one way or another, in the next few days, you are going to be outed as the author of the *Eve of Equality* blog. Your cover will be blown, right?"

"Right. I guess."

"Then let's take the initiative away from him. Let's not put him in charge of how that happens."

Shelley Hunter's strategy was still in its formative stages as she laid it out for me. It evolved as we kicked it around. We refined it. With my blessing, she called in her communications director, Leslie Bandler, and some of her team to help with the logistics. A phone call was made to the NOW research team. Fifteen minutes later, a young woman stuck her head in the door and handed Leslie a couple of pages. She scanned them before speaking.

"Okay, the media speculation about the identity of the blogger behind *Eve of Equality* has been gathering strength for the last three weeks, and it's not going away. It's not front page, but it's still quite prominent. This analysis suggests that Candace Sharpe has been the most significant driver, not just on her program, but through all her social media channels, as well. Stories speculating about who the anonymous blogger might be have appeared in seven major print dailies, on twenty-six radio stations, on twenty-one regional TV stations, and on four national TV network news or talk shows, including *Good Morning America* and *The Today Show*. Finally, there's considerable speculation on Facebook and Twitter as to the identity of the EofE blogger. There's even a hashtag, #WhoisEofE?"

Wow. I'd seen a few stories when grazing on the Internet, but I was not aware that so many mainstream media outlets were interested in this, interested in me. It seemed that the mystery behind who writes the blog might be a more important factor in the media's fascination with the blog than the posts themselves. That was fine with me, as long as it pushed people to the site.

After the others had left to put the wheels in motion, I turned to Shelley.

"Can I just ask, why are you doing this? You could have just sent me on my way. What's in it for you?"

"Well, it's not unadulterated altruism, if that's what you mean," she replied. "Beyond the fact that I do happen to think this is good for NOW, and it's definitely good for the cause, I also have a longer-term agenda and there's an idea crystallizing in my frazzled brain. Besides, linking NOW with a hugely popular feminist blog will help our numbers, too. Oh yeah, and you're Bev Tanner's friend."

I nodded. She didn't offer any more by way of explanation and I didn't push it.

By 4 p.m., the plan was in place. We all had our marching orders. We all knew what we were doing. As a group, we agreed that it was already too late to do anything that day. Better to keep our powder dry until tomorrow morning. We'd execute the strategy then. The NOW communications team would need to burn at least a little midnight oil, but it would all get done. They'd been there before and knew what they were doing. Finally, Shelley and I discussed what I planned to say the next day, and we both took advice from NOW's in-house attorney to make sure our words wouldn't get us into any legal hot water. Mason Bennington was born to be litigious. I also asked the lawyer to review the blog post I'd already written and was poised to post the next day.

I realized that the plan we'd developed was pretty close to the one Beverley had forecast. And she was right. Shelley was an unstoppable force.

———

I managed to find a room at the Renaissance on 9th Street NW, not too far away from NOW. After an early steak in the restaurant, I sprawled on the bed, reached for the phone, and called my dad.

"Dad, it's Ev."

"Son! Hang on. Your mother's here, too. I'm going to put you on the speaker if I can figure out how to do th—"

I called back.

"Hi, Dad. I'm back."

"Yeah, sorry about that. I got it this ti—"

I called back.

I heard the audio change as he somehow managed to switch to speaker-phone mode.

"Sorry about that," Dad said. "Are you still there?"

"I'm here."

"Hi, honey. I'm here, too."

"Hi, Mom."

"How was Washington?"

"Well, no need for the past tense, I'm still here and will be until tomorrow."

"Is that good news?" Mom asked.

"We're going to find out tomorrow," I said. "How's everything in Orlando?"

"Everything is just peachy," Dad said. "In fact, we got some news of our own, today. Look's like they're springing me on Saturday. I'm getting out of this joint. I'm going home."

"Hey! Congratulations, Dad. That's great news!"

"Yeah, well, try telling that to Kenny Chevy," Mom piped up. "He's been moping around since the news broke this morning."

"That's no different from how Kenny acts every day, Mom," I said.

"Yeah, well, he's dialed it down another notch, now," Mom explained. "He's going to miss your father. No one else knows enough about cars to go anywhere near him. It's going to be ugly when your father moves out."

"What about Beverley? Is she around?"

"She turned in early," Dad replied. "She hasn't been feeling too shit hot today. I think she might be coming down with something."

"She still has her sense of humour, though," Mom noted. "She had your father on the ropes earlier tonight. It was hilarious. I like that old bird."

"That's what she does. As her books says, she's the funny one," I said. "Is everything okay at the company, Mom? You haven't seemed quite as frenetic these days. And I haven't seen the ever-efficient Nathan around much either. Is everything cool?"

"The company is just fine. We're on track. The digging has started. That's what's been so consuming. Now that the shovels are in the ground, we just have to build the damn thing," Mom said. "Oh, and I turned Nathan in for a newer model. Barclay, I think it is, starts next week."

We chatted for a few more minutes. I told Mom and Dad what we had planned for the next day. Then Dad ended the call as the dinner gong sounded in the background. He hates to miss dinner.

I was just lying there thinking about what was about to go down in the morning when my cellphone rang.

"Hello?"

"Young Everett, it's Beverley."

"Hi, Beverley. I was going to call you, but Dad said you'd gone to bed early, not feeling well. Are you okay?"

"I'm fine. Just a little tired, and just a touch out of sorts. But I wanted an update. Did you see Shelley?"

"Sure did. And she's everything you said she was."

"And did she propose what I thought she'd propose?"

"Yep. Pretty close. We're on tomorrow morning at ten."

"Perfect. Early enough to get the noon newscasts, right?" she asked.

"Absolutely."

"And how do you feel?"

"Strangely serene. It's like the grown-ups have taken over and if I do my part without passing out, all will be well."

"Good," she replied. "And don't give a thought to Mason Bennington. I think what you're doing tomorrow will put you out of his reach. The world will be watching."

"I hope you're right. But I think I'm going to have to move out of my apartment anyway, on principle, much as I like it."

"Oh, by the way, I should be finished my little guest post for the blog later tonight or in the morning. I'll send it to you then."

"Hey, that's great! You decided to write it. I'm thrilled. Readers will be thrilled, too, I know."

"You might wait till you read it before elevating expectations to an unreasonably high level."

"No need. I already know."

———

Media started showing up at 9:30, a full half-hour before show time. That was a good sign. The NOW media relations team had been burning up the phone lines since 8 a.m., driving attendance. It seemed to be working. The big sprawling NOW boardroom had been turned into a media briefing room. The board table had been moved out, and rows of chairs moved in. Risers were placed at both ends of the room. At the front, a skirted table was positioned on the risers with two chairs and two microphones. Behind the table, mounted on the wall was a very large high-definition TV monitor bearing the NOW logo, the date, and the start time of the media briefing. In the best of all worlds, the risers at the rear of the room would soon be occupied by videographers from various news organizations. I wandered around with not much to do. I had already rehearsed what I was going to say in front of my hotel bathroom mirror. None of the reporters filing in, as 10 a.m. approached, paid me any attention. No one knew who I was.

I leaned against the wall off to the side but toward the front of the room. I was dressed in what I guess is called business casual. I wore black pants, black shoes, a dark blue button-down-collared dress shirt, and a dark blue blazer/sports jacket. I thought I wouldn't look out of place in a Madison Avenue advertising agency. By 9:55, there were twelve reporters in their seats, and five cameras were stationed on the riser along the back of the room. I noticed that one of the cameras was from the *Candace* show. The reporters were chatting with one another, wondering why they were there. The media advisory had not been explicit about the story, but counted on a sense of mystery to enhance the draw. It seemed to have worked.

Shelley walked into the room, nodded once at me, and made her way to the table at the front. Her name and title appeared on the TV monitor. As she sat down with no notes or paperwork of any kind, the room fell silent.

"Good morning, ladies and gentlemen. Thank you for coming in response to an invitation that I know was not just short on notice, but short on details, too. For those of you who might not know, I'm Shelley Hunter, president of the National Organization for Women.

"As you might imagine, we are very interested in any new developments that bear on the fight for gender equality in this country. We're interested when issues arise that set the movement back, like the growing popularity of Mason Bennington's chain of XY clubs that simply exploit women in a more exclusive and expensive setting. And of course, we're excited when something new breaks on the scene that helps advance the cause of women's equality. For instance, in the last several weeks, an anonymous blog, *Eve of Equality*, has captured the attention and the minds of hundreds of thousands of readers around the world. Candace Sharpe promoted the blog on her show, and the media and the Internet took care of the rest."

The screen behind Shelley now featured the home page of the EofE blog.

"This morning, after long and careful consideration, the anonymous writer behind *Eve of Equality*, for reasons that will be shared shortly, has decided to come forward."

Now that Shelley was too far down the road to turn back, I used my cellphone to publish the rather incendiary blog post I'd finalized the day before. There was no way back now.

"I'm pleased now to introduce the gifted writer, thoughtful advocate, and committed feminist who created and writes the *Eve of Equality* blog, Mr. Everett Kane."

Because it was a media briefing, there was no applause that you might expect to hear after such an introduction. Reporters generally don't clap. With the room so quiet, it was much easier to hear the sudden intake of breath from the reporters, when she said my rather gender-specific name. It wasn't Kelly, or Kerry, or Alex, or Avery, you know, where it could go either way. No. It was Everett. I pushed myself off the wall where I'd been leaning, made my way to the front table, shook hands with Shelley, and sat down next to her. I didn't fall, trip, burp, or toss my cookies on the way up. My hair looked okay. Nothing was hanging out of my nose – at least not that anyone mentioned. So I managed to plant my ass in the chair at the front of the room without embarrassing myself, though there was still plenty of time left for that. I was nervous – very nervous – yet, at the same time, I also felt a certain calm fall upon me like a blanket. I took a deep breath as I looked out at the assembled journalists. I had no notes but had rehearsed what I wanted to say about thirty-six times that morning until it sounded spontaneous, conversational, even casual.

"Good morning. I'm Everett Kane. I created the *Eve of Equality* blog several weeks ago and have written every word in every post. My goal with the blog was simply to make a modest contribution to the ongoing fight for gender equality, something I've been interested in since my feminist awakening many years ago in the national student movement. I also decided the blog would be anonymous. I didn't think a man credibly could, or publicly should, be in the vanguard of the women's movement. It just didn't seem right to me. But I did believe there was room in the online world for a feminist blog that offered real substance, reason, and advocacy, but was leavened with humour. And that's what I've tried to write. We don't seem to appreciate the power of humour in social movements, and I wanted to explore that. The blog was shaped by many conversations I had with the feminist icon Beverley Tanner, whom I was blessed to meet and come to know recently. She remains very funny and very committed to the cause.

"While many readers likely assumed I was a woman, I think a close reading of the blog will reveal that I did not intentionally mislead or misdirect in my writing. I just never commented on my own gender. I hope those who might feel that I was not entirely honest will appreciate the dilemma I faced when my humble little blog suddenly became a very big deal.

"The way I see it, we're here this morning for two reasons. Firstly, Candace Sharpe somehow stumbled on my blog and promoted it on her talk show. This changed my life in an instant, driving hundreds of thousands of visitors to *Eve of Equality*, many of whom then subscribed and kept coming back. Overnight, it became one of the most popular feminist sites on the Internet. Secondly, we're here because of a post I wrote early on about Mason Bennington and his chain of high-end 'gentlemen's clubs' known simply as XY. Mr. Bennington didn't like what I'd written and launched an all-out effort to identify the writer behind the *Eve of Equality* blog. In keeping with Mason Bennington's business practices, he relied on money and muscle, a potent and proven combination, to discover that I was the creator of the blog and the author of the particular post he really didn't like.

"Just before sitting down in this chair, I posted a more detailed overview of my dealings with Mason Bennington. I need to be careful about what I say, but I'm here today in response to what any fair-minded observer would call threats, perhaps even blackmail.

"I did not want my identity as the creator of the *Eve of Equality* blog to be revealed, and I worked very hard to protect my anonymity. Unfortunately, with Mr. Bennington threatening to blow my cover, control over that secret was no longer in my hands alone. So here we are. Despite what has happened, I intend to continue to write the blog, though for obvious reasons, the focus will shift to the critical role enlightened men must play in the continuing fight for gender equality. I strongly support NOW's efforts and hope that we can work together more in the future.

"Finally, my sincere thanks to Shelley Hunter and the great staff here at NOW for helping me through this."

I sat back from the microphone.

"Thank you, Everett," Shelley said. "And now we'll open the floor for questions."

Leslie Bandler walked to the podium beside the table at the front of the room to manage the Q and A, directing questions as appropriate to Shelley or to me. It all worked quite well.

"Judy Franklin, CNN. Everett, are you saying that Mason Bennington found out you were the writer behind the blog?"

"Yes. That's exactly what I'm saying. He threatened to reveal that I was the blogger behind *Eve of Equality*, unless I wrote a post retracting my earlier essay about him and singing his praises. I wasn't prepared to do that but believed he would make good on his threat. So it seemed the news was going to get out, one way or another. We decided to preempt him and announce it this morning."

"Won't he just deny your allegations? Isn't it just your word against his?"

"He might deny it, but what he doesn't know, at least until now, is that I have an audio recording of our confrontation where he threatened me," I said, holding up my cellphone.

"Can we hear it?" another reporter asked.

"I'm afraid I cannot share it publicly. But for my own security, there are multiple copies of the MP3 file, including one here at NOW. I'm not expecting to hear from Mason Bennington again, and I certainly hope not to. But having this audio recording gives me some protection, if I ever need it."

"Connie Abrahams, ABC News. Are you scared? Bennington has a well-earned reputation as someone you don't want to mess with."

"Scared might not quite capture it fully. I'd describe it as a few white knuckles short of terrified. But I think this is the right thing to do under the circumstances. It's not comfortable. But we think it's the right call at the right time."

"Tom Grinaldi, NPR News. What's a young man doing fighting for feminism? It seems a little odd, and a little, I don't know, counter to your own interests, doesn't it?"

"I don't see it that way. I think we'll all benefit as a society when equality is finally achieved. There were plenty of white folks involved in the civil rights movement. There are plenty of straight people fighting for gay marriages. These are movements that can only succeed if more than the constituency directly affected get engaged. I don't think it's odd at all to want women to have the same rights and opportunities as men."

"Follow-up, please," the NPR reporter said. "What has all this cost you? And I don't mean financially."

"I try not to think too much about the costs. Social movements all require sacrifices. But remember, I'm a charter member of society's most privileged demographic. I'm a white man. And for my entire life so far, I've enjoyed all the benefits that naturally accrue to white men. So I don't think I've given up much to write my anonymous feminist essays. I do regret that the nature of the *Eve of Equality* blog meant that I couldn't be quite as forthcoming about it with, um, certain friends as I would like to have been. So I guess there's been a minor cost associated with that. But really, my paltry challenges are dwarfed by the obstacles women face in this country, and in every other country, day in and day out."

I paused.

"Okay, I know that sounded a little preachy. But strange as it may seem, that's actually how I feel about it all. I can't really help it."

It went on like this for quite a while. Shelley bailed me out a few times and kept the session moving. By 10:45 all the journalists had left so they could file their stories. I followed Shelley back into her office. She sat on the couch and I dropped into a chair across from her.

"I thought that went rather well," she said.

"Well, my standards are quite low right now. I'd consider anything better than falling on my face and responding to reporters' questions in monosyllabic grunts as success. So I'm quite pleased with how it all unfolded."

"You did well for someone who isn't used to this kind of thing," she said. "I think the coverage will be positive and plentiful. I also think you need to be careful when you get back to Orlando. I don't think Mason Bennington will be very happy with you. I'm going to phone a friend in Orlando and call in a favour or two, that might help keep you safe."

"I'm not sure what that really means, but I'm grateful. I'm very much in favour of being safe."

"Now that the newser is over, I want to plant a seed. Something for you to think about."

I nodded but said nothing.

"We've been wrestling for years with how to bring men into the movement in a thoughtful and productive way. We've been searching for a Director of Men's Programs for about six months now and have come up empty. I think we need to go down this path if NOW is to remain relevant."

"I like the idea of integrating men's programming into the work of NOW, provided it's always in the service of gender equality and not just a way to make men feel better about the power they'll – er – we'll be losing," I replied.

"My, you are certainly earnest about all of this."

"Kind of you to say, but 'earnest' isn't the adjective I usually hear."

"I like 'earnest.' I like it a lot," she said. "So would you be interested in applying for the role here at NOW, the Director of Men's Programs position?"

CHAPTER 15

As Shelley had predicted, the coverage was positive and plentiful. It started with several stories on the noon newscasts, was sustained all afternoon by frequent radio hits and plenty of online pieces, and finished strong with multiple supper hour and nightly newscast segments. I still didn't know why it was considered news. Clearly it was a relatively slow news day. If the pregnant giraffe at the Washington Zoo had given birth that day, I doubt we'd have had any local coverage at all. But what do I know?

Mason Bennington was almost certainly inundated with interview requests but seemed to have dropped off the face of the earth. Not a peep from him was heard. Most of the stories simply noted that he did not respond to interview requests or was unavailable for comment. The EofE blog, Twitter stream, and Gmail account were flooded with supportive messages. A few comments did arrive suggesting I'd hoodwinked my audience by not owning up to the male genitalia I'd carried around with me for my entire life. But the negative shots were minuscule in number relative to the positive reactions.

After lunch with Shelley at a small Italian restaurant nearby, where she talked a lot about the Men's Programs position, I returned to the NOW offices to say thanks and goodbye to the team who made the media briefing happen on such short notice. Then I hopped in a cab and headed back to the airport for my 5:30 flight. Unfortunately, a front of thunderstorms rolled in just as we were taxiing out to our runway. The pilot was trying to get off the ground before the lightning started striking the ground. She wasn't quite successful. So we taxied back to the gate and sat for three hours as the rain pelted the plane. Several people had recognized me in the airport from the media coverage but, thankfully, no one on the plane gave me a second glance.

It was nearly midnight when I finally made it back to the apartment. As I approached the building, I saw a police officer standing near my separate entrance. A cruiser was parked not too far away. That was strange. I saw no yellow tape cordoning off the area, so I figured it wasn't too serious. The nightly community rally was underway, but its intensity and energy seemed to have waned. Very few cars were pulling up to the front doors of XY.

"Is everything all right, officer?" I asked as I slipped my key into the front door.

"Are you Everett Kane?"

"I am. Why?"

"I've been asked to secure your apartment and stay close for the next little while."

"Really? You're kidding. How come?"

"I don't really know the full story, but I've been led to believe you made somebody very angry. I'm just here to make sure you stay safe."

"But how did you know about it? Who gave the order?" I asked.

"My lieutenant got a call from a buddy on the force in DC. And here I am."

"Wow. I guess it pays to have friends in the nation's capital."

"You got that right," the young officer said. "Why don't I go upstairs with you just to make sure everything is how it's supposed to be? Okay?"

"That would be great," I replied. "Thanks."

Ten minutes later, he was back down on the street patrolling a tight circuit that circumnavigated the building. We'd uncovered nothing unusual in the apartment. It was all just as I'd left it, including a few stray corn flakes on the floor. I wasn't sure how long I'd have personal police protection, but it did kind of make me feel like a big deal.

I sat down on my couch. I was wiped. Sitting in economy class of a commuter aircraft for three hours before even taking off doesn't sound like an enervating experience, but somehow it was. Still on the couch, I had closed my eyes when I heard footsteps hustling up the fire escape. I wondered if it might be my Orlando Police Department bodyguard again. The footfalls stopped as the banging on my kitchen door started. I don't know why I wasn't nervous, but I wasn't.

I opened the door, and there stood Shawna Hawkins dressed – some might say, undressed – as Sheena, Queen of the Jungle, and behind her the very large Lewis Small. Shawna came through the door first like a runaway train, locked me in a bear hug, and started dancing me around the kitchen.

"I can't believe you write *Eve of Equality*. I just can't reconcile it all in my brain. It's been my new favourite blog for six weeks now! And you live right here!" she gushed, rocking me back and forth. "When I'm dancing tonight, I'll be thinking, I'm just a pole apart from an A-list feminist blogger! It's just so awesome."

She was big and strong. If she wanted to keep hold of me and swing me around like a rag doll, she could do it . . . so she did. She eventually slowed the rocking and let me go just before I began to think about the benefits of Gravol. Through all of this, Lewis just leaned on the kitchen door and smiled. I know he always smiles anyway, but there were a few more watts in his grin that night. We then just stood there beaming at one another.

"No wonder Batshit Bennington was so pissed. You live right above the club! What are the odds?" she asked rhetorically. "Lewis brought me up to speed on your visit with the little man a few days ago. Isn't Lewis just the bomb with a blush brush? The man's an artist, a real artist."

"Come on. With the symmetry in your face, a blind man with no arms could make you look good every night," Lewis said.

"No, I have to agree with Shawna. You are a make-up maestro, Lewis," I said. "I parked in the handicapped spot at the airport just by showing off my cosmetic rib contusions."

"Really? You did that?" Lewis asked.

"Well, no. But I could have. I'm sure I could have," I replied, and then opened the fridge. "Who wants a beer?"

"No thanks," they answered in unison.

"Don't mind if I do," I said to myself as I grabbed one and twisted off the cap.

I took a long haul on the bottle before turning to Lewis.

"Any word from Mr. B as to what his next steps might be? You know which extremity of mine he plans to break first?" I asked. "Do I need to enter the witness protection program?"

"I think you're safe for a little while," Lewis replied. "We haven't seen him or heard from him in a few days."

"We think he might be busy with his accountants, lawyers, and business advisors about this place," Shawna added. "The numbers are apparently way down and still heading south. The crowds are smaller each night. I'm trying not to take it personally."

"You think it's the demonstrators out front?" I asked, tipping my head toward my living room window.

"Bingo. Them and their cameras," Lewis said. "They've now mounted them permanently on private property across the street. We can't do squat about them. It's not good."

"Well, I no longer care," Shawna said. "I'm out of here in a couple weeks for good. It's dissertation time and then I'm hanging up my dancing shoes for the bright lights of academe."

"Good for you, Shawna," I said. "I'd take a women's studies class from you anytime."

"Are you kidding? As soon as I land a gig in some tiny Midwestern college, I'll be calling up my buddy – you know, the creator of the best feminist blog on the web – and asking you to guest lecture in my class. I'm not shittin' you on that. I'm serious!"

"And I'll be there. Just tell me when and where, and I'll be there."

"Thanks, Ev."

I looked at Lewis and an idea crash landed in my mind, out of the blue. I suppose it should have come sooner, but I'd been a little cerebrally compromised the last few days.

"Lewis, I need a favour that I think might be in our mutual interest," I said.

"Lay it on me."

"I'd like to profile you in an upcoming issue of *Make-Up Artist* magazine. And we'll need to move quickly on it."

"What are you on about, Ever-man? What profile?"

"I owe the mag a biographical profile of a leading make-up artist. The guy I was supposed to be covering won't return my calls, and I'm tired of trying to nail him down. You're one of the most talented cosmetics czars I've ever seen. So let me put you in the magazine. We don't have to say you work at XY. We'll just say you're a much-sought-after freelance artist. We'll throw in some great shots of Shawna and maybe the twins, you know, before they do what they do, and it'll be great! It might even get you some new gigs on the side."

"What about Mr. B?" he asked.

"I don't think his make-up skills warrant a major magazine profile. I'd rather write a piece on you."

"I mean I'd rather not have the big man find out about my make-up moonlighting. You know?"

"Come on, Lewis," said Sheena, I mean Shawna. "Do you really think Mason Bennington is ever going to come into contact with *Make-Up Artist* magazine? I'm not even sure he can read. Come on, do it!"

They both left a few minutes later after we'd set up a time for me to interview Lewis. I was quite pleased with this inspired solution to a problem I'd been ignoring for far too long.

———————

In the morning, I finally got around to checking my email. I should have checked sooner. With my little secret now well and truly out there, my inbox was under siege. I scanned and then ignored almost every email except for the one from Beverley Tanner. It had arrived the day before, while I'd been lounging on the tarmac in DC with my ass growing numb.

Young Everett,

You are now a star! And I guess I can't keep you to myself any longer. I can't believe the media coverage the story has spawned already and it's only the afternoon. This is just the beginning. I'm glad Shelley stepped up, as I thought she would. Congratulations on such a wonderful coming-out party!

I'm very proud of you and what you've accomplished. The cause is so well served by you and your glorious creation. Speaking of the blog, I've attached my attempt at a so-called guest post. Writing a short and punchy piece that still tells a story, and makes a point, was harder than I thought. Feel free to have your way with it.

I'm tickled about all of this and that you'll finally be getting the recognition you deserve. The movement faces as many challenges now as we did in the very beginning. You can help. So write on, young Everett. Write on.

Yours in equality,
Bev

I had a quick scan of her post. It was wonderful, witty, thoughtful, and smart, and imbued with a sense of hope and optimism. It nicely captured not just what Beverley believed, but who she was. I thought it was perfect.

———

It was close to noon by the time I arrived. Something wasn't right. I knew it as soon as I walked into the hospital. I could feel it. It was quiet in the main corridor. Too quiet. Yolanda was not at her post. I walked into Dad's room and found him sitting fully dressed in the chair next to the window. Mom was in the chair next to him, holding his hand. Dad didn't look good. Neither of them did.

"What's wrong?" I asked. "What's happened?"

Dad slowly tilted his head to look up at me.

"She checked out, son. I'm sorry," he said.

"Who checked out?"

"Beverley."

"She checked out? That's weird," I replied. "She thought she'd be here for at least a couple more months."

Mom shook her head and looked down.

"No, son. Listen, I mean the big check out," Dad explained.

I sat down on the bed. I needed to sit down on the bed.

"You mean she's gone? She died?"

Dad just nodded.

"When? How? Where?" I asked. "What . . . what happened?"

"Yolanda found her this morning, in bed. She must have passed in the night, in her sleep," Mom said. "I'm so sorry, Ev. Everyone is shocked."

"I opened an email from her just this morning. She wrote a guest post for the blog. How did this happen?"

"Yolanda said it was probably a massive stroke," Mom said. "She likely never felt a thing."

"The one she was always joking about," I replied. "She was always 'waiting for the big one.'"

I got off the bed, left Mom and Dad, and walked down to Beverley's room. The door was ajar. I pushed it open. They'd already taken her away. Yolanda was making her bed – making *the* bed – and had already started loading Beverley's clothes into a big cardboard box. She turned when I arrived. We just looked at one another. She pulled a Kleenex from her sleeve and wiped her eyes.

"This is the worst part. You think you're going to get used to it. But you really don't. There's no time just to sit and feel bad. We have to get the room ready for another patient on the waiting list. He arrives tomorrow morning. It's not right. In a half-hour it'll be as if she was never even here," she said, stopping and sitting on the bed.

I sat down beside her. Without even thinking, I put my arm around her. She leaned against me.

"I'm sorry she's gone," I said. "I didn't have a chance to say goodbye."

"Nobody did. The night staff said she seemed okay when they looked in on her. She was in bed a little earlier than usual. But thanks to you, she was in very good spirits. She was telling everyone about you and what you did yesterday. She was very proud of her young Everett."

Yolanda stopped talking then. She pressed the Kleenex to her mouth. She looked up at me, then reached for another Kleenex from the box on the night stand. She handed it to me.

I gathered myself.

"Have you let her family know? She has a son."

Yolanda just looked at me for a few seconds.

"No. That's the real tragedy. She has no family. No next of kin was listed on her admission form. She was all alone. I know she would often write to her son, but we have no forwarding address or any information to confirm he actually exists."

———

It didn't take us long to load Dad's belongings into his Ford Escort. I was going to miss that car, though Dad wasn't supposed to drive until his doctors gave him the green light, likely sometime in the coming weeks. We pulled away from the hospital in silence with Mom, in convoy, driving her car behind us. I was not used to being with my father when he was quiet. It hadn't happened very often.

"Despite a few years of being whisked around by chauffeurs, I'm glad to see Mom still knows how to drive her own car," I said, glancing in the rear-view mirror and grasping for conversation starters.

He said nothing. We drove in silence for a good five minutes. That's a long time.

"She was quite a woman, wasn't she?" Dad said, almost in a whisper.

"Yeah, Dad. She sure was."

Mom and I spent the afternoon getting Dad settled. His condo still looked presentable after my initial deforestation initiative the day I'd arrived in Orlando. It seemed so long ago, but could still be calibrated in weeks. Dad seemed happy to be home, but the melancholia that descended earlier that morning wouldn't be lifting any time soon. When I left in the early evening, Mom was cooking dinner for them both in my father's underused galley kitchen. Dad let me take his car.

I still couldn't bring myself to start dealing with the mass of emails, tweets, and blog comments unleashed by the NOW media briefing. It could wait. Instead, after chatting with Shelley Hunter for a while on the phone, we agreed that I would write an obituary for Beverley Tanner. The NOW communications team would ensure that it was sent to every major newspaper, network, and media conglomerate on the continent. With no family, who else would do it? I spent a lot of time on Beverley's obit. I wanted it to do her justice. I sent it off to Shelley around eight o'clock Saturday evening and promptly fell into a deep and dreamless sleep.

The next morning, there was still some dwindling coverage from my little revelation two days earlier, though the story had pretty well run its course by then. I was pleased to see that there was plenty of media pickup on the obit I'd written for Beverley Tanner. Most publications ran it verbatim alongside file photos from her glory days in the movement. I was pleased. She deserved it.

I then spent the entire day, Sunday, wading through emails and interview requests, and managing the EofE Twitter feed and incoming comments to the blog. It was an arduous task that left my mouse finger suffering with exercise exhaustion. But it had to be done.

———————

Still no word from Mason Bennington. Lewis was off on Sunday, but as agreed, he popped up in the afternoon to do the interview for *Make-Up Artist* magazine. He reported that no one downstairs had heard from Mr. B either. After the interview, we went downstairs so I could take some shots of Lewis in action, making up the dancers, Shawna included. Two years earlier, the magazine had given me a fairly decent DSLR camera and I'd learned how to use it to a reasonably competent level. Lewis outdid himself and the resulting photos, particularly those of Shawna, were amazing. She was happy to let me submit them along with the piece. You couldn't tell where the shots were taken. No one would know that Lewis's models would soon be disrobing and then swinging on a pole before the hungry eyes of upper-crust men.

I called Dad to check in and Mom answered. All was well. They'd had a quiet day. Dad was watching a NASCAR race on TV. She told me with considerable shock that Dad wanted to handle the cooking that night. I asked for a full postprandial report.

By ten o'clock Sunday night, I was again exhausted. I was still processing Beverley's passing. My way of dealing with grief seemed to be to ignore it. In theory, I knew she was gone. I think I even accepted she was gone. But was there something else I was supposed to be feeling or doing? Was this the full extent of my grieving?

My last act before turning in was to write a few words of introduction to Beverley's guest post and then to publish it on EofE, along with the obituary I'd written. It seemed a fitting tribute.

————

The next morning, just as I was about to head off to the airport, Yolanda phoned me.

"Your father has left a couple things here and there's a package for you from Beverley that we found in her dresser. Can you come by?"

It was on the way to the airport anyway. Yolanda was at her station. She saw me and smiled. Then she grabbed one T-shirt and one baseball cap from the counter, both bearing Ford Mustang logos.

"I don't think there's any question about who owns these," she said, holding them up. "They were in the laundry and came back this morning."

I took the hat from her.

"Be right back," I said. "Don't go away."

I dashed down the hall and out the door onto the grounds. He was where I knew he'd be, staring aimlessly into the distance.

"Hi, Kenny."

"Hi."

"My Dad wanted you to have this, but it was in the laundry," I said, holding the hat out to him. "He wasn't sure whether you'd want it or would wear it. But he wanted you to have it, anyway."

Kenny took it and looked at it, nodding slightly. Then he took off the old, ratty Corvette hat he'd been wearing for years, and slipped on the Mustang cap.

"The Vette's a way better car, but I guess this is a better hat," he said. "Tell your dad, thanks."

"I will. But you can tell him yourself, too. He'll be back to visit."

Yolanda was still standing where I'd left her. I took the T-shirt from her.

"Thanks, Yolanda. I'll get this back to my father. But I doubt he's missed it."

"I doubt it, too. He's got quite a few of them."

"Thanks for everything, Yolanda."

I turned to go.

"Hang on," she said. "Don't forget this."

She handed me a package wrapped in brown paper. It felt like there was a shallow cardboard box inside. A Post-it note on top said "Young Everett" in handwriting I'd come to recognize.

"We didn't see this until after you'd left."

"Thanks. I don't think I can open it right now," I said.

Yolanda reached out to pat my wrist.

"I hear you, honey."

I wrapped it in the Ford T-shirt and turned to go when my eye caught a glimpse of something in the corridor, outside of what had been Beverley's room. It was the pine box that she kept.

"Where's that going?" I asked, pointing to it.

She sighed.

"We have no choice. With no next of kin, someone on the jan-itorial staff just comes and takes it away. I don't really know where it goes. Doesn't seem right."

"You can't do that," I said. "Okay, Yolanda, if you just look out the window over there for one minute, I'll take care of it. Are you with me?"

She nodded and turned quite formally to look out the window.

I walked down the corridor, placed the T-shirt and package on top of the box, leaned down, and hoisted the whole thing up. I managed to get my arms underneath it and rested it against my midsection.

"Was Beverley a blacksmith in her spare time? This thing weighs a ton," I said.

Yolanda didn't even turn my way but maintained her position looking out the window.

"No one knows what's in there. She always kept it locked," she replied. "Take good care of it."

I made it to the car with only the faint first signs of a hernia. I opened the hatchback and slid in my precious cargo. No one had seen me walking out with Beverley's pine box.

I dropped in at Dad's on the way to the airport to return his T-shirt. It was about 10:30 by this stage. I rang the bell twice, then knocked twice. Nothing. I was about to pull out my own key fearing something had happened, when I heard noises inside. A moment later, the deadbolt slid back and the door swung open. Dad was standing there, in his pyjamas, his hair looking like he'd spent the last hour in a Force 8 gale.

"Oh, Ev, it's you," he said. "Is everything all right?"

"Dad. I was about to ask you the same thing. Have a nice little sleep-in? It's nearly eleven."

I stepped around him into the condo. He shut the door but stayed in the foyer.

"So what's up?" he asked.

"I just came by to drop off the shirt you left at the hospital. Yolanda called me this morning."

"They didn't find a Mustang cap, did they?"

"Oh, um, well, yes, they did, but I kind of gave it to Kenny," I said. "Sorry about that."

"Good idea. I got a couple more of them lying around," he replied, while re-opening the front door. "All right, then. Well, thanks a lot, son, for driving it over. I don't want to hold you up."

Just then my mother peeked around the corner to Dad's bedroom, and it all made sense.

"Geez, Evelyn, you couldn't just stay in the room for another five seconds? I almost had him out the door," Dad said, in a tone of benign resignation.

"I just wanted to see our son. Nothing wrong with that," she said, emerging and smiling, the duvet wrapped around her.

"Well, isn't this an interesting development," I said. "I got to say, I was not expecting this."

I gave them both hugs and headed for the car.

"I've got a plane to catch. Pardon the interruption."

Holy shit. I certainly did not see that coming. I wondered if it had surprised them as much.

————

I'd pretty well made my mind up when she'd first raised it. It sounded perfect to me. Just perfect. But you don't want to appear too eager. Just play it cool. So I said I'd think about it for a few days, which meant I'd simply delay telling her how excited I was at the opportunity before asking "Where do I sign and when do I start?" We were back in her office that Monday, just three days after the media briefing in the boardroom down the hall.

"First of all, I'm so sorry about Beverley. It seems impossible that she's no longer part of this," Shelley said.

"It was quite a shock. But perhaps it shouldn't have been," I replied. "After all, she'd been warning all of us that this was coming sooner or later."

"I wish it had been later."

"Me too."

"Friday seemed to be a big success. I hope you feel the same way about it," she said. "I thought you handled yourself very well. You completely surpassed my expectations."

"Thanks. It was all so much easier with you and the heft of NOW behind it. It added a whole new level of credibility and put lots of reporters in the room. It couldn't have happened without you. I'm grateful."

"All right. Now that we're finished buttering one another up, have you given any thought to the idea I mentioned after the newser?"

"Other than, you know, Beverley's passing, I've thought about nothing else," I replied. "If I were going to design my dream job, I'd stop because you pretty well laid it out for me on Friday."

She clenched her fists and did a little upper-body shimmy in response. I assume it was a positive reaction and not some kind of seizure.

"Wonderful! That's just fantastic. When can you start?"

We spent the next two hours hammering out a job description, the compensation package, benefits, vacation, a six-month plan, and of course what would happen to *Eve of Equality*. Shelley insisted that I maintain control of the blog and carry on with it just as I had been. She also said I could take one hour a day on the NOW payroll to deal with anything blog-related. She asked only that somewhere on the front page there be a reference to NOW and a link to the NOW blogs. As well, you would soon be able to find your way to *Eve of Equality* from the NOW home page. We also decided that in light of our little media briefing, the blog would now be called *Everett of Equality*. We even talked about the design. She suggested a graphic designer from the NOW web team could ink in the letters "rett," on an angle, literally by hand, next to the existing "Eve" in the title. So the look of the blog would be almost the same as before, except for this graffiti-like addition of the rest of my moniker. Of course, we'd add a bio page with my photo and a brief overview of my questionable past.

I didn't care much about the salary as I planned to continue raking in the online ad revenue through the blog and, of course, handing over half the proceeds to NOW, as promised. Shelley gave me plenty of latitude in the job, which was nice, and rare. I'd report directly to her, which was also nice. We had the whole thing wrapped up in principle by lunch. She'd have the paper-work drawn up and emailed to me in the next few days.

"So, again I ask, when can you start?"

"I'll need to get out of my apartment in Orlando, make sure my dad is settled, and find a place in DC. But that shouldn't take too long. Could we say two weeks?"

———

I sat alone in a restaurant not far from the NOW offices. I was thrilled, almost overwhelmed. Without going all melodramatic, it felt to me like this was the job I was destined to do. This role was built for me and I was built for it. I just hadn't realized it for a decade or so after university. But I'd caught up now.

But there was still one huge loose end I felt compelled to tie up, for better or worse. I dialed the number and hung up. I stared at my phone, waited for a few seconds breathing deeply, and dialed the number again.

"Mackenzie Martin. How may I direct your call?"

"Yes, um, I'd like to speak to Megan Cook, if I could,"

"I'm sorry, Megan Cook is no longer employed by the firm. Could I pass you on to the lawyer who has taken over her files?"

"She no longer works there?" I said. "Where did she go?"

"I'm sorry, I'm not at liberty to provide her forwarding address."

"But you have her forwarding address."

"But I'm not permitted to disclose it."

"I see. Thank you, anyway."

Good news, bad news. She was no longer working for that firm, but I didn't know how to reach her.

Idea. I searched on my phone for a florist in the area. It took me about thirty seconds to identify a flower shop, a block and a half from the restaurant. I was there in four minutes. I ordered a bouquet of freshly cut flowers. Or perhaps you just call it a bunch of freshly cut flowers. Bouquet has a mildly matrimonial ring to it. In a perfect storm of serendipity, the store's delivery driver pulled up outside just as I left. He not only drove the florist's van, but he drove a hard bargain, too. A minute later, I handed him $40 and he handed me his ball cap emblazoned with the store's logo. I wanted to look the part. But more than that, a few days ago my face had been plastered all over the newscasts. I pulled the florist's cap down low on my cranium and took another cab the sixteen blocks to the swanky offices of Mackenzie Martin.

I might not have mentioned this, but some people think I have a slightly Slavic look – something about the placement of my eyes and the size of my forehead. Frankly, I don't see it. My eyes are just where you'd expect them to be, as far as I'm concerned. And I like my forehead. I think I'm kind of average looking. But since I was about to address, in person, the receptionist I'd just spoken to on the phone, I figured I'd go with the Slavic thing.

It's actually not that difficult to speak English with a slight Russian accent, even if your only exemplar is Boris from the *Rocky and Bullwinkle* cartoons. I thought I could pull it off, provided the receptionist wasn't named Ludmilla or Ekaterina. I took that chance and walked into the sixteenth-floor lobby of Mason Bennington's law firm bearing my bunch of freshly cut flowers. I know this sounds like something out of a TV sitcom, but at that moment, I was short on alternatives, short on time, and, apparently, long on chutzpah.

The receptionist looked up as I approached her station in the way I hoped your average floral delivery guy would.

"Yes, hello. Good afternoon. I am havink flowers here for, let me see now, Ms. Megan Cook. Yes, dat's de name." I checked the piece of paper I held in my hand.

"I'm sorry, but Megan Cook no longer works here," she replied.

And yes, her voice confirmed it was the same receptionist I'd spoken to on the phone not twenty minutes earlier.

"Oh, I see. She has moved. Dat's not good for me. Could please you tell me vere she now vorks?"

"I'm sorry, but I cannot give you her address. I'm not allowed to."

"Please. Zis is quite important. I took zis order myself, and wrote za card myself," I said, worried slightly that I was morphing into a German accent. "I can say dat it is a serious matter zat is urgent, very urgent. And a matter of za heart."

I gave her my most earnest look, before continuing.

"Zis delivery, I need to make. Please," I said, now worried that I sounded like Yoda with a German accent. "Please. No one vill know, and Ms. Cook vill be happy. You vill be happy. I vill be happy. We all vill be happy."

I could see she was thinking about it.

I pulled two tulips from the bunch and handed them to her. "Please."

She took the tulips and stuck them in a cup filled with pens on her desk. Then she heaved a heavy sigh, looked one way, looked the other, and typed on her keyboard.

"I'll deny giving this to you, but she's working at the Anacostia Community Legal Aid Clinic, you know, in the southeast quad."

"Tank you. Tank you."

I turned and got the hell out of Dodge.

I should have guessed. I remember her telling me she'd worked there during law school. I flagged down another cab and gave the driver the address, courtesy of Google. I had no plan, just some romantic notion that if I showed up on her doorstep, apologized, and handed her the flowers, I might just have a fighting chance. That seems to be what always happens in the rom-com flicks I'd seen.

I watched the cityscape change as the taxi crossed into Anacostia. He pulled over in front of the nondescript low-rise building. I paid and got out, leaving the florist's cap in the back seat as an extra tip for the driver. This truly was a rough part of DC. I entered the clinic. The waiting area was crowded. Really crowded. I approached the frazzled-looking woman behind the glass.

"I'm here to see Megan Cook."

"Is she expecting you?"

"No, probably not."

"Are you a client?" she asked, eyeing my flowers.

"Would it be easier to see her if I were?"

The woman was not amused.

"Um, then no, I'm not a client. I'm a friend of hers."

"Will she want to see you?"

"Your guess is as good as mine, but that's why I'm here. That's why I'm hanging way out here on this limb."

"You got a name?"

"Well, yes, yes I do. But I wonder if it might be more effective just to tell her that someone is here with flowers and not give her my name."

"I think I'd better give her your name."

"Right. Yes, of course. I think that would be best," I agreed. "It's Everett Kane."

"I know that name. And you seem kind of familiar. Do I know you?"

"I have a very average face. Lots of guys look like me. I'm sure we've never met," I said. "Um, don't forget to mention the flowers. That could tip the balance my way."

She nodded and smiled at least a little.

"You can wait over there." She pointed to a small alcove a little away from the mayhem of the waiting area.

I did as I was told and sat down on the wooden bench beneath the window.

I was looking out the window when she appeared. I hadn't heard her approach.

"Everett? What are you doing here?"

She wasn't smiling. But my heart did something anyway, when I turned to see her.

"Oh, hi, Megan. Um, I was in the area, and just thought I'd pop in to say hi."

She sighed but said nothing.

"Okay, that's not exactly true. I just thought we kind of left things a little unresolved and I wanted a chance to explain, because I think you have the wrong impression of me. I just want a minute to explain," I babbled. "Oh, and these are for you."

She took the flowers I offered and smelled them.

"They're really very nice," she said. "You didn't have to do that. In fact, it makes this all a little awkward."

"Sorry. I don't want this to be awkward. I was really hoping for un-awkward."

"How did you find me?"

"Well, it took a little creativity and some serious thespian prowess before the receptionist at your old firm caved. But here I am."

She sat down on the bench.

"Well, you sure made a splash yesterday," she said. "I can't turn on a TV or open a paper without seeing your face."

"Sorry about that. I have no idea why it's been such big news. There's so much other stuff going on in the world that's more important."

"I thought you handled yourself very well. And you took the initiative right out of that asshole Mason Bennington's hands," she said.

There was a lull in the conversation during which she looked at her watch. Great.

"Look, I'm sorry, but I have clients waiting," she said, starting to stand up.

"Wait. Look, can you just listen for a moment? I wanted to tell you that night we had dinner that I wrote the blog. I really did. I almost got the words out. But I just couldn't. I didn't want to put you in that position. So, if you remember, I gave you my 'Canadian' cop-out instead. If I'd told you the truth, you would have had to disclose it to your client. But what's most important for you to understand is that I wasn't using you to get info on Bennington. I didn't offer you safe refuge from that violent rally just to pump you for intelligence on your client. I just acted on instinct. And then I liked you. I didn't intend for that happen. But it did. That's all it was. I had no plans to write any more blog posts about Bennington. That was a one-shot deal, and it hap-pened long before I even met you. I wanted to see you again because I just found I was thinking a lot about you."

"Well, you put me in a really tough spot. When Mason Bennington found out we had dinner together, he was not pleased. Do you have any idea what he's like when he's not pleased?" she asked.

"As a matter of fact, I do," I replied. "Did you get fired over it?"

"No. I just couldn't take the charade anymore," she said. "I didn't feel like being used by Bennington and my own firm to help put a more enlightened face on a first-class jerk of a client. So I just quit. Best thing I've ever done."

"Good for you."

"I still believe everyone deserves legal representation. But I decided I didn't have to be the one providing it to Mason Bennington."

Silence reigned for a moment or two.

"Do you believe me when I say I wanted to tell you, that I tried to tell you? Do you understand why, in the end, I felt I couldn't, at least not then?" I asked her.

She sighed, again, and nodded.

"I think I knew the truth long before now. But it's nice to hear it from you. I should have called you before now, but I've been on a bit of a roller coaster this last week or so, and I could only handle so much at once," she said. "I was just so shocked that you were the mystery blogger. I wasn't expecting that. No one was. Personally, I was impressed. But professionally, I was livid. I felt stupid and I felt used. I didn't react well. I jumped to what I thought were logical conclusions, but I never did my due diligence to see whether I was right. Turns out I wasn't. Sorry about that."

"Thank you," I said. "Wow. This is going better than I expected." Finally, she smiled.

"Megan, I know you've got clients to see," I started. "But I also wanted to tell you that I've just accepted a position at NOW. I'm moving to DC in the next two weeks."

———————

I flew back that night and somehow managed to lug Beverley's pine box up the stairs to my apartment. Actually that's not quite true. The police officer on duty that night, apparently for my own protection, helped with it. She was quite strong. All was quiet on the street that night. I saw no sign of the nightly pro-testors, and no sign of any cars pulling up to disgorge well-heeled XY members.

I'd forgotten about the brown paper package Yolanda had given me that morning. I sat down at my kitchen table and picked it up. I peeled off the brown paper to reveal a shallow white card-board box. The note taped to the top of the box said:

My dear young Everett,
I can think of no one who deserves to cherish this as I have for so many years. I know you will.
Yours in equality,
Bev

The lump entered my throat, hard and fast. I could feel my eyes water. I opened the box. I think I knew the instant before I saw what was inside. Perhaps I should have seen it coming. Her treasured first edition of John Stuart Mill's *The Subjection of Women* lay there in all its crimson glory, resting on some tissue paper. I picked it up and held it in my hands, tightly. I then placed the book carefully on the table before spending the next several minutes no longer ignoring the passing of my friend. It felt good. It was a release.

In time, I recovered my faculties enough to turn my attention to the pine box sitting on the table. It was locked with kind of a metallic flap that swung down from the top and latched in front. No key had turned up. I examined the lock. It was very old, but what I knew about picking locks, I'd learned watching cop shows on television. There was almost always a bobby pin involved, and seconds later, after some deft and delicate manipulation, the lock would magically spring open. I had no bobby pins. Why would I? So I turned the box around and examined the hinges. Those I thought I could handle. I used the blade of a butter knife I didn't even know I had in my cutlery drawer. It took me under five minutes to remove the three slot-headed screws from each of the two hinges. I carefully lifted the lid and rested the free side of it on the table, still connected at the lock.

The box was filled to the top with letters, all in envelopes and stacked neatly. There were hundreds, no, thousands of them.

PART FOUR

THREE MONTHS LATER

CHAPTER 16

My plane landed in San Francisco on time. I shouldered my carry-on bag and walked over to Special Services where I picked up the other piece of my "luggage." With some effort, I loaded it onto a baggage cart and pushed it to the car rental counter. Fifteen minutes later I was loaded up in my Hyundai Elantra and headed for US 101-South. Other than its blinding white colour, the car was really quite nice, though my father would not be pleased at all that I had not insisted on a Ford, or at least an American car.

I'd never been to California so I was relying on my cellphone map app to get me to my destination. It would take me about an hour and a half to get there, maybe more if I ended up zigging when I should have zagged. I have a tendency to do that when driving in strange new lands. I stayed on US 101-South when it merged with I-280 South. Then, near Cupertino, I took the CA-85 South exit for a brief stint before cutting onto CA-17 South near Los Gatos, for the final push to Santa Cruz. It was a lovely day, as they always seem to be in California. I was feeling good. I was content. I was downright happy, with a dollop of anticipation thrown in. Driving down the highway in the bright sunshine always puts me in a reflective mood. I turned off the car radio so I could just think for a few miles with no distractions, no interruptions, save for the disembodied, mechanized, but I think woman's, voice of the navigation app on my cellphone. For some reason, I called her Tabitha.

A lot had happened in the preceding few months. About three weeks after I moved to DC, XY in Orlando closed. One evening it was open. The next it was shuttered. Dancers, who the previous night had been earning good money in a clean, well-appointed, and safe workplace, were now out on the streets looking for work. According to Shawna, it's quite possible some of them ended up working the streets until they could catch a gig in some rundown strip club in a rough part of town. Were they as individuals better off after XY closed? Arguably, no. Were women in general, as a gender, better off with one fewer XY Club on the planet? Arguably, yes. But it's not always an easy argument to make. It was the old micro versus macro debate that seemed eternally unresolved. The problem was, there wasn't really one fewer XY Club on the planet. You see, the day XY Orlando closed, XY Seattle and XY Houston opened their doors for business, with oversubscribed memberships. One step forward, two steps back.

No one suggested that my Mason Bennington posts on *Eve of Equality* had anything to do with the demise of XY Orlando. Rather, it was the local community group's creative use of webcams that ultimately put the club out of business. On the Internet, you can monitor LA freeway traffic patterns, Bay of Fundy tides, and even the progress of the giraffe's pregnancy at the Washington Zoo, all courtesy of permanently placed webcams. It turns out you can also monitor in HD and living colour exactly who is entering the front and even the back doors of XY Orlando thanks to these tiny, relatively inexpensive cameras. And many did. It was enough to close the place down.

I happened to be back in Orlando tidying up the apartment and clearing out the last of my possessions when the tear-down below began. The noise brought back memories of when the club was being built. At one point, a contractor just walked right in to my apartment.

"Oh sorry, man, I was told you'd moved out," he said, backing out of the room.

"No worries. Come on in," I said, waving him back in. "I actually *have* moved out. Just snagging the last few things I'd left here before closing the door behind me."

"Do you mind if I remove some hardware from the floor?"

"Not at all."

I went into the bedroom to grab two pillowcases I'd left in the closet. When I came back, the guy was on his hand and knees with a giant wrench, loosening the big nut. He unscrewed it, lifted it off the threaded end of the dance pole below, and set it on the table above him.

"Okay, Leo. It's clear," he shouted through the floor and banged the pole twice with the wrench.

Almost immediately, the angle of the pole changed and the threaded end slowly disappeared. In seconds, there was a circular five-inch diameter hole in the kitchen floor.

"Okay, my work here is done. Thanks, buddy," he said.

He stood up, grabbed the big nut off the table, and headed for the door.

"Um, excuse me," I piped up. "Do you have plans for that big nut?"

"Not so much. I was just going to sell it for scrap. Why? You want it?"

"I've kind of grown attached to it. What's it worth as scrap?"

"Well, what's it worth to you?"

"Would you take five bucks for it?"

"Ten and it's yours."

"Done."

I pulled a ten from my wallet, and he handed me the big nut in return.

"It'll be fun explaining this to the always understanding folks at airport security," I said, slipping the heavy memento into my overnight bag.

When writing posts for the newly constituted *Everett of Equality* blog, I'd missed my hexagonal metallic footrest. It would enjoy a treasured position, on the floor, directly under my desk in DC.

Speaking of the blog, it was still doing just fine. Under its new name, *Everett of Equality*, I shifted the focus to try to build a supportive constituency among progressive men while I hope maintaining at least some appeal to mainstream women feminists. I'd kept up the pace of posts and was happy with the sustained stream of mainly supportive comments to the blog and through Twitter and a few other social media channels.

As expected, I did lose some readers when the "Eve is really Everett" news broke, but the decline wasn't nearly as significant as I'd feared. No doubt the lion's share of my readers were still women. But I was convinced the community of men reading the blog would grow. At least that was the plan. This broadening of the blog's target audience also opened up new online advertising opportunities and, therefore, increased ad revenue potential. Good for me. Good for NOW.

I had worried that Random House might not want to proceed with the book when my cover was blown. But they seemed more committed than ever. Who knows why? They asked me to write a long preface that told the story of the *Eve of Equality* blog and how my identity came to be revealed. Now I'd almost finished the manuscript. Megan and Shelley were both very helpful throughout, given that I was an authorial virgin. Random House was happy with the early draft. It was actually going to happen. I pledged half the book royalties, as modest as they were likely to be, to NOW.

I still hadn't heard from Mason Bennington. No comments on the blog. No emails. No phone calls. No threatening Twitter chatter. Nothing. I was just fine with that but still found myself looking over my shoulder.

Thanks to the advertising earning power of my humble blog, I was able to buy a condo in DC a week after I accepted the new job at NOW. I don't mean I bought it with cash. I wasn't earning *that* much from Google Adsense. I have a sizable mortgage. But the new job and the blog ad revenue on the side made it an easy approval at the bank. It's a one-bedroom in an interesting building on E Street NW, just east of the White House. The building used to house the venerable Hecht's department store. But now there were twenty-nine condo units, including mine on the eighth floor.

I also bought my first brand-new car. Not too flashy. A red Ford Escape. I really wanted the Mazda CX-5, but unfortunately, my father hadn't spent his entire career working at Mazda. In a two-week span, I found myself with a new job, a new apartment, and a new car. For the first time in my life, I felt like a grown-up.

As soon as I settled in DC, Megan and I re-started our relationship, this time with no secrets. It's now been nearly three months. So far, so good. I'm as happy as I've ever been, and by all accounts, so is she. Of course, I remain a little paranoid about how my last few relationships had ended. Well, how *all* of my relationships had ended. I didn't want history to repeat itself one more time. I'm not sure I could take that. But so far, I'm pleased to report that the intensity of my feminism is surpassed, just marginally, mind you, by Megan's. Wooo-hooo! That bodes well. I'd never dated anyone who was more ardent than I on gender equality. I took this as a good sign.

She also helped me understand that being a feminist in principle is easy compared to being a feminist in practice. For men and women, living each day in practical defiance of thousands of years of gender-based streaming is so much harder than walking in marches, running workshops, and writing blog posts. It means questioning everything you do, moment by moment, day by day. It means thinking differently and making dozens of conscious decisions every day that you might have made on auto-pilot before. It's hard. It's taxing. It's tiring. But it's a little easier when you're doing it with someone else who's equally committed. I was doing it with Megan.

Of course, working at the Anacostia Community Legal Aid Clinic provided Megan with a daily dose of the barriers women face. She is fulfilled by her new job at the clinic in a way she never was at Mackenzie Martin. She represents women, mostly, often single mothers. Sometimes, it means appearing at the Office of Administrative Hearings about a rent-control dispute. Sometimes she's in court on custody hearings and other wrenching aspects of family law. Sometimes she's coordinating counselling for women on parole. She says it makes her feel like she's doing something important and helpful for these women, every day. That makes her happy. And that makes me happy.

My reverie was interrupted by my chirping cellphone. I hit the hands-free button.

"Hello?"

"Ever-man, Ever-man, wherefore art thou, Ever-man."

"You got the job!" I said.

"I got the job!"

"Lewis, that's great news! Congratulations!" I said, thrilled for him. "New York. Wow!"

"I can't believe it. It's part-time to start, but if it all goes right, I could be on full-time by the end of the year," Lewis said.

"That's so great, Lewis. Have you told Mr. B?"

"I told him this morning."

"And?"

"Well, he wasn't jumping for joy. But he thought I might be better at it than trying to be a tough guy."

"So it's done. Congrats."

"Yeah, well, Ever-man, it wouldn't have happened if you hadn't pumped me up so much in that magazine. I can't thank you enough, man. I don't know how to thank you."

"What's the first production you're working on?" I asked.

"*The Taming of the Shrew* opens in six weeks."

"How about you get me tickets for opening night?" I suggested. "Megan and I will hop on a shuttle and see your artistry first-hand. Does that work?"

"That's an easy one, Ever-man. Consider it done," he replied. "So, catch me up. Are your parents really back together?"

"Well, they still have separate residences, but as far as I can tell, only one is being used at a time," I explained. "I don't know what to think of it all. And I'm not sure who's having the tougher time. My dad is still getting used to courting a bona fide business superstar. But I'm sure my mom finds it strange when my dad actually cooks something and then cleans up the kitchen. I'm sure they're both reeling."

We chatted for a few more minutes, but he was at work at the time and had to get back at it. I was thrilled for Lewis. The profile piece I wrote on him for *Make-Up Artist* magazine had run three weeks before. He had two calls for job interviews on the strength of the article. He landed at the Royal Shakespeare Company America, in New York. They'd been particularly impressed with the photos of Shawna's make-up in the story. She was in her Marie Antoinette role. Lewis also had landed a few freelance gigs with Manhattan fashion houses and more were promised.

By then, I was about half an hour out of Santa Cruz. Talking to Lewis made me think of Shawna. I still often thought of her. She'd successfully defended her dissertation about a month ago and was now a fully fledged Ph.D. She'd already lined up three interviews for academic postings at various mid-sized colleges. Only one of them was a tenure-tracked position. They were harder and harder to come by. But she was on her way. I was proud of her. Even Chloe had taken to calling her "perfessor Mom."

I was on my way to Los Angeles. But rather than flying directly to LA, I had decided to take the "land in San Francisco, rent a car, and then drive for eight hours" route. Why? Because I had an errand to run on the way.

I didn't read all the letters in Beverley's pine box. I couldn't. I just couldn't. Even reading the first dozen or so felt like a supreme invasion of privacy. So I stopped as soon as I'd read enough to get the lay of the land. As she had always said, they were all letters to her son. She just didn't know where to send them. She didn't know who he was, where he was, or even if he were still alive. She carried that uncertainty with her for nearly all of her adult life.

The letters were all neatly, painstakingly, filed in chronological order beginning in October 1972. There were just over 2,500 of them, each with the salutation "My son," and each folded precisely in an unsealed envelope. In the bottom of the pine box, slotted just in front of the first letter, was the key to the mystery. I found a birth certificate and an adoption certificate both dated October 6, 1972, and both issued at a hospital in San Francisco. Paper-clipped to the two certificates was a faded note in Beverley's hand that simply said:

"Should my son ever come forward, these letters are for him."

The first few letters described the angst that so often comes with carrying a child for nine months and then, almost overnight, giving him up for adoption. In the fifth letter, written about a month after her son's birth, Beverley recounts her meeting with her son's adoptive parents. She liked them very much. She said that while she was not supposed to know their names, the man had referred to his wife at one point in their meeting as June. Beverley noted that she felt an instant comfort and almost a kinship with them. The rest of the early letters were more about how Beverley was feeling and what she was doing. She was trying to let her son know what her life was like. In fact, this was the pattern she followed until she died.

I'd been moved by what I read and by what she'd endured. The uncertainty of it all, the not knowing if he were alive, or safe, or well, or married. The letters seemed to help her cope. I decided I owed it to Beverley to learn what she never knew.

I decided to find her son. Of course, deciding to find him was easy. Actually finding him was not so easy.

I tried to be systematic and logical in approaching the task. I started by searching online archives for birth/adoption notices in the San Francisco area around October 6, 1972. There was nothing that seemed to match quite right in the month following his birth. I was almost ready to try something else when I found an adoption notice in the *Santa Cruz Sentinel*, dated November 21, 1972, about six weeks after the birth of Beverley's son. It caught my eye because the notice announced the "arrival of bouncing baby Tanner Wilkinson," born October 6, 1972, in San Francisco. That seemed like too much of a coincidence. "Tanner" was certainly not a common given name, then or now.

I Googled Tanner Wilkinson. There were quite a few listed on LinkedIn and Facebook. But only one of them was the right age. I clicked over to his Facebook page to find that his birthday was listed as October 6, 1972, even though the adoption notice had been dated six weeks later. Eureka! He had to be Beverley's son. Who else could he be? Even though he was now in his early forties, I thought I saw glimpses of his mother in the various family photos he'd posted. It might have been my wishful thinking at work, but at certain angles, I thought he had her eyes.

I then surfed through several adoption reunion websites that allow birth parents and adopted adults to list their names in the hopes of connecting with one another. I pursued this because I questioned whether I had the right to introduce an adopted child, now an adult, to his birth mother, even posthumously. Who was I to do that?

But all the pieces seemed to be falling into place. It was as if the whole endeavour was charmed in some way. You see, I found Tanner Wilkinson's name on three separate California adoption reunion websites. The path seemed clear. The Internet is a wonderful thing. When you have a name, a photo, and a birth date, finding an address is only a matter of time. I immediately visited 411.com/California and was rewarded. Thankfully, Tanner Wilkinson did not have an unlisted telephone number. I found him. I found Beverley's only son, the son she never knew.

———

I rolled into Santa Cruz in the midafternoon and found the house without incident. It was a nice house. According to Facebook, Tanner Wilkinson was a high school math and physics teacher. He was happily married with three daughters. Beverley had grandchildren. I parked up the road for a few minutes just to gather myself. I really had no idea how this would unfold. After about ten minutes, I decided there was no reason to put it off any longer. I started the car, drove up the street, and turned into the driveway.

He must have seen me pulling in because when I got out of the car, Tanner Wilkinson was out on his front porch waiting for me.

"You must be Tanner," I said, extending my hand. "I'm Everett Kane. Thanks for agreeing to meet a complete stranger. I didn't think this was the kind of discussion that should be handled over the phone."

He shook my hand and smiled while doing it.

"Nice to shake your hand, Everett. You've made quite a name for yourself the last little while. As the father of three amazing daughters, I'm pleased to meet you. And your call certainly piqued my curiosity."

"Is the rest of your clan at home?" I asked.

"They've headed down to the boardwalk for the afternoon. I thought it might be easier that way."

Tanner helped me with the cargo in the trunk. We carried it around to the shaded back deck. He fetched us both beers and then we settled into chairs in the sunshine.

"Look, I know this is kind of strange, but as I said on the phone, I think you'll want to hear this."

"I'm in your hands," he replied.

"I know that you have placed your name on adoption reunion websites to try to connect with your birth parents," I started.

He nodded.

"Well, through some research I've undertaken, I believe I know who your mother is, or rather was, I'm sorry to say. I have no information about who your father might have been."

It's hard to pinpoint the look on his face. He tilted his head a little to the side, placed his beer on the table beside him, and leaned forward slightly.

"How certain are you about this? I've tried for a long time and have always come up empty. I don't want to get my hopes up just yet, so you'd better tell me your story."

"Of course. I understand. I'll try to do it succinctly, but bear with me," I said.

I paused for a moment and then started talking, as I'd rehearsed it yet again in front of the bathroom mirror that morning.

"I believe your mother was a woman named Beverley Tanner, a prominent feminist and a co-founder of *Ms.* magazine back in 1971. She gave birth to a boy on October 6, 1972, in a San Francisco hospital."

His eyes widened at Beverley's name, but he said nothing and nodded for me to continue. I lifted the lid on the pine box resting on the deck next to me and extracted a few sheets of paper.

"This, I think, is your birth certificate and adoption certificate." I handed both to him.

"You can see they're both dated for October 6, 1972, which I know is your birthday."

Tanner examined them both, his hands trembling slightly. I reached into the pine box and brought out her fourth letter, wherein she described meeting her son's adoptive parents.

"Tanner, may I ask you, is your adoptive mother's name June?"

He looked at me with his mouth open, said nothing, but nodded. I handed him the letter.

"You'll see in this letter that Beverley mentions that the adoptive father called his wife June in their meeting, even though he was not supposed to."

I waited till he'd read the letter.

"So just to review the evidence so far, Beverley Tanner gave birth to a son in San Francisco on October 6, 1972. She then met with her son's adoptive parents shortly thereafter and learned that the adoptive mother's name was June. You were born on the same date, also in San Francisco, and were adopted by parents, where the mother was also named June. And they named you Tanner."

He briefly held his head in his hands and took three deep breaths.

"Is there anything else I should know?" he asked.

"I've brought some photographs of Beverley Tanner, your mother," I said as I lifted the file out of the pine box and handed it to him. "I'm no expert, but I think you look like her. I think you have her eyes."

Tanner opened the file, and as he looked through the photographs I'd mounted on black card stock, his chin started to quaver at bit. Then tears drifted down his cheeks. I gave him a minute. Hell, I needed a minute.

"Tanner, did your parents ever tell you why they named you Tanner?"

He sniffed once, wiped his eyes, and shook his head.

"No. Not really. They just said it was a name I could be proud of."

"Well, they got that right."

"When did she die?"

"About three months ago. She'd had a series of strokes over the last ten years. She died in her sleep."

I reached into the pine box and pulled out a book. I handed it to him.

"This is Beverley Tanner's, um, your mother's memoir from several years ago. It makes no mention of you but you can sense when you read it that something is missing in her life, as productive and celebrated as it was. I know now what she was missing."

Tanner opened the book and flipped through it, pausing on the photographs. He just shook his head a little, trying to take it all in.

"I think your daughters would really enjoy their grandmother's book."

He just nodded. I reached into the pine box one more time.

"And here's a clipping file I compiled so you can see your mother in action and how revered she was for her activism. She used her sense of humour to broaden the base of the women's movement, to make more women feel like it was their movement, too. That was an important contribution."

"Why do you think she never tried to find me?" he asked.

"I don't know. We never talked about it. It was off limits. But I think she might have felt that she'd already disrupted your life once, at the very start of it. Perhaps she didn't want to disrupt it again. But what I do know is that your mother was one of the warmest, funniest, most intelligent, thoughtful, and committed people I've ever met. Whatever the reason, I'm quite sure it was driven by a mother's love for her son."

He shook his head but said nothing. I nearly pulled a muscle turning the pine box around on the deck so he could finally see inside.

"You might find some answers in these 2,500 or so letters. She was writing you right up to the end. Each letter is addressed to you. I only read the first few to figure out what was in the box. Then I stopped. They're all dated and in order. These are for you. I'm quite sure she'd have been deeply touched to learn your parents named you Tanner."

We talked for a couple of hours that afternoon. I told him everything I knew about Beverley. I told him how funny she was and how she helped drag my dad into the latter part of the twentieth century. With another month, she might have been able to bring him into the new millennium. I told him how she would touch me on my arm when speaking to me. I told her how committed she was to the rights of women. I gave him copies of her guest blog post on *Eve of Equality* and the obituary I'd written. I told him how amazed and proud she would have been to meet him and her granddaughters.

As the sun started to sink, I left him there on the deck. He'd just started to read the letters his mother had spent more than forty years writing to him. I felt strangely liberated as I walked to the car. At the same time, I felt at peace.

———————

I drove onto CA-1 South but didn't feel much like driving anymore. So I found a reasonably nice roadside motel near Los Banos and checked in. Stopping so soon for the night meant an early start the next morning. That was fine with me. There wasn't much going on in Los Banos on a Wednesday evening.

Thursday was yet another beautiful sunny California day. There was not a cloud in the sky as I pulled back onto the highway. I figured I could make it to LA inside of six hours if I kept the Elantra pointed in the right direction and was somewhat flexible in observing the speed limit. There was very little traffic on the road at that hour of the morning. I felt renewed and energized. I had a powerful feeling of accomplishment and of closure. I missed Megan. Despite everything swirling in my mind, there was still room for Megan.

I'd given Tanner Wilkinson my contact information and told him to call me whenever he liked. I'd also told him he always had a bed in DC if he was ever passing through.

I stopped for breakfast around 11:00 on I-5 South, near a town called Buttonwillow, a name straight out of a Dickens novel. As far as I could tell, there wasn't much to commend Buttonwillow. But they did have something you won't find in a Dickens novel. They have a Denny's. I didn't stop for long. I got back on the road after the cardio-compromising breakfast special. Tabitha told me I was still on track to reach my destination on time. Two hours later, her voice guided me up to the security hut at a sprawling lot on the edge of West Hollywood. After I presented my driver's licence to the guard, the barrier magically lifted. I drove in and parked where he'd told me to. I was a little early so I just sat in the car for about twenty minutes, getting nervous. My cellphone bonged with a text.

"Hey Ev. Good luck this p.m. I know you're going to kill it. (That's a good thing, BTW.) I'll be watching and cheering. Oh, sorry, but I *did* call your parents about it. I had to. They'd want to know. They'll be watching, too. See you tomorrow. Love Megan xo"

Great. After I was buzzed into the highly secure reception area, a young man with a headset escorted me into a special room where they fixed me up as best they could. The guy was no Lewis Small, but I thought I looked fine in the end. Then I sat alone in this other rather small room for a time, eating the fresh fruit they'd laid on. Ten minutes before I was supposed to go on, some guy came and fed a tiny microphone beneath my shirt, pulled it out through the gap between my top two buttons, and secured it with a clip. He slid the battery pack into the inside pocket of my jacket. Finally, yet a different person, a young woman, also wearing a headset, led me through a maze of hallways, and then through a big heavy door. She put her finger to her lips to make sure I was not about to burst into my own special rendition of "Crazy Train" at the top of my lungs. I hadn't been. I don't even like that song. So I just stood there amidst some curtains, listening to my own pounding heartbeat.

A minute or two later, I heard music and applause from beyond my field of view. Then, in what was a truly surreal experience, I heard my own introduction in a familiar voice. I thought it was all a bit over the top.

When the woman in the headset poked me in the back and pointed, I figured it was time to go. The curtain was pulled back and I walked out, partially blinded by lights that I'm sure could be seen in San Diego if they just opened the doors. The audience was applauding. At least I assume there was an audience. But I could see nothing out there through the glare of the spots. It was as if a black velvet curtain had descended at the edge of the stage. But I knew where I was going. The floor director had given me rather explicit instructions. I follow instructions well.

We shook hands. I smiled. She smiled. Then I sat down on the couch. The ovation petered out. And here we go.

"Everett. It took us a while, but I'm so glad you're here."

"Um, thank you for having me. I guess it did take some time, but I'm very happy to be with you now, Candace."

THE END

ACKNOWLEDGEMENTS

I spent May 5 to 9, 1981, as a new and naive member of the McMaster Students Union delegation to the National Union of Students Conference held that year at the University of Lethbridge, in Alberta. Over the course of this annual gathering of Canada's student movement, I experienced an awakening of sorts, not unlike the one briefly described by the narrator in this novel. It was my first real exposure to organized feminism, and it sparked an interest in, and a commitment to, equality rights that remain strong to this day. The seeds for this novel were sown that weekend, all those years ago.

As always, I owe more than just thanks to my editor, Douglas Gibson, for his friendship and wise counsel. I also owe a debt of gratitude to my stalwart literary agent, Beverley Slopen, who took a chance on me in 2008. I thank also the rest of the wonderful team at Random House/McClelland & Stewart, Ellen Seligman, Frances Bedford, Bhavna Chauhan, Wendy Thomas, and all the others there who work so hard to bring my words to a broader audience.

Of course, I can never write this section in my books without noting the pivotal role in my writing career played by the Stephen Leacock Memorial Medal for Humour and the wonderful people behind it. They changed my life overnight in April 2008, and I will be forever grateful.

I also thank Michele Landsberg, Judy Rebick, and Elaine Lui, who kindly read this novel in manuscript form, and yet still offered glowing tributes.

Finally, to my wife, Nancy Naylor, and our two sons, Calder and Ben, I offer my love, gratitude, and, I hope, more time, as meagre return for all your patience, forbearance, support, and above all for anchoring me in my most important story.

Terry Fallis, Toronto, December 2014

WOMEN IN THE WORLD

- Globally, women make up just 22 per cent of parliamentarians. *(Source: The Inter-Parliamentary Union 2014)*
- Only 7.4 per cent of countries have had female heads of states over the last fifty years. *(Source: The Global Gender Gap Report 2013, World Economic Forum)*
- Women spend at least twice as much time as men on domestic work, and when all work – paid and unpaid – is considered, women work longer hours than men. *(Source: The World's Women 2010: Trends and Statistics)*
- Women work two-thirds of the world's working hours, yet earn only 10 per cent of the world's income. *(Source: CARE.org)*
- Women account for 70 per cent of the population living in absolute poverty (on less than $1.00 a day). *(Source: GlobalCitizen.org)*
- 603 million women live in countries where domestic violence is not yet considered a crime. *(Source: United Nations, UNiTE to End Violence against Women)*

WOMEN IN CANADA

- In 2014, women held 25 per cent of the seats in the House of Commons, and 31 per cent of the Cabinet portfolios. *(Source: The Parliament of Canada)*
- In 2008, women earned, on average, 83 cents to every dollar earned by men (an increase of eight cents since 1988). *(Source: Statistics Canada)*
- Women spend more time than men on domestic work. In 2010, while women spent 13.8 hours per week doing house-work, men spent 8.3 hours. *(Source: Statistics Canada)*
- Women spend more time than men caring for their children. In 2010, women spent an average of 50.1 hours per week on unpaid child care, more than double that (24.4 hours) spent by men. *(Source: Statistics Canada)*
- Half of all women in Canada have experienced at least one incident of physical or sexual violence since the age of sixteen. *(Source: Statistics Canada)*

Also available from
McClelland & Stewart . . .

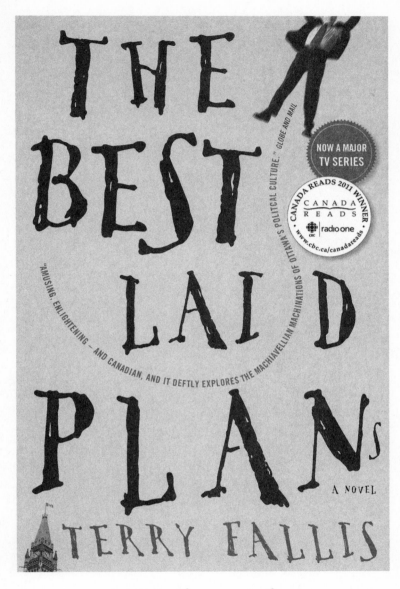

THE
BEST
LAI D
PLANs

A NOVEL

TERRY FALLIS

"AMUSING, ENLIGHTENING — AND CANADIAN, AND IT DEFTLY EXPLORES THE MACHIAVELLIAN MACHINATIONS OF OTTAWA'S POLITICAL CULTURE." GLOBE AND MAIL

NOW A MAJOR
TV SERIES

CANADA READS 2011 WINNER
CANADA
READS
cbc | radio one
www.cbc.ca/canadareads

ISBN: 978-0-7710-4758-9
ALSO AVAILABLE AS AN EBOOK

THE
HIGH
ROAD

AUTHOR OF *THE BEST LAID PLANS*, WINNER OF THE STEPHEN LEACOCK AWARD FOR HUMOUR

A NOVEL

TERRY FALLIS

ISBN: 978-0-7710-4787-9
ALSO AVAILABLE AS AN EBOOK

TERRY FALLIS

UP AND DOWN

A NOVEL

"Another hilarious page-turner. . . . This is satire at its finest."
ALI VELSHI,
CNN anchor and Chief Business Correspondent

ISBN: 978-0-7710-4791-6
ALSO AVAILABLE AS AN EBOOK

TERRY

WINNER OF THE STEPHEN LEACOCK MEDAL FOR HUMOUR

FALLIS

Author of **THE BEST LAID PLANS**

NO RELATION

A Novel

ISBN: 978-0-7710-3616-3